Praise for **CRIME MACHINE** and **GILES BLUNT**

"Blunt delivers another twisting page-turner that will keep readers up late at night, proving yet again that he can deftly toe the line between terror and intrigue." *CBC Books*

"As distinctively Canadian as a Tom Thomson painting. . . . *Crime Machine* is as good as Canadian crime fiction gets." Margaret Cannon, *The Globe and Mail*

"*Crime Machine* brings us into contact with a millenarian sect of lethal composition, an ineradicable and sinister past, wanton murder, transborder intrigue, a beautiful compassion mixed with a terrible love, and all kinds of twists and turns of plot and betrayal." *Telegraph-Journal*

"Giles Blunt manages to inhabit the minds of killer, victim and investigator alike, a feat that very few writers can manage. It moves his work to a different level." *The Independent*

"A marvelously controlled writer, equally confident with characters and narrative." *Toronto Star*

"Giles Blunt writes with uncommon grace, style and compassion and he plots like a demon." Jonathan Kellerman, the *New York Times* bestselling author of *Capital Crimes*

"Another winner from one of Canada's leading crime writers." *The Peterborough Examiner*

"Teeming with questions, possibilities, and clever, enticing dialogue." *The Hamilton Spectator*

BOOKS BY GILES BLUNT

The John Cardinal series

Forty Words for Sorrow
The Delicate Storm
Blackfly Season
By the Time You Read This
Crime Machine

Other novels

No Such Creature
Breaking Lorca

CRIME MACHINE

GILES BLUNT

VINTAGE CANADA

Published in Canada by Vintage Canada, a division of Random House of Canada Limited, Toronto, in 2011. Originally published in hardcover in Canada by Random House Canada, a division of Random House of Canada Limited, in 2010. Distributed by Random House of Canada Limited.

Vintage Canada with colophon is a registered trademark.

www.randomhouse.ca

Library and Archives Canada Cataloguing in Publication

Blunt, Giles
Crime machine / Giles Blunt.

ISBN 978-0-679-31434-9

I. Title.

PS8553.L867C75 2011   C813'.54   C2010-904179-8

Printed and bound in the United States of America

2 4 6 8 9 7 5 3 1

To Janna

1

A SMALL CITY THAT HERALDS ITSELF as the Gateway to the North is unlikely also to be known as the gateway to fine dining, and until recently—unless your idea of an evening out involved donuts or poutine—this was pretty much the case with Algonquin Bay. Many an intrepid restaurateur had been brought to ruin by the economic realities of trying to serve fresh Atlantic salmon, not to mention an edible tomato, 340 kilometres north of Toronto. But they kept trying, and this particular year at least three restaurants—two steakhouses, as well as Bistro Champlain—were vying for the attention of local gourmands.

Of these, Bistro Champlain was by far the most successful. Partly this was the work of Jerry Wing, its creative chef, but being located across the highway from a first-class ski resort called the Highlands didn't hurt. When the Highlands did well, Bistro Champlain did well—and right now it was doing very well indeed, owing to the winter fur auction. Buyers from all over the world had descended on Algonquin Bay to bid on hundreds of thousands of furs that would end up in showrooms from Manhattan to Moscow to Beijing. Champlain's dining room may have maintained its luxurious hush, but for a couple of hours the kitchen had been a scene of barely controlled chaos.

It was nearly ten, and Sam Doucette had just plated what she hoped was the last order for the night: the maple venison, accompanied by sweet potato mash and a red wine reduction. The rush was over, and the decibel level of slamming skillets, pans and ramekins had finally settled below the pain threshold. Jerry had already gone home, and Sam was praying that Ken, the manager, would not seat some late arrival with a huge appetite. Working as a cook—a skill her mother had taught her— was supposed to be part-time, a way of subsidizing her art classes at Algonquin College, but for the past few nights she had been doing the work of two cooks, one of her colleagues having been summarily fired for attempting to exit the premises with two hams stuffed in his back- pack. All but two of the waiters, Ali and Jeff, had gone home, and Sam couldn't wait to get out of there.

She rested one foot on the bottom of an upturned pickle bucket and wiped the sweat from her brow with the sleeve of her chef's tunic. Would Randall call? If he called, fine. If not . . . well, she didn't want to think about that. Romance, she was discovering, was not uninterrupted bliss; mostly, it was uninterrupted anxiety. So she turned her mind to Loreena Moon, the heroine of a graphic novel she was drawing and writing just for fun. Well, she told herself it was just for fun—she didn't want to get all worked up thinking about actually selling it—but she was also toying with the idea that it might be a series. She had already drawn lots of images and written several scenes. For some reason, the imaginary Loreena Moon was clearer in Sam's mind than anything about her real life, except Randall and his passionate kisses.

Loreena Moon was cool, aloof, self-reliant—everything Sam was not. She moved through the shadows of the city, a perpetual frown of suspicion darkening her brow. She carried a knife in a fringed sheath on her hip, a quiver of arrows at her shoulder, and a small bow slung across her back. She was always outraged, always righting wrongs and saving helpless people, wronged people. Loreena never looked back and she was never, ever in love. She was the same age as Sam, eighteen, but she didn't live on the reserve and she didn't live in Algonquin Bay. Sam was not yet sure *where* Loreena Moon lived. It couldn't be a house or an apartment; no bills or personal responsibilities for Loreena. The only place Sam could imagine her staying was in hotel rooms, and never the same one twice.

The kitchen clock hit ten, ending Champlain's food service for the night. Sam's cellphone rang in the breast pocket of her tunic and her heart gave a skip of happiness. The tiny screen said *Randall Wishart*.

"We have a place," she said. "Please tell me we have a place. I've missed you so much."

"Me too," Randall said. "Come to the Island Road house. How long will you be?"

"I'm done here. I just have to set up for the lunch crew."

"Park some ways away," he said, "and don't let anybody see you."

Sam turned off the deep fryer, the ovens and ranges. She had already wiped down the counters and cutting boards. Ken McCoy, the manager, stuck his head in from the dining room and gave her the okay signal.

She changed in a supply closet behind the kitchen. The white tunic came off and went into the laundry bin, followed by the ridiculous check pants. Loreena was always in black jeans and tank top, sometimes a black T-shirt, maybe with a cat logo or a lightning bolt. Sam's own jeans were a struggle, she was so sweaty from the stove. She pulled on the soft red sweater that she knew Randall liked, slung her coat over her arm and went out the back door to the parking lot.

The night was fine, the snap and sparkle of December without the face-freezing cold that January would soon bring. Loreena Moon would have hopped on her Kawasaki, but Sam had to be careful getting into her '96 Civic. The door had to be lifted just so as you opened it or the hinge would go out of whack and the thing would refuse to close.

—

The Island Road property was out on Trout Lake, at the tip of a point it had all to itself. In summer there might have been people cruising by in boats, people driving back and forth to their cottages, but this time of year it was dead quiet. Even so, Randall opened the door the way he always did, standing behind it so he couldn't be glimpsed by any chance passerby. He was still wearing one of the dark sports jackets he favoured for work, but he had taken his tie off and, seeing Sam, his face lit up like a hot young actor's at the Academy Awards. The moment Sam was inside, he took her in his arms and hugged her tight.

"Three whole days," Sam said. "I was going crazy."

"Did anyone see you?"

"Nope."

"Where'd you park?"

"The hydro turnoff you showed me."

"Cool."

The house was a bungalow, very open and lots of polished wood everywhere. Too pretty for Loreena, but Sam liked it just fine. She hoped the owners never came back. She took off her boots and hung up her coat in the vestibule and Randall hugged her again. He switched off the vestibule light and they went to the bedroom and got undressed, Sam draping her stuff on a wooden chair by the closet.

"Jane have nice body," Randall said. "Tarzan like."

"I wish I could take a shower. I'm all sweaty."

"Me like all sweaty."

They lay down on the blue blanket Randall always brought to cover whatever bed they happened to use. He kept it in his car and Sam occasionally wondered how he explained its presence there to his wife. He stretched out naked, hands behind his head, showing off his biceps. Sam loved his body. Loved it in a way she was sure you should never love anything of this world. She had always thought love would be a melding of minds, a union of souls, and until she slept with Randall Wishart she had never considered the possibility that you could be positively loony over the sheer physicality of another human being.

Sam straddled Randall's chest, pinioning his arms. Her hands looked dark against his so not-Native skin. "I think about you all the time," she said.

"Me too."

"No, I mean really, really all the time."

"If I could draw like you, I'd draw you over and over again, all day long."

Sam touched his cheek. It was always smooth. Randall never allowed the slightest stubble. He would have considered it unprofessional in a realtor.

"I think about your voice," she said, touching his neck. "Sometimes I even hear it in my sleep."

"Oh yeah? What am I saying?"

"I can't tell you." She covered her face.

"Come on, what am I saying?"

Sam shook her head.

"I know what I say." He tilted her off and put his lips to her ear and whispered a string of outrageous commands and nipped at her earlobe. That started their usual delirious tangle, which after six months still had the power to leave Sam breathless and amazed. Randall always found just the right touch, the exact timing that could drive her pleasure up and over thresholds whose existence she hadn't even suspected. Was it just because he was older? Or did he have some kind of gift? Or was it—maybe, oh, she hoped so—because he really, totally, absolutely loved her? A Force Ten orgasm in no time at all.

He fell away from her, gasping and laughing. "That's it. I swear. That was the one. I'm never going to need another one. That was it for all time."

Sam laughed. "They ought to have an Olympic event. The hundred-metre orgasm."

"Synchronized orgasms."

They were laughing, but Sam was already beginning to feel sad the way she always did afterward. Sad that Randall would be going home to his wife. Sad that she would be going home to her mother and her little brother and her self-absorbed art instructors at Algonquin. Most of her friends had left town for universities farther afield. Her dad was off on one of his winter camping trips, hunting or just being alone, something he liked to be a lot. She turned on her side and touched Randall's pale shoulder. "Can we go away somewhere, sometime, maybe?" she said. "For a few days at least?"

"That would be nice, wouldn't it."

"Can we do it? Just take off for Toronto or Montreal or, I don't know, anywhere? For a weekend maybe? Even just overnight?"

"I'd love to, Sam, but I can't. What am I supposed to tell Laura?"

"Tell her that you've found a beautiful Indian princess who makes you incredibly happy."

"That'd go over real well."

"Well, make something up, then."

"I can't, Sam. I'm a terrible liar and Laura would know like that." He snapped his fingers.

Sam could feel his tension rising the way it always did whenever she talked about life outside whatever vacant house they happened to be in. She knew she should shut up, but she couldn't stop. "Don't you want to spend time with me somewhere else? Somewhere outdoors maybe? Or anywhere—a coffee shop, a bookstore—it doesn't even matter. Just somewhere we could be like normal people?"

"Sam, Laura and I have been together a long time. I can't just up and dump her, and like I say, I'm a lousy liar."

"Well, that's a good thing, I guess." Sam moved her hand to his forehead and stroked his eyebrows. He gave a little moan of pleasure, and soon he was asleep.

He always fell asleep after, out cold like you'd shot him full of Valium. He'd stay that way for five or ten minutes, during which time Sam got to wonder about his other life, his real life. Laura Wishart was pretty and smart—Sam had looked her up on the Internet—the quintessential blond success, some kind of financial expert. She must have been well off to start with, because her father owned Carnwright Real Estate, where Randall worked. Sam wasn't sure why Randall was unhappy with his wife. He rarely talked about her, except to say they never had sex anymore.

She tried to think about Loreena Moon. Loreena was free, always on the prowl. Loreena was cool and untouchable. She was like Pootkin, Sam's black cat that roamed the neighbourhood and sometimes came home and sometimes did not. She had given Loreena Pootkin's green eyes—the only spot of colour in her monochrome artwork. She wasn't sure if you could actually have a single dot of colour like that in a real book, but she liked it.

She wanted her heroine to be essentially good—that is, always helping the underdog and bringing evildoers to justice. But she didn't want her to be bound by petty rules of behaviour. This past weekend she had drawn a series of images of Loreena swiping stuff. She was investigating a rich industrialist whom she suspected of poisoning the water supply of several reserves, and while snooping through one of his mansions she pocketed various valuable items. Sam liked the idea of Loreena being as amoral as Pootkin, but wasn't sure if she could square that with helping the underdog. She loved Pootkin, but not because the cat had shown any inclination to altruism.

Randall woke up, and picked up his watch from the bedside table. "God, I gotta go. I'm supposed to be watching the game at Troy's place. I did see most of it."

"Better check the score before you get home."

"I'll check it on my phone. Not that Laura cares."

They got dressed and Randall folded up the blue blanket. In the vestibule they put on coats and boots. Randall switched off the light. His hushed voice in the dark as if people might be listening right outside the door. "Give it two minutes, right?"

"Okay."

"And make sure the door is shut properly. Lock seems to be screwed up—everything sticks in this house."

He gave her a quick kiss, said he couldn't wait until next time, and then he was gone. A cloud of cold air, smells of snow and pine. His car starting in the drive. It shouldn't hurt this much, she told herself. You're a big girl. Supposedly. No cat-hearted Loreena, though, that was obvious.

She watched through the door window as his tail lights winked through the trees. It was a long drive back to town and then up the highway to the reserve; she decided she'd better visit the bathroom before hitting the road. She wiped her boots on the mat until she was sure they wouldn't leave water on the hardwood.

As she was coming out of the bathroom, she heard a key in the front door. A man's voice. Not Randall. Stomping of boots and voices answering.

Sam stepped into the bedroom. If these are the owners, she said, or even another agent showing the place, I am in shit city, and so is Randall. But the owners weren't supposed to be back yet, and why would an agent be showing a house at this hour of the night? It didn't make sense. The toilet was still running, and she prayed it would stop.

Voices and movement deeper into the house. Hall light going on.

Sam got down on the floor and slid under the bed. There is no kind of serious person, she said, that would be in this situation.

Several minutes of quiet, then the man's voice louder and footsteps coming her way. Dulled sound of stocking feet. Did that mean they would be staying?

The man's voice from the hall. "Got a nice bathroom. Nothing luxurious, but it's the location you're paying for. The tranquility."

The bedroom light came on and Sam held her breath. She couldn't see anything, the bedspread hanging almost to the floor.

"Good-sized master bedroom. Room for a queen-size bed, obviously. Decent closet space. You might want to pick yourself out a different colour."

Sound of closet doors sliding open.

A woman's voice, some kind of accent. "It was built when, you said?"

"Early sixties."

"So new. Looks older, the style."

Closet doors sliding shut.

"Character," the man said, closer now. "They didn't just reach for the cookie cutter." He crossed the room and there was the sound of curtains being pulled back. "You got the lake out back, snowmobiling in winter, canoeing, water skiing or whatever's your fancy in summer. It's the view makes the place. I gotta get you-all out here in the daytime. Smack dab on the water, out on a point—it's a postcard, there's no other word for it. Pretty unique. Got two more bedrooms."

"Is only one bathroom?" Another man's voice. Again a foreign accent.

"Yessir. You mightn't consider it for your primary residence, but for a northern getaway? I think you'd be hard put to beat it."

Their footsteps thudding toward the hall and the light going out.

"You-all check out the other bedrooms," the man said, "and then I got a little something to warm us up."

Sam shifted her position under the bed. She could hear the man and woman in the hall, some foreign language. How long could it possibly take you to check out a little bungalow? *Leave,* she told them. *Just leave.*

Footsteps moving back toward the kitchen or living room, no longer in the hall anyway. The people didn't leave, but she couldn't hear them anymore.

She tried to regulate her breathing, to calm down. They would go soon. Another few minutes maybe.

From the living room, the clink of glasses. Laughter. Sam prayed they were not planning on an all-night booze-up.

She waited, thinking about the window. The house was such an open style there was no chance of getting to the front door without being seen. She had never seen the back door, but it would have to be somewhere near the kitchen. That meant the window.

Is there one single solitary thing I have to be grateful for in this situation? she wondered. One single solitary thing to justify that famous "attitude of gratitude" her father was always encouraging her to cultivate? Maybe one. Got to the bathroom before all this. Otherwise there'd be a whole other layer of anguish.

Gunshot.

Sam's head hit the box spring. Her father had taught her to shoot when she was nine. There was no doubt in her mind, not for one instant, that someone had just fired a gun.

Another shot.

A man shouted. The kind of yell a man lets fly when his team has just scored a goal.

When you get lost in the woods, her father told her—and everyone gets lost in the woods, even Indians—the first thing you do is what you don't do. You don't panic. Panic will kill you faster than any wolf, faster than any bear. Panic is the quickest cause of death known to man. What you do is you notice it, you name it for what it is, and you lock it away in a little safe where no one can get at it, not even you, understand?

Don't panic, she told herself. Maybe no one has been shot. They were looking at a house—why would anyone shoot anyone? Maybe someone's shooting blanks for some reason. Maybe they snorted some coke or something and they're going a little wacky. Don't panic.

She tried to get control of her breathing, her heart rate. No one knows I'm here. Whatever's going on, it'll be over soon. They'll leave, I'll leave. Life will be normal and no one will be dead. Not me, at least.

None of this slowed her heart rate. Blood thundered in her ears.

She eased herself out from under the bed. There were two windows side by side, one with an air conditioner fixed into it. Outside, moonlight on snow. She turned the lock on the other one and lifted. It didn't move. Her heart jacked itself up even more. It was all she could do not to scream.

This is panic. Heaving up on the window grips, pushing on the sash, nothing moving. Thinking, this is panic, get back under that bed.

Grabbing the chair. To this moment still having made no sound.

I do this and there's no going back. It's one chance and no more. I should get back under that bed.

She swung the chair with all her strength, spinning her weight into it. The noise was terrifying.

One knee over the sill and onto the slight ledge outside. Hands on the sill and glass slicing into her in many places at once. She pushed herself off, coat ripping, and hit the ground hard, knees and hands. Then up and running, and bullets spitting snow in front of her before she even heard the first shot.

She made straight for the darkness of the trees, thinking, my tracks in fresh snow saying shoot me. She dropped down behind an outcropping of granite and looked back. Someone had turned on the bedroom light, but there was no shadow in the window. Think, she said. To her left, the platinum lake, the ice still too thin for anyone heavier than a cat. There's only two ways back to the car, one on either side of the drive and then the road. He saw me come this way. He's going to bust out that front door and head for this side and he's going to hear me even if he can't see me and then I'm dead and I really do not want to die.

The open ground between her and the house looked like the worst place in the world. She left the rocks and ran right back through it, keeping close to the rear of the house, and then into the woods on the other side. Every instinct told her to run all out. I'm fast, she said, but I'm not Loreena Moon and I'm not about to outrun bullets. The trick is not to run fast but to run silent.

She tried to remember all of the tracking lessons her father had given her. How to move in on your prey without being detected. Keep your steps to the rocks, right on them or close by. Ease your weight by grabbing low branches close to the trunk. Don't step on twigs. Great bit of Indian lore there, Dad. I'd never have thought of that. Being a good tracker was not the same as being good, meaning living, prey.

When she was well past the front of the house, she crouched amid a stand of pine and listened. She could see the drive, could hear the man crashing through the woods on the far side. How dumb was this person likely to be, was the question. How long would it take him to see that there were no tracks over there, no footprints in the night's thin layer of snow. Then he would either wait or head down to the back of the house and see her trail doubling back.

He came out of the woods and turned slowly, conning the snow, the woods. Sam reached into her pocket for her cellphone. Not there. She felt her other pockets. The man moved back toward the house, the gun long in his hand. Sam took off again. A few moments later the road was in sight through the trees. Her car was down the road a little toward town. To avoid crossing the open driveway, she would have to get to the far side of the road and into the woods, which climbed a steep hill, or risk the open road.

The man was crashing through the brush behind her. Sam broke for the road and ran for it. If he saw her, he would have trouble getting a shot, and by the time he reached the road, she would be at her car. A bee whizzed by her face and then the following *crack* told her everything she needed to know. She got to the hydro utility road and her car parked maybe fifty feet in from the road.

If he's made it to the road, the noise of me starting this thing up is going to tell him where I am.

She kept the lights off. The Honda started first try. She took it slow on the service road; the slight rise would have been enough to render those bald tires useless. As she rolled up to Island Road, she saw him coming and gunned it, back tires spinning but drifting up onto the road. It was agony to ease off on the pedal, but it was the only way the tires were going to grip. A bullet slammed into the back end, and the man was yelling, running toward her in the rear-view.

The tires caught and she eased her foot down, keeping low in the seat. Another bullet slammed into the trunk. She rounded a curve and breathed a little easier. He couldn't get a shot and he wasn't going to catch her on foot. His best move now would be getting into the car she'd seen shadowed in the driveway and coming after her all *Terminator*. She had the advantage of knowing Island Road, which had some serious twists and turns, and he couldn't be sure if she was headed to town or farther north.

A car coming the other way blasted its horn and flashed its lights. She put her headlights on and kept it fast, the Honda fishtailing on the hills and curves. Nothing in the rear-view, but then you could only see back to the last curve. Up ahead, the Chinook Tavern on the right and beyond that the highway.

The Chinook parking lot was busy for a Thursday night. People outside, huddled over their cigarettes. A guy was poised to pull out on his Harley, but there was no way she was going to let him. She blasted by and totally ignored the stop sign at the intersection. He yelled something—hurling his outrage into the night.

Then the smooth road and the lights of town in the distance. She patted her pockets again for her cell. Definitely gone. She must have lost it when she jumped. Moonlight on the flat white surface of Trout Lake, the road itself in the deep shadows of trees and hills. The speed limit was

80 kilometres, but she pegged it at 120. You couldn't go faster on these curves. It was a perfect speed trap, of course. The cops often staked it out, hoping to lasso the drunks weaving back to town from the Chinook.

The steering wheel was sticky with blood. Her knee was hurting, and not in a way that was going to fade any time soon. The blood had soaked down nearly to the cuff of her jeans. That was probably going to need stitches. You are in trouble ten different ways, she said, and if you've got some plan for getting out of it, I'd really like to hear it right now—preferably before Mr. Murder decides to come after me.

2

When she got home, Sam parked the car in the garage and inspected the damage to the rear end. The left signal light was shattered and there was a bullet hole in the trunk. Three inches higher and her brain would have been all over the windshield.

She went into the house and removed her coat and boots in the dark. Her mother always slept with her bedroom door open. Sam had to be silent moving down the hall and into the bathroom. The right leg of her jeans was stiff with blood below the tear in the knee. She opened the cabinet above the sink and found a bottle of Tylenol with codeine left over from a tooth extraction. She shook two into her palm and swallowed them, scooping water from the faucet to wash them down.

Her left hand was cut, a two-inch gash at the base of her palm. It wasn't bleeding too badly now. She got some gauze and tape and an old face cloth from the closet by the toilet, then had to go back for the rubbing alcohol. Tremors shook her thighs as she got into the tub. She peeled her jeans down halfway and sat on the edge of the tub to extract her left leg.

She took a few deep breaths and held the last one and rolled her jeans off the cut in her knee. Tears sprang to her eyes and she started to sob but managed to keep it quiet. She pulled her jeans off the rest of the way and rolled them up. Blood welled from her knee. She ran water over it and watched the red and pink swirl into the drain. She washed her cuts with soap and water and dried them with the old face cloth. The alcohol was cold and it stung, but it felt clean.

The cut in her knee needed stitches, but there was nothing she could do about that. A trip to the emergency room would require an explanation, and she might run into someone who had been shot or had done the shooting. She dried her feet and went back to the linen closet and dug around and found an ancient box of Kotex that her mother had got a couple of years ago for some medical reason she hadn't cared to discuss with her children. Sam taped one tight to her knee.

It took some effort to clean up the mess and she kept expecting her mother to tap on the door the whole time, but she didn't. Sam turned off the bathroom light and limped past her brother's bedroom door into her own room and shut the door. She hid her rolled-up jeans and the box of Kotex under the bed. She switched on her bedside lamp and sat on the edge of the bed with her left leg stretched out straight. Pootkin was curled up on the end of the bed. She raised her black head and blinked and went back to sleep.

The top of the bandage was already showing red. Every time Sam bent her knee, that cut was going to open.

The tremors had subsided, the codeine beginning to work a little. It's going to take a roomful of scientists, she thought, to calculate exactly how much trouble I'm in. If Mr. Gun saw the licence plate on my car, it's probably game over. But it was dark, he was far back and he was trying to shoot me, so maybe he didn't catch it. Presumably, when you're shooting people, you have other things on your mind than licence plates.

And you don't know, she told herself, you don't know for a certainty anyway, that the man shot anybody at all. Uh-huh—then why was he trying to annihilate you?

Sam's bedroom was tiny. She could reach her desk from the bed. She got her laptop and opened it and checked a couple of news sites, ABdaily.com and algonquinlode.com. Of course, it was too soon. They had stories about the fur auction and the winter carnival and nothing about any shootings.

She looked at her alarm clock. Call him now, she thought, wake his wife, catch him off guard, and you can kiss him goodbye. The earliest she could call would be after eight in the morning. He said his wife was at her office from eight until six every day. Randall didn't have to be in until ten.

Lights from a passing car swept over her bedroom wall and she held her breath until they passed. She switched out the light and moved the cat over so she could lie down. Her knee throbbed. When she closed her eyes, she was right back at the Trout Lake house, crashing to the snowy ground, running through the woods. What are the chances of him finding that phone? He's running through the dark with a gun, is he really going to notice it—probably buried in the snow? She opened her laptop again and lay on her side, checking the Web for articles on what to do if you lose your phone. There were some phones you could sync up to your computer so you could wipe out the information the moment a thief tried to access the Web with it. Not a feature that came with Sam's. She had never even set up the password. Calm down, Sam, she said, he didn't find it. Which means the police probably will.

The codeine was really taking hold now. She was thinking of what to say to the police and couldn't seem to keep it straight in her mind.

—

Sam woke up in the morning with her laptop on the bed beside her. Her alarm clock said 8:30. Her mother and brother would have just left. She called Randall on their house phone. He did not sound happy that it was her, but she ignored that and spilled out the whole story.

"Randall, I've never been this scared in my life. I never knew what *terrified* meant until now. I really thought I was going to be dead, and I'm pretty sure there's going to be dead people in that house."

"You didn't see him actually shoot anybody, though."

"No, but he came after *me*, and he tried to kill *me*, and why would he do that unless he'd just killed *them*?"

"I'm just saying it's not like you can report a murder. All you could say was that you heard shots."

"And that some bastard tried to kill me. There are bullet holes in my car."

"And you said he was talking real estate? He was trying to sell them on the house?"

"He was showing them the bathroom and talking about the view."

"That makes no sense at all. I'm the only agent on that property."

"I wanted to call the cops soon as I got home, but I didn't want to get you in trouble."

"Hold on, Sam—you can't be telling the police I was out there. Do you realize what that would do to me? How am I going to explain to Larry what I was doing on that property with an Indian girl in the middle of the night?" Larry was Lawrence Carnwright, owner operator of Carnwright Real Estate.

"Indian girl?"

"First Nations. Stay out of it, Sam. You're talking about the destruction of my career *and* my marriage."

"I can't just not report it. What if there's someone wounded out there? Someone slowly bleeding to death? What kind of person would that make me?"

"It makes you reasonable. Cool under fire. Literally. If he shot people, they're shot and there's nothing you can do about it, Sam. But you've got to think of my situation here. How are you going to explain why you were in that house? How would you even know about that house without bringing me into it? And once my name comes out, that's it. It's the kind of damage, once you do it, you can't undo it."

Sam thought about that. She ran a hand through her hair and encountered a V of pine needles. "I could just call them anonymously. I could call from a pay phone."

"And tell them what, Sam?"

"I was out in the area and I heard shots fired and thought I should report it."

"And you think they're going to go out there ten hours later on the chance that someone may still be firing a gun on the tip of Island Road? They're not going to do anything with information like that. You'd have to tell them what you told me—that you heard a couple of people and then there were shots and you're pretty sure they're dead. That'll get 'em out there. And they're gonna know, what with the isolation of the house and everything, that you were actually there in the house, and they are going to turn over every piece of evidence known to man in order to find you. They're going to find our fingerprints, they're going to find who knows what-all out there. You can't do it, Sam."

"I don't have a criminal record and neither do you—fingerprints aren't going to lead them anywhere."

"Oh, God."

"What?"

"If there's been an actual murder out there, they're going to be questioning me anyway. I have a key to the place. I told you, Sam, I'm not a good liar."

"You could tell them the truth. You were out there some other day. You wanted to check the house for some reason, and that's it—you didn't see or hear anything suspicious. And that's the truth, so you wouldn't have to be nervous. You don't have to mention me."

"Sam, don't call the cops. Do not phone them. I can't be brought into this. Neither can you. I gotta go. I gotta think about this. Don't do anything, Sam."

"I lost my cellphone, and what if he has it? What if he saw my licence plate? What if he thinks I can identify him and he comes after me?"

"If he was that desperate to get you, he could have done it last night. He could have chased you in his car, right? But he didn't. Because he knows you can't identify a damn thing."

"What if he tries to kill me to play it safe? Can you even believe I'm saying that? This is for real, Randall."

"I gotta go. Don't call me. If the police start checking phone records, everything's gonna go to hell. And we better not see each other for a while."

"Oh, don't say that."

"Just to be safe—we don't want to ruin what we have, do we? This precious thing that we have together?"

"No."

"Okay, then. I'll call you soon."

"I love you, Randall. I need to see you."

"Me too. So much. I gotta go."

3

AFTER DINNER, JOHN CARDINAL SAT at the kitchen table and only realized after some time that he'd been staring at his own reflection in the window. He got up and turned off the light and sat back down. His apartment building was on a ridge overlooking the north bay of Lake Nipissing and now, with the lights off, the frozen surface of the lake took form in the glass. The moon, not quite full, was bright enough to wash out most of the stars and lit a wide off-white track across the snow to Cardinal's window. The tops of trees that lined the beach waved in the breeze, but he couldn't hear them through the double glazing.

Mealtimes were still difficult. For the first six months after Catherine died, Cardinal had eaten in front of the television. He didn't like television, but it was better than simply staring at the empty place where Catherine used to sit chatting to him about her students or her latest photography project. Finally he had come to find it intolerable, and he put the little house by Trout Lake up for sale—the house he had lived in with Catherine and his daughter for nearly twenty years. For some reason he had decided that an apartment would suit him better at this broken place in his life. An apartment was un-Catherine. It was un-Cardinal, come to that. At one time he might have thought of himself as an urban type, back when he was living in Toronto decades ago, but not anymore. Now he was just a man whose wife had died and who had trouble seeing much value in his leftover life.

He turned the light back on and reached for the top file of a stack of manila folders foxed and acidic with age. Under the rubber band that held the folder together was a memo from the chief exhorting the investigations department to dig deep in their efforts to clear cold cases. There was nothing like clearing up an ancient mystery or bringing an elusive criminal to justice to restore the public's faith in their local police. They were to seek especially opportunities to apply technologies, databases and techniques that had been unknown or unavailable to the original investigation. Whenever he was seeking to provoke enthusiasm where none existed, which was often, Chief R. J. Kendall was prone to oratory. *We must see ourselves as visitors from the future, travelling back to help our stymied colleagues in the past.*

R.J. had the politician's knack of presenting a policy he had been forced to adopt as the inevitable result of his personal devotion to good works. In this case, the provocation had been the release of a national report on the clearance rates of the various local forces. Usually these were restricted to larger cities with populations above one hundred thousand. This year, some irritating bureaucrat had produced a comparison of smaller cities, and although one could offer fourteen reasons why the results were not particularly meaningful, that did nothing to assuage Chief Kendall's outrage that the Algonquin Bay police service had been ranked just slightly above the median. The chief didn't mention it specifically, but Cardinal knew that what really rankled with him was that Parry Sound and Sudbury, two cities of similar size, demographics and geography, were far ahead when results were averaged out over forty years. It looked bad, side by side, and even *The Globe and Mail* had mentioned it as an interesting anomaly.

Thus the Scriver case, all twenty pounds of it, on Cardinal's kitchen table. D.S. Chouinard had had the six detectives in CID draw three cold cases each from a hat and Cardinal had drawn Oldham (probable but unprovable murder by spouse), Sloane (missing octogenarian, probable misadventure) and Scriver. When the name was read out, Cardinal's colleagues had not made the slightest attempt to suppress their laughter.

Delorme, by contrast, had drawn Lonnie Laird, a missing teenager who had always been presumed but never proved to be a victim of Toronto serial killer Laurence Knapschaeffer. It took Delorme exactly one trip to the Penetanguishene hospital for the criminally insane and a forty-five-minute interview with Knapschaeffer to get a signed confession from him—possibly because Delorme was a first-class investigator, or possibly (and this was the explanation Ian McLeod liked) for the simple reason that Knapschaeffer had never before had the elective attention of such a good-looking female.

Scriver was the oldest and most investigated and re-investigated case in the history of the Algonquin Bay police and their colleagues in the joint effort, the Ontario Provincial Police. It had taken place many years before Cardinal had joined the force. There was no one left on staff who had been around at the time. All of the investigators were long retired, some long deceased.

On or about July 15, 1970, the Scriver family had apparently left their Trout Lake cottage in their small outboard and had never been heard from again. Cottage door unlocked. The remains of dinner still on the table. No signs of violence.

The missing: Walt Scriver, forty-five, a researcher with the Lands and Forests Department (as the Ministry of Natural Resources was then known). His wife, Jenny Scriver, forty-three, homemaker and part-time teacher. Their eighteen-year-old son Martin, who had been home for the weekend from his summer job on a deer census. All apparent victims of a drowning accident.

Cardinal wrote in big letters on his legal pad, *Cleared — Alien Abduction*.

The buzzer rang and Cardinal went to the intercom to open the door for Lise Delorme. One of the unforeseen benefits of moving to this apartment was that he was now just a five-minute walk away from Delorme, his favourite person at work. When he had first moved in, Delorme had come round to help unroll carpets and hang curtains. Pure kindness, Cardinal figured; she would have done the same for anyone.

Now here she was at his door, tomboyish in flannel shirt and blue jeans, and clutching a DVD in one hand, a gigantic can of popcorn in the other. A less cop-like person would be hard to envision.

"Monsters," she said, holding up the DVD. The cover had a picture of giant insects. "Or do you think it'll be too much like work?"

Cardinal put the DVD into the machine and spent a few minutes fiddling with the remote, which never worked the same way twice.

"Man, it's so humid in here," Delorme said. "They still didn't fix your ventilation?"

"Don't get me started. Buying this place may have been one of the dumbest moves I ever made."

Delorme was looking at the pile of folders. "Hey, congratulations. I see you solved Scriver."

"Yeah. Turned out to be simple."

Cardinal on his recliner, Delorme on the couch. He kept a quilt folded up on the back, because Delorme always got cold—those huge plate glass windows facing the lake. She was still in her thirties, passionate in temperament and appealing in form, and it had occurred to Cardinal more than once to reach across the small table that separated them and touch her, but he hadn't. They had fallen into this friendship and pretty quickly it had begun to feel as if it had always been like this and always would be.

She was telling him about a hunter, the subject of two annoying grid searches, who had just been found near the Nipissing reserve, slightly frostbitten but otherwise okay. Hunters got lost two or three times a year and posed a considerable drain on department resources, not to mention on the patience of those who had to look for them. "What's wrong with these people?" she said. "They haven't heard of GPS?"

"Lot of macho types pride themselves on not needing it. How's Shane?" Cardinal muted the TV as they waited for the FBI warning and the previews to finish.

Delorme hoisted the quilt around her shoulders, careful not to tip her bowl of popcorn. "We had dinner Wednesday night. It was okay."

"You don't sound excited."

Delorme shrugged and transported a handful of popcorn from bowl to mouth. "I'm not."

"I imagine you end up talking shop a lot of the time."

Delorme made a face. "To tell you the truth, I don't think Shane's all that good a lawyer. Doesn't seem to get his clients off very often."

"That's because of the uncanny skill of the local police."

"I don't think so, unfortunately."

"Well, he must have something, or you wouldn't keep going out with him." It amazed Cardinal that he could talk to Delorme about her love life. It would have been unthinkable a year ago, but now it seemed natural.

"Shane is someone to have dinner with," Delorme said. "Go to a movie with. Not much more than that."

"That's too bad."

"You should talk. You don't go out with anyone. You don't even seem to consider it."

Cardinal hit the remote and the MGM lion roared.

The first few minutes of the movie were amusing, even to Cardinal, though he didn't normally like science fiction. The chubby friend of the main character had just been yanked offscreen by an extremely slimy tentacle when the phone rang.

—

They drove out to Trout Lake. Out past the frozen beach, past Natural Resources and the marina. Out past Madonna Road, where Cardinal and Catherine and their daughter used to live. A few more kilometres and they made a right onto Island Road, passing the Chinook roadhouse on the left. Delorme took it slow on all the hills and curves, neither of them saying anything, almost as if they were holding their breath.

Island Road, so called because when you reach the end of it, there's just one last house and then the water of Trout Lake—ice, now—and, about half a kilometre out, a pretty island that sits at the end of this peninsula like the dot over an *i*.

White birches flashed by in an endless palisade. Moonlight on cedar and blue spruce. Not what you'd normally call disturbing, but when Delorme stopped at the driveway to the last house in front of the yellow strip of crime scene tape, Cardinal got a bad feeling. And not just the regular bad feeling you got at the scene of a murder. Delorme looked pale and grim, and Cardinal knew he looked the same.

They got out of the car and nodded at the young cop standing just inside the yellow tape. He introduced himself as PC Rankin and pointed with his flashlight at the left side of the driveway. "Those are my tracks," he said. "PC Gifford's by the house. I walked back up here and figured best to walk where no one else had. Whole mess of tracks further down."

"Where's your squad car?"

He pointed with a fat mitten down the curving drive.

They had driven right over tire tracks that might prove crucial later on, but Cardinal couldn't blame them. They hadn't known what kind of situation they were coming into.

He ducked under the tape and continued down the driveway, following the beam of his own flashlight, Delorme right behind. They walked single file to minimize any more damage, both of them looking at the tire tracks. The tread marks cast deep shadows in the snow.

The driveway was long, really its own separate road. And it had enough dips and turns that they couldn't see the house until they reached the last crest and could look down the final slope toward the lake. It was set there in a wash of moonlight that lit the trees, the frozen lake.

Cardinal had never seen the house from this side, although he had often admired it from the lake when he was out in the boat. The owners would have a spectacular view, being at the tip of the peninsula that divided Four Mile Bay from the main body of Trout Lake. It was a long and low bungalow, constructed of brick and stone and lengths of cedar. He didn't know who lived there. All he knew was they had a bright red canoe that was tethered to the dock all summer. Cardinal stopped and Delorme stopped too and looked at him, her breath turning to steam.

"What's the first thing you think of when you look at this?" Cardinal waved his arm to include the woods, the lake, the island.

"Isolation."

"Me too," he said, and continued down toward the house. The snow squeaked with each step.

A young policewoman standing in front of the house raised her flashlight to look them over. Cardinal had noticed her around the station before.

"PC Gifford," she said. "I know who you guys are."

Cardinal pointed to the kludge of footprints on the stoop. "I hope none of those are yours."

"No, but those are." She pointed to footprints beneath the plate glass window. "I was trying to see if there were any survivors. I thought I should go in—the back door lock has been jimmied and there's a broken window—but Staff Sarge said no, keep it secure and wait for you guys, so that's what I did."

"Who called it in?"

"Couple of boys out for a hike along the shore. They swear they didn't break the lock or the window, and I believe them."

"A hike in the pitch dark?" Delorme said.

"I know. They're like thirteen, parents away for the weekend, and I'd guess the older brother is the world's worst babysitter." She said their names and that they lived on Water Road, which was on the far shore, back toward town. "I put 'em in the squad car."

Delorme stepped up to the front window of the house, holding her flashlight to the glass.

"Take a deep breath before you look," Gifford said. "I've never seen anything like it."

Delorme stepped back from the window, and turned away.

Cardinal went next, also holding his flashlight to the glass. The bodies were toward the back of the house, little more than silhouettes at this distance. "Jesus," he said, and stepped back.

He started toward the back of the house, Delorme following.

"We probably should have left the car back at the road," Gifford said. "But far as we knew, it could've been anything from a prank call to a hostage situation. I tried not to run over those, though." She pointed to the tire tracks between the house and the squad car. "Those were already here."

"Two vehicles," Cardinal said. "Clear tracks, too."

"Should I come with you inside?"

"We need you to stay here and make sure no one steps on that porch," Cardinal said.

—

Sandy and Doug were thirteen and fourteen years old. Best friends. A lot of people might have expected them to be traumatized by what they'd seen, but Cardinal knew they'd be bright-eyed with excitement. He and Delorme took separate statements from them, the only difficulty being trying to slow them down. They had been walking along the south side of the peninsula, not on the ice but on the shore. They weren't up to any mischief, just out for a hike around the shore. But curiosity got the better of them and they decided to take a peek in the windows of this house on the tip of the peninsula.

As soon as the boys had looked in the back window and "like finished puking our guts out," they had called the police. Constables Gifford and Rankin had arrived, checked out the window and made them wait in the car.

Cardinal pointed his flashlight at the tracks leading from the lake to the house, the tracks leading back. "Were any of those tracks here before you went up to the house?"

The boys looked at each other and shook their heads.

"The back door lock has been jimmied and there's a broken window," Cardinal said. "Would you know anything about that?"

Again they shook their heads.

After a few more questions Cardinal gave them his card. "Did you tell anybody about this yet?"

"Nope," the younger boy said.

"Good. Don't tell anyone until tomorrow—we don't want the bad guys to hear anything until it hits the news. You did the right thing calling it in. Wait in the car and we'll have someone drive you home."

The boys looked disappointed. "We'd kind of like to stay and watch the CSI guys, if that's okay," the older one said.

"Sorry. Can't allow any unnecessary personnel on the scene."

"*First* on the scene," the younger one said. "We're material witnesses!"

"Right you are, Inspector—if there's a trial. But for now, you have to vamoose."

As he and Delorme turned toward the back of the house, Cardinal said, "Let's get someone to tape off the back perimeter. We don't want any more *CSI* fans poking around."

—

Ident arrived, and all of them—the two ident guys, Cardinal and Delorme—struggled into paper suits with rubber feet that would keep their influence on the scene to a minimum. Bunny suits, they called them.

"We're lucky in one thing already," Cardinal said. "We've got good footprints that haven't been snowed on. Before we go in, we're going to get photos and videos of all the tracks at the front door, the sides of the house and at the back. When we look back on this, we want to be a hundred percent sure what was here and what wasn't."

Paul Arsenault, the senior ident man, was switching on his video camera as he spoke, and his partner Bob Collingwood had the two young witnesses come out of the squad car and make fresh footprints, which he photographed under bright light. The boys co-operated in a state of solemn excitement.

When they had photographed everything up to the back door, Cardinal went in, followed by Delorme and the coroner.

"The heat's off," Cardinal said. "Owners would turn it down, not off—first big freeze, the pipes are going to burst."

The dead, two of them, were seated at the dining room table, on opposite sides, fixed in the moonlight as if in conversation. Cardinal felt the hairs on the back of his neck stir. He turned on the lights and moved closer to the bodies, looking at one then the other. One male, one female, both hideously foreshortened, both dressed in beautiful fur coats, one sable, one mink.

"First thing," Cardinal said, "we have a holdback." He pointed to the knife handle sticking out of the dead man's back. "Let's keep the knife to ourselves for the moment."

Various grunts of agreement from around the room. Collingwood took a few shots close up. Arsenault had remained outside to continue recording exterior evidence.

Cardinal checked the man's pockets for ID, Delorme checked the woman's. Nothing.

"Nobody's pockets are that empty," Cardinal said. "No keys, no change, no receipts." He knelt to pull leather gloves from all four of the victims' hands. The skin had the same hue as that of a frozen turkey. He didn't want to look above the shoulder line on either of them, where their faces should have been. "Who are they?" Cardinal asked of the room at large. "Anybody know?"

"Ruth and Joseph Schumacher." It was Neil Dunbar who spoke. He was coming in through the kitchen, plump in his paper hood and coveralls. "I looked them up in the reverse directory before I hopped in the car. They've owned the place for twenty years."

"That doesn't mean it's them," Cardinal said. Dunbar was new on the CID squad, young, and what their detective sergeant liked to call self-motivated.

Cardinal moved toward a country pine buffet with framed photographs all over it. There was a picture of a couple standing in front of the house in summer.

"The woman in the picture is wearing a simple wedding band, same with the man. These two," Cardinal said, pointing at the four dead hands, "are a little more flashy, wouldn't you say?"

Dunbar moved forward and peered at the hands. "That doesn't mean it's *not* them."

"Also, her skin. This person is a lot younger than the woman in the picture." He pointed at their feet. "The man's wearing shoes. Why isn't she?"

"Took 'em off at the front door," Delorme said. "Expensive pair of leather boots for her, galoshes for him. I'd say these are not the people who broke in the back door."

"What do you think his wingtips cost? Three hundred? More? Not a cop, obviously."

The coroner, Dr. Beasley, was done in ten minutes. He scribbled on a form, tore off the top sheet and handed it to Cardinal. "Preliminary finding of foul play. You're going to need everything Toronto has to offer."

"That's it?"

"All I can give you on time of death is more than eight hours, less than forty-eight. You're going to have to get 'em on the table in Toronto to narrow it down. The knife in the back was post-mortem, as was the trauma to the neck."

"That's the fastest I've ever seen a coroner leave," Delorme said when he was gone.

"Guess he didn't like the atmosphere," Cardinal said.

Delorme turned her attention to bullets, perhaps unconsciously keeping her back to the two dehumanized shapes. There was a slug embedded in the wall behind the male, another under the sideboard. She made out marker cards for Ident to photograph.

Collingwood was examining the corpses, going over the fur coats with the concentration of an ape grooming his mate. Cardinal was contemplating the table, trying to make sense of the set-up. Three shot glasses. A bottle of Stolichnaya.

"Judging by the position of the bullets," Delorme said, "it looks like they were shot by someone sitting here." She indicated a chair that was pulled away from the table.

"We don't know for sure they were shot yet," Cardinal said. "But since the rest of it is post-mortem, yeah, I could see it. He shoots the man first, possibly right in the face, and the bullet ends up in the wall behind him. Then he shoots the woman, maybe through the side of the head, and it exits this way and ends up on the floor. Then he pulls out the axe."

Cardinal looked briefly over the living room, which was neat and undisturbed. He went down a gleaming hallway, his paper suit making swishing sounds with each step. Two of the bedrooms appeared not only undisturbed but underfurnished, as if no one lived in them. Lots of the houses in this area were vacant most of the winter, their owners having another residence in town. He checked the bathroom briefly, and finally the master bedroom.

He stood in the doorway, arms folded. One window completely smashed—outward, not inward—the chair it had been attacked with lying on its side. No other signs of violence. The bed was made up, but when Cardinal lifted the corner of the bedspread, there was only a mattress pad underneath. The closet was virtually empty, as were the dresser drawers. No sign of any suitcases.

He went to the window and looked out. Arsenault had set up so many lights, it looked like a movie set. He was on his knees, bent low over something.

Cardinal asked him how it was going. Arsenault stood up. "Fantastic. I'm taking moulds before it melts."

"Give me the short version."

Arsenault pointed to two sets of tracks coming up from the lake. "Those are the two boys'. The prints right by the house—up to the back door at least—are mostly ours. I'm betting all the rest are crime related. That window you're standing in? Someone came out of there pretty hard. Cut themselves up, too—we got blood on the left hand, blood on the knee. Fairly small person. Took off that way. Comes back this way."

"Really."

"Yeah, there's a whole story out here, if we can just get it down before it melts or it snows again."

"I'll send Collingwood out."

He went back to the dining area. The scene didn't get any easier to take.

Delorme held up her notebook. "Clothing labels are all American. Barneys, Bonwit Teller, Lord & Taylor."

Collingwood, the younger half of Ident, was plucking invisible items from the man's coat with a pair of tweezers.

"Hair?" Cardinal said.

Collingwood nodded. He almost never spoke.

"Arsenault needs you outside. He's hit the motherlode."

Delorme pulled back the sleeve from the dead man's arm. "Rolex watches, both of them. Fur coats, expensive labels. I'd say we're dealing with some seriously wealthy people here. Whoever killed them took their wallets but left all this stuff."

"Idea being to hide their identities rather than get rich, maybe." Cardinal looked around. "Where's Dunbar?"

"He went to canvass the neighbours on either side. See if they saw anything."

"Nearest house must be two hundred yards away. If they were even here. Not too many people live out here in winter. I don't think it even gets ploughed this far, unless you want to pay a private contractor. Did you tell him to canvass the neighbours?"

"That was his idea."

"Self-motivated," Cardinal said.

"Probably just wanted to get away, like the coroner. Can't say I blame him for that."

"Not for that. No."

Cardinal was beginning to feel a peculiar ache in his bones. Not from cold—the house was warming up now—but from whatever it was that emanated from the two headless beings seated at the table.

Cardinal and Delorme stayed silent for a couple of minutes. Cardinal was waiting for that big picture to develop, but at this moment it was all detail and no picture. He went to the front vestibule. He opened the door and examined the outside lock. There were scratches around the keyhole that could mean it had been picked, but he couldn't be sure if the scratches were new.

When he came back to the living room, Delorme said, "Not much blood. Considering."

"Considering. Pretty gory next to the chairs they're sitting on, but nothing like what it'd be if the heads had been removed before they were dead."

"We've got those." Delorme pointed to two circular smears of blood, one near the entrance from the kitchen, one on the other side of the table. "But no drips moving away from the table, or away from the blotches. So the killer puts them into something—plastic bag or whatever—before he leaves. What did you mean before? When you looked at the house and said 'isolation'?"

Cardinal shrugged, making the paper rustle. "That we're probably not looking at a sudden explosion of violence."

"We're looking at—what—the end result of a plan?."

"The end result of a plan. Exactly."

Delorme went into the kitchen and there was the sound of cupboard doors opening and closing. She came back with a small green box. "No garbage bags. Just these."

Compost bags. The dimensions were printed on the top.

"Might hold one head," Cardinal said.

"It might. But these aren't really leak-proof. You ever see the inside of your compost container?"

"I try not to."

"I think he brought his own box, bag, whatever."

"That's why I've always found you to be extremely intelligent, Sergeant Delorme. You have exactly the same thoughts I do."

Arsenault called Cardinal's cell and asked him to come up to the road. "We're in a hydro access about a hundred yards before the driveway."

There were already a couple of reporters trying to get by PC Rankin, who had moved his perimeter to the far side of the access road. They yelled at Cardinal for a comment as he went by. He told them he couldn't say anything just yet.

Snow glittered under the lights the ident team had set up. More tire tracks.

"Our runner," Arsenault said. "We follow his trail through the woods on the west side of the drive. He comes out to the road and then it gets hard to see, but we've got blood—not a lot, but enough to see he hits the road, comes this way, and bingo—car."

Cardinal and Delorme stood looking at the tire tracks.

"Much smaller car," Cardinal said, "and there's hardly any tread. Are we looking at a third vehicle?"

"Very good," Arsenault said. "Could be a glamorous career waiting for you in Ident. Notice also we have four tires, four different treads, which probably means an old vehicle in pretty bad repair."

"Tail light," Collingwood said. He was holding up a fragment of red plastic.

"Show him the casings," Arsenault said.

Collingwood held up a Baggie. "Found 'em at the top of the drive."

"So we've got a chase that starts at the broken window and ends here?" Delorme said. She put her hands on her hips. "Got a lot to work with, anyway. Hair, fibre, ballistics, footprints, tire tracks . . ."

"We may have something even better," Arsenault said.

"Oh?"

"Might have a survivor."

THE NEXT DAY WAS SATURDAY, but Detective Sergeant Chouinard had cancelled everybody's weekend and they had a morning meeting just like any other day. They began with a quick rundown of smaller cases. Szelagy was working with the fire marshal on a suspicious blaze in an old warehouse. McLeod was working on a fraud artist. Delorme had a couple of ATM robberies.

Chouinard sat at the head of the table, making the odd note and looking unhappy. "We have the fur auction in town, people, and after that the winter carnival. We need to be quick on this one, and we need to be good. Cardinal is lead investigator."

"Cardinal's not available," McLeod said. "He's too busy with Scriver."

"Very funny. Listen, it's not the carnival I'm worried about so much as the fur auction. It's still a big deal in this town, and they're expecting protesters. We're going to have to be a presence. I've already talked to Staff Sergeant Flower, and there'll be uniforms, but the chief promised the Fur Harvesters we'd have people stopping by too."

"Harvesters," McLeod said. "You gotta love it. What's wrong with *trappers*?"

"Most of the furs come from farms these days. Listen, we're talking millions of dollars in a tight economy, so let's do some serving and pro-tecting. Cardinal, where are we with Schumacher? Have we contacted any actual Schumachers yet? They're not the victims, right?"

"No, but they seem to be away—we stopped by their town residence last night. We don't have an ID on the victims yet. At this point, we don't even have a best guess. We've got stuff from the scene that has to be run down. Partial list: blood, fingerprints, footprints, tire prints, spent rounds, hairs and fibres."

The D.S. shifted in his seat and frowned. "Explain something to me."

Cardinal looked at him.

"I thought we were going to have a holdback on this case. Why did I hear Detective Dunbar on CKAT this morning telling the world that the guy had a knife in his back?"

Cardinal looked at Dunbar. "Why the hell would you tell them that? What were you doing talking to the media in the first place? When did this happen?"

Dunbar winced. "I was coming back from canvassing the neighbours. He caught me off guard."

"That's great. And now if another corpse turns up with a knife in its back and minus a head, we're not going to know if we've got a serial killer or a copycat. To say nothing about ruling out false confessions."

"Like I say, he really caught me off guard."

"There's going to be a lot of press, and I want to control what goes to them. Nobody else speaks to them."

"Cardinal's right," Chouinard said. "What else have we got?"

"Ident," Cardinal said. "Maybe Arsenault can tell us the plan there."

Arsenault took a sip from an enormous Tim Hortons mug. "We're waiting in line for a pathologist. They've had three murders in Toronto since Friday and they're short-staffed."

"Two beheadings," Chouinard said, "and we're waiting in line?"

"Give 'em a call—they don't care what I think. Preliminaries: female in mid-thirties, male in mid- to late sixties."

Chouinard shook his head. "Damn it. We should have a holdback. We're already all over the radio, the *Lode* is going to have it on the front page this afternoon, and we've had calls from *The Globe and Mail*, the *Toronto Star*, the wire service. Do you have any idea how big this is? This'll make papers in the States."

Dunbar winced again. "Sorry, D.S."

Arsenault flipped through his notebook. "Footprints. We have two size twelves and one size five, the woman."

"In what? Snow?"

"Yeah. It was just a thin layer, but we managed to get great moulds. Same for the tire tracks. We're putting all this stuff through the databases, but it'll be a while."

"We're looking for a third party, too," Cardinal said. "Someone busted out a back window and left in a big hurry. Got cut pretty bad and then took off into the woods. So that's going to be our new holdback."

"Not a word to anyone," Chouinard said, "or heads will roll." He paused a second. "I wish I hadn't said that."

Arsenault picked the story up. "Tracks indicate a small person, maybe around five-four, five-five, and not too heavy—maybe 120 tops. Tracks head into the trees—running—followed by some size twelves. Much bigger, heavier person. We've got blood from the broken window, so if there's DNA on file we'll nail the runner.

"Runner makes it to the road, where we found some nine-millimetre casings, so presumably size-twelve took a couple of shots at runner. Tracks pick up again at a utility road a hundred yards away. And lo and behold, another set of tire tracks. Can I go to bed now?"

"No, you may not," Chouinard said. "But that's damn fine scene work."

"Of course, we don't know for sure what relationship the runner has to the others," Cardinal said. "Intended victim? Fellow perp in a scenario that went bad? We're still trying to piece together what happened inside the house. Today's agenda is almost totally Ident: they prepare fibres, blood and hairs, and I'll take them down to T.O. later in the day. Delorme, you can come with me. In the meantime, you can track down the Schumachers, and I'll get to work on ViCLAS. "

—

Delorme drove over to the Schumachers' town residence on McGibbon Street. This was a good neighbourhood of old houses and neat lawns. Delorme had been through it a lot recently, because one of her ATM robberies had taken place just around the corner. And late last night she had shoved her card through the Schumachers' mail slot, noting that there were no footprints around their house and no car in the drive. The house was a large red-brick Edwardian, nicely restored and maintained. Now there was a late-model Lexus in the driveway.

She knocked on the front door. It took a while, but a man eventually opened it. He looked about seventy-five, with a badly sunburned face. "Yes? Can I help you?"

Delorme identified herself and asked if he was Joseph Schumacher and if he owned the house at the end of Island Road.

"Yes," he said. "That's me."

"Were you away yesterday, sir?"

"Yes, we were on a cruise round the Mediterranean. Just got back to Toronto last night. Flew back from there and just got in"—he looked at his watch, then back to Delorme—"half an hour ago."

"Did you find the card we put through your mail slot?"

"Haven't had a chance to look. I just tossed all the mail on the kitchen counter."

A woman appeared on the staircase behind him. "What's going on, Joseph? Why are you standing there with the door open?"

"This young lady's from the police. Wants to ask us some questions. See, I told you we should never have joined the Hells Angels, but no, you had your own ideas."

"Mr. Schumacher, maybe we could sit down for a couple of minutes. It seems you haven't heard the news, and I'm afraid I have something bad to tell you."

"What do you mean?" Mrs. Schumacher said. "Has there been an accident? This isn't about our son, is it? His family? No, surely we'd get a phone call—"

"I don't think it concerns your son," Delorme said.

"Well, you'd better come into the kitchen."

They went in and pulled out chairs from the Formica table and all three of them sat down.

"Who has keys to your house on the lake?" Delorme asked.

"Just us," Mr. Schumacher said. "We each have a key. Far as I know, we're the only . . ."

"The only ones," his wife said. "We're the only ones with keys."

"And have you lent the house to anyone recently? Or rented it out?"

"No, we don't rent it out," Mr. Schumacher said. "No one even goes out there unless . . ."

"Unless we're there," Mrs. Schumacher said. She completed her husband's sentences almost as if it were an act they had rehearsed together.

"Well, people went out there," Delorme said. "We're not sure when exactly, but within the past two days at least three people were in your house. Two of them ended up dead."

The Schumachers looked at each other. They looked back at Delorme. Finally Mr. Schumacher said, "You're telling us people were murdered out in our lake house?"

"Yes, sir."

The Schumachers turned to each other again.

"I don't know what to say," the man said. "We've—this is—we lead ordinary lives. There's never been any . . ."

"Discord," the woman said. "No discord."

"But you have to tell us," Mr. Schumacher said. "Who are these . . ."

"People. Victims."

"We don't know," Delorme said. "We were hoping you might be able to help."

"But we need something to go on. We need to know what they . . ." Mr. Schumacher looked at his wife.

"Look like," she said.

"The man's in his late sixties. The woman's in her mid-thirties. They were both dressed in expensive fur coats."

"We don't know anybody like that," Mrs. Schumacher said. "Nobody who owns furs. You said the man was wearing a fur too?"

"Yes, ma'am, the man too."

"We don't know anybody like that. Not that I can think of."

"But your place is for sale, no? You have a sign up. Carnwright Realty?"

"That's right," Mr. Schumacher said. "Carnwright's son-in-law's looking after it for us. Randall . . ."

"Randall Wishart," Mrs. Schumacher said. "That's right, we did give Randall a key. To be honest, we're asking too much for the house—on purpose to discourage actual buyers. Mr. Wishart doesn't know that, of course. We're actually trying to prod Michael—that's our son—to move back here and decide to buy it. He lives in the States, but he keeps saying he's going to move back."

"Aside from Mr. Wishart and your son, who else knows the house is empty?" Delorme said.

"Well, anybody who goes by on a snowmobile, of course," Mrs. Schumacher said.

It was too early in the winter for snowmobiles. The ice on the lake wasn't nearly thick enough.

—

The Violent Crime Linkage and Analysis System, ViCLAS for short, revolves around a national database that categorizes crimes, both solved and unsolved, according to MO. Most murderers not thinking to leave bits of nursery rhymes or other riddles at the scene, investigators have to rely on things like choice of weapon, victim, location and a host of other variables. But before the investigator can glean any information from the system, he or she is first required to fill out a form demanding answers to a great many questions about the current case.

When Cardinal got fed up with trying to answer them, he headed over to Carnwright Real Estate. The Carnwright family had been a force in Algonquin Bay's housing market for three generations. Lawrence Carnwright, the current avatar, was a highly active public figure, constantly turning up on committees and associations, a handsome white-haired gent who would appear on the news when an opinion was wanted on the economic future of the city. Lately his daughter seemed to be following in his footsteps.

The office was located in an exquisitely maintained corner house on Woodrow at Sumner, with a wraparound porch and casement windows and a well-tended lawn. It looked like a set from a TV series about a happy family; all it needed was a swing set on the side lawn. Cardinal had been here several times, when Larry Carnwright had handled the sale of his house.

The receptionist informed him that Randall Wishart was representing the Schumacher property. Wishart came out and shook hands with him and led him back to an office decorated with flattering photographs of Algonquin Bay houses that the Carnwright firm had sold. This being a high-end outfit, there was also a fair bit of art around the place. A small, squat Inuit sculpture of a polar bear sat on top of a bookcase full of binders, and a large, colourful painting or print—Cardinal was never quite sure of the difference—had one wall to itself. There were also plenty of pictures of a sharp-eyed blond woman—in a skiing outfit, in a poolside lounge chair, and a professional portrait in a blue pinstripe suit. She had the startling blue eyes of the Carnwright family.

"Have a seat," Wishart said, indicating a chair. He was handsome in a conventional way, late twenties or so, with something of the look of a politician. Not a hair out of place. "Are you here on police business or about a house?"

"Both. I have some questions about the Schumacher place out on Island Road."

"Don't tell me they've had a break-in."

"Why do you say that?"

"Happens all the time with lake properties—well, I'm sure you know. Was there a break-in?"

"You didn't hear the news on the radio this morning?"

"What news?"

"You're the Schumachers' agent, correct?"

"I guess so."

"You're not sure?"

Wishart smiled. "Well, this is confidential, but the Schumachers are not serious about selling. I knew that right off. I wanted to take a video of the place—it's standard for the online listings—but they wouldn't let me. They're asking way above market, and I think it's really just a ploy to get their kids to move back to Algonquin Bay. Kind of an empty-nest thing. I took them on for goodwill—if they ever really decide to sell that place, I'd love to handle it."

"Have you been out there recently?"

Wishart pursed his lips and shook his head. "Not recently. Not for a few weeks, anyway. I'm gonna go out there and take that sign down. It's just an invitation to trouble, obviously."

The key was not a crucial matter—the back door of the house had been jimmied, after all—but Cardinal asked anyway.

"Yes, I have a key. I should probably return it. They're a nice old couple, the Schumachers, but believe it or not, we do actually like to sell houses, not just put up signs." Wishart sat forward and opened a desk drawer. He rattled around and pulled out a key and put it on his desk. "That'll remind me to get it back to them."

"Have you shown the house to anyone?"

"Not a soul. Had a lot of inquiries, though."

"Phone calls? Or did you actually meet with anyone?"

"Lots of calls. The asking price put 'em off pretty quick. And a few people looked at the picture out on the veranda and came in to ask about it. That stopped soon as I added the price to the posting, though."

"Did any of the inquiries strike you as suspicious?"

"Suspicious in what way? People are always inquiring about houses they can't come close to affording."

"Perhaps someone just trying to determine if the house was unoccupied at the moment? Asking after the owners' whereabouts or habits, for example?"

"No one like that. Just people who like the idea of owning a house out on Trout Lake. No shortage of those."

"All right. Is there anything else you can think of to tell me?"

"Well, no. I mean, it could be anybody, right? We're talking about a break-in."

"Actually, two people were murdered and had their heads cut off."

Wishart went very still and blinked a few times but didn't look away. When he spoke again, his voice was solemn. "Did I hear you right?"

"You did."

"My God. You said they were . . . decapitated?"

"That's right."

"My God," he said again. "But—so, are you looking for some insane individual, like a psycho of some sort?"

"Of some sort."

"My God."

"Just for the record, Mr. Wishart, can you tell me where you were Thursday night?"

"Thursday night? That's easy. I was watching the game at a friend's place. Leafs lost, of course. Troy was destroyed. He's a serious Leafs fan. I mean *serious*. God, I can't get over this."

"Troy?"

"Troy Campbell. We went to high school together."

"I'll need his address. Home and work."

"What? Oh, of course."

Wishart gave him the addresses and Cardinal wrote them down. Then Wishart went with him to the front door, still a little stunned.

Cardinal asked him about the Acura parked outside.

"Pardon me?"

"The black Acura. It's yours?"

"Oh. Yes. Speaking of things we can't afford. God, I can't get over this. It's horrifying. Let me know if I can do anything to help."

"You can. We need you to come down to the station to be finger-printed."

"Sure. Absolutely. I'll try to get down later in the week."

"Today, Mr. Wishart."

⁓

On his way back to the office, Cardinal stopped off at the local hockey arena, which was called Memorial Gardens, although no one knew in memory of what. It was only a couple of blocks from work. Cardinal couldn't remember the last time he'd been to a game, but even though the concession stands were not open at this hour, the smells of popcorn and caramel hadn't changed. A janitor mopping the front lobby directed him to the security office.

A lot of security people are former police officers, or people who want to be police officers. Troy Campbell was neither. A tall man with shoulders that looked like they could support a small cathedral, Campbell was a former captain of the Algonquin Bay Trappers, the local Junior A hockey team. A photograph on the cinder-block wall showed him swooping away from a goal, stick high in the air. He still had the blond hair of the photo-graph, but it was thinner now, unlike the rest of him.

"What can I do for you, Detective? The only time I see police is when we have to charge some drunk for throwing bottles on the ice." Campbell had the easy confidence of a man who is used to being the biggest in the room.

"I'm investigating a major crime, and right now I'm just nailing down a few corroborating details."

"Nothing at the Gardens, I hope."

"No. But I need to know where you were Thursday night."

"Where *I* was."

"That's what I said."

"I don't understand. Why do I have to tell you where *I* was?"

"You don't have to. But it's pertinent to our investigation, so it depends how helpful you want to be. Or not."

Campbell laughed. "Sorry. Don't get me wrong. I'm just mystified. I'm glad to help. Thursday night I was here. Intramural game."

"You were here."

"Yeah. No, wait. Thursday? Thursday I was home. Watching the Leafs on TSN. Total, blatant robbery. You see it?"

"Leafs lost, I take it."

"It was obscene, no other word for it. There was no way Komisarek threw the first punch. Five minutes for fighting and they go from one-nothing to a three-one loss. Ref that called it was Desrosiers. Biased much? Anybody but a French Canadian could see that fight was started by Laraque. I mean, look at the tape, for God's sake. I'm telling you, some people think refs don't know what they're doing, but refs know *exactly* what they're doing. They know *exactly*."

"Anybody watch it with you?"

"Yeah, Randy Wishart. Buddy of mine. Ask him. I nearly threw my beer at the TV screen, and I'm not gonna tell you what I paid for that sucker."

Cardinal got a few more details, and then thanked him for his help.

"Hey, any time. Let me give you some free tickets to the Trappers."

"Thanks, but I really can't. It makes me too crazy."

"Crazy?" Campbell's wide brow furrowed, and he rubbed a hand through his thinning blondness. "You mean cuz of all the fights?"

"The refs. It's just too painful."

"Well, yeah, but up here when they make a mistake, it's cuz they're old or blind. Montreal, it's an outright conspiracy."

5

WHEN CARDINAL GOT BACK to the station, Ident's walls were covered with photographs. Images were tacked to the bulletin board, to the shelves, and taped to the windows, making their cramped quarters even more claustrophobic than usual. The pictures showed every conceivable angle on footprints and tire prints. And the arrangement didn't make much sense to Cardinal until Paul Arsenault started explaining.

"The fresh snow gives us a pretty clear picture of who's who," he said. "We've got tire tracks from two vehicles." He pointed to a photograph. "These were there first. We're checking the databases, but for now we know that it's a mid-size car, not too heavy. The second vehicle is smaller and lighter, pretty new treads. Its tracks are on top of the other car's, but we can't say anything more than that in terms of timing.

"Now, shoe prints. Again, the initial sorting is easy because we were able to take moulds from the shoes of the two victims. The woman's boots—tiny triangular front, small square for the heel, size fives. The man's are size twelve galoshes—note the shallow tread. Hers are Manolo Blahniks, his are Cole Haan—didn't have to look those up, obviously, since they were still at the scene. Took some fibres off the tread of the man's galoshes, but fibres, you know—that's out of our league.

"Which leaves our headhunter. Same size, but a totally different kind of boot. Look at that: deep tread on heel and toe. We're talking serious outdoor footwear here, and I'd say they're pretty new. We should be able to get a make on those pretty quick."

"Tell him about the master bedroom." Collingwood spoke from his desk without looking at them.

"Well, we've got the broken window and the blood. And we've got clear prints from the sill and the chair. Blood type is different from the other room.

"Under the bed, even more interesting. Good layer of dust under there, and look at this. We lifted the bed out of the way to shoot these. You can see where someone's hands were—not the kind of prints you might make pulling something out from under the bed."

"No, looks more like someone slid under there to hide."

"Handprints this end, facing out. And this way you've got leg and toe. Yeah, we think someone was hiding. Picked up some hairs from the top of the bed. A couple of them short, brown. Another one long, black. Now, I've met the Schumachers—they came in right away to give prints—so I know these hairs have nothing to do with them. We also know that some of the prints on the bedside tables are theirs and some of them are not. One set matches whoever broke out the window, the other set matches some we found on the front door but nowhere else—not on the table or the glasses."

"Let me get this straight," Cardinal said. "You're saying we're looking at *five* different people now, not just four?"

"Looks that way."

"We've got all these prints but nothing that matches any criminal record?"

"Not yet. Could still happen, though. Problem for me and Bob is too much evidence, not too little. For example, we pulled a whole bunch of blue fibres off the top of the bed. No big deal, except we didn't find any blue blankets—we photographed the linen closets and the other beds, you can see for yourself. Plus, I asked the Schumachers and they say they don't own any blue blankets."

"I'm still trying to get my head around five people," Cardinal said. "One of them hiding under the bed."

Collingwood spoke from his desk. "Tell him about the wood."

Arsenault pointed to another photograph. A boot print. Beside it, an extreme close-up. The short dark line that appeared in the heel of the first image showed in the second image as a fragment of something. Cardinal leaned closer. When he stepped back, he bumped into Arsenault, who was holding up a small plastic Baggie with the fragment in it.

"This'll have to go to Toronto too. It's a splinter—not big enough for us to figure out what kind of wood, but take a sniff." He held the Baggie open and Cardinal sniffed.

"It's pretty faint. Gasoline? Or maybe oil?"

"Yeah, something like that. We figure maybe someone who works in a garage."

"Really? It's not like we had all sorts of grease stains at the scene."

"Szelagy's got that warehouse arson—maybe this guy is connected with that. Not that we got any boot prints from that scene."

"I'm going to have to think about it," Cardinal said. "We can't just be looking for someone who wore boots in a garage."

Loud voices and the scrape of furniture. Sounds of an altercation out front.

Cardinal left Ident and went to the front desk. Delorme was already there, along with McLeod and Dunbar, watching a street cop struggling to hold on to a man of about fifty who was handcuffed at his side.

The man was yelling over and over again, "You're arresting the wrong guy. I'm not the one committing the crimes. Do you have any idea what they do to those animals?"

The uniformed cop wasn't letting it ruffle him. "Act your age. You'll get your say in court."

"Let me go. You're holding the wrong person, for Chrissake." The man twisted around and kicked at the officer.

"All right, that's it. You're going in the cell now."

Two other street cops took hold of the man and dragged him away, still shouting. "It's not even real blood! It's paint—just paint, you Neanderthal. Haven't you ever heard of free expression?"

The Neanderthal took off his parka and tossed it on a chair while he gave his information to the duty sergeant. He looked around at the audience. "Chad Pocklington. Every year he stomps right over to the fur auction and throws paint on the cars. Every single year. Guy's got a serious case of Noone's."

This was a reference to an ancient line of graffiti that had long decorated the men's room in Algonquin Bay's former, now demolished, police station: *Sparky Noone is full of shit.*

6

ONE OF THE HEADACHES OF BEING a detective in a small city is that there is no forensic science centre nearby. Almost every homicide case requires numerous trips back and forth to Toronto, and it pretty much has to be the lead investigator who does this, along with a backup to make sure there is no question about chain of evidence.

Cardinal and Delorme didn't get away until after lunch. It being Saturday, the traffic was not too bad, but they ran into blowing snow in Muskoka and a near whiteout around Barrie, and it took more than four hours to get to the Forensic Sciences Centre in downtown Toronto. They didn't have to stay for an autopsy; there was still no pathologist available to do one. But it took them over an hour to nudge their evidence through the central receiving process before they could get back on the road for the trip home.

That night, Cardinal ate a late dinner at his kitchen table, flipping idly through pages of the Scriver file. Some of them—thermal faxes from the eighties—had gone perfectly blank. He put his dishes in the sink and shoved the massive file back into its box. He wouldn't be getting to it any time soon.

He sat up for a while in his underventilated living room watching the late night shows, even though he found them neither funny nor informative. He switched them off and read for a while in a self-help book about how to never get upset about anything. Delorme had highly recommended it, but Cardinal found the author's relentless optimism irritating, not least because it was expressed in exclamation marks. What use was advice that suggested you shouldn't be upset about unsolved cases, decapitated corpses?

He went to bed sweaty and grumpy and woke in the middle of the night. The red glow of his alarm clock said 3:50. For months after Catherine's death he had woken up every hour. But this was different. The wisp of a dream was still hanging in the darkness. He had seen himself standing by Arsenault in the ident room. They had been examining the sliver of wood in the Baggie, holding it to their noses and sniffing.

"Some kind of solvent, maybe," Arsenault had said.

Then Cardinal had taken the Baggie from him, held it under his own nose and sniffed. "I know what it is," he said. And that was what woke him up.

He got out of bed and went into the bathroom and splashed cold water on his face. He thought about phoning Arsenault to tell him his idea but decided not to wake him. He got dressed, put on his Kodiak boots and his North Face parka and went out.

It wasn't as cold as it had been, maybe ten below, but Cardinal hadn't had breakfast and it felt much colder. He set the car heater to blow onto the windshield, backed out of his parking slot and headed out through the brick gate that marked the boundary of his condominium's property.

The government dock was less than three minutes away by car. Main West, a residential area of oversized houses and ancient trees, was deserted. Only one house had any lights on, and a car was warming up in its driveway, plumes of grey exhaust billowing from its tailpipe.

Cardinal made a right turn toward Lake Nipissing. He parked on the shoulder of the road near the wharf, switched off the car and got out. The thin layer of snow had mostly either blown away or melted on the wooden dock. Cardinal stood for a moment and sniffed. Even in the minus-ten air the oily smell of creosote was strong.

He wasn't sure what he expected to find. Even in winter the dock attracted a lot of people: joggers, dog walkers, people taking in the sunset. There wouldn't have been any sunset last night. A layer of cloud had formed over the lake and the islands and the town. The only light on the dock came from the high lamps set every twenty yards or so.

He passed the old *Chippewa Princess* cruise ship that was now a restaurant in permanent dry dock. Farther up, there was a bait and souvenir shop that cast a shadow three times longer than the shop itself.

Cardinal moved slowly, keeping his eyes on the wood just in front of his feet. The dock was old, and there were soft splinters on many of the thick slats. If the Trout Lake murderer had been here, Cardinal was not likely to find the exact spot. And there was a marina out at Trout Lake he planned to check out as well.

The wharf was L-shaped. Cardinal didn't even glance up as he made the turn. Beneath his feet the sound of ice grinding against the dock. The smell of old fish, mixing with the creosote. Light glinted on the stems of old fish hooks embedded in the wooden safety wall. It felt five degrees colder out here.

A third of the way along the foot of the L, he still hadn't seen any damaged patches of wood that might have been more likely than others to yield splinters. He glanced up and saw people at the end of the dock. It took a second for him to realize they weren't people.

The heads were on the wooden wall of the dock, which ran about chest high. Cardinal approached the female first. Long blond hair hung down over the wall. On the side nearest Cardinal, it was matted with congealed blood. On the left, a small-calibre bullet hole. She was facing the wide, dark expanse of the lake, as if waiting for a lover, long absent, to return across infinities of wind and night and snow.

The male was a few yards farther on, at the end of the dock wall, facing east. The back of the skull was bloody and misshapen from an exit wound. A breeze ruffled the grey hair.

"Jesus," Cardinal breathed.

He had his hands in his pockets and kept them there as he leaned over the end of the dock to get a look at the face. The closed eyes, the meditative stillness, might have lent the features an air of repose, were it not for the bullet hole over the right eyebrow.

Cardinal walked back the way he had come, undoing his parka to dig out his phone from his inside pocket—keep it anywhere else and the cold would kill the battery. He dialed Delorme. He walked slowly as he talked, trying to calm down. Then he called Chouinard and the staff sergeant. When Delorme arrived a few minutes later, Cardinal was waiting for her by his car.

"Get ready," he told her. "It's even worse than the other night."

After they got there and Delorme looked at the dead faces, she said, "What made you come out here in the middle of the night?"

"Arsenault found a sliver of wood that smelled like oil or gas. I didn't realize till just now it was creosote. These people are likely from out of town—I thought, what do visitors do when they come here? They see the cathedral, the railway museum, the government dock. That's about it."

"Well, obviously the heads had to be brought here in the dark, but that splinter of wood—that was in the killer's footprint?"

"Right."

"Which means he went sightseeing on this dock *before* the murders?"

"I don't know about sightseeing, but I'm guessing he was here, yeah. Somebody might have seen him, even if there was no one here when he came back to hang up his trophies."

Delorme gestured toward the end of the dock. "He must have kept those things somewhere between the murders and now—they can't have been here more than a few hours."

"And why bring them here anyway? Why take the chance of being seen? Why set them up in those weird positions?"

"Once you start cutting people's heads off, probably a lot of other stuff isn't going to seem that weird," Delorme said. "But the bullet wounds—they fit with the scene at the cottage, right? The male was sitting to the left of the killer, the female to the right. The killer pulls out his gun, shoots the male before he can even react, *pow*. Then he shoots the woman in the side of the head. Makes sense, no?"

"Except I wouldn't vouch for the order they were shot in. That's just not knowable. Not yet, anyway."

Cardinal took a few steps back the way they had come, toward the long part of the dock. He stopped and stood with his hands in his pockets. He turned and looked out over the lake in the same direction as the dead woman. He thought about who these people might be and who their killer was. He stared across the frozen lake, beyond the patches of black ice and the dry granules of snow that skittered across them. His eyes watered from the cold. The cloud cover had shifted and the moon was out, lighting the vast bleak plain of the lake. In the distance, black on black, the silhouettes of the Manitou Islands, and above the Manitous, an even blacker sky where cold stars winked and throbbed.

—

Later, when there was nothing more for Cardinal to do at the scene, he walked back along the dock. It was blocked off with crime scene tape now, and even though it was Sunday morning, a crowd of reporters pressed up against it. The beheadings had made the news services across the country, and there were journalists from Ottawa and Toronto in town, as well as locals from Algonquin Bay and Sudbury.

Cardinal had been preparing a statement in his head.

"All I can tell you right now is we have found some body parts that may belong to the victims who were discovered out at Trout Lake. We don't have any identities, and because of that, we don't know who might have wanted to kill them. Even when we do identify them, you know the drill—you'll have to wait until we've notified next of kin."

A barrage of questions. Were the victims really American? What was the crime scene like? Had they found the heads?

"We have just as many questions as you do at this point."

"Will you be bringing in the OPP?" They always asked this, every time there was a high-profile case, as if only a police force of province-wide heft could handle it. They always asked and it always irritated him.

"I don't see any need for the OPP."

They shouted more questions.

Cardinal held up his hands as if pressing back a billowing sail. "That's all for now. When I know more, you'll know more."

He pushed his way past them and hurried toward his car. A woman came up behind him. She was small, her blond head just level with Cardinal's shoulder.

"Detective, could I just talk to you for a minute?"

"Talk all you want." He kept moving toward his car, the woman following.

"I want to ask about the other scene, not this one. It's extremely interesting that the victims were beheaded—and the knife still in the man's back. It's all so theatrical, so high-profile. Aren't you worried about copycats or false confessions?"

"I appreciate your concern," Cardinal said. "We'll still be able to eliminate false confessions. I can't say any more just now."

"And suppose, God forbid, you should get a copycat?"

Cardinal stopped and turned to face her. "Are you hard of hearing? I said I can't talk to you. What is it with reporters?"

Her response was a single, slow blink. She had grey eyes, very wide set, that gave her a look of imperturbability. A quick smile, then: "Now that you have heads, are you able to make an ID?"

"I didn't say *heads*."

"I can do the math, Detective."

"What paper are you with, anyway?"

She took off a leather glove, reached into her pocket and pulled out a business card and handed it to Cardinal. Donna Vaughan. *New York Post*. "The card's out of date. I'm not actually with the paper anymore. I'm freelance."

"Why is a reporter from New York interested in a murder in Algonquin Bay?"

"I think you'll figure that out pretty quick. I'm working on a story—not for the *Post*, for someplace national, hopefully—a story that's taking me all over. And I think maybe we could help each other. Did you get anywhere with the tire tracks at the Trout Lake scene?"

"We're running down a lot of leads. It takes time."

"And the footprints?"

"Like I say, we're following up a lot of threads."

She looked him up and down. "Maybe I was wrong. It doesn't look like you can help me at all. Thanks for your time."

Cardinal got into his car and switched on the ignition to warm it up. He pulled out his notebook and started jotting down a list of calls he had to make. Ms. Vaughan pulled up beside him in a tan Focus and rolled down her window.

Cardinal pressed the button on the armrest.

"You know, Detective, I bet I know more than you do at this point."

"For instance?"

"For instance, the identities of the victims." She flicked a strand of hair out of her eyes. Her brows were dark, and the contrast gave her eyes an added intensity. "Their names are Lev and Irena Bastov. Russian extraction, but they're both U.S. nationals."

"Uh-huh. And how would you know that?"

"The story I'm working on? It's about the Russian mafia—and please don't spread that around, because I'd kind of like to stay alive." She drove away before her window was finished closing.

7

"WE KNOW WHO THEY ARE," Delorme said when Cardinal arrived in the squad room. "We've got IDs!"

"Let me guess," Cardinal said. "Lev and Irena Bastov."

Delorme looked deflated. "How'd you find out?"

"Doesn't matter. How'd *you* find out?"

"Woman up at the fur auction called in a missing person. They were staying at the Highlands Lodge. We should head up there right now."

"Let Ident get started on their own. We've got the autopsy this morning. Just give me a minute and we can catch the next plane—I'm not driving on the 400 again."

Cardinal sat at his desk without removing his coat, pulled out the business card Donna Vaughan had given him and dialed the *New York Post*. It being Sunday, there was no upper management available, but Cardinal finally got connected to an editor.

"Donna Vaughan? Yes, she used to be on staff here."

"Why did she leave?"

"I can't discuss anybody's work history, Detective—too likely to end up on the wrong side of a lawsuit. I can confirm that she was on staff and that she left about a year ago, and that's it."

Cardinal had googled Donna Vaughan as they spoke. Several stories popped up with her byline, mostly about fashion.

"You coming or what?" Delorme was standing beside his desk, looking annoyed.

—

They caught an Air Canada flight to Toronto and arrived at the morgue a little early. Cardinal made a few calls, but Delorme just sat staring at the row of wellington boots lined up on a high shelf. A list of funeral homes and phone numbers was tacked up next to the door, and a hand-lettered sign above the sinks said *Caution: Chlorine + Ammonia = Poison!*

Eventually the door opened and Dr. Elmer Spork was saying hello and introducing his assistant, a petite, intense woman named Tranh, who was about half his height. He took off his sports coat and threw on surgical scrubs and a plastic apron. He didn't look anything like you might imagine a pathologist would look. Although he must have been fifty, he had curly blond hair and the youthful, robust air of someone who has just won a game of tennis. A memory stick dangled from a cord around his neck.

The two bodies were already laid out in the autopsy room, with the heads, which had been flown down earlier. "We put them through the X-ray this morning," Dr. Spork said. He snapped on the light boxes, and ribcages, femurs and arm bones lit up. "As you can see, we didn't pick up anything unusual. No blade or bullet fragments." He snapped off the light again and went over to the male body.

"I have a dumb question," Delorme said. "How do you know a particular head belongs to a particular body? How do you know there isn't some other corpse somewhere minus a head?"

Dr. Spork pointed to the neck area. "Skin tone is the first thing we go by. As you see, we have a perfect match here. Also, the width of the neck. Again a perfect match. Plus, we already took blood samples from each part and we have a match in blood types. That's not definitive, but we've sent the samples to the lab for DNA analysis. But the crucial thing, at least with well-preserved bone and tissue, is the matching trauma. "

He tipped the head neck-up, and Delorme's stomach did a half turn.

One minute the body looks like a young woman, then he's turning the head upside down without moving the trunk.

"We can pair up the damage on both sections of cervical spine," Dr. Spork continued, "same as a broken chair leg. Severed between C5 and C6, in this case, with matching damage to 5. Obviously with decayed remains it'd be a different story."

Dr. Spork switched on his overhead mike. He announced the date and time, case name and number, and the names of those present. "I'm sure your coroner already noted that the severing of the heads took place post mortem. There's no bleeding into the bone."

He examined the female first, from head to toe. He raised his voice to say, "Lividity indicates she was killed where she sat." Then he made the Y incision and removed the organs. By the time the chest was turned inside out, the body ceased to look human and Delorme's stomach settled down. Dr. Spork didn't address them directly again until he had finished with the torso and extremities.

"Negative for disease or trauma," he said. "The head, obviously, is going to be another matter. We have two bullet wounds—entry wound in the left parietal region nine millimetres in diameter, ragged exit through the right parietal approximately fifteen centimetres in diameter."

His assistant started up the Stryker saw. Dr. Spork removed the cap of the skull with its beautiful hair. Smell of burnt bone. Dr. Spork placed the brain in a pan and dissected it with a few swift strokes. "Bullet ricocheted around in there, crossing both hemispheres and ripping a hole in the brain stem. That would have shut down pretty much all the vital organs, so that's our cause of death."

He turned his attention to the male, muttering into the mike, raising his voice when he had any finding of interest. Lividity again indicated death in the seated position. "Liver's enlarged. This guy liked a drink." A little later he held up a cross-section of heart. "Left ventricle's virtually closed. Short of a transplant, he didn't have a lot of time left."

Once again the finding was death by gunshot wound to the head.

"Not much so far," Delorme said as they got into the elevator. "Hardly worth coming down here."

"Ah, but now we get to see Cornelius Venn," Cardinal said. "The wizard of firearms and toolmarks. I think I'll let you handle Mr. Venn."

"I can't believe we've got that guy for both ballistics and toolmarks. He's such a dork. And you always make me deal with him."

"Because you look so cute when you're upset."

"That's inappropriate in so many ways I'm not even going to count them."

"I know. I've been studying under McLeod."

Outside, they breathed in deep lungfuls of cold air—even Toronto's atmosphere could be refreshing after the morgue—and headed around the corner to the Forensic Centre.

"I don't have anything for you." This from Cornelius Venn, a bony little stork of a man who always spoke in a strange sub-glottal whine, as if there were a small bottle lodged in his throat. "If I did have anything for you, I would have called. That would have been the proper protocol."

What was it with Venn? He always came on as if you had committed against him some well-known outrage, unaddressed by the proper authorities. Delorme made an effort at Buddhist serenity—otherwise she might have smacked him. "Could you just tell us what you have so far?"

"All I can say is that the heads were severed by a weighted blade. An axe or an axe-like object."

Cardinal laughed. Venn beamed a level-four scowl at him.

"You must be able to tell more than that," Delorme said. "You have photographs of the wounds. What do you see under the microscope?"

"Detective, are you aware of *Crown versus Toft* in New Brunswick?"

"No, Mr. Venn, I am not up to date on New Brunswick case law."

"You should be. Rudiger Toft was convicted of stabbing a man to death five years ago, largely on toolmarks evidence. The superior court overturned the conviction, because the so-called expert had testified that the wound in question had been caused by a certain knife—i.e., a particular knife *to the exclusion of all others*, as the law books have it. Which was far beyond his actual expertise. And if you think I'm going to join him in the thin-ice club, you are grossly mistaken."

"I'm not asking you to swear to anything. I'm just asking for what you've got."

"I won't have anything useful until you have an actual weapon for me to compare with the wounds. I can tell you that both decapitations were performed using the same blade. And it was obviously not the knife in the male victim's back."

"There you go, Cornelius. See, you do have something after all. Don't sell yourself so short. And you know this how?"

"There are crush marks in the damaged tissue, which you'd only get with the weight of an axe or something similar. Striations in the neck cartilage are identical in both cases, but totally dissimilar to test markings with the knife."

"And what about that knife?"

"It's a Bark River Upland hunting knife. Barely used, I'd say. Fixed blade, not folding, in the so-called skinner style."

"So the sort of thing a trapper would use?"

"Let's not go leaping to conclusions. Yes, it is designed to field dress and skin large game. But point two, it's also expensive, and point three, it's a popular item with survivalists. Most trappers these days would be more likely to go for the newer drop-point style of blade."

"So it might be the choice of an older man?"

"Leap, leap, leap, Detective. I'll just stay on solid ground, if you don't mind."

"Detective Cardinal, did you have any questions for Mr. Venn?"

"No, indeed."

"Okay. Well, I guess I have just one last one."

"Really," Venn said. "How pleasant."

"Have you ever considered taking antidepressants? Zoloft? Prozac? Might make your life a lot easier."

"Perhaps you're unaware, Detective Delorme, that the SSRIs have the known side effect of interfering with sexual function."

Delorme had to leave before he said any more. She checked her watch and said something about making their plane.

"Good to be out of there," Cardinal said when they were out on the street again. "That was terrifying."

"Yeah. Weighted blades and all."

"No, no. The thought that Cornelius Venn has a sex life."

8

SAM DOUCETTE HAD SPENT THE entire weekend shuttered in her room, only coming out for meals. From the first moment she had heard that word, *beheaded*, she had barely been able to move. She told her mother she had a big art project due for class—and she did work on her drawings—but she kept switching obsessively from the radio to the Web, checking the news reports for any mention of witnesses or "persons of interest."

She picked up Pootkin, small warm bundle, but the cat squirmed away and leapt onto the windowsill and sat there whapping the wall with her tail.

Randall hadn't called. He would have to know about the murders by now; he must know how frightened Sam was. But he didn't call. She wanted him to put a strong arm around her shoulders, to tell her everything would be all right. She wanted a police car with two burly officers in it to park outside her house twenty-four hours a day and follow her at a not too discreet distance. She wanted a muscly bodyguard in a black turtleneck and an earpiece to walk beside her looking intimidating.

Reason told her that the best policy would be to go about her normal routine as if nothing was wrong. She opened her closet and dug out a mid-length denim coat with a woolly collar and lining. Her down coat, torn and bloodied, was jammed in the back of a shelf. She dug out a beret she hadn't worn this year. Her father had given it to her and she had to admit it was pretty cute. But one day Lisa Culkin had said, "Hey, you look great, Sam—just like a Girl Guide." Which was probably why her father liked it, the serious air it imparted to his frivolous, wayward daughter who only wanted to study art and nothing, as he put it, "real."

She grabbed her backpack and went out to the garage and looked at the back end of the Civic. Beret, backpack, different coat—it's not me he's going to recognize, she figured, it's this damn car. The garage was her father's domain—when he was home. The walls were covered with shelves full of tools, hardware, bits of lumber and parts of machines he intended to fix but never did. He also kept his hunting gear out here. Not his guns, but his tents and sleeping bags and a canoe hoisted up on ropes. There was the Vixen Excalibur crossbow he had taught her to use, his longbows, and arrows in various states of repair. His current walkabout must be just a hiking trip, because most of his hunting stuff seemed to be there.

She rooted around on the shelves and the workbench and found an open tub of Polyfilla. She had to pry the top off with a screwdriver. The stuff inside looked usable.

The how-to sites said you were supposed to fill the hole with mesh or wire wool first, but the hole was so small that didn't seem necessary. She scooped out some of the compound and smoothed it over the damaged metal. It looked about as much like a bullet hole filled in as a bullet hole could look. It would be hard to match the paint, but she planned to bring a couple of tubes back from the college and give it a try.

The tail light was another matter. She had called the Honda dealership and they'd told her they could have the part in two days and it would cost her more than a week's pay. They took a deposit off her credit card, which with her student credit limit left her about fifty cents' further flexibility.

She caught the bus up to the college and spent the afternoon in drawing class. They had a nude model—a girl from the drama department with big shoulders and beautiful breasts. Sam wondered for a moment if she might be a little bit lesbian, but then she remembered Randall's body and the things he did to her and decided it was not possible.

Raffi March, the instructor, went from student to student. It always took Sam quite a while to know what she thought of a drawing, but Raffi always knew right away. He was an enthusiastic teacher, had a boundless affection for young artists, and he was by far the gayest person most of the students had ever met. The boys, in particular, never tired of imitating his flamboyant manner of speech.

"*Tisk-tisk-tisk*, Miss Doucette. *Tisk, tisk, tisk.* This is not an illustration class. Algonquin College does not offer an illustration class. This is not Comics 'R' Us. We're here to draw, draw, draw."

"I am drawing."

"You're illustrating." He pointed with a graphite-grubby finger at her work. "Hard shadows and simple lines will work on a poster or in a comic book, but you're not developing your skills with light and shade—and you must, must, *must* develop a finer touch. You'll never be able to capture subtleties of expression otherwise."

"Can't you just use a camera for that?"

"I'm going to pretend I didn't hear that." He turned to the entire class and spread his arms theatrically the way he always did when making pronouncements. "This is *fine* art, people. *Fine* art. Subtlety is not your enemy. Subtle is not the same as boring. Dare to be dull!"

"But what if I'm not a subtle person?"

"Well, I suppose you could stick to crayons and Magic Markers."

"Really? Could I?"

Raffi put his face in his hands and wept with a gusto and conviction that made the class laugh. Only the model, half hidden behind her waterfall of blond hair, remained silent.

—

The Highlands Ski Lodge was just outside the city limits off Highway 11. It was the newest of Algonquin Bay's hotels, and by far the most expensive. It was not visible from the highway. To get to it, you had to drive up a winding road to the top of Highland Ridge, an outcropping of the Precambrian Shield that dropped down toward Trout Lake in the north and offered a lofty view of Lake Nipissing to the south.

The lobby was a grand, high-ceilinged vista of cedar and red carpet. Cardinal and Delorme introduced themselves to the pretty Native girl at the front desk and waited there for the manager. He finally appeared, absurdly young and dressed in a sombre suit that would have looked good on a man twenty years older. His name was David Dee, and he reeked of Scope.

"Mr. Dee, we need to see your registration records for the past week."

"May I ask what for?"

"We're following up on a missing person report."

"Under what name?"

"Bastov. Lev and Irena."

Dee went behind the counter and stood at a computer terminal and typed in a few letters. His right hand nudged the mouse a couple of times and twirled the scroll button.

"They checked in, let's see . . . on Wednesday."

"They booked as part of the fur auction, right?"

"That's right. They got a discount, even though they booked our most expensive suite."

"Have they checked out?"

"No, they haven't." Mr. Dee frowned at the screen, his eyes scanning up and down.

"May I see the screen please?"

Mr. Dee swivelled the monitor around. It wouldn't turn all the way and Cardinal had to lean over the counter to see. There were no entries for car and licence plate; he often didn't give those himself when he checked into a hotel. "There's a note here. They ordered room service, breakfast for two for Friday morning, but no one answered the door when it was delivered?"

Mr. Dee swivelled the screen back. "Yes, that's right. The room service manager charged it to the room and attached this note to the guest file."

"Mr. Dee, we need to search their room, and we need to do it right away."

"Do you have a warrant?"

"No. But we have reason to believe—"

"You must know that's not possible. We can't have police searching guest rooms without a warrant. As long as our guests are registered here, the Highlands is their home. They have the same rights as they would have in their own household."

Delorme stepped closer and leaned across the counter. "Mr. Dee, the Bastovs' right to keep their heads connected to their bodies has probably already been violated. They're not going to get upset if we search their room."

The manager looked from Cardinal to Delorme and back again. "Oh, my God. These are those people?" His hand rose to cover his mouth. "Oh, my God."

⁓

Room 217 looked out over the ski runs. Outside, the lift was hoisting people in goggles and colourful jackets into a sky of deep blue that flashed against the white glare of the slopes. There had been no serious snowfall yet this winter, but the snow-making machines had taken care of that. The room itself was overheated and smelled of perfume.

"I don't know what that is," Delorme said, sniffing, "but it's expensive."

Mr. Dee stationed himself by the door, hands clasped before him as if he were presiding over a funeral.

In the bathroom, Delorme pointed to a tiny atomizer of Jean Patou and said, "That costs at least two hundred dollars an ounce."

There was a white leather toiletries case beside the sink on the left, and a tan leather one beside the sink on the right. Delorme examined the woman's things and Cardinal the man's.

Cardinal held up a prescription bottle of blue pills.

"I bet those have saved more than one marriage," Delorme said.

They moved into the main room and surveyed the tops of the dressers, opening and closing the drawers. Clothes were folded neatly. There were several woman's watches, cufflinks, even a tie pin.

"Guy's really old-school," Cardinal said. "I haven't seen a tie pin since the sixties."

"They were very thorough about unpacking," Delorme said, "like they were planning to stay quite a while. I don't think the fur auction has even officially started yet, has it?"

"The Highlands is a destination resort," Mr. Dee said from the doorway. "A lot of the fur people book extra time. Especially if they like to ski."

Two pairs of top-of-the-line K2 skis were propped up against one wall, still with store tags attached. In the closet, a neat array of clothes on hangers, woman's on the left, man's on the right. New York labels. Sweaters folded on the shelves, shoes and ski boots paired up in rows on the floor.

"No wallets anywhere," Delorme said. "And there were none on the bodies."

"We're going to need that opened," Cardinal said, pointing to the safe on a lower shelf.

"Sure," Dee replied. "I can do that."

"Hold it." Cardinal pulled out a ballpoint pen. "Use this."

Dee got down on one knee and used the tip of the pen to key in an override code. There was a whirring sound, the door popped open, and he stepped back to his former position, folding his hands as before.

"No wallets, no cellphones," Cardinal said. "If the killer took them, let's just hope he uses them." He extracted two passports from the safe. One Russian, one U.S.

Delorme came to look as he opened the American passport. Lev Petrovich Bastov, sixty-three years old. "That's our guy," she said. "Definitely looks better all in one piece."

Cardinal opened Irena Bastov's passport. The Cyrillic alphabet stalled him, but the birthdate was clear and there was a U.S. visa attached that was filled out in English. Maiden name, Divyris. Country of origin, Ukraine. "Not even thirty," Cardinal said. "That's quite an age difference. The guy's handsome, I guess. But not that handsome."

He turned the pages slowly.

Delorme pointed to the U.S. visa, the words *Permanent Resident*. "That could be why she married him."

"You don't think it was love at first sight?"

"Maybe on his side." Even the photograph's harsh monochrome could not mar the shining hair, the regal cheekbones, the erotic intelligence in Irena Bastov's eyes.

Cardinal slipped the passports into a Baggie, put them in his pocket and knelt to take a closer look at the clothes. Health conscious, the two of them. Running shoes and gym gear for both. Then, under a stack of cashmere sweaters, a fifteen-inch Apple laptop.

Cardinal carried it over to the desk and opened it up next to the telephone. "Mr. Dee, do you have records of phone calls made or received?"

"We'll have any long-distance calls. Local you'll have to get from the phone company."

"Could you check for us, please?"

Cardinal spent some time with the computer, starting with Irena Bastov's browser history. The most recent activity was at Yahoo! Mail. E-mail could be a gold mine, but they would need her password. Before Yahoo!, there were searches for local restaurants, and sites that rated different types of ski boots. Before that, a search of real estate listings. Cardinal clicked on that. There were a couple of pages for Algonquin Bay and another in Huntsville.

"Seems like they were house hunting." Cardinal opened her address book application. Many of the entries consisted of a single name and an e-mail address, starting with Anton and ending with Zara.

"Come and take a look at this," Delorme said.

Cardinal joined her in the closet.

"You have to get on your knees to see it."

Cardinal got on his knees.

"Look at the hem of her skirt there. The long one."

Cardinal had to put on his reading glasses to get a good look. "Sawdust," he said. "She looks like such a princess. Where would she pick up sawdust?"

"Oh, that's easy." Mr. Dee had once again taken up his post at the doorway. "The lift shack and skyway are under renovation. The work was supposed to be done a month ago, but they're using all different kinds of woods and there was a delay in getting the cedar and mahogany. Anyway, sawdust everywhere. They probably went to check out the facilities when they arrived. And the front desk says there were a couple of long-distance calls. I had them print out the numbers for you." He held out a sheet of paper.

Cardinal took it from him and looked it over. "Hey, there's a bit of luck," he said to Delorme. "First number they called is the first number in her address book. Guy named Anton."

He took out his own cellphone and dialed the number. Voice mail. A deep voice, indeterminate accent, cultured. *This is Anton Bastov. Leave a message and I'll call you back.*

"I don't mean to rush you," Mr. Dee said, "but are you guys about done?"

Behind him in the hallway, Paul Arsenault and Bob Collingwood appeared in identical bunny suits, each holding a black ident case.

Cardinal and Delorme left the ident team at the hotel and drove over to the Algonquin Bay Fur Harvesters' warehouse, which was located on the edge of town between the city proper and the Nipissing First Nation reserve.

The warehouse consisted of a front office, a large, echoing showroom, and several smaller showrooms for the display of different lots. Cardinal and Delorme were shepherded around by manager Hank Stromberg, a man with a neatly trimmed grey beard and hair the colour of nicotine. He was treating them with courtesy, but it was the strained courtesy a car dealer shows to someone who is never going to buy.

The bears—their hides, that is—were spread out on a large table: black and brown and tan with legs outstretched and chins upraised, as if they were doing the breaststroke. A nearby table displayed a dozen polar bear hides.

"But they're endangered," Delorme said. "How can you still sell them?"

"The polar bear is not endangered," he said. "Not in this country."

"What can anybody do with a polar bear hide? Who buys them?"

"Russians, mostly. They stuff them. Put them in the office lobby. Make an impression."

Men in white lab coats were moving from lot to lot, touching hides, making notes.

Cardinal pointed. "Who are the guys with the clipboards?"

"Buyers. They have until this evening to check out the merchandise. Friday was beaver. Bidding on the rest continues through tomorrow."

"And Irena Bastov was a buyer?"

"She was."

"For whom?"

"That I couldn't tell you. You'll have to ask our Russian agent. All I know is she bought a lot of fur."

"Russian agent?"

"A woman on staff here who works with the foreign buyers. A lot of them don't speak English. She translates for them—and for us, of course. These are the minks. Oh, and seal."

Stromberg led them through the main showroom where mink pelts hung from display poles. The air was redolent with fresh hide.

"Eighty percent of these are farm raised," Stromberg said. "You can feel the difference in the fur." He held out a pelt of chestnut brown for them to touch. Cardinal had never felt anything so soft. "Amazing what good care and regular feeding will do for an animal. Far superior to trapped fur. Here's the seal."

Seal hides took up perhaps a quarter of the space, spread flat on tables and on the floor. Delorme pointed to a stack of small hides. "They're so tiny. I thought it was illegal to kill baby seals."

Stromberg shook his head. "You're thinking of harp seals. These are ring seals. Not as photogenic."

The next room was devoted to wolves. Hundreds of pelts hung from a rack that snaked around the warehouse like a vast coat check. The wolves were strung up by their snouts, fluorescent light gleaming through the holes where their eyes had been.

"Those weren't farmed," Cardinal said.

"No. Trapped."

"If a buyer checked in Wednesday night, when would you expect to see him or her?"

"If they were interested in beaver, I'd expect to see them here for the preview Thursday afternoon, and Friday for the bidding. I saw the Bastovs here Thursday, but I didn't talk to them other than to say hello. They seemed happy. Cheerful. They were shooting the breeze with people. Laughing. Scoping out the merchandise like everybody else. You can check the sign-in sheet for exact times."

"Did you notice anything unusual about them? Anything at all?"

Stromberg stroked his beard for a moment and stared at the floor. "Nope. Strictly business as usual. Mind you, auction time, I'm rushed off my feet—I don't stop moving from morning to night, so I wouldn't be the best person to ask."

"Is it weird to arrive on Wednesday for an auction that doesn't start until Friday?"

"Depends what you want to get out of it. It's called an auction, but in a way it's kind of like a conference. People get the lowdown on what everyone else is up to. And they might combine the trip with a little vacation, who knows?"

"Did either of them have any enemies?"

"Not that I know of. Lev's a pro, been in this game for decades. So, yeah, it's possible he pissed some people off in his life. And they're wealthy—people might be envious. But serious enemies? None that I know of."

"You've been running this place eight years, you said?"

"That's right."

"And the Bastovs have been coming here all that time?"

"Irena's been coming the past four years at least, Lev just the past two. But Lev's not really a buyer at this point—he just comes to be with his wife. And for the skiing maybe."

"If he's not a buyer, what is he?"

"Lev is money. He's a manufacturer. Plants all over Russia. He'd be selling to the big furriers—the designers, the big department stores. Lot of dough in that part of the trade."

"How did you come to be running this place?" Cardinal said. "What were you doing before?"

"I was a trapper. Not full-time—nobody in this town's full-time. But I'd been doing it a lot of years. Me and my partners took the place over when the last bunch went belly up. Figured we could do a better job. Believe me, a double murder is not going to help our balance sheet."

"What happened to the former owners? Why did they fail?"

Stromberg shrugged. "You'd have to ask whatshisname—Don Rivard— he was the head guy. I'm guessing expenses outran revenues. We work strictly on a percent of sales. You have a few bad years, a few bad debts . . . It doesn't take much. Ah, here's the lady in question."

A small blond woman with sharp features and a pixie haircut was standing by a set of glass doors, talking on a cellphone. She put it in her pocket and smiled at Stromberg.

"Nat, this is Detective Cardinal and Detective Delorme. They're working on the Bastov thing."

"Natalia Kuritsyn," she said, shaking first Cardinal's hand then Delorme's.

"You're the one who called in the missing persons?" Delorme asked her.

"I am."

"Presumably you tried to call the Bastovs first. Do you have their cell-phone numbers?"

"I do. Come. We can talk in cafeteria." Her Russian accent was strong, as if she had strayed off the set of a Bond film.

"I'll be on the floor if you need anything else," Stromberg said.

The cafeteria consisted of a few tables in a chilly room. Coffee was available at a counter where a dark-eyed girl wearing a head scarf was arranging muffins on a tray. They got their coffees and sat at a table in the corner. The other tables were empty.

Cardinal decided to let Delorme handle Ms. Kuritsyn. He burned his tongue on his coffee and spent the rest of the interview surreptitiously sucking air between his teeth. Delorme got some general background first. Ms. Kuritsyn was a former fur buyer who had come to Algonquin Bay many times before deciding to make it her home. Immigration had not been a problem because she had fallen in love with a trapper and married him.

"Judging by the people on the floor," Delorme said, "there aren't a lot of women in this business."

"Is true. Same in your business, I think."

"I would have thought two women in the fur industry would gravitate toward one another. Especially since you were from the same country."

"Same country? Irena Bastov is from Ukraine—born there, anyway. More important, she is Moscow. I am Kaliningrad. Not same country. Is like

Paris and Marseilles, only worse. Someone like Irena Bastov is not going to spend time with someone like me. So, no, not friends. Not enemies."

"What about other enemies? She was a beautiful woman. Maybe she caught the attentions of the wrong man?"

Ms. Kuritsyn shrugged. "Possible. I wouldn't know."

"You sound a little hostile."

This elicited a big smile. "Not hostile. Russian."

"What does that mean?"

"Always people misunderstand. Always they think we are with a problem. From television. From movies. They think we are Communist, they think we are gangsters, poets, dancers, drunks. Always they expect big emotion, big gesture. The truth is we are like Canadians—not so boring, maybe—but like you, we are wrapped up inside ourselves. Probably the winters cause this. We are slow to open. Slow to warm."

"What about Irena Bastov? Was she—"

Ms. Kuritsyn pointed a slim finger at Delorme. "And I will tell you other thing. We don't like questions. In my country, questions get you killed. Yes, still. And answering them . . ." She shook her head. "Not good."

"Irena Bastov. Was she slow to warm up to Lev Bastov?"

Ms. Kuritsyn laughed. "Not at all. Was *coup de foudre*. Instant love. On both sides, I would say."

"I can understand Lev Bastov falling for Irena. Irena was young and beautiful. But he—"

"He was rich. He adored her. Of course she loved him back. Who wouldn't?" She leaned across the table. "Forgive me, but I think Russian women are a little more practical on this point. A little less romantic. A wealthy man in love with you? Is like winning lottery."

"No guarantee of happiness then."

"Please, if you know where to find this guarantee, tell me. I will divorce my husband and marry you."

Cardinal laughed. Delorme did not look amused.

Ms. Kuritsyn leaned even closer and touched Delorme's wrist. Not so slow to warm after all. "You are single, I think, Ms. Delorme. Can you honestly tell me you would turn down offer of marriage from a rich, handsome man just because you weren't crazy-mad in love?"

"Let's focus on the Bastovs, all right? Who is Anton Bastov?"

"Anton is Lev's son from earlier marriage. He's maybe early thirties. Used to be a buyer, now he's in fashion industry—Donna Karan, I think. Nice guy, close to his father."

"Okay, now please think about this: did the Bastovs have any enemies? They made a lot of money. Maybe somebody thought they didn't deserve it. Maybe somebody felt cheated."

Another shrug. "I heard Irena's brother is not so crazy about Lev. At first he was all for this marriage. Totally excited. Telling whole world. Then, I don't know, some business deal goes bad, something like that, and . . . not so happy. This is what I hear—I never met him."

"What about jealousy? Maybe someone more romantic than yourself was in love with Irena Bastov."

Ms. Kuritsyn turned to Cardinal but gestured toward Delorme with the slightest toss of the head. "She's good cop, no?"

"You should just answer the question," Cardinal said. He kept it deadpan. He seldom got to see Delorme wrangle with another woman and he was enjoying it.

"You two see each other outside of work?" Ms. Kuritsyn asked.

"Please focus on the question," Delorme said.

"I think you do." Ms. Kuritsyn sat back with the smile of one who has just won a hand of poker. "I didn't really know Irena Bastov. I wasn't interested in Irena Bastov. But I hear things. Things maybe true, things maybe not true."

"Things like what?"

"A bush pilot, comes here a lot. Ron Larivière. Everybody in this business knows Ron. Supposedly he was fucking her. Why do you look like that? You don't use this word? All right. Supposedly they were *making love*," she said, giving it ridiculous emphasis. "You like better? Supposedly they were *making love*. If true, I think this would upset Lev. Who knows? Maybe he got upset and someone got upset back."

"But why would he kill Irena too?"

"In your job I suppose you must try and understand people. Is necessary maybe. But for me?" Ms. Kuritsyn shook her head. "Waste of time."

10

It was dark when Cardinal and Delorme came out of the fur warehouse. The temperature had dropped, and blades of cold pressed against Cardinal's face. The parking lot was empty except for three or four cars and a red pickup with a bumper sticker that said *I ♥ Country Music*.

"Lev Bastov's been in this industry forever," Cardinal said. "It may be his killer has too. At some point we're going to have to talk to some real old-timers. Get background on him and the local biz."

"What did you think of our Russian agent?" Delorme said. She pulled her hood up against the cold.

"I think she liked you."

"Are you kidding? She was completely hostile."

"Funny thing, Lise—you don't seem to have any trouble understanding men, but women are a whole other story. I meant she *liked* you."

Delorme looked back toward the warehouse, then at Cardinal. "No way. She has a husband."

"Touching your hand, saying she'd marry you."

Delorme shook her head. "You are so wrong."

"Well, why don't you wait in the car a minute." Donna Vaughan was waving to Cardinal from across the parking lot. "Someone I have to talk to."

The reporter was by her car, notebook in hand. She had bought herself a thicker parka since the other day.

"Just leaving?" Cardinal said. "Or just arriving?"

"Leaving. Man, I get tired of Russians. These people are paranoid with a capital *P*."

"You talked to Natalia Kuritsyn?"

"Yesterday. Kind of frisky, that one. Today I was interviewing Russian buyers. Four of these guys, all built like trucks. All from Kalinin. Spoke five words of English between them."

"How were you able to ID the Bastovs before we were?"

"Trade secret." She held out her wrists together. "You can tie me up and beat me. I'll never tell."

"I don't think that'll be necessary."

"Actually, it was just dumb luck. I happened to be interviewing Natalia Kuritsyn when she was waiting for the Bastovs to show up. She got more and more worried, called the hotel, called the cops. Did you find the car yet?"

"We're running that down. They may not have bothered renting one."

"Mercury Grand Marquis. Red. Current model. They rented it from Hertz at the airport. You want the licence number?"

Cardinal laughed. "You're good."

"I try to be, Officer."

As Cardinal headed back toward his car, she caught up to him from behind. She spoke breathlessly, words colliding into each other. "Listen, I hate to sound forward and everything. I'm really not a pushy person, despite how it may look. But I'm sick of eating at the hotel and I'm hoping you'll go to dinner with me. Someplace nice. I realize you're married and I'm not trying to pick you up. In fact, I'd love to meet your wife, so bring her too and it'll be my treat, okay? What do you say? I can put it on expenses and it won't even be a lie. Say yes. You can explain Algonquin Bay to me. You can talk about hockey. It'll be fun."

It had started to snow, and a flake landed on her eyebrow and melted there.

—

When Cardinal and Delorme got back to the station, McLeod told them how his unrelenting devotion to duty had led him to canvass the airport rental agencies and determine the make of the Bastovs' car. An all-units alert for the Mercury Grand Marquis was already in place.

Cardinal dialed Anton Bastov's number again. No answer. He looked up Donna Karan, dialed the DKNY corporate headquarters and finally ascertained his whereabouts. Anton Bastov had been overcome by severe food poisoning after a return flight from Paris. He was expected to recover but was still in hospital. Cardinal got the name of the hospital and called them and was told the patient was not well enough to receive bad news or be interviewed.

Cardinal typed up his supplemental reports, wondering if he should mention Donna Vaughan in them. He decided against it. She was press, not a witness, and others had garnered the same information through the usual police footwork.

D.S. Chouinard stopped by Cardinal's cubicle on his way out. "Word to the wise. Just had a call from the FBI's New York office. They're going to be sending a man up here. Special Agent Mendelsohn."

"What for?"

"We've got a couple of dead American citizens and they want to have a look-see. Naturally, we're going to be the model of international co-operation."

At seven-thirty, Delorme put on her coat. "You want to watch a video later, or are you too tired?"

"I'm pretty beat," Cardinal said.

"You staying all night?"

"Nah, I'm just about done." He didn't feel like telling Delorme about his dinner date, he wasn't sure why.

"Who was the blonde at the warehouse?"

"Donna Vaughan. Reporter from the States."

Delorme's brown eyes lingered on him for a moment, then she was gone.

—

DeGroot's restaurant had opened up on Main Street the year before. It couldn't boast the elegance of Champlain's but, with its snug wooden booths and its red plush banquettes, it did offer a pleasant mixture of privacy and conviviality. It didn't hurt that the food was good too. When Cardinal had warned Donna that it was a steakhouse, she said, "Fine with me, Detective. I'm good with red meat."

She was already seated in a booth when he got there. "Typical pathetic single, right? Asks the guy out, gets there first, already into the wine."

"Pathetic is not the word that comes to mind," Cardinal said. "You look amazing."

He hadn't said anything like that to any woman other than Catherine for nearly thirty years. It was completely true, of course. He wasn't sure if it was the colour of her sweater, or something she had done to her hair, or the silver earrings.

"I'm really embarrassed now about being so forward," she said, "and suggesting you bring your wife. I looked you up on the Internet and, boy—brilliant move, Donna."

"You couldn't have known," Cardinal said. He twisted his ring. "I know I should take it off. It's been more than a year now. But we were married a long time."

"Yes, you would be. You're definitely the type. Stable. Steady. Secure." She took a sip of her wine. "Tell me something. Your last name is Native American, right? Sorry—Native Canadian."

"In my case it comes from Scotland. My grandparents were from Fife, wherever the hell that is." Cardinal pointed at the glass of red in her hand. "Should I order a bottle of that?"

"Definitely."

DeGroot's was busier than usual. It was a cold night, and diners had been drawn by the lure of comfort food, candles and a roaring fireplace. When the wine came, Donna told Cardinal how she had become a journalist. It had been a toss-up between politics and journalism, and since she couldn't stand politicians, that had pretty much sealed her fate. After college she had worked at various small-town papers, and eventually got hired at the *Post*, only to get downsized out a couple of years later.

Their salads arrived, and Cardinal told her how he had become a cop. He had been young, just finishing university, studying psychology. His life had then been touched, peripherally, by a murder—a friend of a friend—and the detectives handling the case did not seem to be very good. Cardinal became involved and helped them catch the killer.

"Don't tell me," Donna said, holding up her salad fork. "There was a woman involved. A damsel in distress."

Cardinal smiled.

"I knew it." Candlelight glittered in her eyes, and something else Cardinal couldn't quite place.

He smiled. "We got married a year later."

Donna shook her head. "You are so Canadian."

The waiter whisked away their salad plates and replaced them with their steaks.

"Why did you say that?" Cardinal said. "About being so Canadian?"

"Because you do these amazing things, live this amazing life, and you don't even realize how amazing it is. How rare. An American would be telling you the high points within five minutes. He'd have a ghostwriter working on his memoirs. He'd be a consultant on a TV show."

"In that particular case, I didn't do anything that wasn't completely obvious. I was still a kid, really. It's just the detectives assigned to the case were substandard. Missed stuff they shouldn't have."

"Yeah, but it's how you met your wife. And then you're married for the next God knows how long and you act like it's just the most normal thing in the world." She touched his hand. "Don't ever change. Why are you looking at me like that?"

"I'm trying to figure out if you're always this friendly. Or if it's because you're a journalist and you think I can help you with your story."

"I'm American. We're pushy."

Cardinal shook his head. "My wife was American and she wasn't like that at all. But you seem to say what you're feeling and the hell with it."

"Go ahead. Try it."

"Try what?"

"Say something you feel and the hell with it. Don't worry about being a cop or being proper or being whatever. What are you feeling right now? Just tell me without thinking about it."

"Nervous. Wary."

Donna sat back against the booth. "You mean about my motives? Okay, that's fair. You're right that I definitely want all the information out of you I can possibly get. But that's always true. I could have just made an appointment to talk to you at the office, or cornered you again at the next press conference. So if you mean my motives in asking you out to dinner, well . . ." She shook her head. "You'll just have to keep guessing."

Cardinal tilted his wineglass, studying the ruby light within. "This is the first time I've been out for dinner with a woman other than my wife in . . . decades. I don't have a clue what to do or say."

"Nonsense. In fact, you seem suspiciously smooth."

"Also because you must be about a dozen years younger than me and you're, I don't know, radioactive or something." Cardinal shrugged. "Why don't you tell me what else you know about the Bastovs?"

She pushed her plate aside and sipped her wine. "Lev and Irena Bastov. Small-time buyer Irena falls in love with big-time manufacturer Lev. Two months later she marries him and moves to New York, just as her own little Russian furrier business goes belly up. What can I say? She's a lucky girl."

"Was everybody happy for her?"

"Ooh, you should be a reporter. Irena has a brother named Yevgeny. Apparently he was over the moon when the marriage was first announced—telling everyone Lev was going to buy his failing fur farm and set him up somewhere better, maybe get him eventually into manufacturing. His ship had finally come in. Unfortunately, he managed that fur farm into the ground and now things are not so lovey-dovey. Didn't Ms. Kuritsyn tell you this stuff?"

"Some of it."

"So, cut to the chase. All is connubial bliss, the Bastovs are the wonder couple of the fur trade. You see them in New York, you see them in Copenhagen, you see them in Seattle. All the major fur auctions, the two of them are there. Then, a couple of years ago, a funny thing happens on the way to the auction. This was in Copenhagen. A harvest of 460,000 mink and God knows how many other pelts goes up for sale, and guess what? Nobody bids."

"Nobody? They hold an auction and nobody buys anything?"

"Not one fur is sold. True, we live in a globalized market, and true, we've had several warm winters recently. But not one fur?

"Then we get to Seattle, last year. The furs sell as well as ever. But the prices—the prices go through the floor. Even though demand—except for the Copenhagen anomaly—was more or less stable. Global warming can't account for a drop like that. That's when I started getting interested. I got into this fur stuff through fashion. The paper had me covering the garment industry—I can't tell you how boring that was. Before that, they'd had me covering the art market briefly. Anyway, one day I'm doing background on the Russian fur biz and I hear a rumour that Lev and Irena have organized a bidding ring. It was just a rumour at that point. You've heard of bidding rings?"

"Sure," Cardinal said. "People want to sell a painting, they get friends to bid the price way up."

"Exactly. Difference being, here, the point was to keep the price way down. Very good position to be in if you're a Russian manufacturer trying to compete with cheap Chinese labour. But boy, when I started asking around about that, you wouldn't believe how people clammed up."

"And you think they're Russian mafia?"

"Do I think Lev's *vor*? No. But some connection, definitely. Who else is going to scare an entire industry into not buying a single pelt? Could be they were pure victims. Could be they were acting on behalf of the mob and someone else got irritated. But who else is going to cut heads off and stick them on a public wharf?"

"Last I heard, the Russians were going legit."

"They go wherever money and Russians are gathered together. Banking, energy, hockey, you name it. As far as the fur business, there's Marat Melnick—a Brighton Beach don who has a stake in at least three major fashion houses."

"One thing I do know about the Russian mob," Cardinal said, "they don't hesitate to knock off journalists."

Donna nodded. "Fifteen, at last count."

"That doesn't scare you?"

"It terrifies me. In fact, if I ever publish this thing, I'll probably have to do it under a pen name. In the meantime, as you may have noticed, I want to stay close to cops."

Cardinal asked her if she wanted coffee or dessert, and when she said no, he signalled for the check.

She grabbed his wrist. Her fingers were hot. "Hold on a second. I gave you some pretty good information here, now you have to give me something back. That's how this game works. You do play fair, don't you? And it's my check, by the way." She produced her notebook and clicked her ballpoint several times.

"You realize I'm not allowed to talk about an investigation in progress."

"I do."

"You can't use this in any paper, book, magazine, blog—anywhere—until *after* there's a trial. Only after it's part of the public record, understood?"

"Absolutely." She raised two slim fingers. "Scout's honour."

"All right," Cardinal said. "We just got this back from Toolmarks in Toronto. The weapon used to sever the heads was an axe."

She put her notebook down. "That's it? An axe? You call that a fair trade? Boy, you really play hardball, don't you."

"And the knife at the scene? You already heard about that. But it's a Bark River Upland, a skinner's knife—solid, not folding. The kind of blade used by hunters or trappers."

"Hunters and trappers. Very cool." Donna scribbled in her notebook. Cardinal was good at reading things upside down, but not this time.

"We're not telling anybody about the make, model or type, so if this hits the papers, I'll know who's responsible."

She snapped her notebook shut. "The only way I'll be in the news, Detective, is if I get killed."

11

When Sam got home, her mother looked up from the kitchen table. "Where's your parka?"

"It got torn. It got caught on the locker at the gym."

"Bring it to me later and I'll fix it."

Sam got a plate and put some lamb stew on it. Her brother, Roger, was at a small computer desk with his back to the table and earbuds plugged in both ears, a thing his father would not tolerate at dinnertime.

"Roger, say hello to your sister."

"Don't bug him. You know he can't hear you." Sam poured herself a glass of skim milk and sat down opposite her mother. She took a bite of the stew and pointed at it. "Phenomenal, Mom."

"Why are you so late?"

"Car wouldn't start. I had to take the bus and I missed the four o'clock."

"That car is more trouble than it's worth."

"Except the bus takes forever and I don't see how I can ride my bike up to Algonquin once the snow gets serious."

Mrs. Doucette reached over and took hold of her son's arm above the elbow. He jerked away. She reached again and he whirled around. "What! Stop plaguing me!"

"Your sister's home, Roger. Act human. Acknowledge her existence."

"I acknowledge your existence," he said to Sam, and turned back to his game.

"Cute, isn't he?" Sam's mother was a small, slim woman, still attractive, who worked as a nutritionist for the school board, overseeing cafeteria offerings at the local high schools. It wasn't as exhausting as her previous life as a chef, but it still left her looking tired at the end of the day. "I wish your father would get home," she said wistfully. "I don't know why he insists on wandering off in the bush."

"Keeps him in touch with the spirit world."

Her mother laughed. "He doesn't believe a word of that stuff. I don't know why he's always going on about it." She picked up a TV remote and clicked on the countertop television.

The murders were still the top news story. They showed footage from the house and stuff from the government dock that Sam had already seen. When the announcer gave the names of the victims, Sam thought, Yeah, the woman had an accent. The announcer finished by saying the police were asking anyone with information to call the Crime Stoppers number at the bottom of the screen.

—

"What can you possibly tell them?" Randall wanted to know. "You don't have any information. You didn't see anything. And obviously you're not going to save any lives at this point."

"Except maybe mine," Sam said. "He saw me, Randall."

"He didn't get close enough. He saw your car from a distance, you said. In the dark. There aren't even any street lights out there."

"There's one at the hydro turnoff—right where I was parked."

Randall was driving home. She could hear traffic and his car radio in the background.

"Sam, you're not calling me from home, are you?"

"I told you, I lost my cell. I'm afraid to use my car, and there's no pay phone for about three miles."

"Jesus. You're really playing fast and loose with my life here. I told you I'd call you."

"But you didn't. If that maniac has my cellphone, he's gonna find me for sure. This is a guy who cuts off heads, Randall. I'm fucking scared."

"There's no reason to think he's coming after you. He's probably not even in the country anymore. He's probably gone back to Chechnya or Brooklyn or wherever the hell he's from."

"He didn't sound foreign. The woman did, but he didn't. See, that's something the cops don't know. And if he does have my cellphone, maybe they can find him with it. You know, trace it."

"Just sit tight, Sam. Let the cops do their job."

"Well, when am I going to see you?"

"Not for a while, obviously. I mean, I don't feel like sneaking into an empty house right now, do you?"

"We don't have to sleep together. I just want to be near you. I need you, Randall. Don't you care at all?"

"Of course I do. We just have to be careful with this, Sam. We can't afford to go playing hero. There's too much at stake. Okay, I'm turning onto my street. Don't call me. You know I'm crazy about you, Sam. I'll call your home number as soon as it's a good time."

Sam tried to distract herself for the rest of the evening by working on Loreena Moon. A series of night scenes, Loreena's dark, lithe figure vivid against the snow. Moonlight through trees and the bright silver tips of her arrows. Green-eyed hellcat on the quest for justice. Every once in a while Sam could hear her brother exclaim at some score or setback on his cyber-battlefield.

Her mother went to bed early with a migraine. Sam shut herself in the bathroom with the gauze and rubbing alcohol. The cut on her knee was beginning to close at the ends, but in the middle it was still open. It would leave a scar, and the first time she wore shorts her mother would want to know how it happened and why she never mentioned it. It was one thing to have the private story world of Loreena to escape to now and again, but Sam didn't like how her own life seemed to be splitting in two.

She was getting into bed when the phone rang, and her heart immediately started to pound as if she'd been going all out on the treadmill. She reached for it from the bed and knocked the handset to the floor. She had to get under the desk to find it, and her knee sent a sting all the way up her body.

"Hello?" Her voice to her own ears like the voice of a timid, fearful person. "Hello?"

The line was open, she could tell by the sound. There was someone there. "Hello?"

A few more seconds of dead air and then the click of disconnection.

Her mother's voice from the hall. "Who is it, Sam? Who's calling at this hour?"

"No one. Wrong number."

"Thank God. I thought for a second your father was in an accident or something."

Sam lay in the dark, pressing gauze on her knee. You're quivering, she said. You're actually quivering. Her black cat was outlined on the windowsill against the blind, dark ears angled and alert.

12

NORTHERN ONTARIO, AS THE TOURISM office is fond of declaring, is a land of lakes. Algonquin Bay itself sits between Lake Nipissing, one of the largest bodies of water in Ontario after the Great Lakes, and Trout Lake, which is small and bottomless. But there are many more within a hundred-mile radius, often linked by streams and rivers that were the traditional highways of the Nipissing First Nation and other Ontario tribes. Some are extremely isolated, rarely visited by anyone other than wildlife or the occasional lost hunter. Most lie within designated preservation areas controlled by the province. A few of the tinier ones are actually private property.

One of these, not so small, was Black Lake—accessible, but just barely, via a former logging road. Black Lake was owned by a man in his seventies named Lloyd Kreeger. He had made a lot of money in the fur industry, and his intention had been to build himself a perfectly comfortable place of retirement where he would spend his time fishing and reading and keeping a watchful eye on his investments via iPhone and Internet.

Kreeger was a man who liked his solitude. He'd had a wife or two along the way. One had divorced him because he basically ignored her and the other, to whom he had become much more warmly attached, had died. He never developed the inclination to pursue a third.

But it turned out Kreeger had overestimated his capacity for solitude, and underestimated his attachment to business. His solution to the first problem was to hire a full-time assistant, a skilful handyman named Henry, to help look after the place. His solution to the second was to turn his property on Black Lake into an exclusive hunting lodge. It was still mostly in the planning stages—construction would not begin until the spring—but it was good to have the feel of a future again, however short that future might prove to be. He certainly didn't care to think of his life entirely in the past tense, and a few months alone in the woods had made it clear to him he was not someone who could live entirely in the present.

One night shortly after the murders at Trout Lake, Lloyd came out of the bathroom wearing his plaid robe. His skin was pink from a hot bath, and his white hair was damp and slicked back. He went down the stairs to the living room, not gripping the banister exactly but letting it glide under his hand.

The lower floor was an open-plan arrangement and he could see Henry setting out the breakfast things in the kitchen. Lloyd lowered himself into his favourite club chair and put his feet up on the ottoman. The big toe of his left foot was visible through a hole in the top of his slipper that had been developing for about a year. He heard the cereal box being set on the table, and the bowl and spoon.

"Do you need anything else tonight?"

"No thanks, Henry. You go on to bed or whatever it is you do out there in the bunkhouse."

"Okay, then. Good night."

"Listen, Henry . . ."

Henry was reaching for his big parka by the kitchen door. He stopped, with his hand poised above the hook..

"I was thinking maybe you should set two places for breakfast."

Henry turned around and looked at Lloyd, at the silent house, and at the night-black kitchen window. "You're expecting company in the morning?"

"Naw." Lloyd fanned the air in front of his face, banishing the idea of visitors. "I was just thinking maybe it's not right that you eat out there in the bunkhouse all by yourself."

"Why not? You eat in here all by yourself."

"Exactly. Seems kind of dumb. Also, I may have been fortunate in my life, made a lot of money and so on, but the fact is I wasn't raised that way.

I never had a servant the entire time I ran the company—unless you count a cleaning lady—and I never intended to have one now."

Henry shrugged on his parka and folded his arms, making the fabric rustle. "You see a servant around here? I don't see a servant. I see an old guy lives out in the woods needs things done. I'm ready to do them and he's got the money to pay me. It's just work. Doesn't have to be called anything else."

"I know, but it doesn't seem right. Mind you, I don't want chatter. Chatter's what I came out here to avoid."

Henry looked down at the floor for a moment then back up. "I appreciate your thoughts, but on the whole I think I'd prefer to keep things as they are. It's a good arrangement. I like my bunkhouse. It's the nicest place I've ever lived."

"All right, if you're comfortable being my slave, I'm not going to moan about it. Good night, then."

"Good night, master."

"Master." Lloyd nodded. "Funny."

Henry went out the door. It took a minute or so, but the wall of winter air eventually reached the living room and chilled Lloyd's damp head. He clutched his robe together over his bony chest and picked up his book. His feet were already getting too hot from the fire Henry had built in the grate, and he shook his slippers off.

He heard the door of the bunkhouse open and looked up to see the wedge of light illuminate the snow before the door closed once more. He went back to his book. Now the only sound was the creak of various joints in the structure of the house, adjusting to the cold.

—

Even before he took his coat off, Henry knew the bunkhouse was much colder than it should have been. The wood stove was still glowing and he could feel its radiant heat from ten feet away, but the air inside was chill and fresh. He hung his coat on a peg and hung his scarf over it, and then took off his boots and put on a pair of moccasins decorated with beadwork.

The main room was basically a den with a kitchenette, a dining table and a lounge area with a couple of armchairs and a sofa. It would house four male staff members when Lloyd's lodge opened two years from now. There were two bedrooms, each with two bunks. Henry could feel the cold air coming at him from the right, so he headed for that room. When he touched the light switch, a large hand grabbed his wrist and the muzzle of a gun was pushed up under his chin. The intruder must have broken in through the bedroom window, which faced away from the main house. Henry had seen no tracks outside, despite the fresh snow.

The man forced Henry back at gunpoint toward the eating area. Henry had been strong at one time, but his years as an alcoholic had taken that from him.

"Sit down," the man said. He was young, maybe mid-twenties, with the kind of square moustache actors put on when they play bank robbers in the Wild West.

Henry sat on the chair closest to the door. It didn't make any difference, though, because two other men came out of the second bedroom. One was a kid of about sixteen, the other a man in his late fifties, something military about him.

"Good job," he said with a nod to the first man. He sat down opposite Henry and asked him his name. Not threatening, not friendly either. Just a request for information.

"Henry."

"Henry? That your original name? You're an Indian, aren't you?"

"First Nations."

"Oh, First Nations," the man said with a deep sigh, as if this information had ended a long and exhausting search. "Not much of an Indian name, Henry."

"I'm not much of an Indian."

The man folded his forearms on the table and leaned forward, scanning Henry's face. "Let me guess. Quit the reserve. Headed for the big lights. Discovered you had no immunity to firewater. Came crawling back here to dry out."

"You got the order wrong. The grape juice came first. And I didn't quit the rez, I was banned."

"Is the old man alone up there?"

Henry shook his head. "He's got me."

The man sat back in his chair, making it creak. "So he's alone."

"If I told you he had a couple of bodyguards with forty-four Magnums, would it make any difference?"

"No."

The boy was leaning against the counter near the fridge, no particular expression on his face. The young man with the gun had moved out of Henry's line of vision, but Henry could feel his body heat on the back of his neck, he was that close.

The man sitting across the table didn't take his eyes off Henry. Nor did his expression—an expression of interest, nothing more—change one iota as the two last words Henry would hear in his life came out of his mouth. "Kill him."

Lloyd heard the shot and lowered his book to his lap. It was near. He was a long way from town out here, but he got hunters passing through now and again, even in winter. Their occasional shots were usually not much louder than a twig snapping, and they didn't come at night.

He stuck his bookmark in the novel he was reading, closed it and put it on the side table. He got up, pushing himself up from the chair, and went to the picture window. The heavy curtains were closed, not because there was much chance of anybody breaching his privacy out here but because even the double glazing wouldn't keep out the northern Ontario cold when winter got into its more serious stages. Lloyd parted the curtains about face-width, feeling the cold from the glass, and looked out.

The lights were on in the bunkhouse. The curtains in Henry's small windows were closed, and Henry's shadow moved across them. Lloyd thought Henry would come out on the stoop to take a look, but he didn't. Nothing much visible out there, other than the thin coverlet of snow between the house and the bunkhouse, and Henry's tracks between them.

Lloyd let the curtains fall back and went and switched off his reading lamp and the kitchen light, and then he switched on the outside lights. Nothing. Nothing on the dock. Nothing by the boathouse. And no tracks anywhere. Just the white snow and the still trees and the near edge of the frozen lake. Snow clouds hung low. No moon or stars. Beyond the lake the world fell away to darkness.

Lloyd switched off the outside lights and went back to his chair and his reading lamp and his book and settled down again. Hunters. The only thing you could hunt this time of year, legally, was pheasant and rabbit, and even the most avid hunters don't do that at 10:45 on a moonless, starless night. Occasionally they'd let rip with their shotguns after drinking too many beers, just to make a noise. Trying to fill up all that darkness.

But he hadn't heard any trucks or snowmobiles or anything like that all day.

He opened his book again. *Bleak House* by Charles Dickens. It was one of Lloyd's retirement projects—along with building Algonquin Lodge—to read the entire works of Charles Dickens. To his surprise, he had discovered that Henry knew Dickens' work very well. Though why that should have been a surprise, he didn't like to think. Sheer prejudice probably.

Anyway, once he found that out, he started ordering two copies of the books from the online outlets, and he and Henry talked about the story and the characters almost every day. Henry was a little ahead of him in *Bleak House*, but that was because Henry slept even less than Lloyd.

The old man sat in his chair reading for a few more minutes, but standing by the window had chilled him, so he got up, finger holding his place in the book, and took it with him to his bedroom. He was just taking off his slippers when the front door burst open and three men he had never seen before made their entrance into his world.

13

RANDALL WISHART WAS ON THE PHONE with a young couple named Jessup. The wife was at home, but Randall had set up a conference call with her husband, who was in Toronto on business. Every so often two of them would speak at the same time and there would be audio dropouts, leading to confusion and repetition.

Randall was underlining the importance of presentation—you had to make a place look both homelike and yet depersonalized so that people could imagine themselves living in it—when his wife and her father pulled up in the parking lot. He had a sudden panic that they knew about Sam, but they waved to him as they got out of Mr. Carnwright's Mercedes, both smiling like crazy.

"I'm sick of fluffing," the wife said. "We've been fluffing the place for weeks."

"And you're doing a great job," Randall said. "Trust me, Brenda, all your hard work is going to pay off. Now I told you I want to list it low. I'm thinking two eighty-five."

"Two eighty-five!" Mr. Jessup had been mostly quiet until now. "That's ridiculous. Out of the question."

"I know, I know," Randall said in his most soothing voice. "It's a shock to you because you know and I know that it's worth quite a bit more than that."

"A bit?" This from the wife.

"A significant amount. And you'll get it. Trust me, this is the smart way to go. We'll hold an open house, and that low price is going to get people bidding against each other. Once that starts happening— . . ."

"Yeah, but what if it doesn't?" Jessup said. "We have to sell, we're moving in two weeks, but we can't take any two eighty-five."

"It's much less than Thatcher's Realty was suggesting," the wife said.

"Well, then they're wrong. They may be used to a different market— they take on properties we wouldn't touch. By all means go with them if you think they'll do a better job. But I'm telling you, a lowball asking is the way to go. You've got a charming house, beautifully cared for, and a sizable lot. I'd hate to see you take any other route. I've gotta go. You think about it, and let me know your decision."

That was good; you didn't want to look like you cared too much. He got up and crossed the reception area to Lawrence Carnwright's office. His father-in-law was standing with his back to the window. He was not a big man, but he had an authoritative manner that made him seem so, and today some triumph was making him look particularly tall. Laura was sitting in a wing chair, blond powerhouse in blue pinstripe.

"What's up with you two?" Randall said.

"Tell him, Laura."

Laura was a woman who prided herself on her ability to keep cool, a considerable asset in her daily dealings with the stock market. But now she jumped up and grabbed Randall by the biceps. "You're not going to believe this," she said. "The Conservatives want me to run for office."

"You're kidding." Randall found he was grinning, although he was not at all certain this was good news. "That's great."

"We've just come from Bob Sloane's office," Carnwright said. "He approached me last week and asked me what I thought Laura might say, and I said I didn't know but I thought she might be pleased."

"Bob Sloane? You'd be running for federal office?"

"For MP," Laura said. "Isn't it fantastic?"

"It is. It really is. Congratulations, honey." He hugged her tight. She didn't usually like to be rumpled, but she hugged him back. "Wouldn't you have to be in Ottawa all the time?"

"Part time. And that's only if I win."

"She'll win," Carnwright said. "I've never been so certain of anything in my life. You'll win."

"But I can't sell Algonquin Bay real estate from Ottawa."

"You could do a lot from there," Carnwright said. "And you and I have to talk about this, something I've been mulling for a while now."

"Dad's been thinking of expanding. Opening offices in other cities."

"And why not start with Ottawa?" Carnwright said. "Listen, Randall, you're the only agent I'd trust with something like this. And of course it could mean a lot more money for you. But you and I'll talk. It's Laura's day, and you two have to sort out how you feel."

"I know how I feel," Laura said. "I'm pumped."

Randall could see this was true, and it touched him to see his wife—normally beautiful but ungirlish—alive with almost adolescent high spirits.

"We'll have to be on our toes," Carnwright said. "Absolute top of our game, all of us. No parking tickets, know what I mean?"

"I know what you mean," Randall said.

"And it wouldn't hurt if you produced a couple of grandkids along the way."

"Dad, they're hardly going to want me to run if I'm pregnant."

Carnwright put his hands up in instant surrender. "I know, I know. I'm just thinking long-term. Thinking big. Did we take that sign down out at the Schumacher place?"

"I drove out there, but it was already gone."

"Good. It burns me up to see our name every time they show a clip from the crime scene. Talk about bad PR. Ten to one they're going to want to unload that place after what's happened, and you know what?"

"We shouldn't handle it," Randall said.

His father-in-law cocked a well-manicured finger at him and said, "Right on, pardner. Anyway. Whatever you two decide to do, I think this calls for a toast." He opened a Bombay Company sideboard and pulled out a bottle of Macallan eighteen-year-old, something he hadn't done since two years previously, when Randall had sold the local senator's house for two hundred over asking.

14

CARDINAL WAS HEADING INTO THE meeting room when Delorme called him over to her desk. "You have to hear this." She switched on the speakerphone and replayed her voice mail. The synthetic voice gave the time stamp as 11:45 the night before. Then a girl's voice.

"Hi. I don't want to give my name, which is why I'm leaving a message instead of speaking to an actual person. I have information about the murders on Island Road. I was there. I was in the house and I heard — I heard people talking and I heard shots fired. I don't know anything more than that except that the guy who did it did not sound Russian — the woman did, but he didn't. I can't come forward because — I know I shouldn't have been in that house. I'm a thief. I steal stuff sometimes. I was looking for stuff to swipe and then I heard voices and hid. When I heard the shots, I ran. That's all I know. Please don't try to find me. I hope you get this."

"What do you think?" Delorme said. "You think she's for real?"

"She certainly sounds nervous. More than nervous."

"We know someone ran. We know someone hid under the bed."

"A girl burglar. She sounds, what, sixteen? Seventeen?"

"I don't know," Delorme said. "Could be early twenties."

"Let's hear it again."

Delorme replayed the message.

"I'm not sure I buy it," Cardinal said. "Not all of it, anyway."

"No one knows about the runner."

"'I'm a thief,'" Cardinal said. "'I steal stuff sometimes.' Does that sound real to you?"

Delorme shrugged. "Kind of."

"Lise, I've been fighting for truth, justice and the Canadian way for thirty years and I've never heard anyone say 'I'm a thief.' And a kid?"

"Maybe not a kid."

"Someone that young? 'I'm a thief'? Do you get a lot of thieves calling you up to confess?"

—

When they were all assembled in the meeting room, D.S. Chouinard issued a stern reminder that they could not afford to let other investigations slide—particularly any involving weapons or violence. "So Szelagy, for example—I'll be expecting you to bring me a plan on your warehouse arson sometime today. Same with Delorme and the ATM robberies. The citizens of this town do not lie awake nights worrying they're going to be attacked by Russian mobsters. They worry about being mugged taking cash out of the ATM."

"I don't think we should do anything else," McLeod said, "until Cardinal has wrapped up Scriver."

After that, the meeting turned into an ident show and tell. Arsenault manned the digital projector—he was vain about his technical virtuosity—and Collingwood manned the flip chart, writing things in wildly coloured fluorescent markers. For someone so reserved, he was surprisingly effusive with circles and arrows.

"This is a case where we have a ton of leads," Arsenault began. "We're practically buried in leads. With any luck they may eventually turn into evidence. We've got blood, hair, fibre, fingerprints, shoe prints and tire tracks. We're running every single item through all available tests and databases. We've made some progress and some connections, but so far . . . well, you can judge for yourselves where we are. You're gonna want to take notes.

"All right. Blood first. Since we live in the real world and not on *CSI*, we do not have DNA back. No surprise there. But we do have blood types.

Lev and Irena Bastov are both B-negative. Blood on the windowsill and outside is Rh-positive. Schumachers are A and Rh-positive, but I don't see Mrs. Schumacher smashing that window and diving into the snow."

Collingwood wrote locations and blood types on the chart, Magic Marker squeaking.

"Next, hair. Irena Bastov's hair is faux blond, brown roots. Lev Bastov's is short, salt and pepper, mostly silver with some black at the back of his head. We didn't find any hair at the table or on their clothes other than their own. However, in the master bedroom we found a long black hair on the window side of the bed, here." He indicated a space between the pillow and the bedside table. "Obviously it does not belong to the Schumachers, so it would be good to know who it belongs to and how it got there. In the meantime, fingerprints. To answer the question I know you all want to ask: no, we do not have a match on any known evildoers. But there's some interesting stuff. The last supper."

He clicked his remote and the screen showed an image of the table where the victims and their killer had been sitting.

"Prints on the glasses belong to the Bastovs, matching the set we took from them, and the prints in their hotel room and on their passports. Far as we can tell, they don't seem to have touched anything else at the scene. Prints on the bottle could belong to as many as three people, but you have to expect that with people in the liquor store, warehouse, et cetera.

"The thumbprint, which is right where it would be when you're pouring—left-handed, I should point out—matches a thumbprint we lifted off the knife in the male victim's back. This individual did not seem at all concerned about leaving prints, which makes me pessimistic about our chances of finding a record on him. Or them—we have no evidence that there was more than one killer, but this could well be the work of two or three. We have matches to that thumbprint with one on the front door knob, and partial matches on the back door, and the door to the master bedroom."

He flashed close-ups of the vodka bottle and images of the various doors one after another. Collingwood drew circles and arrows.

"As you know, most of the house appeared undisturbed, except for the rear door, which was jimmied, and the master bedroom, where a fourth party smashed out a window and took a runner. First the window."

He clicked on an image of the broken pane, then a close-up of the sill. "We have a very good print in the blood on the sill. No matches in the databases so far. But perhaps not surprisingly, that print does match the latent we lifted off the chair that was used to smash the window. Now, here's the interesting part. We also have a match with the bedside table on the window side of the room. Not the table itself but the bedside clock radio. All the other prints on that table belong to Mrs. Schumacher.

"As you know, our very tentative theory was that some individual fled the scene and was chased by the killer. We don't know what said individual was doing there, but it appears they may have been hiding under the bed—we didn't get any usable prints from under there—so that may mean a person who was at the scene in some separate capacity, maybe a break and enter. I know it seems unlikely—two separate criminal enterprises at the same time—so if you have any better ideas . . ."

Images of the chair and the clock radio appeared, followed by a wide angle that took in the bed, the chair, the smashed window.

Delorme spoke up. "Someone left a message on my machine last night. A young woman maybe around twenty? She claims she's a thief and she was in the house when she heard people coming. She hid, and when she heard shots, she ran."

The air in the room was suddenly charged. People shifted in their seats, everyone looking at Delorme.

"Why didn't I hear about this?" Chouinard wanted to know.

"I just picked it up now," Delorme said. "She called in the middle of the night."

"Why'd she call you? Why not Crime Stoppers? Why not the general mailbox?"

"I don't know. A lot of people don't believe Crime Stoppers is anonymous. Maybe she just wanted a female."

McLeod, uncharacteristically quiescent up to this point, came to life. "That clock radio is about thirty years old. I've met some desperate junkies in my time, but none of them would bother stealing that piece of crap. Even the most disadvantaged of our criminal adversaries have standards."

Arsenault was contemplating the floor. When he looked up, he said, "She said she hid under the bed?"

Delorme shook her head. "She just said she hid."

"Well, it kinda jibes with what we have so far . . ." He looked at Collingwood, who shook his head and wrote on the whiteboard: *For Sale.* "Yeah, exactly," Arsenault said, and changed the image. An exterior shot of Island Road, the driveway entrance. The mailbox that said THE SCHU-MACHERS, and the sign that said FOR SALE, CARNWRIGHT REAL ESTATE. "Notice there are no tracks around the For Sale sign or the mailbox. Call me anal retentive, but I decided to take prints off both of 'em anyway. Lifted a good thumb and a couple of partials off the sign. And get this: they match prints we found in the master bedroom—on the headboard of the bed."

As circles and arrows flew from Collingwood's marker, Arsenault changed the image to show first the bedside table, then the headboard. "We found a nice thumbprint here." He pointed to an area near the upper left corner of the headboard. "And it doesn't match the Schumachers or any other individuals we have so far."

"Well, the realtor usually puts up the sign," Chouinard said. "Have we ruled him or her out?"

"Him," Cardinal said. "Randall Wishart over at Carnwright's. Did he come in to get printed?"

Arsenault said no.

"I told him to."

Dunbar sat up and cleared his throat. "I have some information that might help. I took the Schumachers out to the house."

"Before it was cleaned up?" Chouinard said. "Who told you to do that?"

"We needed to know if anything was stolen—especially now we've got a self-confessed thief on the scene."

"As of five minutes ago," Cardinal said. "Why didn't you clear it with me?"

"I didn't think it would need clearing. I mean, we're all supposed to be investigators, right?"

"We're working a *coordinated* investigation. Do not go off interviewing people without telling me." Cardinal felt the heat spreading up his neck and into his face. "I should not have to be saying this."

"Okay, I hear you. Can I tell you what they said?"

"After they'd finished throwing up?"

"They weren't that bad, considering. They didn't see anything missing. Nothing. Also, I asked them about their routine for closing up the house in winter. They lock doors and windows, turn the heat down, shut the water off, all that. Main point, Mrs. Schumacher strips all the beds and puts on fresh bedspreads. They don't have a cleaning lady, so that long black hair could be crucial."

"Okay, that's good stuff," Cardinal said. "I'm still annoyed at you, but let's move on."

"What do we know about this Wishart?" Chouinard said. "The realtor."

"He's been with Carnwright just a couple of years," Cardinal said. "He's married to Carnwright's daughter."

"Laura Carnwright?" Delorme said. "She's a high flyer. She must be on every committee in town."

"Wishart seems like a real go-getter himself. Hasn't been out to the Schumacher house for a few weeks. Or so he says." Cardinal looked at Arsenault. "Do we have anything back on the tires?"

"Tread marks," Arsenault said. He flashed a picture of the hydro utility road. "Our runner seems to have got into her car here—if it really was a her—and shots were fired, damaging her tail light. Treads on this vehicle are all different, all old and worn, and could belong to any number of subcompacts: Honda, Mazda, you name it. Same with the shards of tail light. The driveway's more promising."

The image changed again. "Vehicle One got there first. Or put it another way—Vehicle One was the first car there after the snowfall Thursday morning. Vehicle Two tires aren't going to get us far. Wheel base gives us a compact, tires are the most common Goodyear snow tires, all four wheels. Vehicle One is a mid-size with Bridgestone Blizzard Grips, again all four wheels. Width and load rating would suit a range of pricier sedans: BMW, Saturn and Acura. The tires were discontinued three years ago, but you know the tire stores keep records of what they sell, and if it's local we might get lucky."

Chouinard pointed at Cardinal. "You didn't happen to get what Wishart is driving, by any chance?"

"Yeah, I did. He drives an Acura TL."

"I knew there was a reason I hired you," Chouinard said, getting up.

"You didn't hire me."

"Well, somebody must have had a reason."

15

Cardinal and Delorme pulled up in front of Carnwright Real Estate just as Randall Wishart was getting into his car.

"Mr. Wishart?" Cardinal said. "Could you hold it right there, please?"

Wishart looked annoyed, until he realized who Cardinal was and then he flashed a smile. "Detective—what can I do for you?"

"You can stop bullshitting me for a start."

The smile vanished. He looked from Cardinal to Delorme and back again. "I don't know what you mean."

Cardinal opened the rear door of the unmarked. "Or we could do it right here in your office—maybe bring your father-in-law in on it? Or how about your wife's office? Would you prefer that?"

"Hey. I sell houses for a living. I don't kill people."

"Just get in the car."

On the way, Wishart called a lawyer.

—

Dick Nolan was known around the CID as Dr. No, the reason being that he never agreed to anything if he could avoid it—certainly not to anything that might be construed as disadvantageous to his clients, of whom Randall Wishart was now one. He arrived at the station fresh from court, Burberry overcoat flapping, red polka dot tie flying over one shoulder, thinning grey hair shooting out from his scalp like a seeding dandelion about to blow away. His colour was high, not due to the cold but to a state of outrage that, as far as Cardinal knew, was permanent.

Nolan stormed into the interview room where Wishart was waiting and slammed the door. Moments later his shouts of disbelief could be heard all the way down the hall.

Cardinal gave them fifteen minutes. When he and Delorme finally sat down across from Wishart and his counsel, he asked if they had any objection to the interview being videotaped. He knew what the answer would be.

"No tape," Nolan said. "Why have you brought my client here against his will?"

"We believe he has knowledge pertinent to the investigation of a double murder," Cardinal said. "By law we have to interview him and—by all means check with your client, but I believe he would rather speak to us here than in his office or his home."

"You're threatening his reputation and his peace of mind without cause, not to mention invading his privacy."

"All right." Cardinal closed his notebook and stood up. "If Mr. Wishart doesn't want to talk to us today, we'll talk to him another time."

"Hold it. Hang on a second," Wishart said. He leaned over to whisper to his lawyer.

"We're prepared to proceed on a limited basis," Nolan said.

Cardinal flipped the pages of his notebook. "Mr. Wishart, you told me you hadn't been out to the Schumacher place for a couple of weeks."

"The house was broken into. The rear door was jimmied," Nolan said. "My client, as you very well know, has a key. Why would he need to break in?"

"To make it *look* like someone who didn't have a key," Delorme said.

"You were there on Thursday," Cardinal said. "The day the Bastovs were murdered."

"Do you have some evidence that puts my client there? Perhaps a security video? A witness?"

"We have tread marks that match the tires on his car. We have fingerprints on the For Sale sign. And on the bed in the master bedroom."

"Prints that you matched to my client how? He has no criminal record. He has never been in the armed services. He has never had a security check. How would you have his prints?"

Cardinal folded his hands on the table and studied his thumbs. "Mr. Nolan, how uncooperative do you wish your client to appear? People who have recently been to the Schumachers' were asked to provide fingerprints. He chose not to. Are you advising him to continue down that road? You know where it will lead."

Nolan let out a long, slow exhalation through his nostrils. "Suppose my client—purely hypothetically—were to admit that his prints are likely on both the For Sale sign and the bed. There are any number of explanations for this. He's a real estate agent who was asked to sell the house."

"But never showed it," Cardinal said. "So how do his fingerprints end up on the headboard and bedside table in the master bedroom?"

"I can clear this up," Wishart said.

"You don't have to say a word," Nolan said. "Let me do the talking."

"No, there's a simple explanation. I'm sorry," Wishart said to Cardinal. "I wanted to take a video of the house. The Schumachers had said no before, but I went ahead and did it anyway. I may have straightened the bed a little. You know, you want it to look the best possible."

"That video is evidence," Cardinal said. "You're going to have to produce it."

"I'm not sure if I still have it. I may have recorded over it."

"You went out there against the Schumachers' wishes to shoot a video—and broke the law by entering without their permission—but you may have recorded over it?"

Nolan looked at his client. "Now will you let me do the talking?"

Wishart slumped in his chair.

"There's no reason why a video of an empty house is of evidentiary value," Nolan said.

"Excuse me," Delorme said. "A video taken the same day as the murders?"

Wishart sat up fast. "I didn't say it was the same day. I told you where I was that day. I thought you were going to check with Troy."

"I did," Cardinal said. "And I just may talk to him again."

Nolan put a restraining hand on his client's wrist and glared him into submission. Then he turned to Delorme. "Now you're implying not only that my client was there, but *when* he was there. Fingerprints—even if they are his, which we are a country mile from granting—do not, as far as I know, come with a date stamp. Kindly tell us the nature of the evidence that puts my client at that particular house on that particular day."

"Are you denying it?" Cardinal said to Wishart.

"He doesn't have to deny or admit anything."

"Hey, Counsellor, here's an equation for you. I'll let you do the math." Cardinal had sworn to himself he wouldn't let Nolan get to him, but he had to struggle to keep his voice calm. "The snow was fresh on Thursday, putting Mr. Wishart's Acura with the Bridgestone Blizzard Grip tires there on that day. Either he was there for some entirely unrelated reason, in which case he's only obstructing justice, or he was there to commit or abet a double murder. So rather than have him face a life sentence, I'd suggest you encourage him to admit *one*, that he was there on Thursday, and *two*, the reason he was there."

"Do you have moulds from his tires?"

"We will soon enough."

"Do you have any blood? Any hair? Any fibre? You don't—or he'd be charged. Do you have evidence of prior association with the victims—these Russians from New York? You do not. So unless you have a security tape or an eyewitness who puts him there on Thursday night, you have absolutely nothing and you're wasting everybody's time."

"If you weren't at the Schumacher house," Delorme said softly, "suppose you tell us where you really were."

"I worked late—till six-thirty or so—and then I went over to Troy's house. We watched the game and then I went home, around eleven-thirty. My wife was in bed, so she can't confirm that, but Troy will."

"Who won the game?"

"Montreal, 4–1 over the Leafs. Lost it all in the third."

"What did you think of Rosehill's penalty?"

"Rosehill didn't get any penalties. He's still out with a torn ligament."

"Nice try," Nolan said.

"Let me lay it out for you, Randall," Cardinal said. "I think you have a girlfriend. I think you have a little something on the side. I think you have hot little rendezvous with her in empty houses."

"No, no, no." Nolan put up a hand like a traffic cop. "Unless you have this hypothetical other woman outside, that is totally inappropriate."

"Randall knows what I'm talking about, don't you, Randall? What's her name, Randall?"

Wishart shook his head. "There isn't anyone, I swear."

"You've got a high-powered wife and you're sitting pretty in her father's firm. If this comes out, all of that could be blown sky-high. You can tell us now, or you can wait for us to find her, and if we do—"

"That's all, Detective." Nolan put his legal pad into his briefcase, snapped the locks on it and stood up. "My client has been more than co-operative."

"Oh, good. I guess that means he'll be supplying us with a set of fingerprints."

"No, it does not."

"And I guess it means he'll be handing over that video of the house he took."

"No, it does not. Not if it's been recorded over."

"Are you available for another meeting tomorrow morning at ten?"

"No. I'm in court. What possible reason could there be for another meeting?"

"There isn't. I just wanted to hear you say no one more time. Something about the way you say it, Counsellor. I just can't get enough."

"Keep breaching my client's charter rights and you'll be hearing it a lot more."

16

Curtis Carl Winston, who called himself Papa, knocked on the bathroom door. He had disabled the lock, but he gave it a moment before entering. The old man was standing in the corner, hands folded before him, secured by the plastic ZipCuffs that bound his thumbs. He stood erect, a certain nobility to his posture, but even this impressive front couldn't hide his fear. Much that was wrong in the world could be traced to a shortage of fear, and Papa did what he could to supply it.

"How are you doing, Lloyd? Got enough to read?"

"Mister, I'm seventy-five years old. Why don't you just take what you want and leave? I can't do anything about it."

"Did you have enough to eat?"

"Yes. Look, I'm an old man, I can't sleep in a bathtub."

"If there was room for a mattress in here, I'd requisition one for you, but there isn't. And I can't have you needing the bathroom every five minutes, can I?"

"Lock me up in the master bedroom. It's got the ensuite."

"And probably a lot of sharp objects. I'll think about it. I don't want to cause you unnecessary pain."

Papa gestured at the door. He walked the old man down to the basement office and sat him in front of the computer.

"I don't understand why you're here," Lloyd said. "Or what you want."

"Let's just say winter camping gets a little hard on the nerves, Lloyd—
even when you know what you're doing. Like everybody else in the world,
we appreciate warmth and comfort."

"Uh-huh. And how long are you planning on staying?"

"That's strictly need-to-know, Lloyd. You're not going to be able to type
with the cuffs on. If I take them off, you're not going to give me trouble, are
you? I need your word on this." He placed a hand on his sidearm.

"How am I going to give you trouble? You're the one with the platoon."

"Just give me your word, Lloyd."

"No trouble. You have my word."

Papa bent and undid the cuff.

The old man rubbed his thumbs and placed his hands in his lap.

"Call up your calendar."

Kreeger put his bony hand over the mouse and did so. The screen lit
up with the month of December.

"You're shaking, Lloyd. You don't have anything to be afraid of. I have
no intention of hurting you. None whatsoever."

"It's a frightening thing to have your home invaded."

"I know. I'm sorry. But it had to be done." He squeezed the old man's
shoulder. Thin cord of muscle. "Relax. Really. I'm not a violent person.
I wish I could convince you of that, but I understand you're going to be
skeptical. Who's Greener and Greener, coming on Thursday?"

"Landscaping outfit."

"Why would you have landscapers coming in December?"

"An estimate. Work they're going to be doing in the spring."

"Send them an e-mail and cancel."

The old man called up his e-mail and addressed a message.

Gentlemen,
Something has come up and I have to cancel Thursday.

"Don't just cancel. Make some arrangement to reschedule. Otherwise
they'll keep calling."

The old man typed a little more. He was surprisingly good with the computer.

> I'll give you a call early in the new year and we'll arrange
> another time. I apologize for the inconvenience.
>
> Sincerely,
> Lloyd Kreeger.

"Good. Hit Send. You've got two more appointments this week. Do the same with them. Then we're going to set up an Out Of Office reply. Not that you get a lot of e-mail. Bit of a recluse, Lloyd?"

"Not a recluse. I'm retired. I stay in touch with my family, and if they don't hear from me, they're going to be worried and call the cops. My daughter's a worrywart—she's done it before."

"Wrong approach, Lloyd. I don't like lies." Papa spoke softly. A little bit of fear was one thing, but he didn't want the old man to panic. A couple of Papa's former recruits had made that mistake in the past, terrifying their targets, and it had gone badly for everyone. "Your daughter lives in Colorado Springs, way down in the good old U.S. of A., and you hear from her once a month. So let's not pretend she's going to be any kind of factor."

The old man looked up at Papa, his face hard. Old, yes, but not dumb, not a pushover. "If you're so honest, why don't you tell me what you did with Henry? You killed him, didn't you?"

Papa gave him a look of worried sincerity. "Henry would be your Aboriginal friend? Henry is safe and sound in the bunkhouse. I didn't kill him. I didn't kill anybody."

"I heard the shots." Those watery eyes looking at him, eyes that had seen a lot, maybe, but not enough to understand the kind of man he was dealing with.

"Relax, Lloyd. You're letting your imagination run wild. The truth is, I've never killed anybody in my life."

"Maybe not you personally. Maybe one of your associates."

"You're referring to my boys. Lemur's only sixteen and he's a good-natured kid—hardly your natural-born killer. And wait'll you meet Nikki, my youngest. She'll be here tomorrow. Jack's a bit of a commodity—I'll admit Jack can be a handful—but it's not his fault. He runs on adrenalin the way you and I run on oxygen, the way you and I run on food and water. But Jack is no berserker and he doesn't go around shooting people, and I won't hear him accused of it. So stop worrying about Henry, Lloyd. When this is all over, the two of you are going to be telling stories to your grandchildren. Now call up that Vacation Response and then we'll move on to financial matters."

—

The old geezer had a high-def seventy-incher in his living room, and Jack and Lemur were totally into an episode of *24* when Papa came upstairs and asked Lemur to turn it off. He and Jack would need some privacy. The kid didn't say a word of protest, just switched the thing off and headed to his bedroom. "And don't stay up all night," Papa called after him. "You rendezvous with Nikki at the airfield at 07:00."

Papa's word choices amused Jack sometimes. The guy hadn't been in the military for it must be thirty years, but airports were still "airfields" and train stations were still "railheads." He had the bearing to carry it off, though, you had to admit.

Papa stood in silence for a few moments, his back to the living room, hands clasped behind his back, staring out the window. He had turned off the lights—turned them off on the entire ground floor. The fire burned low in the grate, casting long shadows across the floor and up the walls. Jack loved this place—all the wood, and the thick carpets and expensive furniture, and the peace and quiet of the forest. The past week they'd been bivouacked in the woods, and God knows Papa had trained them well for that sort of thing, but it sure made you appreciate a comfortable house. Part of Jack hoped they could stay there forever, and part of him knew that it would never happen.

The plate glass window, large as a movie screen, looked out across the lake, the black patches of open water. It was snowing hard now, and a high wind whipped the flakes across the window in wild swirls. Every few moments lightning detonated and lit up the blizzard with a flash that made the world leap then fade to mauve, then black.

Jack—his full name was Jackson Michael Till—had been with Papa for six years. Long enough that sometimes he thought he knew the man, understood him even. Sometimes he thought he never would.

Papa turned from the window, placed a hand on his chest. "Storms speak to me," he said. And he said it in that confidential voice, that soft voice that implied he would never talk to anyone else in quite this way. Jack would never have admitted it, but he loved that voice. He waited for it with anticipation, even yearned for it, and having those feelings probably put him at some kind of disadvantage, but it didn't stop him loving that voice.

"Lightning, thunder—especially in winter," Papa said. "They get to me in here"—he patted his chest—"in a way that nothing else does."

"Me too," Jack said, realizing this was true only as he said it. Papa often got him to say things that were both true and yet surprising to him.

"Will you have a brandy with me? Mr. Kreeger has a bottle of Delamain in the sideboard."

"Yeah, sure." Jack's voice and words sounded ugly and low-class to his own ears after Papa's slightly formal manner of speech. Being around Papa made you want to improve everything about yourself, even the way you spoke. Jack had never in his life drunk a brandy except when he was with Papa, but he cleared his throat and said, "Brandy would be perfect."

Papa went to the sideboard and poured out two glasses. Firelight glittering in pale amber. "I'd like to propose a toast."

"Okay."

"I feel a little formal about it, Jack. Could you stand up?"

"Sorry." Jack got to his feet.

"No apology necessary," the older man said. "The last thing I want to do is make you uncomfortable. I propose a toast to Jack—a man who has his own code of behaviour and follows it to the letter. A man with a mind of his own, who nobody can tell what to do if he doesn't want to do it. A true soldier—with a sharp, discerning intellect, who doesn't just blindly follow orders but who fights for what he believes in. In short, to you, sir . . ." He clinked his glass against Jack's. "In gratitude for everything you've done for this family. For being my right hand. I owe you more than I can say."

Jack took a sip. The brandy had a bite to it that almost made him cough.

"Okay, enough of this formal stuff," Papa said, and clapped a hand on Jack's shoulder. "What say we sit by the fire and you tell me your damn war story!"

There was one leather wing chair close to the fireplace. Papa lifted up another and carried it across the room. He placed it at an angle to the other.

"Take your pick," Papa said. "And tell me everything."

Jack sat down. He stretched his feet out and looked at them. Then he looked at Papa. "You sure? I already told you everything."

"I know you did. But I'm like a kid with this—I want to hear it over and over. Or not a kid. It's like in the old days. The days of Viking warriors. They'd sit around the fire and try to outdo each other with wild tales. Well, son, I can't hope to outdo you, I'm just here to listen. And let's face it, it's not the kind of thing you get to tell a lot of people, so let me have it. I've got my brandy, I've got my fireplace, and I've got a total man of action with a hell of a story. You can't beat that."

So Jack tells him again how really it was Papa himself who laid the groundwork for the operation by telling the Bastovs he'd have a good realtor friend call them. Tells him again how he called the Bastovs with the news that he had the ideal house for a couple who liked winter sports. Tells him again how he drove them out to Trout Lake and showed them around. Tells him again how he pulled out the bottle of Stoli.

"Oh, that was smart," Papa says. "A very good touch. Who knows—maybe one day you can retire to a life of selling real estate. You'd be good at it."

Jack holds his snifter up in the firelight, watching the upside-down flames flicker in his glass.

"So you're sitting down, the three of you having a drink," Papa says. "What were they saying? What were they like? Were they suspicious at all?"

"Not really. The woman was real excited—about the lake, not the house. The location. The guy was, like, noncommittal."

"Tell me again how you did it, Jack."

So Jack told him again. The words came out and he couldn't believe he was saying them, even though he'd done this before—told Papa other stories, about other "targets," as Papa called them. Told him how he pours the third round—how those Russians like to just toss it back, not into sipping, those people. How the woman's eyes are getting brighter, her laugh a little louder. And as they're tossing it back, how he reaches into his shoulder bag and pulls out the Browning. How he whips it out and points it across the table at the man.

"How'd he look, Jack? How'd he look when you did that?"

"He looked like . . ." Jack had to think how to describe it, not sure what to call the emotion or state of mind that was so plain on the man's face. "He looked like, just, 'oh.' You know?"

"His mouth dropped open."

"It did," Jack says. "His mouth actually did drop open. Anyway, I shot him right then and there. Just bang, no hesitation, right between the eyes. Well, forehead, I guess you'd say."

Papa nodded. "Again smart. Neutralize the man first."

"It's how you always told me, Papa."

"Yes, but you did it. The pressure was on and you did it right. And the woman?"

"I didn't give her no time to scream. Place was isolated enough, but I didn't want no screaming. Bring people running. So I just whipped around again . . ." He held his gun arm out, finger pointing, and showed Papa how he pointed to his right. He closed one eye as if aiming anew. "Like so. And I let her have it."

"Between the eyes also?"

"She was looking at the guy, so she was turned a little—like so? Caught her in the temple and went right through."

"Two shots, two down. You're good, Jack. They're going to be talking about this. Russian mob circles? The oligarchs? This is not going to go unnoticed."

"They really Russian mob, those two?"

Papa raised his hand level above his head, as if showing deep water. "Up to here, Jack. Up to here. When the Communist system imploded, they basically handed Lev Bastov the industry. Those people have no concept of our values. All he had to do was pay off the right commissars and it was his."

"They didn't seem like gangster types to me. They didn't have the tone of it. Not to my ears. Leastwise not the woman."

Papa put his glass aside and leaned on the arm of his chair. "And there were no witnesses, right? No one saw you with them? No one saw you at the house?"

"Hell, you saw that place, you found it." Lying had always come easily to Jack. He couldn't even remember a time when he didn't lie. But he did not like lying to Papa. "There's nobody out on that damn point *to* see."

"You're right." Papa's blue eyes looking into him, sparks of firelight in the irises.

"How'd you know that place was out there, anyway? How come you knowed it'd be for sale and all?"

"I didn't. Not until we reconnoitred. You could call it luck. But luck will always favour those who study the terrain. Tell me the rest."

So Jack told him how he put on the raincoat he'd brought with him. Zipped it up and took out the axe. Then the skinner. He didn't mention the sound of a window shattering. His shock and terror. A witness that got away? He wanted to confide everything to this man who had taught him so much, given him so much. But part of him knew he couldn't. Papa already knew about the heads in detail—they'd planned all that out together, from the axe to the bags to the local wharf—but now he insisted Jack tell him anyway. So he did, and somehow the telling of it made it weigh less inside him.

"Beautiful job," Papa said. "Terror and confusion, Jack. We've sewn terror and confusion—and you pulled it off. Flawless. Absolutely flawless. And the woman—Irena Bastov was quite a looker."

"Really? That your assessment?"

"Be honest now, Jack. We can tell each other these sorts of things."

"Truth is, I don't get all fired up about Slavic sorts of women. But yeah, you could say she was good-looking."

"And after you shot Bastov—how did you feel about her? You know you have a problem with lust—we've discussed that. You didn't go after her sexually?"

"Never even thought of it. I just shot a guy and I'm about to shoot her. Never crossed my mind."

"Didn't cross your mind? Or it did cross your mind but you chose not to do it? It's two different things, Jack. Think about it before you answer."

Jack took a deep breath and let it out through his nose. He drank down the last of his brandy and could feel the room tilt a little. "Okay," he said at last. "You're right. As usual. I did want to mess with her. I can own that. But I remembered what we discussed and I chose to stay focused."

Papa reached over and squeezed Jack's arm. "That's my man. I know that was difficult for you."

Jack shrugged.

"Discipline," Papa said, sitting back. "God, I admire discipline. And to think how wrong people were about you. I can't get over it."

Jack couldn't either. The schools he had been thrown out of, his pathetic attempt to become a cop, how even the army—an institution staffed entirely by maniacs and retards—had turned him down. And those reports in the juvenile detention facility. He wasn't supposed to see those, but he snuck a look when the psychologist got distracted one day: low impulse control, emotional disturbance, personality disorder, all kinds of crap. That day marked the first of several suicide attempts. He had never thought about suicide since meeting Papa. Not once.

Papa stood up and they said good night. Papa shook Jack's hand, looking him in the eye as he said it, as if saying good night was some special manly ceremony.

Jack went to bed in one of Lloyd Kreeger's many rooms. He lay on his back for a time with a cellphone in his hand, flicking through images that were almost all of grinning teenagers, quite a few of them Indian-looking. Dark-haired girls making faces or laughing like crazy. The images weren't labelled, but he was pretty sure which one was her.

17

Delorme came into the squad room and stood in front of her desk, which was next to Cardinal's. It was her habit to check her e-mail without sitting down and before even taking off her coat. She did that now—Cardinal knew the sound of her keystrokes by heart—in a penumbra of cold air and the smell of snow. Then she took off her coat and shook it, sending tiny water droplets onto his desk. She always did that, on purpose, and she always said sorry, as if she hadn't.

"I'm having an idea," Cardinal said. "I realize I haven't had an idea since 2006, but I'm having one now."

"No, remember in August that time? You said, 'Let's stop at Tim Hortons'? That was totally you. Me, I would never have come up with something like that."

"I've been replaying that phone message over and over in my head, and here's what I'm thinking. I'm thinking this girl sounds First Nations—not strong, not obvious—but you know, that slightly compressed sound they sometimes have? Vowels a little flat, and maybe a little more in-the-nose kind of sound?"

"Nasal, you mean?"

"I'm not describing it right. Listen to it again. Try it with headphones."

They both had the message on their computers now. Delorme sat down and put on her earbuds and listened again. "You could be right," she said, a little loudly, before it was even finished. She put her hands over her ears and listened to the end. She took off the buds and swivelled to face him. "Definitely. I should have heard it before."

"So if Randall Wishart is having an affair with a First Nations girl, the question is, how did they meet?"

"They could've met anywhere. It's not like she's going to be living in a teepee."

"A wannabe real estate tycoon married to a hotshot financial whiz has an affair with a First Nations kid, and you think they could've met anywhere? You really think we're that multicultural? Not to mention the age difference, which sounds substantial."

"Maybe she moved and he sold the family's house."

"Possible."

"So let's check Carnwright's recent sales. Or maybe there's something on the *Lode* online or ABDaily.com."

Cardinal shook his head. "Already did. Nothing useful. But it occurred to me that there's going to be more Web stuff on Laura Carnwright than on him. That's the thought I was having when you came in and shook snow all over my desk."

For the next few minutes there was the sound of the two of them tapping at their separate keyboards. In the far corner of the squad room Ian McLeod was yelling at his lawyer. McLeod, as Delorme had once put it, was born for divorce the way some men were born for the army or the priesthood.

They announced the various headings to each other as they clicked on them: *Laura Carnwright on the recent upturn . . . Laura Carnwright on rezoning the west end . . . Laura Carnwright talks to the Canadian Club on the country's prospects for a green economy.*

"Here we go," Delorme said. "Aboriginal art show."

"I don't have that," Cardinal said.

"It's under Images. She's at the Macklin Art Gallery. Kind of dumb to have an affair when you have a wife who looks like that, no?"

"He's got pictures of her all over his office." Cardinal leaned over to look at her screen. "And you know what else he's got in his office? He's got

Native art." He stood up and took his coat from the coat tree and put it on. "I have a sudden urge to visit an art gallery. What about you?"

"Can't. I've got to set up my ATM stakeout. Don't look like that." She put on her Chouinard voice. "'The citizens of this town do not lie awake nights worrying they're going to be attacked by Russian mobsters. They worry about being mugged taking cash out of the ATM.'"

—

Jane Macklin turned out to be much younger than Cardinal had expected. And she didn't resemble his—admittedly vague—idea of a gallery owner. She was thirty at most, and looked like someone who might cut hair in an upscale salon. Her own hair, dyed jet black, was styled in a pageboy that looked as if it had been cut with a laser. The Aboriginal art, she told him, had been taken down several months earlier.

"It was probably my most successful show," she said. "Sold practically everything. We had artists from all over northern Ontario. If you're interested, I can arrange to show you some interesting work. I just need a little advance notice."

Cardinal told her who he was. "We're trying to find someone—a young woman. We don't know her name, but she may have been one of your artists for that show."

"And I thought for sure you were an art lover when you walked through that door."

"No, my wife—" He caught himself about to use the present tense. "And my daughter's an artist down in New York."

"New York. Wow. Tough town. You said you're trying to find a young woman?"

"Around nineteen or twenty years old."

"We had a few younger artists in the show. They're taking the traditional forms in some interesting directions. But twenty—I don't think we had anyone that young. This would be someone local?"

"Probably."

"There was a woman from the Nipissing reserve, but I think she must be late twenties at least. She sold a big piece about two minutes after we opened."

"Oh, yeah?" Cardinal took a leap. "Would that be Laura Carnwright who bought it?"

Miss Macklin gave him a funny look. "You know Laura?"

—

Cardinal drove out of town along Main, past the residential area, past the turnoff to St. Joe's—formerly a Catholic girls' school, now a home for retired nuns—past the Fur Harvesters' warehouse. Cars were circling the lot, looking for parking, and others were parked along the shoulder of the road. Three men were huddled around the side door, smoking and laughing. He made a left and drove past the sign saying NIPISSING FIRST NATION.

Sandra Kish lived in a tiny white bungalow with a single sapling out front that looked in danger of shivering to death. A blue Chevy Echo gleamed in the driveway. Cardinal pulled in behind it, noting the snow tires and undamaged tail lights.

Ms. Kish might have been in her late twenties as Ms. Macklin had said, but it was impossible to tell. She was the kind of fat that flattens the features and smoothes the skin. She could have been twenty-eight; she could have been forty.

Cardinal had interrupted her working on a painting and she was not pleased to see him. He told her who he was and that he was investigating a major crime.

Miss Kish showed no interest. "Ugh. Crime. I stopped reading the newspaper years ago." She was dressed in paint-spattered jeans and an enormous T-shirt that had once been yellow but was now dotted and streaked with many colours, mostly red. A headband creased the doughy skin above her eyebrows. "I just can't afford to absorb all that negative energy. It interferes with the work."

Her front room had been turned into a studio, rich with the smells of paint and wood and mineral spirits.

"That looks familiar," Cardinal said, pointing to a panorama-shaped canvas propped against one wall, a fantasia of animals linked together by whiplash-shaped tongues. "I saw something a lot like that in a real estate office the other day. Except the tongues were blue."

"Carnwright's, I bet."

"You're right."

"She put it in the office, huh? I thought she was going to put it in her home. Well, I guess the office is better. More people will see it."

"This would be Laura Carnwright we're talking about, right? She bought it at the Macklin Gallery show?"

"That's right. She's a lovely person, a powerful spirit. Very knowledgeable."

"And you know her husband too, of course."

"Not really. Laura introduced him—but she had to pry him away from the catering table, and he went right back to it, far as I know. I had the impression she was the art lover of the two."

"Did you see him talking with anyone else?"

She shook her head. "I barely noticed him."

She flipped through the lean-tos of canvases, pausing now and again to show Cardinal a painting, as if that had been the sole purpose of his visit.

"That exhibition was amazing," she said. "I sold all three of the pieces I had up. See, that's the hard part about art, not making it, not selling it. What's hard is getting it out there where people can see it. They should have more First Nation shows like that. I mean, this was world-class—they had Champlain's catering it, for God's sake. People see class like that, they want to buy."

Her voice was low, with a smokey rasp to it, nothing like the panicky teenager's they'd heard on Delorme's voice mail. You think you have a great lead and it turns to dust in your hands. As he was heading for the door, Ms. Kish seemed to pick up on the fact that he had asked her almost nothing.

"That's it?" she said. "I thought you were working on a major case."

"Unfortunately, I'm having kind of an uninspired day. You ever experience those?"

"It's been known to happen. When it does, I find by far the best thing is to curl up on the floor and cry."

"Thanks," Cardinal said, stepping out into the cold. "I'll have to try that."

18

SAM HAD NO DOUBT RANDALL WOULD be missing her by now. Two people could not touch the way they had, love the way they had, know such passion, feel such joy, and simply abandon it as if it had never happened. Okay, maybe she was addicted to those orgasms he seemed to engineer so effortlessly, but it wasn't just sex. It was his eyes, the way he seemed to liquefy at the sight of her tawny skin, the way just seeing her seemed to take him over some threshold. No one could be that loony about just sex. He had to be missing her.

But there were lots of good reasons for him not to call. Which was why Sam was shivering in a phone booth across the street from Carnwright Real Estate, actually quaking with cold. Even with its fleecy hood, her denim coat was no match for the cold winds that blew uptown off the lake, and she couldn't ask her mother to fix the bloodied parka.

Sam had bailed out of drawing class early to get here before five. Now it was a quarter after and it was dark and the cars were crawling up Algonquin with their headlights on and no doubt their heaters going full blast while she stood huddled in a phone booth waiting for the love of her life to appear. At least the phone booth cut the wind a little.

An old guy in a long grey coat came out and got into a flashy car parked in the small lot beside the house. Mr. Carnwright maybe? A few minutes later a woman in a black down coat that made her look like a carbonized waffle emerged, cellphone pressed to one ear. Phyllis. Randall had mentioned Phyllis a couple of times, not exactly in what you'd call positive terms.

The windows of the real estate office went dark and the porch light went on and Randall came out at last. He turned around to check that the door was locked. The traffic was moving again, and Sam had to dodge through it, causing people to honk.

She caught up to him in the parking lot.

"Sam." He looked over her shoulder and around the lot. "Jesus Christ, Sam."

"I know. I'm sorry. I had to. I miss you."

"Jesus Christ." Randall pointed his key at the car and the locks chirped open. "Get in before anyone sees you."

Sam got in and he hit the ignition. "Heat, heat," she said. "I'm freezing. God, I'm so happy to see you."

She touched his arm and he shook his head. "Not good, Sam."

"Come on—just a few minutes? I have to be at work soon. Maybe we could just drive around?"

"Uh-huh. Someone sees us and I explain it how?"

"You were showing me a house. Come on, show me a house. I'll tell people I just won the lottery and I'm buying it for my mother. No, I'll tell them I sold *Loreena Moon* for a million bucks. Take me anywhere. I just want to be with you."

Randall waited for a gap in the traffic and pulled out onto Algonquin. He took the first right onto a quieter street. A darker street. After two blocks he pulled over in front of a building that at one time had been a bakery. Shuttered now. Weeds in the parking lot and graffiti all over the brick.

"You told the police about me, didn't you."

"No! I didn't say a word, I swear."

"They know about me, Sam. How could they know about me if you didn't tell them?"

"They're police. They're not retarded—they find stuff out. I love you, Randall—why would I do anything to hurt you?"

He looked her up and down the way you might look at a defective purchase. "Maybe to stir things up with Laura. She leaves me, and then you have me all to yourself."

"I do want you all to myself." Sam placed a hand on the sleeve of his coat. She traced a pattern in the fabric with her index finger. "But only if you want me."

"So why did you go to the police, Sam?"

"I didn't. I called them."

"I knew it. I fucking knew it." Randall pounded the steering wheel.

"It was totally anonymous. I called at night, from a pay phone—I've never been in so many pay phones in my life—and I left a message on someone's voice mail. A woman detective. I didn't say anything about you. I just said I was in the house—actually, I said I was there to rob the place."

"Not smart, Sam."

"Well, how else am I going to explain what I'm doing there? I told them I heard the guy's voice and he wasn't Russian like the victims. They need to know or they'll be looking in the wrong places. They have to catch him—he has my cellphone, Randall. Somebody's been calling our house."

"From your cell?"

"The number was blocked. But I pick up, or my mom picks up, and there's someone there—you can tell there's someone there—but he doesn't say anything. He's going to figure out where I live, Randall. He probably already knows."

"If it wasn't from your cell, I don't see any reason to worry. It could be anyone. It could be a malfunction on the line, for all you know."

"It's him. The police have to catch him."

"Well, this is great great, Sam. All you've succeeded in doing is putting them on to me. Laura is running for office. They haven't made the announcement yet, but she's going to be a candidate for MP. If this gets out, all that'll be over."

"If what gets out? That you visited a house you're trying to sell?"

Randall grabbed her shoulder and shook her. "On the same day as a double fucking murder, Sam. With a hot little chick from the Indian reserve? How do you think that'll play in a political campaign? How do you think that'll play with my pillar-of-the-community father-in-law? Don't you ever think of anyone other than yourself? Jesus Christ, Sam. How selfish can you be?"

He let go and Sam rubbed her shoulder. It was the first time Randall had ever touched her with anything other than affection.

"I thought you loved me," he said. He was staring out the windshield at the snow that was beginning to sift down through the street light. "I really thought you did. But frankly, now I have to wonder."

"I do, Randall. I do love you. You really don't believe me?"

He gave a snort. "You've got some way of showing it."

"Do you really hate it that I'm First Nations? I'm just asking—I won't be mad, if it's true. I just—does it bug you that much?"

"Oh, Sam . . ." He turned to her again, his expression softer. He took her hand and rubbed the woollen mitten with his thumb. "I actually love that about you. It makes you interesting—exotic, kind of. Sexy. Unfortunately, a lot of other people don't think that way. They just think—well, you know how they think. And that makes me very sad."

Sam buried her face in his shoulder. "Let's go to a house. You must have another empty house somewhere. Please. I want you so bad."

"I told Laura I was on my way home."

"So you'll be late. And I'll be late for work."

"Sam, we can't do this anymore."

"Don't say that."

"Sam, we can't."

"Ever?"

"Not until this is over, that's for sure. I'm not going to ruin Laura's career. I may not be the world's best husband, but I'm not going to do that to her."

"So you mean I don't get to see you until they catch the guy and there's a trial and he's in prison? That's *years*. Is that what you're saying?"

"We'll see each other when it's safe. When we can relax and have a good time together. Which we can't do now, obviously. It won't be forever."

A kind of nausea swirled in Sam's chest. The word *heartsick* drifted into her mind. This is what they mean by heartsick. She started to cry.

Randall reached into the glove compartment and handed her a small package of Kleenex. "Come on, now. Take it easy. There's nothing to cry about. They'll catch the guy and it'll all be over and things'll be fine. You'll see." He kissed the top of her head through her hood. "And then I'll get to kiss you all over your beautiful body again. Because I love you,

Sam. Call me crazy, but I honestly, honestly love you. Listen, did you replace your cellphone yet?"

"I'm borrowing my mother's on the nights I go to work. She likes to check up on me before she goes to bed."

"Give me the number. I'll try to find a way to call you—not from home, obviously, and not tonight. But I'll call. I promise."

—

The bus made a million stops, ensuring Sam was late getting to Champlain's. Ken, the manager, gave her hell, as did Jerry, the chef, but she didn't let it bother her for too long. She felt so much better after seeing Randall. Her fears seemed to be shrinking down to some manageable size. She focused on her work and turned the dishes out efficiently without sacrificing presentation. When there was an unexpected slack period, she cooked up a couple of days' worth of the cranberry glaze she knew they'd be serving with practically everything now that the Christmas holidays were approaching.

She didn't let it get to her when Ali brought back a steak saying it was overcooked.

"It's not overcooked," she said. "You asked for medium, that's medium."

"You want to go out there and argue with them?"

Sam put another steak on the grill. She kept a close eye on it, but all she could think about was that Randall still cared about her—cared so much, he was worried *she* didn't love *him*. When Ali came back, the new steak was on the plate, practically bleeding.

"It's medium?"

"The last one was medium. Tell Geoff to pick up his sole almondine— it's been sitting here for five minutes."

At ten o'clock, her mother called. "Can't you get a ride home? I don't like you having to take the bus late at night."

"It's okay. I have the timing down, so I don't have to wait long."

"What exactly is wrong with your car, anyway?"

"It's got asthma or something. It won't start. I gotta go, Mom, it's really busy."

"Okay, hon. Good night, then."

Jerry Wing came over, wearing his parka. "I need you to make the cranberry glaze."

"It's done." Sam pointed at the two bowls on her chopping board. "I'll put them in the fridge before I go."

"You already made them?" Jerry put his hood up, even though it must've been eighty-five degrees in the kitchen, Chinese eyes blinking out at her from the fur.

"Think you'll be warm enough?" she said. "You're dressed for Inuvik."

"I evolved for a different climate." He raised a mitten in farewell. Sam was glad he wasn't mad at her anymore. Relieved, anyway.

The trouble with having a passionate nature, she reflected as she was shutting down her station, is that you can't win either way. Even when you're happy, it's more like a kind of relief—relief that you're not feeling the alternative. The sting of Jerry's anger. The agony that would take over her life if Randall dumped her. It's the happiness of not falling off a cliff. Is Loreena Moon happy? No. Because Loreena Moon doesn't love anybody. Loreena doesn't worry about falling off any cliffs either.

Sam looked at the kitchen clock. Eleven-fifteen. She had exactly three minutes to make the bus. She ducked into the supply closet and changed out of her cook's outfit, threw on her coat, and ran out the door and across the parking lot, reaching the bus stop with less than a minute to spare. It was not as cold as before. The earlier snow had melted, leaving the parking lot and the highway gleaming blackly in the street lights.

The bus was overheated. Sam sat near the middle exit, sweating after the kitchen and her run. She wiped an arc of clarity on the fogged windowpane and rested her head against the cool glass. The fast-food joints and the shopping malls slid by, impossibly bright oases along the slick, dark road. There were only three other passengers and they got off one by one along the route through town, long before the bus passed the Fur Harvesters' warehouse and approached the Nipissing reserve.

She got out at the turnoff. The intersection was brightly lit, but after that the street lights along the access road were spaced far apart until you actually got into the residential area. Sam had never in her life worried about walking along this road, even late at night, but she worried now.

She walked quickly, trying to put herself into a Loreena frame of mind. Cool. Brave. Not brave—fearless. She was managing quite well, keeping her breathing fairly normal and her heart reasonably quiet, until she went up a slight rise and rounded a curve and saw the car parked on the shoulder.

She stopped. Smells of trees and wet road. Sounds of trucks on the highway not far off.

It's just a car, she said. The lights aren't on. The motor isn't running. There's no one in it. Those are headrests.

Sam crossed the road to be on the far side from it. Courage would be a nice item to list in one's catalogue of virtues, but if it was not available she would just have to make do with caution. She continued up the road, the lights of her street visible at the top of the rise.

She was nearly even with the car. Glancing toward it. Yes, empty. She made a pact with herself that she would not look over again as she passed by. She would keep it in her peripheral vision, but she would not actually look.

It wasn't a vow she had to keep long. The driver's-side door opened and a man got out—a really tall man. He had to have been hunched down for her not to see him. His face was covered in a black woollen thing with holes for mouth and eyes.

"Come here." There was something long and metal dangling from his hand.

Sam ran.

His steps were right behind her, his stride matching hers. "You didn't see anything," he said. "You didn't see anything. You don't know anything."

Something nicked the back of Sam's coat. She kept running, forcing her legs to move faster. She thought about making a dash for the trees—he might have more trouble keeping up there—but she stayed right in the middle of the road, praying for headlights, a car, people.

He wasn't behind her anymore. She heard the car start, and his headlights threw her shadow the length of the road to the top of the rise. Then her shadow began to shrink. She feinted left, ran right, the darkness of the trees.

She wasn't going to make it. He was going to run her down. She stopped and dodged left, the car cutting her off. He was out and after her again.

Legs, lungs, heart, all straining at their physical limits. She simply could not run any faster. Her street came up and she made as if to go by it, then took a sudden right. Her house was the third on the right. She ran past it to the fourth, the fifth, dodged right again, and then she was in Cal Couchie's backyard. Sweet old guy, but about two hundred years old and stone deaf.

Sam ran back to her own backyard. Her keys were in her hand. She couldn't hear the man behind her anymore. She could stay in the darkness of the backyard and scream for help, but that might just bring him right to her. She pulled out her mother's cellphone and hit 911. It rang three times before someone picked up.

"Emergency services, location please."

"1712 Commanda Crescent. A man is after me."

"Can you speak up? I didn't hear you."

"Oh, God. 1712 Commanda Crescent. Send someone now. He's going to kill me."

She shoved the phone back into her pocket and peered around the corner of the garage. No one.

She made for the side door and he came from around the front, black and featureless. She wouldn't make it to the house. She veered back to the garage and got her key into the lock and got the door open and inside and turned the lock again as he slammed into it with a noise like thunder that made her scream. It didn't come out as a scream but like a noise her cat might have made. He wouldn't be able to bust through that door— that was only in the movies, right? Doors don't break that easily.

There was a splintering sound, and she remembered that long thing he'd been carrying. A crowbar.

It was dark in the garage, but she was afraid to turn on the light. She felt her way around to the far side of the car. Not locked, thank God. She opened the passenger door and the dome light came on, just enough of a glow to make out her father's workbench, the shapes of hammers and saws and wrenches.

That splintering sound again.

She shut the car door and moved through the dark to the workbench and got up on it, damaged knee screaming. She felt on the wall and pulled down the crossbow, felt to her right for the leather quiver. She got behind the car and fitted an arrow into the groove, and wound it back until the loud click told her it was cocked. The Vixen had an automatic safety that she now pressed into the Off position.

Sam saw it in her head before it happened. She knew how it would look—dark silhouette against the glow from the moon and the street lights. After that he would find the light and he would kill her.

The door crashed open. The dark shape. Sam stood up and released the arrow. The man doubled over and made a sound like he was puking. He fell back, got up, staggered, fell against the garage. Then his footsteps— uneven, dragging—moving away.

She waited behind the car. Her breathing was rapid and shallow. She'd seen squirrels breathing like that when Pootkin stalked them.

After a time she heard a distant siren, and closer, the sound of voices and car doors slamming. The squawk of a radio.

Flashlight beams playing over the surfaces outside, and then a man's voice, cautious, saying, "Police. Police. Hello?"

A cop's face and hat flashed in the doorway and disappeared again.

"I'm going to have to ask you to put down that weapon, miss. Now."

"Did you catch him?"

"We have an individual in custody."

"Tall bastard with a mask on?"

"He also has an arrow sticking out of his liver. Now put down the weapon and step to the front of that car and place your hands on the hood. I'm not asking."

Sam looked at the bow. She didn't even remember doing it, but there was another arrow in the bow and it was cranked all the way back.

19

CARDINAL HAD BEEN IN BED BUT NOT asleep when the call came. He got out of bed and got dressed and drove up the hill to City Hospital. The shock of moving from the warmth of his bed to the cold of a December night was still reverberating in his bones when he found the patrol officer waiting for him outside a recovery room.

"Girl claims he's the guy did the murders out at Trout Lake. He denies it up the wazoo, of course."

"Where's the girl now?"

"Down in emerge with PC Gifford. Bad cut on her knee, but you know how it is with emerge—if you're not dying, you're there for eternity."

Cardinal had to get by the nurse on duty in the recovery room.

"This man has just come out of surgery," she said. "You can't be cross-examining him."

"Just a couple of questions," Cardinal said.

She led him past a row of beds, all but two of them empty. "Five minutes," she said. "I'll be timing you."

The man on the bed was hooked up to an IV and a pulse monitor, but other than that, he looked in pretty good shape. His blond hair needed a wash, but his powerful shoulders, where they emerged from beneath the sheet, looked wider than the pillow he slept on.

"Troy Campbell," Cardinal said. "I've been meaning to talk to you again."

Campbell opened his eyes and contemplated Cardinal with medicated calm. After a while he said, "I didn't touch that girl." His speech was slow but clear. "And she shot me with an arrow. She perforated my spleen. I plan to press charges."

"Troy, you want to tell me again where you were Thursday night? Keep in mind that we already know where Randalll Wishart was."

Campbell's features maintained their contemplative cast. "I was at work that night. Ask my supervisor. We have a time clock that'll show I clocked in."

"So you weren't in fact at home with your buddy Randall."

Campbell shook his head, making the pillow rustle. "We have a TV at work." He lifted his hand and encountered the handcuff that secured him to the bed frame. He squinted at it for a good thirty seconds. "You're kidding, right?"

—

PC Gifford, standing outside Exam Room 3, gave Cardinal the particulars. "Samantha Doucette. Eighteen years old. Art student up at Algonquin. Her mother and brother are in the exam room with her. Mother won't let her out of her sight. Got a pretty tall tale, if you ask me."

"The doctor in there with her?"

"Yeah, they must be about done by now."

The doctor came out and Cardinal identified himself. "How's she doing?"

"She has a deep laceration to her left knee. Wouldn't have been so bad except she didn't get it treated for so long."

"So it didn't happen tonight."

"No, no. Days ago. But she'll be fine. I stitched her up and gave her a scrip for ampicillin."

Cardinal went in and identified himself to Sam and her mother. The girl had put on a fresh pair of jeans and was shoving the others into a shopping bag. Her brother was entranced by an iPod or some other cyber-drug.

"I want to stay," Mrs. Doucette said.

"Your daughter's eighteen," Cardinal said. "I need to talk to her in private."

"She should have a lawyer."

"Officers at the scene are satisfied that she was responding to an attack. I don't anticipate charging her with anything—provided she tells me the truth."

"Of course she'll tell you the truth. Why would she do anything else? Don't worry, honey, I'll be right outside."

When her mother and brother were gone, the girl sat on the edge of the exam table. "She doesn't know the real story. She just thinks I was attacked by a complete stranger out of the blue."

"And that's not what happened, is it?"

The girl folded her arms across her chest and stared at the floor, shaking her head.

"You were coming home from work, is that right? Where do you work?"

"A restaurant. Part-time. I'm a cook."

"Don't tell me," Cardinal said. "Bistro Champlain."

"That's right." A puzzled look crossed her face. Her features were small, perfectly formed, and she had a dark-eyed intensity that without too much effort on her part might cause a married man to lose his head.

"Okay," Cardinal said. "Why did this man attack you?"

"Because of what I saw. In the Trout Lake house. Not saw—heard."

"You're talking about the couple that was murdered."

"Look, I admit I was in the house, okay? I steal stuff once in a while and the place looked empty. But I didn't have anything to do with any killing. I didn't know any of those people. I was checking the place out when I heard voices, and I hid."

"Where'd you hide?"

"Under a bed."

"How'd you break in?"

"What?"

"How'd you break in, Samantha?"

"The back door. I used a credit card. So I heard these voices and I hid under the bed. It sounded like the guy was trying to sell them the house, pointing out all the good points and stuff. I figured they'd be there a few minutes and then go, but then there were gunshots. I thought, That's it, I'm outta here. So I smashed the window and climbed out."

"How'd you smash the window?"

"I used a chair. I swung it as hard as I could."

"Which is how you cut your knee. Climbing out."

She nodded. "I jumped out and ran. He came after me. My car was a little ways up the road."

"At the hydro turnoff?"

"Yeah. I got to it and he actually shot at me. He hit the car a couple of times and I took off. I don't know if he got my licence plate or what. I lost my phone when I jumped and I'm pretty sure he has it. I've been getting calls."

"What kind of calls? Threatening?"

"Hang-ups. He stays on the line awhile but doesn't say anything."

"Do you know for a fact these were from your cellphone?"

"The number was blocked. But who cares what phone he used? You've got him locked up, right? You better. He cuts people's heads off, for God's sake."

"The man who attacked you is under guard and handcuffed to a hospital bed—you don't have to worry about him right now. But listen, Samantha, only part of what you're telling me is true. I know you hid under the bed, and you ran like you said. And damage to your car matches our findings at the scene. But I also know about Randall Wishart, so you don't have to hold anything back in order to protect him."

Her eyebrows went up, her dark eyes went perfectly round. "I'm not protecting anybody."

"Samantha, I know you're not a thief. And I know you didn't break into that house with a credit card. You went out there with Randall, who of course has a key."

The innocent expression vanished. She looked at him with dark, implacable eyes.

"Wishart got a friend to cover for him, in case his wife found out. Troy Campbell? To say they were watching the game together. But it turns out Troy was actually at work that night."

Cardinal waited. Eventually she said, "We didn't have anyplace else to go. We didn't take anything or hurt anything. Randall was super careful about stuff like that. Even the bed—we put a blanket over it so it wouldn't get messed up."

"I know you did. A blue blanket."

"It sounds bad. I know it sounds bad. But it isn't like that. Do you know what it's like to be in love and not be able to see each other?"

"Why don't you tell me."

"It's horrible. It's agony. I hate it. Everybody else gets to go places together, do things together. Kiss. Hold hands in public. Whatever they want. Even couples that aren't that happy together. But here we are, crazy about each other, and we have to skulk around like criminals and wait until some special opportunity comes up. We get to see each other like every three weeks or so. I can't even call him hardly. And he can't call me too often either."

"You ever wonder why Randall doesn't leave his wife?"

"He's going to. He just doesn't want to hurt her, and he's waiting for a good moment. He has to be careful—I mean, he works for her father and all. It's not like it's something he can do right away."

"Samantha, you've been through a lot, but I'm afraid I have to tell you something that's going to upset your life even more."

The dark eyes lost their implacability. The black eyebrows went up again, and suddenly she was a kid and Cardinal wished he could protect her from what he was about to say.

"You're right that the man who attacked you wasn't a complete stranger. It wasn't out of the blue. But it wasn't the man who chased you out at Trout Lake."

"It was. He kept saying, 'You didn't see anything! You don't know anything!' Who else is going to come after me with a crowbar, for God's sake?"

"Well, you're right—it was definitely because someone doesn't want you to testify. Someone who knows where you live. Someone who knows what time you got off work. Someone who knew you'd be taking the bus home."

"I told you—the guy has my cellphone."

"Which might give him your name and address."

"The other stuff too. Champlain's number is on there."

"What's it listed as? 'Where I work on Wednesday, Thursday, Friday, from six to ten p.m.'?"

"What are you getting at? I don't know what you're trying to tell me. Will you please just tell me?"

Cardinal could hear the rising panic in her voice, the same panic he had heard in her phone message. She gripped the edges of the exam table, and her mouth opened as if she would say more—something that might stop this horrible cop from ruining her life. But some other emotion— perhaps her sense, not yet acknowledged, that dread was about to be transformed into grief—made her lower lip tremble and the dark eyes fill, and Cardinal could not remember the last time he had seen a human being so vulnerable.

20

"How am I supposed to get down?" Nikki said. She was hanging by her knees from a tree branch. She was high enough that, even upside down, her face was a foot higher than Lemur's. He was looking up at her, shaking his head in his solemn way. A frigid breeze blew across her belly where her jacket and sweater had fallen open.

"Cover yourself up," Lemur said. "Your stomach. Don't show yourself like that."

"Perv. You getting turned on?"

"It's not our way. You've heard Papa talk about modesty."

"You just don't like to look at girls cuz you're a faggot."

"Don't call me that."

"Chill, Lemur—I'm just kidding."

"Don't call me names. I don't call you names. We're here to respect each other. You're not gonna get a lot of that outside the family, and neither am I. Not yet, anyway."

Nikki didn't like that talk of respect. The only thing people had ever respected about her was her ass. Soon as they saw her face, it was a whole other story. She pulled herself up so that she was sitting on the branch. The sensation of all the blood now draining from her head made her woozy. She looked up to where she had climbed to loop the rope over a high branch. "I can't believe I went up that high. I haven't climbed a tree since I was a kid."

"You're thirteen years old. You still are a kid."

"You're three years older. Big deal."

"Toss me the rope, then come on down."

"I told you, I don't know how." She let the rope go and it slithered down through the branches.

"Just swing down and hang from the branch by your hands."

"Uh-huh. And if I break my ankle? Papa will kill you. You're supposed to protect me."

"You're family, Nikki—I will always protect you. But you have to be self-reliant, too."

Still holding tight, Nikki slid back and down until her heels caught on the branch so that she was swinging under it, clinging almost upside down from hands and ankles. She let go with her ankles so that she was stretched out full now, hanging just from her hands, the cold bark biting into her fingers. She let herself dangle, feeling the stretch all the way down to her toes. Cold air on her stomach again. She wanted Lemur to touch it. Eight months with this weird family and she still had no idea how to be with a male who didn't try to fuck her. Lying down in the dark, they couldn't see her stupid face.

"You're showing yourself again."

"Don't be such a tard. I'm hanging from a fucking tree."

"You have to take care for yourself, Nikki. Watch your language, too. You can't be using the F-word. Men have strong desires."

"You don't. Not for girls, anyway."

"Don't start with that again. I'm trying to be nice to you."

"I know all about men's desires," she said from between upstretched arms. "I bet you all had a good laugh about it when Papa took me in that night." She let go. Her feet hit the ground hard and she staggered backwards.

Lemur steadied her, strong hands gripping her biceps.

"You can let go of me now, perv."

"Nobody laughed at you," Lemur said. "Night he brought you in, Papa said, 'Nikki's been doing what she has to do to survive. I won't hear her criticized for it.'"

Nikki imitated Papa's tone. "'I won't hear her criticized for it.'"

Lemur smiled. He had a good smile—the gap in his front teeth made him look like a little kid—but he didn't use it much. "Okay, I'm going to tie this to the rear axle."

Ignoring the snow, Lemur got down on his back and slid under the Range Rover. All Nikki could see were his legs and the rope jerking beside them as he tied it. She thought about making a grab for his crotch, going down on him right here in the snow. See exactly how faggoty he might be.

"Why are we doing this, anyway?" she said to his legs. "Who in their right mind is going to come out here?"

Lemur emerged from under the car and stood up, swatting snow from his pants. "You want to question Papa, you go right ahead. But you may have noticed, if you're going to stay in this family, you don't ask too many questions." He got into the Range Rover and started it. He rolled down the window and said, "Let me know when the rock's about twenty feet up."

The car inched forward, pulling the rope taut. The huge rock Lemur had fixed to the other end with many complicated knots began to rise in the air. When it was about twenty feet up, she called out, "Stop!"

Lemur got out and showed her how to tie the loop, how to set it to be tripped by an unwary footstep. "Okay, let's try it out. Step in the loop, there."

"I'm not stepping on that thing."

Lemur gave her a look. He didn't have to say anything. It was the family look. It said, This is family business and you just get it done.

"It's not gonna hurt, right?"

"No."

Nikki stomped one foot on the hidden trigger. The loop slithered closed round her ankle and she was hoisted into the air as the counterweight slammed to the ground. "Ow, Lemur. What the fuck."

"Watch your language."

"I hit my head, you jerk-off."

"Nikki, you have to stop cursing. It's a sign of weakness, and members of this family are not weak. You use language like that, Papa's gonna go berserk."

Nikki was dangling upside down from one ankle, the snowy forest floor swinging crazily beneath her. "Just get me down before I throw up. The thing works, okay? Anybody comes along this trail, they're totally fucked—sorry!—trapped. Don't wanna hurt those virgin ears of yours."

—

In the kitchen, Papa had just finished his lunch and was sitting at the table picking his teeth and listening to the radio. There were a lot of local ads, but it kept promising news. Jack was staring out the window, where a light snow was falling.

Papa put the toothpick on the plate and pushed the plate aside. Then he rested his elbows on the table and leaned his face into his hands, like a man suffering a tragedy. After a while he said, "God. I have such thoughts."

His words were muffled. Jack turned from the window and said, "What'd you say?"

"Such thoughts come to me," Papa said, his face still in his hands. "Such images."

"I'm aware of it," Jack said. "It's not like you're the one got to deal with it."

"Picture this. Neighbours hear a barking dog. As far as they know, the people who live in that particular house are away. The barking goes on all through the night. Finally the police come and, after trying the doorbell, after trying to see in the windows, they bust the door open. What they find inside beggars the imagination. A dog is barking all right, but the dog is sewn inside a human body, his dog head emerging where the human head should be."

Jack turned back to the window. "Personally, I don't get the attraction of headless bodies—having seen 'em up close and all."

"Shh. Listen."

The local newscast opened with an item about a First Nations girl who had shot an assailant with a crossbow.

"A crossbow," Papa said. "Have to give her points for that."

A police spokesman related that the girl was not being charged with anything, and her alleged attacker was in hospital but expected to survive his injury.

Meanwhile, residents of Algonquin Bay continue to live in fear, wondering if they should expect more murders following last Thursday's grisly double slaying. Police believe they have now identified the victims, but that information is being withheld pending notification of next of kin. As to the killer or killers, police still seem pretty much in the dark. We spoke to Detective John Cardinal of the Algonquin Bay police service earlier today.

The detective's voice came on. *"This investigation is still in its beginning stages, but at least it's now on solid ground and we have a number of different leads to follow up."* CKAT will keep you updated as further developments unfold.

"'In fear,'" Papa said. "I like that, 'in fear.' In fear is exactly the way people should be living. Fear is healthy. Fear is good. There's a new world coming, and it's nothing like the old world."

"Chaos is coming," Jack said. "Hold on to your hats." He traced K-OS in the condensation on the window.

"Guided chaos. Exactly right."

Jack drew a happy face in the O. "Lemur is taking an awful long time to set that trap. Maybe I should go find them."

"Lemur knows what he's doing."

"You trust him with Nikki? Girl's got a hot body for a thirteen-year-old. Terrible face. But I'd have swore she was sixteen."

"Lemur will behave like a gentleman. I've trained a lot of kids over the years, and he seems to get it more than most."

"Including me?"

"Including you."

"That's the thanks I get."

"I'm referring to the gentleman part, Jack. Each kid responds to one part of the code more than another. In your case, it's loyalty. For Lemur, it's manners."

"I've never understood why you're so all-fired missionary on the subject."

"Because no situation is made worse by good manners, and many are made better."

"I still don't see why it's taking them so long."

"Jack, that's just lust talking. You know it's a problem for you and it only brings you misery and pain. But I don't define you by it, and I hope you don't either. You're such a strong guy, I can't imagine you're going to let it get the better of you."

Jack turned from the window. He opened the fridge and took out a can of the old man's ginger ale, opened it and took a drink. He wiped his mouth and said, "I didn't say nothing about lust. That girl don't even turn me on, tell you the truth. That face of hers."

"Let's not be shallow about people's looks. Nikki's face is perfectly fine."

"It's not to my taste is what I'm saying. So it's not lust talking, Papa. It's concern. We're supposed to look after each other, and I'm concerned about Nikki."

"Nikki's in no danger with Lemur at her side."

"It's Lemur I'm concerned about."

"Then you don't know human nature. And you don't know Lemur."

Jack drank down the rest of the ginger ale and crushed the can in his fist. "Lemur this, Lemur that. What's he ever done? What're you always going on about that little faggot for?"

"Jack, please. We do not call each other names. You've spent years in institutions—have I ever called you psycho?"

"No."

"Crazy? Disturbed? Wacko? I have not. And no one else in this family ever has or ever will. Because we respect you, Jack. And we respect your ability to give as you receive."

Jack felt he should have a reply to this, that there was something unfair about it. But there was a lot right about it too, and now he felt bad for letting Papa down, letting the family down. After a time he said, "You always told me loyalty was the most important thing. Now all you go on about is manners."

"Loyalty is second nature in Lemur. His manners, on the other hand, needed a lot of work. When we first took him in—don't you remember?— it was 'fuck this' and 'motherfucker' that, and now he's a model of polite speech. With you, loyalty has always been an issue. Lemur is like a hunting dog, but you—you're a wild stallion. Magnificent, yes, but liable to gallop away at the first chance."

"You question my loyalty? After what I just done for you? Everything you said, down to the letter—when you said and how you said. Do you have any concept what that took?"

Papa stood up and opened his arms wide. Jack hesitated then stepped closer, and Papa closed his arms around him in a bear hug. "Jack, your courage is never in doubt. Not for one minute. You're our samurai. Our warrior. Our knight. Some poet said, 'Lonely are the brave.' Well, not in my house. You are crucial to this family and I trust you with my life, Jack. With my life." Papa stood back, hands still gripping Jack's shoulders. "When it comes down to it, Jack—when it comes to sheer guts?—I think you've got me outclassed. Maybe one day I'll prove myself wrong, but I don't think so."

Jack did not feel brave. If he had any guts, he'd tell Papa that a girl, some kid, had seen him out at that house and it had panicked him so bad he couldn't see straight. He should have killed her—run her down, shot her, whatever it took—but it hadn't been part of the operation and he'd just panicked. But he couldn't say it. He pulled away and folded his arms. "So when's Lemur going to face his big test? He's been part of this family a long time now. Is he gonna do the old man?"

"If I ask him to, he will."

"You think so? I wouldn't have said the odds favour it."

Papa smiled. "That's because you're a man of action, Jack. Understanding people is not your strong point."

21

THE CRIMINAL WHO CALLED HIMSELF Papa had locked Lloyd Kreeger back in his master bedroom, having removed anything that might be construed as a sharp object. That, at least, was a positive development. Lloyd's hands were still cuffed together in front of him, but this didn't restrict him too much. He had a comfortable bed and lots to read, but he couldn't stop thinking about Henry. Even Charles Dickens couldn't stop him from picturing the worst.

He was trying to decide if there was any hope to his situation, or if he should risk escape and a bullet in the head, when this "Papa" came and got him and led him once more to the basement office. This strange man now knew some of Lloyd's passwords, and had made notes of different account numbers. They sat beside each other now on two office chairs, as if one were teaching the other about software.

"Look what I found, Lloyd."

Lloyd leaned forward to peer at the screen. His New York investment accounts. "A discount brokerage site," he said.

"I know what it is, Lloyd. My point is, you didn't tell me you had these accounts. Add up these different funds, we're looking at a couple of hundred thousand U.S."

140

Giles Blunt

"I forgot I had them. Those were set up must be thirty years ago, back when I was working in New York. I never touch them."

"I know. I checked your transaction history. But you didn't tell me about them. That's my point."

"I never think about them."

"They send you statements once a month. Which you file away in those neat blue binders I found. You're keeping things from me, Lloyd. You're chiselling me. I try to help you out, I put you back in your room, I make you as comfortable as possible . . ."

"You steal everything I have . . ."

The man's eyes on him expressed nothing but mild disappointment. He turned back to the computer screen. "Well, we're just going to have to empty these out, aren't we."

"Those are for my grandchildren. My daughter has three kids, and all three of them are going to be in university at the same time. She is a copy editor, her husband is a freelance journalist. I doubt if they make fifty grand a year between them. Those funds are to see their kids through college."

"It's not letting me move anything."

"Well, I can't help you, I haven't touched those funds since they were set up. I wouldn't know where to begin."

The man unholstered his sidearm, took aim at a lamp, and fired. The base of the lamp shattered, and Lloyd's ears rang as if they were made of brass.

"Apply yourself to the problem," the man told him. "I have every faith that, together, we can get past this."

—

Sometimes it seemed to Nikki that this "family" was a real thing, and not just some make-believe game they were playing. Tonight was one of those times. Papa had asked the three of them—not ordered them, asked them—to refrain from turning on the television. He wanted them to light a fire, a big one, while he was downstairs with the old man, and he would join them a little later.

"And then what?" Jack had wanted to know.

"You keep your eyes on that fire and tell each other everything you see."

Which, in Nikki's opinion, had worked out great. Jack had built up a big fire, fat logs criss-crossed over each other, and the flames flapped and swayed and you could hear the hot air rushing up the chimney. The furniture was arranged at angles around the fireplace, as if it were a TV. Nikki had an arm-chair to herself on one side, Jack had the other, and Lemur was lying on the couch, propped up on one elbow. His face glowed orange in the firelight.

At first they just pointed out different shapes that shifted among the logs and flames. Lemur saw a hooded monk, Nikki saw a fat man on a bike, which made the other two guffaw, and Jack saw seven little dwarves, all carrying axes and saws over their shoulders. Nikki had seen that in a car-toon somewhere, but she didn't mention it. They played this game for a time and even Jack, a world-class grouch, was smiling, teeth gleaming in the firelight. His shadow leapt and shuddered on the ceiling.

Then Lemur suggested they try to see their futures in the flames. "Try to imagine where you'll be in ten years. What your situation will be. Who you'll be with."

"We're gonna be in the north," Jack said. "K-OS will be in effect. All the underclasses are gonna rise up and the rest of the world will try to crush them—they're already trying to crush them. But this time the losers are gonna win—the blacks, the Aboriginals, the Muslims—because they've been down so long they don't see no downside to fighting to the death and lopping heads off. That's why we're commandeering the Jeeps and the snowmobiles. Ten years from now, hundreds of members of this family from all across the continent will be hid out in the north—small communes, self-sustaining. Rest of the planet, K-OS reigns. North is going to be the best place to be, because blacks and Muslims obviously don't care for cold and the rest of the planet's gonna burn."

"Is Papa from up north?" Nikki said. "Is that why he's so crazy about it?"

"He was raised somewheres up north," Jack said, "but that is not what this is about. Haven't you heard about global warming? North's gonna be the only place habitable."

"That's right," Lemur said. "That's how Papa sees it."

"How Papa sees things got nothing to do with it. It's the way things are."

"Well, however it goes, I'm with this family to the end," Lemur said. "But right now that's not what I'm seeing in those flames. Well, maybe a little bit." He pointed to part of an ashy log that had fallen away from the flames. "See, there's my igloo right there."

"Kinda hot for an igloo," Nikki said.

"But all that heat in there? All that beauty? That's coming from the loving home I'm going to put together with my wife."

"Oh, sure," Jack said. "That's crystal clear."

"I'm telling you, I can see her. She's got long brown hair. Down to her shoulders. A little bit of curl to it. And when she smiles, she's got those little curvy things either side of her mouth."

"Dimples," Nikki said.

"Is that what dimples are? Then she's got dimples. She's tall—at least as tall as me—and she's got a nice figure. Not too full. She's real smart, too. Smarter than me."

"That is likely true," Jack said.

"And she wears turtleneck sweaters and corduroy jeans that fit real nice. Because it's cold up there. And she has a white coat with a fur hood and a sky-blue scarf. I'm telling you, I can see this girl. I can see her so clear. When we meet? I'm going to know who she is right off. And I'm gonna fall in love with her, because I'm already in love with her."

"Aww," Jack said. "That is truly beautiful."

"It is," Nikki said. "It really is, Lemur."

Nikki was wishing she'd seen something like that. She'd forgotten about that north business. Papa's K-OS vision. It made sense to her, from what was on the news and all, but it didn't stick in her head. Sometimes she thought Papa himself didn't really believe it, that he believed something else entirely, which he kept to himself.

Lemur looked over at her, the whites of his eyes gleaming. "What do you see for yourself, Nikki?"

Nikki shrugged. "I guess I see music. I know I have a voice like a frog, but I hear songs in my head all the time. So I see, like, a studio of some kind. Do they have those up north where we're going?"

Lemur sat up. "If they don't, we'll build one. We'll look it up on the Web, get some books on it."

"It'd be like a combination music studio, like for recording, and a TV studio. So you could make the videos while you record the songs."

"Oh, sure," Jack said. "Those Eskimos are some fine singers. Famous for it. Have you ever heard the Eskimo Boys' Choir?"

"We'll have all sorts of family up there," Lemur said. "Some of them'll be singers for sure. Anyways, chaos is only gonna reign so long. Sooner or later the blacks and the Muslims and all the rest of the, like, downtrodden are gonna come to us to run things. They don't have the experience with it—not with running a civilization like ours. They're gonna need help, and they're gonna come to us that know how it works."

"Well, aren't you Papa's parrot."

"It makes perfect sense, Jack. If you don't believe it, why are you part of the family?"

"I just don't see it word for word, note for note, one-hundred-percent-copycat-perfect in Papa's exact words, is all. I still have a mind of my own, is what I'm saying."

Lemur hunched himself up in a corner of the couch, eyes on the flames again. "Well, anyway. There's no reason why Nikki can't be producing records or videos ten years from now. Or managing some really cool band. Why not?"

Jack knelt in front of the fire and poked at it, clattering and bonging in the grate as he spoke. Sparks darted and swirled. "Getting back to your own personal vision quest there, Lemur. I'm interested in this girl you describe. This soulmate business. That sounds about as close to perfect as perfect gets."

Sometimes when Jack spoke, it was as if some malign entity—cold, wet, shapeless—entered the room and sat watching. As if he had custody of some alien creature that fed on anger and tears. Jack's tone was cheerful, but Nikki sensed that ugly little creature in the room with them. Watching. Drooling.

Lemur didn't pick up on it. "I never put it into words before. Just sitting here watching the fire, it just seems so . . ."

"Real," Jack said. Leather creaked as he got comfortable in his armchair again. "She have a name, this princess?"

"I don't really care what her name might be. But if I was gonna guess, I'd say she looks like—I don't know—maybe a Jennifer? Or a Melissa?"

"I'd have said you was far more likely to find yourself cuddling up with a girl named Jason, or Buck. Something like that."

"Very funny."

"Listen, Petunia, you ain't the kind of ace ends up with any Melissa. Reason being, Melissas don't come supplied with cocks. And you are a natural-born cocksucker if ever I saw one, and that's the truth."

"Don't talk to me like that." Lemur folded his arms across his chest. His face had gone all tight. "We don't call each other names in this family."

"No need to get all hissy about it. Your proclivities is your proclivities. I'm just pointing out what's obvious to everyone except you—that you are a solid gold, one-hundred-percent certified faggot."

"It's Lemur's future," Nikki said. "He can imagine it any way he wants."

"The world's ugliest whore defends the world's dumbest fudge packer. Christ, how'd I end up in this freak show? Tell you what, Lemur, I got the perfect line of work for you. We get up north? You learn yourself some carpentry and go straight into cabinet work. Building closets. 'Cause you are locked up in a closet even Fort Knox got to envy."

"Just shut your mouth," Lemur said. "I'm not gay."

"Is this the kind of family I'm living with?"

None of them had heard Papa come in. He stood looking at them, hands clasped behind his back the way he always stood, measuring them.

"We call each other names? Accuse each other? Tell each other to shut up?"

"Jack was giving Lemur a hard time," Nikki said. "About being gay."

"Is that a fact."

"I was just suggesting he might want to stop lying to himself about it. Be a little more honest with hisself."

"He was calling me a faggot," Lemur said.

"And why is that upsetting, if you're not one?" Papa said. "Or even if you are?"

"He's punkin' me. Same as if he spit on me."

Papa came around the couch and stood with his back to the fire. "Well, people. I have to say, I'm disappointed."

"Let's not make a federal case out of it," Jack said.

"No, not about a little name-calling—childish as that might be. What bothers me more, Jack—and all of you—and to be honest, it's something that bugs me about myself sometimes—it's just so conventional. So *ordinary*. The idea that a person who has sex with someone of their own gender is somehow worthy of ridicule. Are we born-again Christians in this family? Are we Scientologists?

"Being a member of this family is about being free. Free from the labels and conventions our dying society throws around for its convenience. Faggot. Terrorist. Communist. Liberal. Lunatic. It's the same with all of them. They take the place of real thinking." Papa tapped a forefinger to his temple. "This family thinks. It does not accept ready-made labels. I want us to be free of those conventions that tie the rest of the world in knots. We don't accept the Pope's idea of morality, or Rush Limbaugh's, or Barack Obama's. We make our own.

"All my life my intention has been to free myself, but I don't want to be alone. I want my family with me. So right here and now, in this room, I'm going to defy convention. I'm going to have sex with Lemur right here in front of you. You think I'm a faggot, Jack?"

"No, I do not."

"You think I'm a faggot, Nikki?"

"No."

"Lemur?"

"No. But I'm not either, and I don't want to have sex with you."

"You want to be conventional the rest of your life? You want to hide what you might or might not want to do? I don't think you do. I'm asking you to join me in this little exercise. Exercise makes you stronger. We're going to break this taboo together, and we'll both be stronger. You think I don't feel resistance to it? I do. It's an iron claw inside my chest, an iron band around my mind. I have no desire to have sex with a man. But I choose to not care."

Nikki had seen a lot of things during her short career as a hooker, but she had never seen anything that shocked her more than Papa pulling off his sweater and undershirt right then and there in front of the fire. Removing his shoes and socks and taking off everything else right there in front of them.

He had a good body, however old he might be. Really in shape, with the skin still tight and the muscles ropy. His skin glowed before the fire.

"That's one convention down," he said. "Are you with me, Lemur?"

"What about modesty? You were saying just the other day how we—"

"Special circumstances. Are you going to take your clothes off, or am I gonna do it for you?"

"I don't credit this," Jack said. "This is outright outlandish."

"Yes," Papa said, "it is. Stand up, Lemur."

"I don't want to do this."

"I don't either." Papa took hold of Lemur's wrist and pulled him up. "Not sexually. But as an exercise in freedom, I want nothing more. This is important, Lemur. And it takes guts. I think you've got the guts. I know you do. And I know you care about our freedoms. Take your sweater off."

Lemur hesitated, and Papa took hold of the hem of his sweater and pulled it up over his head. Lemur made some noises of protest but didn't struggle much. Papa started on his belt.

"Tell me this ain't real," Jack said.

"You think I'm a faggot?" Papa said.

"No, I don't, but—"

"I refuse to be a slave. I choose freedom, and I want you people beside me. Take 'em off, Lemur. Don't make me do all the work."

Lemur took his jeans off. The two of them were naked, facing each other, about a foot apart.

"Two men do not get naked in front of each other," Papa said. "That's the rule in our society, right? Unless they're on the same sports team, men do not get naked together. That's the rule. And they certainly don't touch each other, right? Not unless they're faggots. Am I a faggot, Lemur?"

"No."

"No, and you're not either." Papa took Lemur's penis in his right hand.

Lemur put his hands up on Papa's biceps and leaned back. "Whoah, this is . . ."

"Am I a faggot, Jack?"

"Jesus."

"Sounding pretty conventional there, Jack."

Jack shook his head and looked up at the ceiling. Nikki couldn't take her eyes off them. Papa got Lemur to sit back on the couch, legs stretched out before him. Papa took hold of his ankles and spread them out and then he knelt between Lemur's legs and went at it. Nikki covered her face and watched between splayed fingers. Papa seemed like the ungayest person she had ever met, and seeing him going down on a guy was—well, she could feel the furniture of her mind trying to rearrange itself.

She had never thought before that two men having sex could be anything other than comic or disgusting, but now she felt her own body reacting to the two burnished males before her.

Papa didn't ask Lemur to do anything. Lemur just lay back, silent through most of it, moaning toward the end, and gasping when he finally finished in Papa's mouth. Then Papa held him in his mouth, unmoving, for some time after. Jack was staring straight into the fireplace now, but Nikki had caught him looking lots of times. He was acting all perturbed in how he was sitting and everything, but she could tell he was pretty turned on.

Papa stood up and started pulling on his clothes, taking his time about it. "Let's agree on something," he said, tightening his belt. "There are no faggots in this family. And if Lemur wants to have sex with a man, he is free to do so without any loss of respect around here."

Lemur had curled up in the corner of the couch again. He clutched a wad of his clothes over his lap and Nikki could see he was nervous and ashamed and she felt bad for him. She tried to lighten the atmosphere a little.

"Is it just me," she said, "or was that, like, major hot?"

22

Lemur and Nikki were out on another trail. They had been walking for about ten minutes in snow that was nearly up to the tops of their boots. At breakfast it had been decided to set this trap farther away from the house. It was a bear trap of the old-fashioned kind, with iron jaws that clamped shut.

"What if an animal steps in it?" Nikki said, puffing with the exertion of slogging through snow. "Won't it break its leg?"

Lemur smiled, showing the gap in his front teeth. "You worry too much, kid."

"Omigod, how many times do I have to tell you, you're not old enough to call me kid."

"The only animal heavy enough to set this thing off is a bear, and they're all hibernating this time of year."

"So what if a human steps in it?"

"The only human coming along this trail to the house is going to be someone we don't want to see. They'll get what's coming to them. Family rules. All right, this looks good. We'll remember where it is because of that tree." He pointed to an evergreen with one large branch hanging down at a diagonal.

Nikki put the trap down and started kicking snow out of the way.

Lemur leaned his sledgehammer against the tree and started fiddling with the mechanism of the trap.

"Are you going out again tonight?" Nikki said. "You know, like, to work?"

"Probably."

"How come you have to do these jobs by yourself? Shouldn't Jack or me be helping you?"

Lemur shrugged. "Jack's above that kind of stuff now. And you're not ready for it. We each have to carry our weight, so pulling these things is my job, that's all."

"Do you ever wonder about the people you're robbing? How they feel?"

"A dollar of the enemy's is worth twenty dollars of our own. That's what Sun Tzu said."

"Why are they our enemies?"

"Because they're not us." Lemur took up the sledgehammer and held it crossways. "It's about survival too. It's about K-OS. Civilization is going down and we're gonna be the survivors. I don't need to know every detail. And neither do you. Hold the stake."

Nikki knelt in the snow and held the stake with both hands. The iron radiated cold through her mittens. If anyone had told her even three months ago that she would be wandering through the forest planting traps in the snow, she would have laughed. But she was beginning to like the outdoors. She was even beginning to like winter. The shafts of sunlight through the trees, the glitter of ice on the branches, the spears of light cast every which way. And the air, so dry and clean it made you feel transparent.

Lemur swung the sledgehammer, taking care to hit the spike dead-on. Each time, a loud clank ricocheted round the forest and a shudder went up Nikki's arm bones.

"Get back to the house." Jack's voice, behind them. The master of Papa's arts of stealth and survival, standing beside the broken tree, as if he had materialized out of the forest. "You heard me," he said to Lemur. "I'll show her how to set it."

"I'll show her in a second. We're just fixing it in place, then I'm gonna show her. Papa asked me to do it," Lemur said. "Asked me specifically."

"Yesterday it took you the entire afternoon to rig up a simple rope trap. We need this done pronto and it's near lunchtime. I'm going to show her. Now beat it."

"You giving orders now?"

"It's okay," Nikki said to Lemur. "Don't make a big deal out of it."

Lemur kept his eyes on Jack. "You're not the boss of this family. Nobody's boss in this family. Everybody's equal."

Lemur was holding the sledgehammer across his body as if to ward off blows. Jack took a step toward him. Nikki was reminded of a nature program she had seen about apes, males posturing and spitting at each other. Jack was by far the taller of the two—a lot more muscular, too. He grabbed hold of the sledgehammer with one hand and with the other slapped Lemur across the face. The sound made Nikki jump. "Get back to the house," Jack said.

Lemur stood motionless. His right cheek was an angry red, and tears trickled down from that eye. "I'll go," he said. "But not because I'm afraid of you. I'm going because of what Papa says—about loyalty and unity. I'm not gonna fight you." He threw down the sledgehammer and it vanished in snow. He turned to Nikki. "Guess I'll see you back at the house."

"Okay," Nikki said. "See you later."

Lemur tramped back the way they had come, the snow swishing around his feet.

Jack rubbed his hands together and put on a smile that looked as fake as anything you might see on a billboard. "It's you and me, kid. And we are going to set ourselves one hell of a trap."

~

Lunch was over and Jack was carrying away the plates and putting the dishes into the dishwasher—not because anyone asked him to but because he was a neat freak. Liked things in their place. Also, Nikki figured, because he was none too comfortable sitting at the table just now and wanted to get away from Papa's observant eye.

Papa had been telling them about how it was going to be up north. How they would have a whole fleet of Jeeps and snowmobiles, and how they would make a living trading them to people who had not had the foresight to prepare. He spoke about how they would love and respect each other and start an entirely different society based on that. And how, when the blacks and the Natives and the Muslims came looking for their help, they would be up and running and ready to steer the remainder of humanity into the new reality. There was more than a little of the poet in Papa when he got going on the subject.

Today the poetry wasn't working so well, though, owing to what had transpired in the woods. Lemur was the only one responding, and Nikki didn't feel like talking, thank you very much.

Lemur was all excited about Hudson's Bay blankets. He'd been surfing the Internet on the subject of coloured wool blankets and finally figured out the name. He was all for laying in a huge supply.

Papa had a tiny little notebook he carried with him at all times. It had an elastic band around it and a little ribbon like they have in bibles so you can find your chapter and verse. He always made a note when someone had a good idea, and they all liked to see him take that little notebook out and write in it with the little stub of a pencil he carried with him for the purpose. Nikki figured he'd had that thing since like the eighties or something.

"What's that on your arm?" Papa was looking down at his notebook, but there was no doubt whom he was talking to.

"You talking to me?" Jack said.

"There's a mark on your left forearm." Papa closed the little notebook and set the elastic band around it and put it in his pocket along with the pencil. "How'd it happen?"

"I don't know. It's nothing."

"Jack, it's a bite mark. How do you come to have a bite mark on your forearm?"

"It ain't a bite mark. I took a tumble in the woods. Must have whanged it against something."

"You tried to force yourself on Nikki, didn't you?"

Nikki spoke up. "We were just wrestling. I was practising the moves you showed me. I guess I got carried away."

Papa spoke so quietly she had to strain to hear. "You're trying to protect him. Maybe you think that's loyalty, but it isn't. If someone is disloyal to the family and you take his side, you are being disloyal. Do you understand? I know you're young, but you need to get this."

"Okay."

"Jack, you tried to have sex with your sister."

"I didn't have sex with her—and she's not my sister in the first place. You had sex with Lemur right here in front of all of us."

"Nikki is under the age of sixteen. That makes her a child. Also, what I did with Lemur was an exercise."

"Yeah, well maybe the rest of us would like a little exercise once in a while. Child? Sister? She ain't even worthy to be in this family. Were you not in the room when this so-called *child* told us she performed a record 75 blow jobs in one *month*? That girl has fuck—has had sex with 167 men and she didn't even know who they were. She did it with a German shepherd while a bunch of drunk bastards cheered her on. And you think she's too good to be with me? Where's *your* loyalty? That's what I'd like to know. Where's *your* loyalty?"

"You come to this family, you get dignity," Papa said. "All that matters is what we do now. How we treat each other now. You don't get to ruin the family for the rest of us, Jack."

"Not only are you taking sides with a whore against your so-called right-hand man, you fail to notice that this poor girl got a face would stop a Mack truck. She's gotta be downright grateful anyone would *want* to touch her. When the hell else is anyone not afflicted with outright insanity gonna lay a hand on her? I mean, *look* at her."

Back in the woods, Nikki had kicked him and punched him and finally, when he wouldn't stop, bit him. That made him let go and she got away from him. What she couldn't figure out was, why did his words hurt so much? She pressed her chin to her chest and would not cry, but she couldn't speak either.

Papa's tone changed entirely. "How are your new boots, Nikki?"

Nikki had nothing to say to that.

"I noticed you favouring your right leg. Are they pinching?"

"A little." She kept her chin pressed down, but she had to keep sniffing back tears. They all knew she was crying anyway.

"Wait here," Papa said. "Jack, I've finished now, but please, all of you, just indulge me." He left the table and went into the kitchen and clattered around in the cupboards, one after another, looking for something. Jack sat back down, and Lemur just watched with a look on his face like WTF.

Papa filled a huge metal mixing bowl with hot water and brought it back to the table and set it down. He got Nikki to turn her chair sideways to the table and he knelt in front of her. She wasn't wearing any shoes, just thick red socks. Papa took hold of one of her cuffs and rolled it up, slowly, with concentration, nearly to her knee. Then he did the same with her other cuff. He rolled off one sock. Then the other. Normally Nikki would have said WTF like Lemur was obviously thinking, but there was some kind of major pressure in her chest and she mistrusted her ability to say a single word.

Papa took her left foot in his hands. They were cool and dry and felt like a doctor's, but more tender. He examined her foot this way and that, changing his grip. It tickled but felt good too. No one had ever handled her feet before, not that she could remember.

"Left one looks okay," he said, and set it down gently before taking up her right foot. "Little tender there, I bet, huh?" He gripped her ankle where it was sore and she nodded. "And maybe here a little too?" The fat part by her big toe. She nodded again.

Papa stood up and got the bowl of hot water and set it down in front of her. He went over to the bathroom and got some soap and a big fat red towel. He put the towel on her lap and she could smell the Downy on it, a smell she loved. He knelt in front of her again and took her left foot in his hands. Sudden heat of the water as he placed her foot in the bowl. Then the right one.

Hearing her intake of breath, he said, "Too hot?"

Nikki shook her head.

Papa took a red face cloth and soaped it up. Strong scents of lemon and lavender wafting up between her knees. He washed her left foot, the sole, the arch, the ankle, in between the toes. A sexual tingle up the inside of her leg. When the foot was soapy enough, he gripped it with both hands and rubbed the sole with his thumbs, warm swirling circles that made her sleepy even while they tickled. He bent her toes back and rubbed each one, giving each a gentle tug.

Nikki fixed her eyes on the top of his head, the short hair much flecked with grey. She watched his capable hands that handled her feet with such tender firmness. She felt Lemur and Jack staring, but she didn't want to see their faces. Neither said a word. Papa took her feet from the water, first the left, then the right, and dried them and rubbed them with some kind of cream that felt slippery and cool, and then he patted them with the towel.

"Feel better?" His eyes, deep blue, looking up at her.

She nodded and tried to say yes, but nothing came out.

Papa raised her left foot and cocked his head to plant a kiss on her instep. The pressure of his lips just so, then gone. He did the same with her right foot, holding the kiss just a moment longer.

23

NINE P.M., AND DELORME WAS IN THE last place she wanted to be, parked in an unmarked car in the darkest spot of an outdoor parking lot. She had spent the afternoon re-interviewing the two victims of the ATM mugger. They were both young, both women, and Delorme patiently coaxed every possible detail out of them. But in the end it had only served to upset them and she had come away with nothing new. From her dark corner of the parking lot she had a good view of the ATM across the street. It was in an area that used to be well lit, but the new building going up next to it now blocked the street light.

She and Chouinard had discussed at length which ATM would be most likely to be struck next. There weren't all that many in Algonquin Bay, but even so, the police had nowhere near the resources to stake out every one. The two easiest targets had already been hit. The first was in a tiny strip mall at the top of Roxwell Street, a quiet area that made for a pretty soft target. The second had been more brazen, but also made tactical sense. It was downtown, but at the back of a bank rather than the front, beside an alley that ran the length of that particular block, which was where the robber had waited and where he had fled.

The security videos revealed nothing. He was too smart to set foot inside. He came up behind each of his victims as they stepped away from the machines, shoved a gun into their ribs and demanded money. Over in a matter of seconds. Young man, eighteen to twenty-five, they thought. Dark pants, dark hooded coat. The hood had been up, and he also wore a wool cap low on his forehead and a scarf over nose and mouth. No one would be able to identify him in a lineup.

Of the ATMs that remained, this location, central but dark, made the most sense. There was very little traffic around this corner after eight o'clock, which was why Delorme was sitting in an unmarked car with the snowflakes twirling slowly to the pavement around her. Of course, she had pointed out to Chouinard, the mugger could just as easily decide to target the first ATM again; he might figure no one would expect that. That's true, Chouinard agreed. He could.

She shifted her position on the car seat. She was in the back because nobody notices the rear seat of a parked car. A backup unit was tucked discreetly in a driveway nearby. Cardinal and the others were chasing down one of the biggest murder cases ever to hit the province, and here she was stuck trying to trap some dork robbing ATMs. She knew it was important—people have to be able to go about their business without being mugged—but there wasn't going to be any glory in catching this guy.

Only four customers had used the ATM in the entire two hours Delorme had been watching, and there was no sign of trouble, no sign of anybody else watching. She made a note every time someone went by: *9:14 lady walking dachshund wearing tartan coat; 9:36 juvenile about sixteen, skates slung over his hockey stick, hockey stick on shoulder like a rifle; 9:43 Stuart Cort* (a homeless alcoholic well known to police) *lurches by, clutching a Subway sandwich bag.*

Algonquin Bay police service, she said. Be all you can be.

The radio squawked and she had to reach around the front seat to get it. "Get your ass up to Roxwell and Clement," the duty sergeant told her. "He hit the first one again."

I knew it, I knew it, I knew it, Delorme said as she got into the front, started up and headed for the other side of town. She also employed several French Canadian curse words that she usually considered beneath her dignity. She was at the scene in under three minutes. A couple of cruisers were already there, and the whole front parking lot was taped off.

She spoke to a female constable who directed her to one of the squad cars.

A woman was sitting in the back. Her name was Stella McQuaig, and she was in not too bad shape, considering, although there was a tremor in her voice as she told Delorme what had happened. The other two victims had been hysterical by comparison. Her description was no more useful than anybody else's: young man, dark clothes, hood and scarf. She had seen the hood and scarf reflected in her car window.

"Do you think you could show me exactly how it happened?" Delorme said.

"You mean go over there with you?"

"You're safe now."

The woman looked from Delorme to the scene outside and back to Delorme. "All right. I mean, I guess. If you think it would help."

Delorme led her back to the ATM, a free-standing machine outside a convenience store, and Ms. McQuaig showed her how she had put the money into her wallet and headed back toward her car. "He came out of nowhere, just as I was about to get into my car."

"Did he come from a car? From the street? He must have been waiting somewhere."

"I didn't *see* where he came from," the woman said, her voice edging up the panic scale. "There were no cars other than mine."

"What about the phone booth?" Delorme pointed to a phone booth at the edge of the mall's parking lot.

"Could have been. I don't know. Like I say, I didn't see anything. Then, just as I was getting into my car, I heard footsteps—fast steps—and before I could turn, I felt the gun in my ribs. Oh, God . . ."

"It's all right. You're doing great," Delorme said. "You saw his reflection in your car window?"

"Just his hood and scarf. I didn't see his face. Thank God. He probably would have killed me."

"You heard steps. From which direction?"

"That way." She pointed toward Clement Street. Delorme looked at the pavement. The parking lot had been well ploughed. No footprints.

"Then what happened?"

"He told me to hand it over and I did. I just handed him my wallet and he took off."

"And you didn't look at him then?"

"No. I didn't want to see his face. Can I go now? I think I'm having a delayed reaction." She covered her mouth with a mittened hand.

"Did he take off the same way he came?"

Still with one hand covering her mouth, she pointed in the other direction.

"Up Roxwell?"

She lowered the mitten. "That way. Back toward the buildings, but toward that way." She was pointing beyond the ATM, toward the far end of the strip mall.

Delorme thanked her and walked her back to the cruiser, then she headed back past the ATM. They had set the perimeter too narrow. She ducked under the tape and stood on the other side. To her left was the edge of the parking lot, a high hedge and, beyond it, Roxwell Street. To her right was a small gap between an adjacent house and the end of the mall.

Light from the street and the parking lot didn't reach back here, and Delorme called across the lot, "Hey, Benson, lend me your flashlight." Benson brought it over and she shone it down the alley. She had gone barely ten feet when she found the wallet. She picked it up and flipped it open. The driver's licence showed an unflattering picture of Stella McQuaig. No money. Delorme put it in her pocket and shone the light down the alley again.

Beyond a row of recycling bins, she could see the legs of a homeless man.

"Police," Delorme said. "I need to ask you some questions."

The man didn't move.

She went up and tapped his foot with her boot. His clothes were too good for a homeless person, and he was wearing a hood. Delorme stepped back and trained her Beretta on him. He didn't move, and his stillness was not the stillness of the living. Delorme bent down, and in the beam of her flashlight the small black hole in his forehead glistened. His eyes were only half closed, the crooked track of a tear straying down one cheek. The lips were slightly drawn back, as if he had been interrupted in the middle of speech, exposing a sizable gap in his front teeth.

—

When Cardinal arrived, Delorme brought him up to speed. "No wallet, no ID, but we found the ten fresh twenties he'd just taken from the victim. Also a nine-mil Browning Hi-Power with at least one good thumbprint. Clothing labels are Gap, Guess?, Hilfiger. Coroner's been and gone."

Cardinal went over and spoke to Collingwood and Arsenault, who were taking prints from the body. A few minutes later the wagon arrived and the removal guys loaded it in back for the trip to the Forensic Centre in Toronto.

"So what do you suppose went down?" Delorme said to Cardinal. "A vigilante?"

"How would a vigilante know the kid was going to hit this particular ATM again? We didn't."

"We certainly thought it was possible. Maybe it was a chance thing."

"Pretty slim chance."

They left Ident in charge of the scene and drove back to the station. In the silence of the deserted meeting room, Cardinal slotted the security video into the player and sat next to Delorme to watch it. Grainy, dark in some frames, washed out in others. Stella McQuaig comes up to the ATM, makes her withdrawal, puts the bills in her wallet and turns to leave. No robber. No killer. Not so much as a shadow.

"Maybe it was a freak of timing. A good-Samaritan thing," Delorme said. Her voice sounded loud in the quiet of the empty room. "Happens to be going by and sees a woman in trouble, chases the kid into the alley. Kid pulls the gun and *boom*—the guy drops him first."

"But your witness didn't see anybody else. Didn't hear anybody else."

"You're right." Delorme picked up the remote, pressed a button, and the monitor went dark. "Also, the way he was shot in the face, it looks more like he was stopped head-on. Like the person was coming the other way down the alley. Or waiting for him."

The fluorescent lights went out and Delorme and Cardinal both yelled out, "Hey!" The lights came back on and someone down the hall yelled back, "Sorry!"

"If the killer was waiting for him," Cardinal said, "that would seem to indicate someone who works with him. Maybe they had a falling-out."

"Except none of the victims has mentioned an accomplice, and there's no other evidence of one. It would help if we had some idea who the kid was. We don't even know if he was local. Pretty hard to make any sense of it. What? Why are you looking like that?"

"Nothing," Cardinal said. "I was just remembering what the Russian lady said—about not having to understand people."

"That Russian lady," Delorme said, "has Sparky Noone's problem."

24

FOR THE FIRST TIME IN HER YOUNG LIFE, Nikki was experiencing silence. This brand new house out in the Canadian woods didn't creak or rattle like older houses. And no cars, no trucks, no boats, no trains or planes going by. Almost no wildlife. The other night a squirrel or some-thing had scrabbled across the roof of her bedroom and woken her up wide-eyed and scared. She liked the quiet during the day, but at night it put her on edge. Every now and then the furnace would make a muffled *whump*, then a mild hiss from the air vent, then nothing. How could you relax when you could hear every little thing—the scratch of your fingernail on the pillow, a strand of hair falling across your forehead?

And the darkness. She had never known what darkness was before now. When she turned off the light in her bedroom, it was as if she had gone blind. She wanted one of those little lights you stick in a socket, but she didn't want to ask Papa and sound like too much of a wuss. Tonight at least there was a moon, bright enough to cast shadows. She held a hand straight up and turned it, bone white in the air above the bed, and admired the shadow it cast—elegant and slim, the arm of a ballerina, the neck of a swan.

She sat up cross-legged and bunched the pillows behind her back. Smells of lavender and lemon wafted up from her feet. She held each one and rubbed with her thumbs, the soles softer and smoother than usual. Papa's washing them had thrummed a chord deep in her chest, as if there was an instrument inside her—not harp, not organ, no instrument she had ever heard—that had been yearning to be played since the day she was born.

She picked up her watch and tilted it in the moonlight. Two a.m. She got off the bed and stood before the mirror, backed away from it until she was lit by the moon. Her silly pyjamas, blue and white striped and utterly sexless. The first gift Papa had given her, telling her how modesty was the most underrated virtue in the world, the one thing maybe the Muslims could teach us something about, whatever that meant. The pyjamas had felt stupid and clumsy and ugly at first—Nikki had been sleeping naked as long as she could remember—but she had come to love them. There was something consoling about dressing for bed, as if you were going somewhere special, somewhere private, someplace no one would bother you.

She lifted up the striped top, gathering the material with both hands. So cool and clean, the metallic glow of moonlight on her skin, the dime-sized spot of her navel. She pulled the bottoms down a little, exposing the ridge of her hips. I'm hot, she said. I'm a hottie. The ridges and planes of her face, alternately glowing and shadowed, made her look aloof, ethereal—*alluring*, that aching word she came across so often in the vampire novels that were her only reading. The night made her features regular and even, her eyes deep and black.

She went to the door and opened it and listened. Silence. A glow beneath the door of Papa's room. The feel of carpet under her bare feet as she covered the short distance to the door. She raised a hand and held it an inch from the wood. For some reason it was a moment like on the diving board at the juvenile centre, knowing it wouldn't hurt but afraid anyway.

She tapped on the door with her fingertips.

Silence.

Nikki raised her fingers to tap again, when Papa's voice, no louder than conversational level, said to come in.

She opened the door a little and stuck her head in. Papa looked at her over the paperback he was reading, a crescent moon in flames on the cover.

"What is it, Nikki? You should be asleep."

"I need to be with you for a little while."

"You do? Why? What's up?"

Nikki closed the door and crossed the room and got on the bed beside him. She curled up and laid an arm across his belly and hugged him, pressing her forehead into his ribs.

He didn't say anything. He adjusted his elbows, but he was still holding the book up over his chest.

Nikki sent her hand straying up over his chest and belly and down between his legs. She felt the soft outline of his penis beneath her palm and rubbed it.

"Don't."

"I want to. Just lay still. You don't have to say anything or do anything. I just want to suck you off."

He dropped the book over the side of the bed and grabbed her by the wrist and pulled her hand away. She tried to put it back, but he was fast and strong.

"No."

She looked up at him, the blue eyes frowning at her. "Please," she said. "I want to. I want to make you feel good."

"No."

She used the voice that had worked fine with her tricks. "I'll make you come like you've never come before, honey. You just lay back and let me suck your huge cock and blow your mind."

"God, Nikki, you're going to make me cry. That is the saddest thing I have ever heard."

"You made me feel good. I want to make you feel good. Why can't I?"

"Because you already make me feel good. Just by being part of this family."

"You had sex with Lemur."

"I went through an exercise with Lemur. It was something he needed and the family needed."

She rolled away from him. "You think I'm ugly."

"That's exactly wrong, Nikki. The reason I don't want to have sex with you is because you are beautiful and perfect just the way you are. I curse the world that taught you the only way you can be nice to someone is to have sex with them. Sit up, now. Pull that cushion up off the floor and get under the covers, but you keep a good foot between us. Respect my space the way I respect yours."

She did as he said.

"People have harmed you all your life with sex, Nikki. Remember what I told you the first night I brought you home? That I would never harm you? I never will. Not even if you ask me to." He let a little silence go by. "What? What are you thinking? I can see thoughts crossing that perfect little face of yours."

"I've never been in bed with a man who didn't want sex. I wasn't trying to be bad. I just wanted to pay you back. For what you did this afternoon."

"You let me wash your feet. It gave me a lot of pleasure, so you can consider me pre-thanked. You owe me nothing. What's this, now? Are you crying?"

She shook her head and folded her arms and couldn't speak. He asked her again what was wrong and she started to bawl and turned away. He put a box of Kleenex on her lap and lay back and waited for her to settle down.

When she spoke, her voice sounded strange to her. Deeper and more mature. "You don't know how good you made me feel. No one ever made me feel that good."

She cried a little more and he waited, in the patient way he had. Not ignoring, just waiting. She turned on her side to face him and said, "Are you Jesus?"

The smallest of smiles played over his features. "What do you think?"

"I think you might be. You wouldn't even have to know it, necessarily. You could be like a reincarnation or something."

They didn't speak for a time. Outside, the sound of the Range Rover pulling up and the door slamming. A minute later, Jack's big footsteps crossing the kitchen. He went to the bathroom and ran the water and brushed his teeth, and then the sound of his bedroom door opening and closing.

"That's Jack," Nikki said. "Lemur still isn't back?"

"No."

"What's so special about the bunkhouse? The other day I was just on the porch over there and Lemur yelled at me to get away. Actually yelled at me. I wasn't even looking inside."

"There's material in the bunkhouse that doesn't concern you. It's better for you not to know about it. I want you to trust me on this and keep away."

"I will. I'd do anything for you, Papa. I honestly believe I'd do anything you asked me to."

"None of what we do is about me. It's about the family. Our survival. You know, I was lucky. I had a good family, growing up. Unfortunately, they died when I was very young—not much older than you—and I vowed that one day I would try to re-create the happy family I had known. It's become something much bigger than that, of course, something much more important, but it's still my family. Our family. And it makes me happier than I can say to have you with us, Nikki. Happier than I can say."

—

Nikki woke early. There wasn't even a hint of sunrise outside her bedroom window. Nothing out there but darkness lit by scattered stars. Darkness and forest, the boughs of the trees weighed down with snow so that they almost touched the ground. A radio muttered from the kitchen. Nikki closed the curtain again and got out of her pyjamas and into her clothes.

She opened her door, listened to the radio for a moment—it was going on about hockey—and closed the door behind her. She went down the three stairs to the dining area. Papa was sitting at the head of the table with a shotgun across his lap and his hands resting on it.

"Good morning," he said. His voice sounded strange, detached somehow, as if it worked independently of Papa himself. "You're up early, considering."

"I couldn't sleep. Something woke me up."

"Fix yourself some breakfast. Stuff's on the counter."

Nikki poured herself a bowl of cornflakes and skim milk. She got a glass out of the cupboard and a pitcher of orange juice and poured a glass and put the pitcher back in the fridge. Then she took the cereal bowl in one hand and the glass of juice in the other and sat at the end of the table opposite Papa.

He watched her eat.

"What's up?" Nikki said. "What's with the gun?"

Papa looked down at his lap then back at Nikki. "Your brother is dead."

Nikki went still, her spoon in mid-air, milk dripping from it and splashing into the bowl below.

"Lemur is dead. He was shot last night. While he was working."

Nikki lowered her spoon to the bowl. She stirred her cereal a little. An unexpected emotion was gathering inside her chest and she felt the prickle of tears. "How did it happen?"

A bedroom door opened and shut. There were footsteps and then Jack was in the kitchen.

Papa stood up and levelled the shotgun at him. Jack was pouring himself coffee and wasn't even aware of it until he turned around and faced the dining area. He took a sip from his coffee and his eyes went to the shotgun. "What's that for?"

"Did you kill Lemur?"

"What?"

"Did you kill Lemur? Yes or no."

"No. What happened to him?" Jack started toward the table, casual about it, taking another sip from his coffee.

Papa pumped the shotgun, pointed it again at Jack's chest. "Where were you last night?"

"I went into town. To a bar. Had a few beers. Listened to a band couldn't even play in tune. Came back."

"Prove it."

"How am I supposed to do that? Subpoena witnesses? Stop pointing that thing."

"I could end your life right now."

"If the family just lost a man, it's probably not real smart to lose another."

"Getting rid of a traitor is pure gain."

"I'm not a traitor." Jack set his coffee mug down on the table. "Put it down, Papa."

"What time did you get back?"

"I don't know. Two-thirty. Three. What difference does it make?"

"Lemur was killed around nine."

"I can't do nothing about that, Papa. You neither."

"I could blow your head off."

"Well, you'd best do it, then. Because if you don't, I'm gonna rip that shotgun out of your hands and bust your skull in with it."

Papa took three quick steps and hit Jack one sharp blow in the head with the butt of the shotgun. Jack fell sideways out of his chair. His mug twirled to the floor in the opposite direction, and the aroma of coffee blossomed around them.

25

Friday morning, Delorme asked Staff Sergeant Flower to check if any tickets had been handed out in the neighbourhood of Roxwell and Clement. The boy would almost certainly have driven there, and yet there had been no suspicious cars parked in the strip mall lot, or on the street. He had gone into the alley, presumably to get to his car, which should therefore have been parked on Clement Street. So he must have parked somewhere else and they just hadn't found the car. Twenty minutes later Sergeant Flower came back with the answer: Yes, one car had been towed. An irate citizen had called about some idiot parked in his driveway. Right in his driveway, for Pete's sake. For this he pays taxes? Location: third house from the mall.

Delorme put in a call to the city towing service. The man who answered chose to liven up a boring job by speaking in the manner of a Marine on a vital mission.

"Clement Street?" he said when Delorme asked. "That's an affirmative."

"What number on Clement Street?"

"Hold on a second . . ." A distant clicking of a keyboard as a log was consulted. "Number twelve. That's one-two. Number twelve Clement."

"Could you give me the VIN number and plates on that?"

"Plates are Alpha-November-Foxtrot-Charlie-two-eight-niner."

Delorme wrote it down, and then he gave her the much longer and even more military-sounding vehicle identification number. She thanked him and he said ten-four. She typed the VIN into the Ministry of Transport's database. The car, a silver-grey Mazda 3, was registered to Dr. and Mrs. T. J. Walker of Barrie, Ontario. It had been reported stolen two weeks previously from Toronto's Pearson International Airport. The plates didn't match.

Delorme took the information into Chouinard's office and got permission to have Ident tow the car into the police garage for fuming. An hour later she put on her parka and went down to the garage. The garage door was wide open—a necessity when fuming an entire vehicle.

Even with the door open, the place reeked of superglue. Fingerprints had taken the form of ghostly white smudges all around the Mazda's door handles, and over the dash, and on the insides of the doors. They had found prints on the radio and on the rear-view.

"Found a whole bunch of stuff that's probably not related," Arsenault said. "A whack of old parking slips from Barrie, couple of discs full of medical lectures, a *Cat in the Hat* toy. Problem number one is we don't know what we can rule out until we get prints from Barrie. The doctor and his wife agreed to go in and get printed down there, but we don't have them yet."

"And what about our dead thief?"

"No matches so far."

"Come on," Delorme said, and gestured with a sweep of her arm at all the white dots. "In all that? A two-bit mugger maybe sixteen years old doesn't leave a single print?"

Arsenault shook his head. "We've checked inside and out."

"What about that?" Delorme pointed to a Welch's grape soda can lying on the floor on the passenger side.

"Haven't got to it yet."

Collingwood picked up the can in gloved hands and took it to a small Plexiglas box. He put it inside and closed the lid and turned on the fumes. He squatted so his eyes were level with the box. After a minute he turned off the machine, opened the lid, took out the soda can and held it up to the light. He handed it to Arsenault and said, "Thumb."

Arsenault held it up to the light and squinted at it. "Triple tenting in the arch."

"Which means what?" Delorme said.

"It matches the prints we took off your dead ATM artist."

"It's a start, I guess," Delorme said. "Too bad he doesn't have a record."

"We got something better than that," Collingwood said.

An outsider would not have noticed, but Delorme had known Collingwood for going on ten years. For him to utter so many syllables in a row amounted to excitement bordering on hysteria.

"What have you got, Bob?"

He crooked a finger and she followed him over to the counter at the side of the garage. He pointed. Four white arcs of plaster were laid out, each in its own plastic bag. Interspersed with these were four more white plaster arcs, not in bags.

"You made moulds of the tires?"

Collingwood nodded.

"And the ones in plastic are from Trout Lake?"

"You got it."

"Don't tell me we've got our killer."

"Fingerprints don't match but the tires do. Prints on the gun at the ATM show he's a right-hander. The Trout Lake killer is left-handed. But this car was definitely there."

~

Cardinal's first duty of the day was to apprehend Randall Wishart. "Wish I could come with you," McLeod had said. "Hate to miss a pleasure like that."

Cardinal drove up to Carnwright Real Estate and waited for Wishart's client to leave. In contrast to McLeod's sense of fun, Cardinal found the business depressing. Preventing harm to a girl like Sam Doucette was unquestionably a good thing. He could recognize that this was "serving and protecting," as Chouinard liked to put it. But a pleasure?

When he snapped the cuffs on him, Wishart's face turned paper white, and Cardinal thought for a moment that he might faint. He led him through the outer office under the shocked gaze of Lawrence Carnwright and their receptionist, and knew that his action, although just and necessary, was catastrophic to this family. Yes, Sam would be safer, but he took no pleasure in yanking the loosened thread of a young man's unravelling life.

Even a lawyer of Dick Nolan's calibre couldn't keep Wishart from spending a day and night in jail, not with the information Cardinal had amassed from Troy Campbell and Sam Doucette. The Crown would not go for a charge of attempted murder—Campbell had never laid a hand on her—but obstruction of justice and uttering threats were not going to pose a problem.

When that was done, Cardinal went to D.S. Chouinard and asked that a safe house be provided for Sam and her mother.

Chouinard's flat-out no was for him an unusually decisive response. "I don't even understand why you're asking," he said. "Wishart wanted to shut the girl up to save his job and his marriage. But that cat is well and truly out of the bag, so he has no motive to attack her again."

"It's not Wishart I'm worried about. It was the killer, not Wishart, who chased her and shot at her car. And she lost her cellphone at the scene. It has her picture, her name, her address."

"If we were *sure* he had her cellphone, I would not hesitate. There's been no activity from her number."

"No, but it's still pinging. Which means it isn't frozen or dead. If someone picked it up, why aren't they using it?"

"They want to change the SIMM card. I don't know. But I also don't know that the killer has it. We don't know that he caught her licence plate. But we do know that he chose not to chase her. So on the whole, I'm not inclined to think she's in danger."

"I don't think that's a bet we can afford to make."

"Luckily, it's not your decision."

"Uh-huh. And what happened to serving and protecting?"

"Let me tell you something off the record, Cardinal, and I mean no disrespect, but fuck you."

—

Cardinal brought Sam and her mother down to the station for a formal statement, which he videotaped. Sam sat across the table from him, her mother at her side. The girl had lost the passionate, excitable manner of the other night. Her words were matter-of-fact as she described Troy Campbell coming after her, but when she related how Randall had kept telling her not to go to the police, her tone became more and more depressed.

Her mother, neatly dressed in skirt and blazer, stayed quiet until Sam was finished. "A married man," she said softly. "What could you possibly have been thinking?"

"I wasn't thinking," Sam said. "I was feeling." She pulled a strand of dark hair away from her forehead with thumb and forefinger and hooked it behind a perfectly formed ear.

"The story's been all over the news," Mrs. Doucette said to Cardinal. "I'm terrified someone's going to come after her again."

"We've talked to the local media—they're not going to run Sam's name or picture—but I can't promise anything once other places get hold of it. Unfortunately, shooting someone with a crossbow isn't a great strategy if you want to remain anonymous."

"I know. *Indian shoots white man with bow and arrow.*" She turned to her daughter. "Sweetheart, you probably just set us back a hundred years—but I'm glad you did it."

"It's Randall I should shoot," Sam said. "I still can't believe it. I know it's true and I just can't get my head around it."

"I hope you're planning to keep that man in jail," her mother said to Cardinal.

"I'll certainly try."

"You know, if a bear wanders into town and hurts somebody, they kill it."

"Mother, please."

"Bears don't have the right to due process," Cardinal said.

He turned the focus to the night of the murders and took Sam slowly through it, starting from when she got to Champlain's, to Randall's call, to the drive out to Trout Lake. She gave him every detail he asked for and volunteered many he didn't. She emphasized again, as she had in her anonymous phone call, that the man who had spoken to the Bastovs did not have a Russian accent. As she spoke—she hadn't put her finger on it at the time—she realized that the man might be from the South. The American South.

"Why do you say that?"

"He said *you-all* a couple of times. And the way he pronounced a couple of things. He said *nass* instead of *nice*. *Maht* instead of *might*. Stuff like that. It wasn't really strong, but it sounded kinda South to me."

"And he was trying to sell the Bastovs on buying the house?"

"He showed them the bathroom. The bedrooms. Pointed stuff out. Switched the lights on and off. He talked about the view. How he'd have to get them out there in daylight to see it. I wondered about it, because I know Randall and Mr. Carnwright are the only two men in the company."

Sam was precise on the time the shots were fired, and detailed in her description of other sounds—the man sounded tall, fairly heavy, big boots—but she wasn't going to be able to identify him: a glimpse in the night, a man's form silhouetted against a lit room. She described the chase, and the bullets hitting her car.

Sam's mother spoke up. "How are you going to protect Sam from this animal?"

Cardinal tried to repeat Chouinard's reasoning as if he believed it himself. "Maybe you have some relatives you could stay with," he added. "It might be good if Sam could be out of town for a while."

"In other words you aren't going to do anything."

Cardinal said he could arrange to have patrol cars pass by their house as often as possible.

"That doesn't exactly sound like ironclad security. In fact it sounds pathetic." She turned to her daughter. "We could stay with Susanna in Dokis, I suppose."

"Oh, great." Sam said. "I lose my job and my school year."

"No you won't," her mother said. "We're not going to let that happen."

Cardinal tried to remain upbeat as he drove them home. He even gave Sam his cellphone number—something he never did with witnesses—but when he dropped them off, the look on her mother's face filled him with shame.

—

The security video finally arrived from Pearson International just as Cardinal was leaving for the day.

"Hey, Delorme," he said, holding it up. She was shutting down her computer in the cubicle next to his. "You want to watch a video tonight?"

They drove in their separate cars to Delorme's bungalow. The small brick house looked pretty in the snow. She had put up Christmas decorations since the last time Cardinal had visited.

Cardinal sat on the couch in front of the TV with a bowl of tortilla chips beside him, flipping channels while Delorme defrosted some chili. He caught part of a documentary on the discovery of a British frigate that had been sunk in Lake Erie in the War of 1812. A salvage team out of Toronto was testing a new sonar device that used computer technology to translate sound waves into remarkably clear images. Cardinal made a note of the salvage outfit's name.

Delorme brought in their dinner trays and picked up the remote. The video began to play, showing a wide-angle view of parking level five that took in about a dozen vehicles. The time stamp reeled off the seconds in the lower right of the screen.

"Three weeks ago," Delorme said. "A little more."

"Car's third from the left." Cardinal pointed with his fork. "Good chili."

"French Canadians have always made the best chili."

A figure entered from the foreground, his back to the camera, wearing a hood. A bulky knapsack hung from his back.

"Could be our ATM kid," Delorme said. She put her plate on the coffee table and went to sit on the rug, closer to the screen, hugging her knees to her chest like a teenager.

The figure approached the car that was deepest in shadow; his face remained completely obscured. A slim jim appeared in his hand, and with a couple of swift movements he had the lock up and the door open. There was no sound on the video, but the car alarm must have been loud in that concrete space. He got in, popped the hood and got out again. He raised the hood and shut it a moment later.

"So much for the car alarm," Cardinal said.

"He's fast. Must have had some good training."

"We're not going to be able to recognize him from this tape," Cardinal said. "Not unless the Toronto geek squad can enhance it somehow."

"Well, it's got to be the same kid, even if we can't prove it. Oh my, who have we got here?"

Another figure had entered the scene.

Cardinal pointed, outlining the man's head and shoulders. "He looks a lot older. Way older. Just the way he moves."

The two got in and closed the doors. The rear lights went on and then the car backed up, turned and drove out of frame.

"Back it up," Cardinal said. "I think we got a bit of light on the older guy's face when he turned to open the door."

Delorme reached for the remote and froze the image for a second, and then ran it backwards. She clicked the image forward a few frames. The older figure was wearing a baseball cap that shadowed his face. He moved jerk by jerk toward the car. He opened the passenger-side door, and when he turned slightly, Delorme froze the image.

She got up on all fours to peer at the screen. Cardinal sat forward on the edge of his seat. "Definitely older."

"They should be able to enhance that one. Maybe even use facial recognition on it." Delorme ran the recording forward and back a few more times, but none of the frames was any better. She switched off the set and came back to the couch. "So. We're looking for two guys. One's a kid, the other's in his forties or fifties?"

"That's good," Cardinal said. "Two guys travelling together—one of them a teenager—are going to be more noticeable than just one. First thing tomorrow we've got to get on the stick to Pearson. If they can match these guys up with other security shots, we may be able to get names from passport control, maybe even connect with a likely flight."

"Do you know how many million people go through Pearson in a year?"

"That's in a year. Look how we can narrow it down. The Bastovs are American—we can assume their killer followed them here. Assume these two guys arrived within an hour before stealing the car. They can check security tapes in the U.S. arrivals area for that hour. We may even be able to get it down to a particular gate, or close to it. But all of this makes me wonder."

"Wonder what?"

"The victims are American. It looks like the killer or killers are American. So how did they know the Schumacher place was for sale? The sign was up, but it hasn't been listed for some time."

"If they knew the Bastovs were looking for a house in the area, maybe they just did a thorough search of the real estate agencies."

"Doesn't seem likely."

"No, it doesn't."

They let the thought lie. They finished the chili and talked for a while longer about the best ways to deal with the Toronto airport. Then Delorme said, "So. How was your date the other night?"

"Date?" Cardinal said. "You mean with that reporter? That wasn't a date."

"Uh-huh. You seemed pretty evasive. Why be evasive if it wasn't a date? How'd it go? Did you go out to dinner?"

"Yeah, we went to DeGroot's."

"DeGroot's," Delorme said, "is definitely a date."

"It was not a date. And don't look at me like that. Donna doesn't know anybody in town—I figured why not take her out to dinner."

"She didn't look like a charity case to me."

"It was an information exchange. She gave me some good stuff."

"Did you boink her?"

"Lise. For Pete's sake . . ."

"I can ask, can't I? We're buddies, aren't we? If I was a guy, you'd tell me."

"You're not a guy, and—contrary to what you may think—men do not constantly tell each other about their sex lives. No, I didn't *boink* her— what are you, twelve? And before you ask—no, I didn't try. Jesus."

"I'm sorry. I didn't mean to embarrass you."

"Yes you did. How's Shane, Lise? Did you boink Shane this week?"

Delorme laughed. "As a matter of fact, I did."

"That's it." Cardinal stood up and got his coat. "Thanks for the chili. I'll see you tomorrow."

"You asked me, John."

"Jesus, Lise."

26

THE SKY OVER BLACK LAKE WAS astonishingly blue, almost indigo at the highest point of the dome, paler at its fringes. The man called Papa stood in Lloyd's living room, staring out the window, hands clasped behind his back—a pose that seemed habitual with him. His cohorts—his so-called family—were outside somewhere, and Papa had magnanimously allowed Lloyd to emerge from his bedroom, although he was still tethered at the ankle like a goat.

"Astounding," Papa said, "the things that can fall out of a clear blue sky."

"You're referring to unexpected events?" Lloyd said. He felt it prudent to engage in conversation with this psychopath, on the theory that it's harder to kill a man you've gotten to know. No one who had gotten to know Henry, for example, could have imagined ending such a benign life.

Papa spoke in a tone of recitation, without turning around. "Book of Joshua. The Israelites rout the Amorite army and are chasing them all over the map when a rain of stones falls from a clear blue sky and decimates the enemy."

"Oh. Bible stories."

"Cambridge, Maryland, 1828. Twelve days of rain force a man named Muse to stop digging a ditch around his property. When he ventures back outside, he finds the ditch teeming with fish—six, seven inches long, some of them. Perch. Bass. No river within miles of the place. No explanation how they got there."

"A delivery truck," Lloyd said. "A Natural Resources truck on the way to stock a lake maybe. Gets stuck in the storm and has to jettison cargo."

"Wake up, Lloyd—this is the nineteenth century. *Early* nineteenth century. November 13, 1833. Rahway, New Jersey. A rain of fire. Locals describe blobs of burning jelly falling from the sky. Moment they burn out, they turn to white powder."

"There were munitions factories in New Jersey," Lloyd said. He was a U.S. history buff and happened to know. "They come into prominence later, during the Civil War."

"No, Lloyd." Papa turned and spoke as if to a recalcitrant student. "As it happens, there was a meteor shower that same day. It's inconceivable to me, and I hope to you, that the two events are unrelated."

Lloyd was not sure how to respond. Ready agreement might be taken as an insult. Disagreement, however gently expressed, risked violence. He made a noncommittal sound.

Papa turned from the window and came closer.

"What I'm pointing out, Lloyd, is that I happen to be a similar sort of phenomenon."

He took a stub of pencil from his left-hand pocket and a small sharpener from his right. He sharpened the pencil and put the sharpener back in his pocket and took out a small black notebook. He undid the elastic and opened it and made a note and put the pencil and the notebook back into his pocket. He sat on the end of the sofa closest to Lloyd and leaned on the armrest. "You don't remember me, do you."

"Remember you?"

Papa leaned closer, dark blue eyes assessing him. "I've been waiting for you to put two and two together, Lloyd, but it looks like you never will. Not without a nudge."

"I'm sorry," Lloyd said. "You have the advantage. I don't— We've met before? You and I? We met somewhere?"

"Indeed, yes."

"I'm sorry. You look vaguely familiar . . ."

"Here's a little clue for you, Lloyd." Papa reached across the gap between the sofa and the armchair and pressed Lloyd's shoulder as if he were ringing a doorbell. "Seattle."

"Seattle. That's supposed to jog my memory?"

"Mm-hmm."

"I've been to a lot of fur auctions in Seattle. How am I supposed to remember one time?"

"Well, you're right—it was a fur auction. Twelve years ago."

"Twelve years ago. Was it at one of those big dinners?"

"Getting warm. After dinner. Hotel bar. You were with some honcho from Lord & Taylor."

Lloyd snapped his fingers. "Ron Weissman. He was retiring that year. We met in the hotel bar. You came up and asked me something. I remember. You were with a beautiful young woman."

Papa smiled. "Thataboy, Lloyd. That'd be Christine. Broke my heart."

"You came up and asked me a question."

"I asked you a question. Very good. Do you remember the question?"

Lloyd shook his head. "No. No, I can't say that I do."

Papa smiled—a flash of a grin totally unconnected to the neutral expression of the rest of his face, quickly gone. "Of course not. Why would you? I asked if you could spare a minute. You were very polite at first. You said sure. And so I started to fill you in on an idea I'd been working on for months. Years, actually. A concept that involved organizing trappers and buyers—and manufacturers like yourself—into a top-down outfit."

"And I said I wasn't interested."

"You didn't put it so eloquently at the time. How many words was that? Five? Six? You didn't come near to wasting that many words. What you said was, 'Not interested.'" Papa held up two fingers before Lloyd's face. "Two words. As if I was some religious wacko forcing a flyer on you. 'Not interested.'"

"And that offended you."

Papa looked up at the ceiling and shook his head. When he looked back at Lloyd, he said, "When you step on a spider—an ant, a cockroach—don't you think that offends him? When you spit in the face of someone who wants nothing more than to work co-operatively with you, do you not think that might offend him?"

For his entire adult life, Lloyd Kreeger had prided himself on being a down-to-earth, to-the-point sort of man. Honest, reliable, decisive. He valued courtesy, and even coming from a thief and possibly a murderer and certainly some kind of psycho, the accusation that he had been high-handed upset him.

"Perhaps you are not very experienced in business matters," Lloyd said. "The greatest courtesy you can extend a businessman is to respect his time. Whatever the merits of your scheme might be—and to tell you the truth, I didn't consider it long enough to even weigh them—I knew it wasn't for me. I'd worked with trappers, I'd owned farms, but by that time I was strictly manufacturing and retail."

"Naturally. Lloyd Kreeger is far too good to get his hands dirty."

"Got nothing to do with being too good. I gave you the quickest answer possible. 'Not interested.' I apologize if that offended you, but it was the truth. Are you offended by the truth?"

"I live by it."

"Then there's nothing to be offended about."

"It wasn't what you said, Lloyd. It was how you said it. 'Not interested, *cockroach.*'"

"I never said that."

"The insect was implied in your tone. You were in a hurry to get away. A rush to get away from the pesky little bug. Swat him down."

"Not true." Lloyd shook his head. "Not true."

"Did you know the Bastovs are dead?"

"Lev Bastov?"

"It was on the news last night. Both Lev and Irena Bastov were killed last week, right here in Algonquin Bay. Couldn't identify them till now. Had their heads cut off. What do you think—Russian mob?"

"The Bastovs were murdered?"

Papa nodded. "Yes, sir."

Lloyd felt something cold turning in his stomach. "You did it, didn't you?."

Papa smiled. "I could never do something like that. It's not in me. Besides, I hardly knew them. But to get back to our conversation about Seattle, you can say whatever you want, Lloyd. You can tap dance around the issue. Obfuscate and rationalize. Tell us the moon is blue, tell us it never snows in Algonquin Bay, Ontario. It's fine. I am indifferent. Just like you were indifferent. You have to love indifference, don't you think? If I had to make a choice, I'd have to say indifference was the perfect state of mind. The natural state of mind. But everything you say just begs the question, Lloyd."

"What question?"

"Who's the insect now?"

—

In the days since Lemur's death, Papa had begun teaching Nikki how to shoot a rifle. He didn't say as much, but she knew it was to help get her mind off Lemur. And he enlisted Jack as an instructor, which she wouldn't have thought possible after their altercation. First thing he did was to give Jack an absolute apology. Found Jack sulking in the living room that afternoon and called Nikki in because he wanted it to be public, so to speak. *I was in the wrong, Jack — I was upset about Lemur and I just lost it. You were wrong too, but I should never have used violence against a family member. It violates my own principles, and I hope you'll find it possible to forgive me.*

When Jack didn't say anything, Papa went and got the shotgun and handed it to Jack and knelt with his back to him. Told him to go ahead and bash his skull, he had every right. But Jack wouldn't do it, and after a while he seemed to relax a little. Eventually Papa cajoled him into coming outside with them, saying all sorts of good things about him. *I'll let Jack show you the longer-range techniques — he's a much better sniper than I am.* Or, *Watch how Jack does it. He's just got an instinct for this, and it never fails.*

They had good weather; a little warmer than it had been, so Nikki's fingers didn't freeze handling the rifles. Then, just when she was getting used to target practice outdoors, Papa took her and Jack down to the basement, bringing along a couple of handguns. Still in his scoutmaster mode, still deferential to Jack.

"Decisive battles never arise in ideal circumstances. Right, Jack?" he said. "We don't get to choose when or where we have to deal with matters of life and death. The fact is, if you're ever called upon to use your sidearm, it's likely going to be indoors. So you have to get used to shooting inside. What do you think, Jack?"

"Absolutely true," Jack said. "You hit the nail there." If he still harboured any anger against Papa, he was keeping it locked up. Papa got him to show Nikki the proper stance, the crouch, the drop and turn—all of this without firing a shot—while he stood looking on, offering advice and encourage-ment. They had her practise the moves over and over again.

At one point he said, "You know what's stupid about most people owning firearms, Nikki?"

"They end up shooting themselves by accident? Or someone steals them?"

"True enough. But what's the all-out stupidest thing? Jack, I think you know."

"The all-out stupidest thing," Jack said, in a tone Nikki recognized as the sound of rote memory, "is when an assailant just walks right up and takes the gun out of his victim's hands. Because most people, when it comes down to the wire, are just not ready to shoot anyone."

"He's right, Nikki. See, they train boxers by having them hit the bag. Hit it fast, hit it hard, hit it again and again and again. Partly that's to develop speed and power. But more important, it's to overcome our natu-ral reluctance to hit another human being. In matters of life or death or honour, when you're called upon to protect the family, you've got to be able to overcome that kind of reluctance. Frankly, I blame myself I didn't train Lemur well enough—that it came to crunch time and he hesitated that fraction of a second too long. So now I'm going to get you set up so you don't even feel *any* reluctance to shoot. You'll be like Jack—a warrior down to your bones."

What they were saying made sense, Nikki supposed. She had been wondering why Lemur hadn't used his gun. Poor guy. She pulled his iPod touch from her pocket. "Um, I took this out of Lemur's room. Do you think he'd mind?"

Papa looked at Jack then back to Nikki. "I think he'd probably want you to have it." He went behind the wet bar and pulled down a brandy glass. He set it on the mantel and came back to stand behind Nikki. "Weaver stance."

"You want me to shoot that glass?"

"That's exactly what you're going to do."

"Maybe I should shoot a tin can instead."

"You hear that, Jack?"

"Reluctance," Jack said. "Pure reluctance is what I hear."

"Exactly. It's what a criminal, or a terrorist, or a rogue government agent depends on—your reluctance. That is the last time you're going to express it, Nikki."

Nikki adopted the slight crouch, left palm cradling right hand. The handgun packed a bigger thrill than the rifle. It felt so solid, so perfectly contoured for the hand. Even its disproportionate heaviness, once the clip was in, was pleasing.

Nikki fired and the glass exploded. Jack let out a whoop.

"Good," Papa said. "But you hesitated."

Over the next half-hour he set up more glasses, an ornamental vase, a cute old teddy bear, several hats, various shirts and jackets belonging to Lloyd, framed photographs, even a couple of statues. They had to weigh a lot, the way Papa and Jack struggled with them. It was the teddy bear that gave her the most trouble.

"Shoot him," Papa said. "Save your life. Save your family. Shoot him."

Nikki shot the bear and he twirled into the air and landed face down. The stuffing blown out of his back pierced her heart.

The statues were easier. One of them was a Greek god or something. Some dead Roman. Nikki had seen a similar statue in a museum once. Boring thing with a tiny little dick. She shot at the blank eyes and blew away a chunk of forehead and curls. She fired again and half the nose burst into dust. Suddenly the mouth looked delicate, almost feminine—tiny bow up top, plump droop of the bottom lip. A few more shots and there was no face left, not even much of a head.

Papa said wonderful things to her the whole time: *That's our girl. You're Nikki the Kid. You're making me proud.* She never knew words could have such power. She had seen TV images, some frozen wasteland where slabs of ice were breaking off and sliding into the sea. That was the sensation inside her now. Blowing plaster gods to smithereens, a hot automatic in her fist, and she starts to sniffle. Or maybe she was still remembering Lemur.

"Don't even think about it," Papa said. "No reluctance. No hesitation. And most of all, no tears."

He unplugged the television. It was a flat panel like the one upstairs, forty inches at least, and he picked it up like it was made of Styrofoam.

"Aw, not the TV," Jack said.

"She has to learn." Papa set it down in front of the fireplace and plugged it in again. He clicked through channels until he found the kind of image he wanted—a man and woman reading the news. No sound.

"Shoot the man," he said.

"You want me to shoot the TV?"

"Nikki, this kind of hesitation will kill you. Shoot the man now."

Nikki took aim and put a hole through the man's left eye. His mouth kept moving, head bobbing behind a pool of blackness that fanned out from the hole like black blood.

Jack let out another whoop. "Watch out, people. Nikki the Kid's in town!"

"Shoot the woman," Papa said, and Nikki did.

27

CARDINAL PUT IN THE CALL TO Peel Regional and spoke to Sergeant Rob Fazulli, who headed up airport security. They had worked together briefly on Toronto vice "back in the Jurassic Period," as Fazulli put it, but he wasn't happy to hear from Cardinal again. "We already sent you guys the parking video. Do you know the kind of effort that took?"

"Car stolen from your airport—you would have had to do that anyway."

"And now you want us to match a face from the parking lot to U.S. arrivals?"

"Just within the hour previous to the car theft."

Now he's going to tell me about the thirty million, Cardinal thought.

"Cardinal, Pearson handles thirty-two million passengers a year."

"And at least one of them decapitated two people in my town. If you've got more gruesome murders to deal with, by all means handle them first. Otherwise, you know . . ."

"Consider it done," Fazulli said, and rang off. *Consider it done* was a phrase they used to employ in Toronto vice when they had no intention of doing whatever was being proposed. Cardinal, not by nature an optimist, in this case chose to think Fazulli was kidding.

His phone rang as he was hanging up. Toronto Forensics getting back to him on the sawdust. The analyst sounded suspiciously youthful.

"I'm actually just an intern. I'm working on my doctorate in botany," he told Cardinal. "When I saw we had a sawdust sample, I took a personal interest and put it under the scope during my lunch hour."

"I'm already impressed. What did you find?"

"White pine and birch. That's it."

"No cedar?" Cardinal said. "No mahogany?"

"No, no. Just the two—white pine and birch."

Cardinal thanked him and hung up. "Hey, McLeod, what do you make of this?"

McLeod's face rose like a bloodshot moon above the divider. Cardinal told him the results.

"The Highlands manager said they were doing all kinds of work out there, right? Cedar and mahogany, et cetera? So where did Irena Bastov pick up white pine and birch on her hem? We haven't had a lumber mill in town must be twenty years. And somehow I can't see a couple like the Bastovs dropping into Home Depot while they're here for the fur auction."

"Home Depot, you'd get all sorts of cedar."

"So where are two visitors going to pick up white pine and birch sawdust?"

"As it happens, you're asking the right guy, Sergeant Cardinal." McLeod addressed him in the tone of mock formality he always adopted when feeling particularly smug. "I can think of two places. You know Kabinet Kreations out on Cartier?"

"The unfinished-furniture joint? They must handle more than pine and birch."

"Nope. Reason I know, I just ordered an entertainment unit from them. I asked for oak—like I could afford it—and he told me no, they only do pine or birch. I went for birch."

"You think the Bastovs arrive in Algonquin Bay and the first thing they do, they head out to Kabinet Kreations?"

"No, I do not. You know what your problem is, Detective?"

"No. Please tell me."

"Your problem, Detective Cardinal, is that you don't drink enough. If you drank more often, you would go to bars more often. And if you went to bars more often, as I do—purely in the interests of law and order—you would know that the floors of the Chinook roadhouse are covered with sawdust."

"Okay. Why would it be just pine and birch?"

"An excellent question, Detective Cardinal, and once again I can satisfy your curiosity. You know who owns the Chinook?"

"That Greek guy—Jimmy Kappaz."

"Jimmy Kappaz. And guess where he gets his sawdust."

"Kabinet Kreations? McLeod, how would you know a thing like that—assuming it's true?"

"Kabinet Kreations is owned and operated by one Leon Kappaz—Jimmy's older brother. He's got the identical moustache—Greeks, as you know, are born with them. Same hound dog face. I got to asking him about Jimmy, about the Chinook, and he happened to mention that's what he did with his sawdust."

"I always hoped you'd be good for something," Cardinal said, "but you've exceeded all expectations."

"Thank you, Detective—and congratulations, by the way. Delorme tells me you've cleared the Scriver case."

⁓

The Chinook had been through many different incarnations—from inn, to cabaret, to oyster bar—but for the past ten years it had been a roadhouse, meaning the music was always live and loud, the food was down-home (and surprisingly good) and the beer tended toward the more powerful concoctions of the Quebec microbreweries. It had a sizable dance floor, now dark and deserted. Smells of stale beer and sawdust.

Jimmy Kappaz was sitting at the end of his bar with a morose expression on his face, punching numbers into an adding machine. When Cardinal showed him the pictures of Lev and Irena Bastov, he recognized them at once.

"Sure. Exotic couple. Both with huge fur coats. Not my usual customer."

"Why didn't you call us?" Cardinal said. "Their pictures have been all over the newspapers."

Kappaz shrugged. "Who reads the papers?"

"You didn't hear about a double murder just up the road?" McLeod said. "What are you, retarded?" Cardinal gave him a look, and McLeod corrected himself. "Sorry. Are you developmentally impaired? These people had their heads chopped off."

"Sure, I heard people talking about it. But I didn't pay much attention. Like I say, who cares about the news?"

Cardinal asked him if the Bastovs had been with anybody else.

"Sure, yeah. One guy. Nobody I recognized. Guy maybe late fifties. Short hair."

"Think about it. Can you describe him better than that?"

"Not really. I was crazy busy."

"Did they meet him here, or did they arrive with him?"

Kappaz shrugged and shook his head. "Don't know. They were sitting far end of the bar, I was down this end, making a million drinks for the waiters."

"Did they look like they were friends, the three of them?"

"No. The couple left, and the other guy, he looked pissed off."

"Short hair. Late fifties. What else?"

"Who knows what else? I'm a bartender, not a detective."

"Hey, Euclid," McLeod said, "I thought Greeks were supposed to be smart."

"Long time ago." He swung his mournful eyes back to Cardinal. "It's just my feeling, but the guy looked tough—you know, like a Marine or something. Like if you got him upset, he might dismantle you."

"Thanks," Cardinal said. "Listen, can you get someone to cover the bar for you before the evening rush? We need you to go downtown and talk to the police artist."

"I told you, I don't remember nothing."

"Do it anyway. You may be surprised."

—

When they got back into the car, Cardinal drove out along Island Road rather than back toward town.

"I want to take another look at the scene," Cardinal said.

"Fine by me. By the way, I talked to Ron Larivière—the bush pilot Irena Bastov was screwing? He denied it at first, of course, but faced with my priestlike demeanour he admitted that, yes, they had a two-night fling a couple of years ago, and that was the extent of it."

"And you believe him?"

"I actually do. Besides, on the night in question he was drinking with a bunch of trappers at the Bull and Bear."

"What about the guy who used to run the trappers' association?"

"That was more challenging. Donald Rivard left town six years ago and didn't keep in touch with anybody. I tracked him down to Red River, where apparently he died of cirrhosis in 2008. So glamorous, the fur industry."

There was a car parked in the hydro turnoff where Sam had parked. Cardinal pulled into the Schumachers' drive. Crime scene tape fluttered in the breeze, but other than that the house gave no sign of what had taken place inside. They went in through the back door and into the dining room. The blood-smeared floor, the empty chairs.

"Heat's back on," McLeod said. He picked up an unused Baggie from the floor and put it in his pocket. "Makes you wonder who turned it off. And why."

"Probably the killer. Wanted to be sure we found the bodies exactly the way he left them."

"You think it's the guy the Bastovs were with at the Chinook? From Jimmy's description, it could be the older guy on the airport tape."

"Could be. But it was Wednesday night they were seen with him. They were killed Thursday night."

"Well, we know it's not the ATM mugger. The shoe prints don't match. And he was not left-handed." McLeod interrupted himself to point out the back window. "Why, look at that—a suspect."

Outside, a pudgy man in a long dark coat was contemplating the snowy surface of the lake. He was about ten yards from shore, hands jammed in his pockets and shoulders hunched, even though it was a relatively warm day. On his head, a Russian-style fur hat.

"Looks too harmless," Cardinal said.

"Looks like a fucking commissar. Do you suppose he realizes that the lake ice is not exactly the safest place to—"

It was as if, by raising the possibility, McLeod caused it to happen. The ice gave way beneath the man and he pitched forward. In an effort to counterbalance, he tipped back. As his weight shifted to his rear foot, that too broke the surface. Now only his shoulders and head were visible.

McLeod pulled out his cellphone and dialed 911.

"Find some rope," Cardinal said. "And a crowbar or something."

He grabbed a broom and reached the lake in seconds and ran to the end of the dock. He got onto the ice on all fours and lay down to spread his weight. He dragged himself forward and placed the broomstick across the hole. The man was trying to suck in air, unable to speak. He grabbed hold of the broom handle. Cardinal pounded the near edge of the hole, snapping off chunks of the weakest ice.

McLeod was on the dock now. He tossed a crowbar, and Cardinal used it to break more ice until he reached a thicker patch.

"You've got to pull yourself up," he said to the man. "We're not going to be able to haul you out of there without your help."

McLeod had tied some clothesline into a lasso. Cardinal looped it around the man's shoulders and told him to put his arms through. Together they managed to get the rope under his arms.

Cardinal crawled back to the dock. He and McLeod braced the rope around their backs and heaved. The man got first one leg up out of the water, then the other. He collapsed on the ice, and they dragged him to shore.

As the wail of the ambulance grew louder, Cardinal reached into the man's coat. He made a token effort to resist, his hand a white claw. The dripping bills inside the wallet were American, and a government card identified him as Special Agent Irv Mendelsohn, FBI.

McLeod, who had been looking over Cardinal's shoulder, let out a bark of laughter.

28

MENDELSOHN WAS TAKEN TO EMERGENCY, where he was treated with hot tea and an electric blanket. His first words to Cardinal and McLeod were, "So *embarrassing*. Thank you both."

"What are you talking about?" McLeod said. "You made our day."

"So *humiliating*." Mendelsohn's native tongue seemed to be italics. He blew on his tea to cool it.

"What were you doing trampling all over our crime scene?" Cardinal said.

"I know, I know. So *rude*. I wanted to go through proper channels. I did call your HQ. They said you were out, and I thought you might be at the scene. Enthusiasm got the better of me, I guess."

"We found a red Chevy Alero down the road a ways. Would that be yours?"

"It was all Avis had left. I'm just here to help any way I can, fellas. You have a couple of dead Americans. I'm here to observe and assist."

"Sort of a charity thing," McLeod said. "Help out the hillbillies up north."

"No, no, we have our own hillbillies, you may have heard. Say, did I *thank* you gentlemen? I certainly meant to."

"We do actually have running water up here," McLeod went on. "And horseless carriages. Electricity, even. And we have been known to make a case or two."

"Oh, now you've taken offence. The *last* thing I wanted. I've really put my foot in it, haven't I."

"Through it," McLeod said. "You put your feet through it."

"*Wonderful.* Now I'm a figure of fun."

"All right," Cardinal said. "So you head out to the scene. What were you looking for on the lake?"

"Evidence. Often people will go over the *interior* of a scene with a fine-tooth comb, and the exterior . . . who knows? Maybe a perpetrator approached via snow machine. Maybe someone could have tossed a weapon out there, forgetting the lake was frozen."

"Sort of," McLeod said.

"Go ahead, amuse yourself, Detective. I deserve it."

"You're welcome to observe," Cardinal said. "But I don't really see how you can help."

"Similarities," Mendelsohn said. "Your case has certain similarities to another case of mine. Do you suppose my clothes would be out of the dryer yet?"

"No," McLeod said, "our dryers are very inferior up here. What similarities?"

Mendelsohn gave him a mournful look and reached for a Kleenex. He blew into it with surprising force, and then lay back. Eyes closed, he said, "Two cases. I brought copies of the files to show you, but they're in my hotel room.

"About six months ago in Westchester County—that's just north of the Bronx. Swanky area. Family of three found murdered. Shot. Weapon was a nine-mil of undetermined make and model. Mutilated post-mortem. Heads turned up a few days later on some church steps like a trio of gargoyles. Sick stuff."

"Definite similarities," Cardinal said. "But a church is not a dock. An undetermined make is not the same as a Browning HP."

"No, and three people are not two. You're *right*, Detective. You're absolutely a hundred percent *right* about that. It's not *definitive*."

"What's your other case?"

"Long Island. Two years previous. Sam Begelman, sixty-two, retired manager with Bergdorf's, is shot with a nine-mil, *possibly* a Browning HP. Bodies of wife and teenage daughter found nearby. Once again, beheaded post-mortem. Heads turn up in Central Park—Belvedere Castle, if you know what that is—placed on a parapet overlooking the Great Lawn. New York's my hometown, and I'll tell you it absolutely *ruined* the park for me."

"There's been some suggestion the Bastovs may have been connected to organized crime. Or at least victims of it."

"Really. There's nothing like that with the other cases. I can do a run-down on the Bastovs in our database. Would that be useful to you?"

"Very," Cardinal said. "Tell me more about the victims."

"Like I say, Begelman was a former Bergdorf's manager. Wife was an interior decorator. Daughter was a student at the Lycée. They also had a son away at college who survived. Not a suspect. The Westchester family, the guy was a finance type. Venture capital. Wife a CPA. Fifteen-year-old son was a high school sophomore."

"Signs of robbery?" McLeod said. "Any other motive?"

"No obvious one. No robbery."

"With all this head-chopping, was there any consideration given to terrorism?"

"Not really. For one thing, these killings had none of the trademarks— no scimitar, no video, no Great Satan screed, et cetera. Terrorists *advertise*. Terrorists want you to *know* it's them. Anti-Semitism maybe. The Begelmans were not observant, but they were big supporters of Israel. So no, Homeland Security did not get excited about it. And I have to tell you, our HQ does not buy the similarities—not to the extent I do. They're content to leave that case strictly with New York Homicide. Those guys are good, but they don't have our resources when things get out of state, not to mention out of country. It's also only fair to tell you that the NYPD is not on board—so I'm on my own here, pretty much. I hope I won't inconvenience you too much."

"Hell no," McLeod said. "We can use the entertainment."

"Detective Cardinal?"

"As long as you don't go barging into crime scenes unannounced. I want one investigation here, not two."

"Absolutely," Mendelsohn said. "Word of *honour*. I'm at your service, minute my clothes are dry."

~

Lise Delorme was in her cubicle catching up on her reports when her cell-phone chirped, indicating a text message. It was from Shane.

> Lise—sorry 2 do this by txt msg but Im in court all week—
> Lise, I rly like u a lot. Ur a wonderful person and I rly enjoy yr
> company but . . .

"Oh fuck," Delorme said, scrolling down the tiny screen.

> . . . 4 a long time now Ive felt r relatnp not developing. Pls
> understand Im not judging u—the sx is gr8, ur gr8 I just dnt
> think we shd see each othr anymore—I hope we can b
> friends and that ul call me when u feel ok.
> Case up—got2go shane.

Delorme pressed speed-dial. It rang twice and switched over to voice mail. She leaned deep into her cubicle so no one would overhear. "The reason our relationship isn't developing," she said into the phone, "is because you are not developing. That's spelt Y-O-U A-R-E. Really, Shane, what kind of three-year-old breaks up with someone by text message? And for your information, the sex is not great, you are not great, and I feel perfectly okay. So just FUCK OFF."

"Maybe I'll come back later."

Delorme spun round.

Jerry Commanda was standing behind her in his OPP parka. It had been ten years since he'd switched over to the provincial force, but the front desk still let him sail right through as if he remained on staff.

"What the hell do you want?" Delorme said. "You know I'm not good company by the end of the day."

"Way I hear it, you're pretty hard to take the rest of the day too."

Delorme looked at her watch. "Shouldn't you be out catching speeders?"

"Wanted to give you a heads up. You okay? You look a little pale."

"Problem with a lawyer. Take a seat—you look like a totem pole standing there."

Jerry pulled Cardinal's chair over and sat down. He unzipped his parka. "You know a guy named Henry Whiteside?"

Delorme shook her head. "From the reserve?"

"Not exactly. He was banned a few years back. You must have seen him on the street. He used to always be begging outside the Country Style top of Algonquin."

"That guy? Oh, man, he was in terrible shape. I haven't seen him for years. I assumed he died."

"You wouldn't recognize him if you saw him now. Henry turned himself around a few years ago. Did the twelve-step thing, got his head together, and even managed to get a job at Rona—he's quite a carpenter when he's sober. Looked healthy for the first time in ten years."

"You're right—I wouldn't have recognized him."

"Anyway, Henry has a cousin still lives on the rez, and according to her, he's gone missing. He had a small room here in town, and was leading— for him, anyways—a regular life. He's at Rona for a couple of months and then one day he just doesn't show up for work. They didn't think to report him missing—they figured either he'd heard the call of the wild or the call of the bottle. He hadn't been there long enough to make real friends who would check up on him. So it wasn't till his cousin stopped in the other day that anyone realized he'd moved out of his place. Rent was paid up, but one day he was there, next day he was gone."

"When was this?"

"Day she checked in on him was December 1, but he could have left quite a while before. She said he'd been considering a job somewhere out in the bush—just a handyman thing, but she thought it had some connection to the fur business. I figured, with the Bastov case, you guys'd be in a good position to keep an eye out, maybe ask around a little?"

Delorme finished making a note on a legal pad. Then she swivelled back to face Jerry. "You know I can't file a missing person on this, right? It's just too likely he's off on a drunk. Nobody's going to send out a search party."

"I know. I just wanted to bring it to your attention."

"Okay. I'll tell the others in morning meeting to keep an eye out for him."

"Thanks, Lise." Jerry stood and zipped up his parka. "It's just I have a fair acquaintance with recovering alcoholics. You get a sense for who's going to make it and who won't."

"And you thought Henry would."

"Hundred percent. Course, if he turns up frozen solid with an empty can of Sterno in his fist, I'll have to reassess my recovery meter."

When Jerry was gone, Delorme wrote *Henry Whiteside* in big letters on the biggest Post-it Note she could find and pinned it to the corkboard above her desk. Then she picked up her cellphone and opened the speed-dial menu and deleted Shane.

—

Cardinal drove home that night in a state of frustration. They had so many leads—the tires, the make of the car, the shoe prints, the bullets, the parking garage video—and yet it seemed they were still treading around the edge of the case instead of moving closer to the heart of it. Then there were the New York cases that Mendelsohn had brought—with their tantalizing similarities and yet no solid connections. He opened the parking garage with his clicker and drove down the ramp.

It was even darker than usual, and in the corner where Cardinal's slot was located there was barely any light at all. Every day it seemed there was another problem with this so-called luxury building, and Cardinal thought once again—as he thought pretty much every day—that it had been a mistake to sell the house.

He switched off the car and got out and locked it and headed toward the elevator. He had his key out and was opening the door to the elevator room when there was a noise behind him. He spun around and his Beretta was already in his hand with the safety off.

"Jesus," he said. "Are you out of your mind? I nearly shot you."

It was Donna Vaughan, looking uncharacteristically nervous. She apologized profusely. "Can I come in for a while? Please say yes. I think someone's following me."

Cardinal looked past her at the garage.

"I don't think he saw me come in here," she said. "But I'm scared. I thought there was someone following me in the car, after I left the hotel—I just put it down to paranoia. But then, just now, as I was parking, someone pulled over a little ways behind. When I got out of the car, I heard him behind me."

Cardinal picked up his keys with his left hand, keeping the revolver in his right.

He held the door open for her. When they were inside, he said, "Did you get a look at him?"

"Not really. Mid-fifties maybe? Long dark coat."

"What about his car?"

She shook her head. "I didn't see."

"Where was this exactly?"

"On Travis—I think it's called Travis. Near the corner. I saw a gun in his hand—I mean, I thought I did. I was totally freaked at that point."

"And you think you lost him."

"I hope so. I made a sudden rush toward a house as if I lived there and went back between it and the next house. I could see your building through the trees, so I just walked through the back. Got a lot of snow in my boots doing it."

"You're still driving the Focus?"

She nodded. "You've got a good memory."

Cardinal hit the elevator button. "Get out on the ground floor and go sit in the lobby. I'll come back in through the front."

The elevator door opened.

"Maybe I should come with you."

"Wait in the lobby."

He went out through the pedestrian door beside the vehicle entrance. There was no one in sight. He looked for Donna's tracks in the snow between the trees on the far side of the driveway. No one ever came through that way; there was only the one set of tracks. He went back to the driveway and turned up Travis Street, walking a hundred yards or so before he saw her car.

He bent to examine the doors, the windows. No signs of tampering.

The sidewalk was mostly slush, nothing that would hold prints. He walked farther up the street, shifting his glance back and forth from the parked cars to the houses. There were three vehicles. The first was covered in a month's worth of snow. The hood of the second one was cold to the touch, and the third was a pickup—surely she would have noticed if it had been a pickup following her—also cold to the touch. He stopped at the end of the block and turned around. Once again on the way back he watched for movement among the houses, the cars, for anything at all, but there was nothing.

He went back to his building and in through the front door. Donna was in a corner chair that could not be seen through the glass doors. She stood up when he came in. "Did you see anyone?"

Cardinal shook his head. "Now maybe you could tell me what you're doing here. How did you find me?"

"They said you'd just left the office. I thought I could catch you before you got home."

"Why would I want to talk to the press when I'm off duty?"

"I know, I know. Look, I'm freelance—I have to push, okay? I'm sorry."

"You look pretty shaken up. Maybe you better come in for a minute. Just don't make it a habit."

"I won't. God, I'm so embarrassed. Helpless female."

The elevator door opened and Donna went in ahead of him. She was hunched and tense, the former brassy confidence quite gone.

Cardinal pushed the up button. "How did you know where I live?"

"I was going through your local paper's morgue. I came across an unrelated story about your run-in with your co-op board. Some ventilation issue?"

"Awfully thorough, aren't you? What are you looking me up for?"

"Local colour, obviously."

"That story didn't give the building address."

"Are you kidding? There was a picture of you standing in front of it. You can see this building from the government wharf."

The door opened at the third floor and they got out.

"You look like you could use a drink," he said when they were in his apartment. "Whisky okay?" He hung their coats up and went into the kitchen. He called out, "Ice?"

"Please. Quite a view you have here."

Cardinal poured two whiskies and brought them into the living room and handed her one. She took a sip and looked at the glass. "What is it?"

"Rye. You prefer something else?"

"No, it's good. I've never had it before—must be a Canadian thing. What are those lights over there?" She pointed at a spray of silvery pinpoints across the bay.

"Area of town called Ferris. Who do you think was following you?"

"God, I don't know. I hope it's just a random perv and not some bloody Russian."

"There's no sign of anyone at all."

"Hey, he was maybe twenty yards behind me—I didn't imagine the guy."

"I didn't say you did."

She drank down the rest of the whisky. "Now I'm second-guessing myself. Do you suppose it's possible he *wasn't* following me?"

"That's the most likely scenario."

"Could I really be that dumb?"

"You wouldn't have to be dumb—you're writing about guys who kill people like you. Can I get you another?"

She handed him her empty glass. "I could get used to this stuff."

Cardinal went into the kitchen and poured two more.

"In fact," she called after him, "I could get to like your whole country. Everyone's so polite here, it's like they're all on Valium—except you. The way you drew that gun. I thought I was a goner."

Cardinal brought the drinks out and handed her one and sat on the couch. Donna was sitting in his favourite chair, a recliner that she had tipped back to its halfway position. She had small feet, and socks that were perfectly white.

"What else did you find out from the *Lode*? I assume you didn't spend all your time looking me up."

"Local stuff on the fur biz—the Web was useless. A couple of things may interest you. Did you know the fur auction used to be run by a different group than the guys currently in charge?"

"I did. The first group couldn't make a go of it."

Donna reached for her bag on the floor beside the chair, a manoeuvre that caused her to reveal a good deal of cleavage. She struck Cardinal as a cold person in some ways—dry, analytical, obsessed with work—but he also had the sense of enormous emotion held in check, though as to which emotions he had no clue.

Donna sat back up and flipped open her notebook. "A man named Rivard—Donald Rivard—is quoted in this article from a couple of years ago saying, 'It's not just the low prices. Certain people, the big buyers, have a way of holding on to their cash. We have to warehouse the fur and they take their sweet time paying us. Meanwhile we have to pay all the trappers, not to mention our staff. You can't make a living on promises.'"

Cardinal nodded. "We know about Rivard."

"Well, if you don't buy the Russian mob—it's a possibility, right?" Donna sat forward and the recliner reformed itself into an upright armchair. "And now you have another murder on your hands—more people to interview, more leads to chase down. Give me a little help here. A name or two."

"Sorry. Investigation in progress."

"We went over all that. I won't publish a thing until you have a conviction. I swear." She got out of the chair and came to the couch and straddled him so that her knees were on either side of him. Before Cardinal could say anything, she looped her hands around his neck. Warm hands, small. "Are you going to tell me?"

"What happens if I don't?"

"I'm probably going to kiss you."

"And if I do?"

"I'm definitely going to kiss you."

She smelled fresh and clean and weighed hardly anything at all.

"The Bastovs were seen at the Chinook roadhouse the night before they were murdered." He could tell her that. Jimmy Kappaz wouldn't be the only one to remember a pair of rich foreigners—dead foreigners—in such a setting.

Donna leaned forward and kissed him. The sudden heat of her lips on his. She sat back, keeping her hands around his neck. "Who with?"

"God, they should have used you at Guantanamo. A man in his late fifties. And that's all I'm telling you."

"Late fifties. That could be the guy who followed me."

"It could be anybody. Obviously, we want to interview anyone else who was at the bar who might have seen them."

"Thank you," she said. "See, that didn't hurt, did it?"

"Wasn't too painful."

A quick smile, and then a look of concern crossed her face. "You seem a little uncomfortable."

"No kidding."

She leaned forward again, arms around him, her face hot against his. Cardinal held her, too—uncertainly. Her voice in his ear. "Am I the first one since . . ."

Cardinal nodded.

"What about when you were married? You never strayed?"

"Never."

Beneath his hands, her rib cage, taken by a deep sigh, expanded and then contracted again. Her breath hot against his neck. "We don't have to do anything," she said.

"I know."

"I feel good just being here with you. Protected, I guess."

"That's me: to serve and protect . . ."

She sat back. "That serve part sounds interesting."

—

Cardinal took her to the bedroom and there Donna regained all her former confidence. She was small and fine-boned, but with lean muscles palpable beneath the flawless skin—a lithe, intuitive lover. Cardinal felt coarse and ungainly, acutely aware of his age, despite her enthusiasm, which was both athletic and huskily vocal. Afterward he lay beside her in the swirl of sheets, glazed with sweat and thinking about Catherine. He tried to compose his face to disguise this fact, but Donna seemed to know anyway. She gave a small smile and touched his shoulder, but didn't ask him about it.

They talked for a while in low voices. Cardinal asked about her background and was somewhat surprised that she talked about it openly—a horrible father, a nonentity mother, two failed marriages. There was no self-pity in it; she related the bits of information as if they were facts she'd come across on microfilm.

In the morning she roused him with the heat of her mouth and then he was inside her again almost before he was fully awake, so that it felt like an extremely vivid dream. Then a rushed breakfast and awkward good-byes. When Donna was gone, Cardinal stood for a long time looking out the window, coffee mug in hand, watching the darkness recede from the white and grey expanse of Lake Nipissing.

29

THE SUN WAS STILL LOW IN THE SKY, the first rays hitting the grave-stones, slowly turning the light from grey to pale blue. Cardinal pulled to a stop in the parking lot, switched off the Camry and got out. He shut the door but didn't lock it. There were no other cars, and no footprints marred the snow that covered the graves and the paths that wound among them.

He stood for a moment in the pale wash of sunlight. The cawing of a distant crow and, closer by, the obsessive squawk of a squirrel claiming territory. Smells of snow and wet bark. The black branches, the paper-white hills—Catherine had taken many pictures of just this sort of scene. But Cardinal had never shared her attraction to graveyards. He left the parking lot, gloveless hands in his pockets, and took the path over the nearest hill.

The tips of his ears burned with cold. He walked through a copse of blue spruce and beyond it to an oak that spread its branches over the path, so low he could reach up and touch them. Catherine had told him a couple of times that she wanted to be buried under a tree, wanted to feel she was spreading her branches in some kind of blessing on those who were still alive. Not that they had talked about death a lot, no more than most couples.

Cardinal squatted down beside the edge of the path and brushed the snow away with his bare hand. Underneath Catherine's name, the brass plaque identified her as a photographer and teacher, the beloved wife of John Cardinal and loving mother of Kelly. Then there was the date of her birth, some fifty years previous, and the date of her death—the plaque said nothing about murder—some fifteen months ago.

Catherine would not have approved of the plaque. She was never one to make a fuss about herself, and not the least bit sentimental. Cardinal hadn't been sentimental either, until his wife had been taken from him. He had had *photographer* and *teacher* engraved because Catherine, when she was well, had been utterly devoted to being both. Beloved and loving, well, those were understatements, the least you could say. The thesaurus was next to useless when it came to describing such things; Cardinal had checked.

The snow melted on his hand and he let the water drip from his fingers onto the brass plaque, where it immediately began to freeze. He didn't believe in God. He didn't believe in an afterlife either; at least, he told himself he didn't. So it wouldn't be right to say he was talking to the woman who had shared her time in the world with him. But he stayed very still and thought about Catherine's life, and his life, and many things Catherine had said or done. And her face.

—

Special Agent Mendelsohn was nothing if not a hard worker. He asked Cardinal if he could go over missing person reports in case one of these missing persons might turn out to be in fact another murder victim who would lead them to the same perpetrator. Cardinal brought a stack of files to the meeting room, there being no desk available, and there Mendelsohn took off his sports jacket and rolled up his sleeves and fell into intense concentration.

Cardinal checked back a little later and Mendelsohn was in exactly the same posture, files on his left, untouched coffee on his right. It was not hot in the meeting room, but Mendelsohn was sweating. Cardinal's own concentration was interrupted again and again with thoughts of Donna Vaughan. Still, he sat at his desk, drawing diagrams of what he knew, what he thought he knew, what he wanted to know.

One of the things he wanted to know was the location of the Bastovs' rental car. Hertz had not reported it missing—it was merely on their files as overdue. Cardinal had a copy of their records in front of him. Mercury Grand Marquis. Current model. Plate number duly noted.

"Lise."

Delorme rolled her chair back and raised her eyebrows.

"There were only two sets of tire tracks in the driveway of the Trout Lake house, right?"

"Right."

"And they match the ATM kid's car, not a Mercury Grand Marquis. Now, since it's not in the lot of their hotel and it wasn't at the scene of the murder, it seems likely that the Bastovs drove somewhere else—somewhere they met someone who then drove them out to Island Road."

"Makes sense."

"And since our killer is from out of town, it stands to reason the Bastovs might have met him at a hotel—a hotel other than the Highlands. We should check them all for the Bastovs' Grand Marquis."

"I'll get Sergeant Flower to put the street guys on it. If they all stop by the hotels in their sector, we'll get a quick answer."

A little later, Cardinal went into the meeting room to check on Mendelsohn.

"Oh, hey," Mendelsohn said. "This fur auction stuff is *interesting*. I could read all day about this. And this *protester* —this Pocklington—what a piece of work *he* is. I hope someone's keeping an eye on *him*."

"I gave you missing persons stuff to read."

"Yeah, yeah, I went *through* all that."

They were interrupted by Delorme. "They've located the Bastov car. The Belvedere Motel."

﹌

The Belvedere was a grand name for a motel that was little more than a block of red brick offering views of a Petrocan gas station and a discount electronics store. Delorme and the ident team swarmed over the Grand Marquis the moment they arrived. Cardinal and Mendelsohn went in to talk to the manager, a tubby man in his sixties who was aromatic of pipe tobacco. "We get people helping themselves to our parking spaces all the time," he told them. "This time of year we have a lot of vacancies, so we don't call in the tow trucks like we might in summer."

Cardinal asked to see the register, and the manager swivelled a battered and smudged PC monitor so Cardinal could see.

"Only three guests?"

"Yeah. Rushed off our feet."

Two had checked in too late for the fur auction. "This third one," Cardinal said, "the one who checked in a week ago last Wednesday. What can you tell me about him?"

"Not a thing. He signed in and I haven't seen him since. Hasn't given me any reason to worry."

"He have any visitors?"

"I wouldn't know. They don't come through the office."

"Was there anything unusual about him?"

The manager thought about it for a minute, chewing a plump knuckle. "One thing, maybe. He had an accent. He gave his name as Ted Nelson, but he didn't sound like a Nelson. I didn't question it—I mean, lots of people change their names when they immigrate. But to me he sounded more like a Sergei or an Igor."

Cardinal turned to Mendelsohn. "You have any questions?"

Mendelsohn shook his head. "Your show, Detective."

Cardinal made a note of the Chevy Aveo the man had registered, and the licence plate number. "His car's not in your lot at the moment. You mind if we sit in here and wait for him to come back?"

"Why, has he done something?"

"We certainly plan to ask him."

—

Cardinal asked Delorme and the ident team to leave the Mercury and come back later. He moved his own car farther up the street and came back to the motel office. He and Mendelsohn set a couple of chairs to face the windows, and rearranged some plastic plants so they could keep an eye on the parking area.

Cardinal was a little worried about manning a stakeout with Mendelsohn.

Mendelsohn was a talker—not just a talker, an italicizer and a gesticulator—and Cardinal didn't like a lot of chit-chat on a stakeout. He preferred to think about the case, to try to develop ideas for new avenues of investigation. But the FBI man sat in his chair, watching a parking lot utterly devoid of activity, and didn't say a word. He had his notepad out and occasionally flipped a page, made a note. Mostly he sat there, slouched at an angle, twirling his ballpoint in silence.

They sat that way for a good hour and a half. The manager, unasked, brought them coffee and muffins. It was the only time Mendelsohn spoke. He thanked the manager and bit into one of the muffins and called after him, "Hey, these are *good*. You're very kind to share them." Cardinal made a mental note to practise better manners himself.

"I have a colleague or two could take lessons from you," Cardinal said.

"From me? What *in*? My tuba playing is not so hot, and my driving is a constant concern to the Bureau. Yiddish maybe? You have someone dying to learn Yiddish?"

"Not exactly," Cardinal said.

"Can't be much demand for it up here. Jews don't respond well to cold. Deserts. We like deserts. Especially if they belong to someone else. I got a Palestinian colleague, we call him Zippy because his family name is a little like Doodah. One day I told Zippy, I said, 'Doodah . . . Doodah . . . That's so familiar. I got it! I think my cousin moved into your family house in Jerusalem!' Oh boy, did I catch hell from *him*. Such bad jokes I make. I think I could take lessons from that McLeod guy. Now he's *funny*."

"McLeod, yeah. Very dry."

"Dry, no. Funny, yes. Okay, I'll shut up now. I hate people who gas on when you're on a stakeout. The perfect opportunity for reflection and they have to launch this *spielkreig*. So *dismayed* I get. So *disheartened*."

They settled once more into their separate quiets. Half an hour later, the Chevy Aveo pulled into the lot and parked in front of room eight.

"Let's wait till he gets to the door," Cardinal said.

"Long as he doesn't get *inside* the door. That would be a *negative* thing."

The man got out of the car and shut the driver's-side door and immediately opened it again. He reached in and pulled out a paper bag with the KFC logo. He shut the car door again and locked it and carried his dinner to his room door.

Cardinal got up and drew his Beretta. He opened the office door slowly so it wouldn't squeak, and he and Mendelsohn were behind the man before he had his key out of his pocket.

"Ted Nelson?"

The man turned and looked at them both and said, "Fuck."

"I need to see some ID."

"ID why? I have done nothing."

"Just show me."

The man reached into his inside coat pocket. Mendelsohn was behind Cardinal with his weapon drawn. The man dropped the wallet and Cardinal kept his Beretta trained on him while he picked it up. There was a credit card and a New York driver's licence in the name of Nelson, but everything else was in the name Yevgeny Divyris.

"Yevgeny Divyris," Cardinal said. "You're related to Irena Divyris? You're Russian?"

"Ukrainian," Mendelsohn said, his Glock aimed at the man's head.

The man turned and looked Mendelsohn up and down and spat on the ground. "Jew."

"Yes. And please let me personally apologize. I'm so *sorry* you people had to work so hard herding us into the showers. Nice *job* your people did as camp guards."

"Fucking scum. How many in my country you starve to death? Millions."

"Hands behind your back," Cardinal said.

"Millions dead from starving while landlords ate like pigs, and nobody talks about this millions. Only the fucking Jews."

"Both hands," Cardinal said. "Now." He snapped the handcuffs on the man and turned him around. "That Mercury is your sister's rental. You have any explanation why it's at your hotel?"

"I don't have to explain nothing. To you or your fucking Jew friend."

"I'm sure you mean that in a positive sense," Mendelsohn said.

They put Divyris into the back of the car and drove to the station, where he was booked on a charge of credit card fraud. They sat him in an interview room and left him there to stew for half an hour while they dug up all the background they could on him.

"Explain to me one thing," Mendelsohn said, "and then I'll just observe. Explain to me how it is that the Jews, who are supposed to be behind every international plot, who are supposedly manipulating the world's *banking* system through a worldwide network of conspirators—explain to me how these Machiavellian *geniuses* ended up as lampshades and other handy household items."

"Right now I'd rather ask him about his relationship with his sister."

"Good point. *Focus*, Detective. I *like* that. See, I could learn from *you*."

—

Cardinal sat himself down opposite Yevgeny Divyris and silently filled out a form. Divyris sat back with one foot crossed over his knee, cuffed hands in his lap.

"How long you plan to keep me here? You think I don't have better things to do?"

Cardinal didn't look up.

"I asked you question."

Cardinal put aside the form. It was actually just a federal tax form; you couldn't beat the feds for ominous-looking documents. At this proximity he could see Divyris's resemblance to Irena. He had the same deep-set eyes, the same wide cheekbones, and Cardinal wondered if his sister had had the same arrogant attitude.

"You don't have right to keep me here," he said. "You have to charge me."

"You're charged with fraud."

Divyris gave a snort. "Credit card. I thought you were investigating my sister's murder, but no, big detective is worried about credit card. Is nothing."

"It'll do for now." Cardinal flipped back through his notebook. "You owned a fur farm outside Kiev, didn't you?"

Divyris stared at him. "Long time ago. Big deal."

"It was doing quite well until about, let's see, five years ago. What happened then?"

"Market problems. Suddenly no one buys furs. No one in Russia."

"But some people were doing quite well. Lev Bastov, for example."

"Lev Bastov? Is nothing. Nobody."

"Correct me if I'm wrong, but Lev Bastov appears to own several fur farms in Russia, and owns or has a controlling interest in fur factories in

Russia, China, the U.S. and Canada. He sells furs, buys furs, manufactures coats, hats, you name it, and sells them again. Hardly nothing."

"Who cares? Is his business."

"Just before the fur market really tanks, he sells his factory in Russia and buys two in China. That's exactly one year after he marries your sister."

"Maybe you never notice—so busy chasing credit cards—some guys are lucky. Other guys? Not lucky."

"Which brings us to your own fur farm." Cardinal consulted the notes. "A thriving business when you take it over, a disaster when you sell it—presumably for peanuts—two years later. Again, right before Lev Bastov hits the big time."

"You get this from Internet? Internet is always wrong."

"We have witnesses who say you were hot on the idea of Irena marrying Lev Bastov. You were totally excited about it. Lev Bastov was going to buy your fur farm and save you from ruin. Lev Bastov was going to set you up on a new farm somewhere profitable. Or better yet, he was going to make you manager of a fur factory."

"Some guys like to talk big, you know? Some guys like to make promises—especially when they have eye on woman like my sister. If you cannot win her with your looks, you buy her with your money. You make big promise her family will benefit also. He will look after everyone. Then he's married and big promises are forgotten."

"But he did keep one promise. He did put you in charge of a factory in—where was it . . ." Cardinal flipped a page in his notebook, scanning until he found the entry. "Kalinin?"

"Kalinin. Fuck Kalinin. Kalinin, it's like getting charge of auto factory in Detroit. Like getting charge of *Titanic*. Bon voyage, Captain!"

"Sales went down, profits turned to losses, people lost their jobs, and Lev Bastov put it all on you."

"Lev tells me, 'You drink too much, party too much. You pay yourself too much. And you pay too much for furs when no market.' As if I'm supposed to know future. I'm supposed to know China is going to rule universe? Fucking slave owners."

"And he fired you."

"Fuck him."

"He gets your sister, he gets his factories, his profits, his jet-set lifestyle, and you get . . ."

"I hated the bastard, okay? Big revelation: I'm not going to miss Lev Bastov. But if you suppose I killed him, no. Kill *him*, maybe I can imagine. Kill Irena? Never. And you will never prove this, because I did not do it."

"Why are you even in Algonquin Bay, if you're not in the fur business anymore?"

"I buy for couple of Jews in garment district. Pay is shit."

"Where were you the night your sister was killed?"

"My hotel."

"Was anyone with you?"

"Yes, of course someone was with me. Irena and her fucking husband were with me. You saw their car outside hotel. You think I'm going to go out to some house with them, cut heads off, and stay in hotel waiting for you to arrest me? And all this time I leave their car outside my room?"

"You probably didn't know it was their car. They come to visit you, they knock on your door—why would you see their car? Did you call them or did they call you?"

"They called me."

"The memory on your cellphone says otherwise."

"So I called them. Why not?"

"You weren't on good terms. Why did you call?"

"With *him*. With *him* I was not on good terms. I didn't ask Lev to come. With my sister, yes. I call her to come see me, say hello, spend some family time. Is my sister. Also, I wanted to see Anton."

"Anton. Bastov's son from a previous marriage."

"I know, strange I should like him, but he's good guy. Not like Lev. He was supposed to come to auction, but he had to cancel. Got sick."

"Was anyone else with them?"

"No."

"You arranged for someone else to meet them, didn't you?."

"No. They came alone. We were supposed to go out for a drink, Irena, Anton and me. Lev came too, I don't know why. We were just leaving when they get a call. Lev's cell. Some guy wants to show them house."

"What guy?"

"Some guy. I don't know. Real estate guy. I knew they were looking for house, but still I thought was strange, real estate agent calling late at night. Supposedly they met some guy night before was going to set it up. Ten minutes later Lev's phone rings again, guy is outside in car, and they leave."

"What guy? What did he look like?"

"I didn't see him. Phone rings, Lev answers, they go out."

"What kind of car?"

"I didn't see."

"What did you do after they left?"

"I stay in my room. No. First I go out to beer store, buy six beers, come back and watch TV. You can check with beer store."

"What did you watch?"

"Movie. Some porno."

"What movie?"

"You want *title*? Of porno movie? *Pussy* something. Starts with window washer, sees blonde working out on treadmill. Then comes repairman, then comes painter—oh, and her personal trainer—brown hair, tits size of your head. *Spitfire Pussy*."

"Sounds like a classic," Cardinal said. "Okay, so you know Lev and Irena are coming to the fur auction. You know they are thinking of buying a house here—"

"Investment property, they tell me. I don't have house. I rent lousy apartment. They collect houses."

"So you arrange a set-up. Some guy posing as a real estate agent, but he's really someone you paid to kill Bastov."

"Not true. No."

"Lev and Irena have everything. They collect factories, houses, and you've got nothing but broken promises. What's to stop you hiring someone to kill them?"

"I told you. With Lev, yes, I was pissed off. With Irena, no. Is not her fault. You think I hire someone to cut my sister's head off? You are one crazy cop. I hope you got some other suspect, because you can't blame this killings on me. You have to prove, and you can't."

Cardinal put his notebook and papers aside and leaned across the table. "Two questions for you, Yevgeny. One, why didn't you come to the police when your sister disappeared? We couldn't even find you as next of kin. And two, why are you still here nearly two weeks later?"

"I want to find out what happened. This is so strange?"

"And yet you never showed up to help our investigation, or to ask a single question."

"As if you know answers. Lev was not perfect business guy, okay? Is good chance they were killed by *mafiya*. You think he didn't have dealings with *mafiya*? He did. How much, I wouldn't know. They kill whole families, *mafiya*—I don't want to go back to Brooklyn, find some fucking *vor* in my apartment. Okay?"

"So for safety's sake, you hang around in the place where your sister was murdered."

Divyris shrugged. "Is true. You think I would stay here if I *killed* them? Waiting for you and your handcuffs? I am not rich, maybe, but I have business too. I have to make a living. I've been talking to people, setting up deals. You can check."

Cardinal pulled out a sheaf of papers he had printed out and placed it on the table. "E-mails," he said. He pulled out another sheaf of papers and placed it beside the other. "Translations." They were actually Google translations and perfectly hilarious, but close enough that Cardinal could fake it.

Divyris said something in Russian or Ukrainian. When Cardinal didn't reply, he said something else.

Cardinal improvised from the top translation. "'Don't imagine I will forget. I will never forget. Your loving husband made promises and you will make him keep them, Irena, or it will be trouble for you.'"

"Fuck you."

Cardinal read from another one. "'Always the same story. Always these lies. Make him do right, or I will make him myself.'"

"And you wonder why I don't phone police. I am angry, okay? Lev owes me, okay? Bastard has everything. He owns world and all little tiny worlds that make up big world. And me he can't give decent living? His sister's brother? Treats me like dog? Worse than dog."

Cardinal got up and went to the door. "I'll be right back."

Mendelsohn and McLeod were in the next room, watching through the one-way glass. Mendelsohn put down the phone. "Manager confirms he ordered *Spitfire Pussy* and ran it from 11:30 to 1:30 a.m."

"Thank you, Maestro," McLeod said, "but that doesn't mean he watched it."

Cardinal handed McLeod the sheaf of bogus forms. "Get a list of his so-called business contacts and check them out. I want to know what he's been doing for the past two weeks."

"Absolutely," McLeod said. "I also plan to watch *Spitfire Pussy* from beginning to end. Don't thank me, it's just my duty as an officer of the law."

30

CARDINAL HAD NO DOUBT THAT Divyris—despite his alleged fear of the Russian underworld—would flee the country if he could. When McLeod finished with him, he was booked on the fraud charge and installed in a cell. By the time that was done, the day was pretty much over.

Cardinal and Mendelsohn were heading out to dinner, to Morgan's Chop House.

"Oh, hey—old-style chophouse with the red check tablecloths and all that? Sounds like my kind of place," Mendelsohn said. "Sounds like my *ideal*."

"So let's go there and we can toss ideas around."

"Excellent. I could eat an entire cow." He opened the door to his bright red rented Alero. "Oh, wait—sorry, I forgot my galoshes. Hang on a second and I'll follow you in my car."

Mendelsohn went back inside and Cardinal crossed the parking lot and got into his Camry. He backed out of his space just as Donna Vaughan was pulling into the lot. They rolled down their respective windows.

"Is there any chance I can take a few minutes of your time?"

"I'm just heading out to a working dinner with a visitor, I'm afraid."

"Is that him?" Donna pointed to Mendelsohn, who was coming out the side door of the station, now wearing his galoshes and fur hat.

"That's him. FBI."

"Seriously? He doesn't look nearly slick enough."

"Is it urgent? I can postpone dinner half an hour."

"No, that's all right." Her grey eyes were cool, in contrast to her voice. "To tell you the truth, I just wanted to see you. I've been thinking about last night."

"Why don't you come round later?"

"I really shouldn't. I've got to organize all my notes into some usable form, and a friend just FedExed me a fat trial transcript to read."

"Come over when you're done."

"Really? I mean, I'd love to, but—"

"Good. I'll see you later."

~

"Oh, this is *nice*," Mendelsohn said. He looked around over the top of his menu. "Stained glass lamps, waitresses in uniforms, I *like* this. What more could a man *want*?"

They ordered salads to start, even though Cardinal warned him they would be strictly iceberg lettuce.

"I'm old enough to remember when we just called it lettuce. It was *all* iceberg lettuce. Pour some of that Kraft ranch-style on it? Can't be beat."

Mendelsohn had delicate table manners, dabbing at his mouth often with his napkin. Cardinal asked about his colleagues (*wonderful* characters, *good* men), and his boss (not a bastard, but not exactly *effervescent*).

"Tell me about this McLeod," Mendelsohn said. "I get the impression he's maybe not quite the loose cannon he seems."

"McLeod is a solid investigator. Also reliable in court, keeps his facts straight."

"Oh, in *court*. I imagine he has a pretty good *delivery*. And this Delorme. Now there's an attractive woman, and I don't mean just pretty."

"Sergeant Delorme has no idea how attractive she is."

"Which is part of the attraction." Mendelsohn pointed a fork at his food. "Good pork chop. Most places dry them out, but this is just right. By the way, database came back negative on the Bastovs for Russian mob."

"You wouldn't necessarily know if they'd merely been threatened by the mob, though, would you? Most people are going to be too scared to tell anyone, right?"

"You're right. It doesn't rule it out. But I checked with NYPD as well—they're the real experts. Lev Bastov has met one or two connected people in Brooklyn, but not in a way that raised flags. They got a don down there with interests in the fashion business, which gets you to furs pretty quick."

They talked about Yevgeny Divyris. Neither of them thought he was guilty of murdering his sister and her husband. Whether he hired someone else to do it, however, was still an open question, at least to Cardinal. Mendelsohn was skeptical even of that.

"He has the motive," Cardinal said. "And he's got a nasty edge to him."

"Hundred percent. I *agree* with you. But I'm coming at this from an entirely different angle. And here . . ." Mendelsohn paused, fork in mid-air. The expression on his face was as if he were straining to hear a faint melody. "And here, I don't know. There's other stuff I should tell you."

"So tell me."

Mendelsohn winced. "I feel awkward. It isn't that I didn't trust you. It's just—especially in the Bureau—you learn to keep things close to your chest. We've been burned by other agencies, other departments, and the DOJ itself, come to that. Don't even *talk* to me about the CIA. So, we're not real good about sharing information."

"It's pretty much like that between us and the RCMP."

"Oh, good. I mean not *good*, but good you understand—now I don't feel so selfish, so *ungrateful*." Mendelsohn dug into his meal with renewed gusto. The snap peas were downright *refreshing*.

After a few moments of extremely reflective chewing, Mendelsohn leaned across the table. "Okay. Here's the good stuff. My field supervisor and my colleagues would not approve, but I'm going to go out on a limb. Heck, I've already fallen through the ice in front of you—what harm can it do?

"Okay, we have these similar but not identical crimes. I see them as by the same guy or guys; others disagree. Fine. Here's something I haven't even floated by them yet, because I don't want them to haul me straight down to St. Elizabeth's."

"St. Elizabeth's?"

"Psychiatric facility in D.C. Full of agency burnouts. Anyway, here's what I got—laugh if you want to, but hear me out first. These mashed potatoes are delicious, by the way. I sense more than a tablespoon of butter at work.

"Okay, we got the two cases—three, counting yours. I heard about three *other* unrelated cases—unrelated by anyone but me—where the doers are kids. These go back a ways—ten, twelve years. We're talking real youngsters of thirteen or fourteen. No apparent motive. They break into a house, shoot anything that moves—mother, kid, they don't care, it's bang, bang, bang."

"And they're acting alone?"

"No. With other kids. Older kids. Eighteen, twenty years old. Reason we know, in one of the cases there was a *survivor*. This was near Elmira—upstate farming area. They missed this terrified thirteen-year-old daughter hiding in a closet. She hears the older ones giving orders: 'Do it, shoot him,' stuff like that. 'That's how Papa wants it.'"

"'Papa'? They actually said 'Papa'?"

"Yeah. So you think, what, European? New immigrants? But the survivor said they sounded American."

"Was anybody caught?"

"Exactly one guy. He was sixteen, practically a *child*. He's on his deathbed with a bullet in his skull. They can't take it out or his brain comes with it. Lead detective asks him the question on everybody's minds: Why? Why do you break into a house in the middle of the night and kill everything in sight? His answer? 'Papa told us to.'

"Detective says, 'What, your father told you to do this?' Kid shakes his head and says, 'Papa.' It's the guy's name. Nobody knows his real name. Doesn't like to be called anything else. Kid says he teaches them everything—from how to rob an ATM to hand-to-hand combat to outdoor survival. Made it sound like a crime school. A crime *machine*."

"Robbing ATMs is interesting."

"I thought you'd like that. Kid died before he could tell us much more."

"Who shot him?"

"One of his teammates. Apparently he showed hesitation when it came to killing and one of his mentors dropped the hammer on him. Nice, huh?"

"Other than the ATMs, what's the link with our case up here?"

"Same-type firearm—the Browning HP nine-millimetre."

"Same make but not the same weapon? That wouldn't even get you a search warrant up here."

"I'm losing you," Mendelsohn said, dabbing at his mouth with the napkin. "Okay, it's understandable. Here's what I'm gonna do. What time's your morning meeting? Eight-thirty, right? Nine o'clock I'll bring everything in, we'll go over it together. Is nine okay?"

"Sure. Nine's good."

"Rather than try to fill you in on everything over this beautiful meal—thank you for bringing me here, by the way, not everybody would do that for an out-of-towner—rather than talk your ear off right now, why don't I tomorrow just bring you the stuff I've got."

Cardinal signalled the waiter for the check, but Mendelsohn won the battle to pay it.

When they got out on the street, it was colder than before. The wind had picked up and eddies of snow twirled under the streetlights. Mendelsohn raised the collar of his overcoat—a manoeuvre that made him look like a comic-book PI. He thanked Cardinal again and shook his hand. He got into his car, started it and drove away.

—

When Cardinal got home he pulled his curtains so he wouldn't have to look at his fogged-up windows. He went to the fridge and got some ice and put it in a glass. He poured a shot of Black Velvet, then added a little more and took it into the living room.

He sat in the recliner that Donna had occupied. He tilted back and thought about his day and about Mendelsohn. He thought too about the things he had to do the next day, the calls he would have to make, the reports he would have to write. He thought about Donna, about whether she would come. And if she did come, what it would mean.

He dozed off. When he woke up, the ice in his glass was gone. It was too early to go to bed and he didn't feel like reading. He was watching the second half of a nature program when his cellphone rang.

"You're still up," Donna said. "I was worried it might be too late."

"Where are you?"

She was at the front door of his building. He pressed the buzzer and waited for her in the hall. When she came out of the elevator, he said, "Do I look too eager?"

She didn't answer, but when she reached him she put her arms around his waist and rested her head on his shoulder. Snowflakes melted against his cheek. She took a step back, keeping her hands on his waist. "You, sir, are seriously interfering with my concentration."

When she was inside and he had taken her coat and poured her a drink, he asked her about her day. She sat in his chair again. She took a swallow of whisky, set the glass on the side table and looked at the ceiling for a moment, exposing a column of pale throat. When she looked at him again, she said, "Wouldn't you rather just fuck me?"

Afterward, when they were lying side by side, the telephone beside the bed rang. Cardinal propped himself on one elbow and checked the caller ID. Delorme. He didn't pick up.

"Cop's life, huh?" Donna said. "Lots of late night calls?"

"That wasn't work."

"Aha—you exceeded your credit limit again."

"It was a friend," Cardinal said. "My best friend, actually."

"Tell me about him."

"Another time, maybe."

She turned on her side and kissed his shoulder. "I didn't mean to pry. I'm just interested. You can tell a lot about people by their friends. Not that I have any myself."

"I doubt that."

She lay back down. She held a strand of golden hair before her eyes, contemplated it for a moment and let it go. "My husband was my best friend. It's funny—I didn't think of him that way until he left. It was so painful, I wanted to turn to my best friend and say, 'Oh, God, this *hurts*.' But of course, he wasn't there to turn to."

"I'm sure you have other friends."

She shook her head. "I'm curious about people. I like my work. I like to ask questions. Learn things. But I don't want them with me at the end of the day. Husbands I get. Lovers I get. But friends . . ." She turned on her side again. "I'm surprised you have a best friend, actually. I mean, the way you spoke about your wife the other night, I assumed . . ."

He took hold of her hand and held it up. She had small, neat fingers, the nails clipped short. "Why would your husband leave? It's hard to believe anybody would be that dumb."

"Ray was a lot of things, but dumb, no. He just got tired of my being a bitch."

"Were you a bitch?"

"Definitely."

Cardinal looked at her. "I suppose I can see the potential."

She smiled. "I was stupid. He was a very kind man. He looked after me—tried to—didn't drink a lot, didn't chase other women, watched over the finances okay. But, I don't know, somehow he got under my skin and I just had to protest. Naturally, it came out in the worst way."

"You slept around."

"Worse. With his best friend."

"Jesus. You *were* a bitch."

She nodded—once, a simple affirmative. "I actually didn't realize how much it would hurt him till after I'd done it. Ray was devastated."

Cardinal turned on his side and put a hand on her shoulder. "Why are you telling me this? Are you trying to warn me off?"

"Maybe." She gave a wan smile. "I just—you're so different from me, that's all. Loyal to the same woman for thirty years. I'm envious—not just of her, your wife, but of you. I can't imagine what it must be like to be that stable."

"Boring, most of the time."

"I don't think so. Not in your case. But I don't seem able to sit still. Every time life hands me something that looks like it might be steady, comfortable—something that might last longer than a few months—I manage to destroy it."

"But you didn't do that entirely on your own. His so-called friend helped."

She shook her head. "It actually doesn't take two, John. Believe me, I've done it many times."

"There you go, warning me again."

"Or maybe I'm just trying to talk myself into being a better person. Maybe you're worth changing for."

"You don't even know me."

"And pretty soon you won't want to know me."

"Now we're getting melodramatic."

She put her arms around him and held him close. A hot tear slid onto his chest and cooled there.

"People can change," Cardinal said. "I've seen it happen. People turn their whole lives around."

She sighed, and reached up to touch his face. "What a lovely story."

31

BY THE TIME CARDINAL GOT OUT of the shower in the morning, Donna was gone.

After the morning meeting, he checked his phone messages and returned a few calls. Even though he had something of a mental block about responding to e-mail, he spent the time while he was waiting for Mendelsohn answering as many as he could. Of course, Mendelsohn couldn't call to explain why he was so late; his cellphone was on the bottom of Trout Lake.

At ten o'clock, he called the Highlands. No answer in Mendelsohn's room. The FBI man struck Cardinal as a little eccentric, a bit of a klutz, but also completely reliable. Not the sort who says nine a.m. when he means ten-thirty or eleven. Cardinal grabbed his coat and drove to the Highlands and parked next to Mendelsohn's Alero. A maintenance man was pushing a snow blower, blasting geysers of white into the blue of the sky.

Young Mr. Dee was not happy to see Cardinal again. Across the front desk, he radiated clouds of Scope-scented dismay.

"I need to visit one of your guests," Cardinal said.

"Certainly, Detective. What name?"

"Mendelsohn."

The manager checked his computer and got the room number and dialed it. He kept the phone clamped between his ear and shoulder and continued typing away at something the whole time. He put down the phone. "I'm sorry, Mr. Mendelsohn must have stepped out." He pointed toward the house phones. "Would you like to leave a message?"

"I need to see his room."

"Oh, I don't think we can . . ." He scanned Cardinal's face and whatever he saw there changed his mind. "I'll look after it."

In the elevator, he said, "Please tell me this investigation will be over soon."

"It won't."

He led Cardinal down the second-floor corridor to room 218 and rapped smartly on the door. "Weird thing is, our bookings for the next two months are actually *up*, year over year."

"I wouldn't have thought a double murder was great publicity."

"Me either." He rapped again.

"Open it."

"Please—we're not going to have that discussion again, are we?"

"No," Cardinal said. "We're not."

The manager took out his pass card and opened the door. He took up the same position as last time, back against the door, holding it open. "Sounds like he's in the shower."

The mirrors, the windows, even the TV screen, were fogged with steam.

"Mendelsohn?" Cardinal stepped farther into the room and stopped.

Mendelsohn was on the floor between the toilet and the sink, in a half-curled position. Blood had formed a pool above his head in the shape of a thought cloud in a comic book. Cardinal placed a hand on his shoulder. Dead some time.

He knelt down to get a better look. There was a dark hole above Mendelsohn's right eyebrow and an exit wound at the back of the skull that had taken a good chunk of bone and brain with it before it hit the wall above the toilet. Another entry wound below the Highlands logo on his bathrobe seemed to have produced no exit wound that Cardinal could see. That one would explain the hole through the bathroom door. It was about waist-high if you were standing, but if you were sitting on the toilet, as Mendelsohn clearly had been, it was about level with your right lung. That was like him, to get himself murdered while he's about to take a dump.

Cardinal called it in. It was only when he got off his cell that he remembered Mr. Dee, paler than before, but still at his post by the doorway.

"We're going to need your security tapes again."

"That's going to be a problem."

"Why?"

"In response to the last incident, we're having an expert do a thorough review of our security system. The cameras have been down the past three days."

"Fabulous."

"This is going to be another loud, messy business, isn't it?"

"You might be in for a few cancellations."

⁓

While he was waiting, Cardinal turned off the shower and stood in the bathroom trying to picture how it had all transpired. Mendelsohn must have turned on the water to let it get hot before showering. Then he'd sat down on the toilet.

The bullet that had caught him in the chest, after passing through the door, was telling Cardinal something. He spoke, barely above a whisper. "You're in the hallway and listening at the door and you hear the shower running. Somehow you get past the lock and step inside. The shower is running, the door is closed. Why do you shoot straight through the door? Why did you aim straight for the seated position?"

Gloved, Cardinal stepped out and pulled the bathroom door shut. There was barely an eighth of an inch clearance, and even that was obscured by the deep pile of the carpet.

He opened the door again, avoiding the sight of Mendelsohn. "No. You knew he was sitting down. The door must have been open."

He turned to look at the folding closet doors that faced the bathroom. Mirrored from floor to ceiling. The door on the left was closed flat and reflected Cardinal's image and Mendelsohn's lower legs curled on the floor. The other door was ajar. Cardinal could see the shoulder of Mendelsohn's trench coat in the space between the two doors. The angled mirror on the right reflected the bed and part of a nightstand.

"You were under the bed," Cardinal said. He went to stand beside it. The closet door now reflected the toilet and Mendelsohn's bare feet.

"He leaves the door open to let some of the steam out. Then he decides to use the toilet. He sits down, but no—he's not comfortable with the door open—so he pushes it closed.

"You come out from under the bed. You stand outside the bathroom door and fire once. Did you use a silencer? You fire once and hear him fall. While he's still on the floor, you open the door—he wouldn't have locked it—and you put one in his skull."

Cardinal went back to the bed. Mendelsohn slept in the other one and used this one as a desk. Papers were stacked in eight neat piles. Cardinal stood over them, scanning the headings. He tried to judge if any one pile was messier than the others, but the arrangements gave no clue.

Ident arrived with their cases of equipment. Cardinal asked them to pay particular attention to the space under the bed. "I'm taking this," he said, holding up a tiny notebook by the corners. He had just removed it from Mendelsohn's coat pocket.

Arsenault dusted it, but it wasn't of a texture that would hold prints. He stuck a tented number card in the coat pocket and photographed it and then he stuck an evidence tag onto the notebook with the same number, the time and his signature. He handed it to Cardinal. "You're responsible for getting it to the evidence room."

～

The hotel lobby was already full of reporters. There was Nick Stoltz from *The Algonquin Lode*, Brian Murtaugh from the local cable station, even Grace Legault from the CBC. Donna was beside her, looking at Cardinal with expectation but nothing more.

They clamoured around him. Do you have a positive ID? Do you have any suspects? Is it the same killer?

"We have a deceased middle-aged male, not local, obviously the victim of foul play. I can't give you anything more right now."

Donna didn't throw any questions at him. He had been dreading she would say something like, "Is it true he was with the FBI?"—something that would drive the others into a frenzy, and also raise suspicions that she might have a special contact inside the investigation.

In the parking lot, the snow glare made his eyes water. He got into his car and started it. His cellphone rang and he had to slot the shift back in park to answer.

"Mendelsohn had an interesting contact." It was Donna's voice. She was standing beneath the hotel marquee looking out toward the parking lot but not at him.

"How'd you know it was Mendelsohn?" Cardinal said.

"I didn't. Thank you for confirming."

"Where'd you get the name?" Cardinal said, angry at himself now.

"Come on—I do have more than one source, you know."

"Do you use the same technique with all of them?"

"I'm not going to dignify that with an answer."

"All right. Okay, I'm sorry. Who's this contact?"

"A guy who works in New York Homicide. He and Mendelsohn worked together on something a couple of years ago. His name's Stuart Nathan—he's probably a lieutenant by now. Does this mean I'm not going to see you later?"

"Well, it means I'm looking at long hours."

"Call me when you can," she said, and clicked off.

Cardinal drove by the entrance on his way out of the lot. They didn't wave to each other.

⁓

Back at his desk, Cardinal called the New York field office and spoke to the special agent in charge, Wesley Walker. Chouinard had already informed him of Mendelsohn's death, and Cardinal assured him they would do everything possible to catch his killer. He asked for a complete copy of the file Mendelsohn had brought with him.

"You don't have it? Mendelsohn made a complete copy just before he left—we don't let the originals out of the office."

"We have his copy. But here's my thinking: Mendelsohn couldn't have had any enemies from up here. Whoever killed your man likely knew he was going to connect our murders up here with his other cases."

"How would this person know? You're saying he was recognized by someone from a previous case?"

"We've had a lot of press on this one, a lot of coverage. I just did a quick check, and there are pictures of Mendelsohn with me on two local news sites. Whoever killed him didn't take the whole file, because that would give the motive away—he probably took some specific thing. And if we figure out what that was, it may lead us right to him."

"You make big leaps. You and Agent Mendelsohn must've got along well."

"I liked him."

"You'll have the file as soon as possible."

Cardinal hung up and started leafing through Mendelsohn's notebook, a catch-all item in which *Buy new socks* appeared next to *Run Divyris US database*, and *Check Canuck military weapons* was under *Fix bathroom sink*. On the last page he had written, *Interview fur biz old-timers*.

32

LLOYD KREEGER FIGURED he had about twenty minutes, thirty at the most. The one called Papa was out hunting with the girl. The one called Jack had gone out about an hour ago; Lloyd had heard the Rover start and drive away.

His most important asset right now was not his property, not his interests in the fur business, not his mining stocks. His most important asset was a broken wood chisel that a workman had left behind. Lloyd had tossed it in a wastebasket that had subsequently filled up with paper. His captors had overlooked it when they checked his room.

The chisel's blade was not sharp enough to cut butter. Where the handle used to be, there was a stub of steel armature. Lloyd was trying to pry apart the manacle that held the tether to his ankle, but it was hard to get any leverage because he couldn't immobilize the chain. He upended the wastebasket and held the chain across it with his left foot. The links shifted too much for him to get any purchase.

He adjusted the chain so that the link was half off the wastebasket. He thought he had widened the gap a little. He looked around for something else to use as a tool. In the top drawer of the dresser he found a twelve-inch ruler. It was maybe three-eighths of an inch at the thickest part, tapering to the metal straight edge that ran under the measurement units.

He pressed the straight edge into the tiny opening in the link. He placed his foot over it and pressed down, raising himself a little on one leg. That wedged the ruler into the link. He tried to force the chisel in beside the ruler. It was not difficult to work the tip of the blade into place, but it was hard to do much more with the broken handle.

He reached down and lifted the chain, gripping it on either side of the link. He moved as carefully as he could, but the chisel toppled and fell. It took several tries to get it wedged into place again. His back was hurting from bending over from the bed. He raised his right foot, holding the chisel steady with his fingertips. The chain had just enough play for him to get his foot on top of the chisel handle. He put his weight down, and then, with a sudden movement that risked the whole operation, he put all his weight on it, rising an inch from the bed.

He felt the chisel give beneath him. When he took his foot away, the blade was lodged firmly between the ruler and the link. He lifted the whole delicate array back onto the upended wastebasket. He pressed down with his left foot to hold it in place. He pushed the chisel handle to the right and felt the link give a little. He adjusted the chain under his foot and pressed again.

The ruler toppled and the chisel came away in his hand. The gap was wider. He positioned the next link over the gap and stepped on it, pulling up on both sides of the chain. The link gave and he fell backwards on the bed.

He moved quickly to the living room and looked out the front window. Papa and the girl would almost certainly come back the way they had gone. The tracks of their snowshoes led into the woods on the far side of the lake.

He went to the mud room by the side door, ignoring the phone and computer in his office. The invaders had disabled both—he didn't know how. His car keys and snowmobile keys were missing from the hook. It would be difficult for anyone to make it through these woods without snowshoes, let alone a seventy-five-year-old man. He put on his parka and stepped outside.

The footpath between the house and the bunkhouse was snowed over, but not nearly as deep as the drifts out front. He made it across the clearing and found the key Henry always kept hidden under the stoop. He opened the door and the smell choked him.

He closed the door again, on the edge of vomiting. He took a few lungfuls of clean cold air and held the last one. He went in and saw right away there were no keys on the table or on the wall.

Still holding his breath, he got down beside Henry, ignoring the black hole in his forehead, the dark congealed mass beneath him, and felt in his pocket. He pulled out a penknife and a few coins and put them in his own pocket.

Henry was lying on his left side. Lloyd managed to search his jacket pocket before his lungs gave out. He breathed in through his mouth, but even so, the gases of decomposition made his stomach convulse and he vomited on the floor. He kept on retching well after there was nothing left in his stomach to expel.

He managed to roll Henry over so he could get at his other pockets. Chewing gum, a plumber's business card—absolutely nothing he could apply to his present situation.

He got to his feet and retched again. The phone on the kitchen counter looked intact, but when he lifted the receiver, there was no dial tone. Snowshoes would have afforded him a few options, but Henry's snowshoes were gone from their usual hook by the door.

Lloyd looked out the window, across the clearing and into the dark woods. Nothing moved. No sound beyond the hum of Henry's fridge.

He opened the door and closed it behind him and set off at a run. One of Papa's gang had ploughed a path along the former logging track that led to the highway. He hoped Jack had gone to town and not just a curve or two up the road. His troublesome joints would not get him through snowy woods.

Lloyd had been blessed with good health most of his life, but he had never gone in for serious exercise. His lungs threatened to quit on him altogether after a couple of hundred yards and he slowed to a fast walk. Pain had already invaded his ankles and calves and gave no sign of retreat. He kept moving.

If he got to the highway, he could flag somebody down. Old man on the side of the road, someone would realize he was in trouble. Someone would stop.

He heard the Range Rover before he saw it. The suspension squeaked every time it went over a bump.

Lloyd plunged into the snow on his right and allowed himself to fall. He toppled forward, got up and did it again, throwing himself into the snow, twisting hip and knee in the process. Cold seared his wrists, ankles, neck. He sat up and scooped snow over his legs. He lay back down and heaped snow over his midsection to hide the vivid red and blue of his parka.

The Rover rounded the curve, its rattles and squeaks louder. Lloyd lay still. The gearshift was yanked and ground into reverse. The engine revved a couple of times. The truck came into the snow until the plough blade smacked into Lloyd's feet.

The engine revved again.

Lloyd staggered to his feet, brushing snow from his face and hair. Snow melted around his neck and ran in icy rivulets down his back and chest.

The driver was the mean-looking one with the three-day stubble and squared-off moustache. Jack. He rolled down the window. A gun emerged, then his face.

"Move."

"No."

"I said move."

"I'm not going to."

Jack tapped the door panel with his automatic. "You look ridiculous. Old man in the snow, trying to act tough."

"Just shoot me and get it over with."

"Nossir."

"Go on, why don't you. You shot Henry. You're going to kill me too."

Jack narrowed his eyes at him. "Not on your say-so."

"No, it'll be when that insane man you call Papa tells you to."

"That's right."

"You do everything he says."

Jack tapped the truck with his gun again.

Lloyd waded through the snow toward the passenger side. When he got to the door, he tried to run. Jack reversed and cut him off with the Rover. The passenger-side window rolled down.

"Back to the house, old man."

"Let me go. Tell that man I got away while you were out hunting."

"Nossir. You're mistaking me for some kind of Third World customs official—some pathetic, no doubt Negroid flunky can't wait to violate his own integrity for two bits and a pair of Ray-Bans. But at this moment I am the keeper of life and death, and I will not be corrupted by you. You're suggesting I be derelict in my duty and then tell lies about it. I never lie."

"As if that's something to be proud of, when you go around killing people."

"Some people need killing."

"Well, shoot me here, why don't you. I don't want to be chained up day and night, terrified about when it's going to come."

"It'll come when it comes. Stop trying to control it."

"Is this how you want to live your life? Hiding out? Running from the law?"

"Appears so. Otherwise I wouldn't do it."

Lloyd started around the front of the truck, but it lurched forward, cutting him off.

"Understand something, Lloyd. If you force me to shoot you, it's not gonna be in the heart or the head or anywhere quick and convenient. I'll place a round somewhere it'll hurt bad, and you'll have to sit there watching yourself exsanguinate. Blood and pus everywhere. Now you march up that road ahead of this here truck before I put one in your bowels."

—

The far side of Black Lake. Papa and Nikki moving through thick woods. They each carried a rifle and wore light down jackets of a white and brown wavy pattern. When motionless, they were almost invisible. On their feet, gaiters, boots, snowshoes.

Papa led the way off-trail. He knew without being told where Nikki and Lemur had set the leghold trap. At the top of a small rise, he beckoned and she joined him, awkward on her snowshoes. He had been right about the light jacket: with the fleece top she was wearing underneath, Nikki was as warm as if she were indoors. Papa had taken her shopping in Manhattan, the best shopping trip of her life.

But now, having come so near to the place where they had set the trap, she was thinking about Lemur. The newscast had spoken of him as if he were just a common criminal. They didn't even know his name, and it bothered Nikki that they dismissed this brave and friendly young man as if he were just some loser who got what he deserved.

She asked Papa about it. He didn't tolerate questions in the normal course of events, but he was in teaching mode now, and it was like being gathered into his strong arms.

"Lemur knew the risks," he told her. "He came into this organization knowing full well what lay ahead. You get killed, that's just part of the life. That's what keeps your heart pumping, and the blood pounding through your veins. You want an ordinary life? Don't join the family. You fear danger? Don't join the family. You want to work in an office? Punch the clock? Draw a regular salary? Don't join the family. Is that what you want? You want to be ordinary?"

"No, sir."

"I'm your Papa, not your 'sir.'"

"I don't want to be ordinary. Neither did Lemur. Do you really think Jack killed him?"

"Jack would never have come back if he had. He knows I'd know."

"You think it was just some psycho?"

"I have my theories, but let me worry about that. Later on, if it's the correct move tactically, you may be called into play. How are your boots holding up? Are your feet okay?"

"They're really warm."

"Hands?"

She was wearing thin gloves under large mittens. Her hands had never been warmer. "They're almost hot."

"All right. Which way is Algonquin Bay?"

She took off her mitten and held a compass in her right hand. The needle found north and she pointed in the opposite direction.

"Good. And Toronto?"

She pointed again.

"Good. How about the airfield? You remember from the map?"

She pointed west.

"And the railhead?"

A couple of degrees east of due south.

"Bus station?"

Same.

"Good."

"How come you know this area so well?" Nikki said. "Is that just from the map?"

"I used to work in the fur industry. Business brought me up here more than once. Now get out your knife and cut me down a lot of pine boughs. Shake the snow off them and spread them here." He indicated a hollow just below a fallen log.

For the next twenty minutes, Nikki hacked off pine boughs, shook them out and laid them on top of the snow. Papa collected boughs as well, spreading them fussily in the hollow. When there was a thick bed of them, he told her to stop.

He knelt on the boughs and sighted along his rifle over the top of the fallen log. Nikki got down beside him. Papa spoke to her in a low voice, as if they might be overheard. "The boughs are important," he said. "You're warm in your layers, right? Well, doesn't matter how warm you might be, if you lie against a surface with a temperature of thirty-two degrees Fahrenheit, it's going to leach the warmth right out of your bones. You'll be shivering in no time. The boughs keep you insulated."

"They're kind of soft, too. How did you learn all this stuff—was it from the army?"

"Some. But you know, it's really through families that knowledge and traditions get passed down. My father taught me a lot before he died, and now I'm teaching you. Okay, get into position."

Nikki copied Papa's pose, sighting with her smaller rifle over the log. Both of them wore white woollen caps pulled low. The silence was so thorough that Nikki felt it press in upon her, an urgency around her rib cage.

"It's so quiet," she said.

"Way I like it."

"I can hear my own breathing." And that was all she could hear, unless you counted the rustle of her jacket, the barely audible click of her trigger as she adjusted her grip. Her right hand, wearing only the glove now, was beginning to get cold.

They stayed that way for maybe fifteen minutes.

"How do you know we'll see anything?"

Papa pointed off to the right.

"What?"

"Tracks."

Nikki squinted in the direction he had pointed. Faint V-shaped marks, not even fresh. "Wow. I didn't even notice them."

"Rabbit. You can tell by the V shape and the close grouping. Front paws go down, back paws come forward and hit the ground either side. The short drag mark is the tail."

"Papa, I don't think I can kill a rabbit. They're too cute."

"I'm teaching you survival, Nikki, not aesthetics. You want to go back to working the streets, that door is always open."

"I don't. But I don't want to kill any rabbit, either."

"You eat chicken, don't you? Turkey? Pork? Beef? You wear leather belts and shoes. You drink milk. All of those things involve pain and suffering for animals. You don't mind it because you don't see it. You may think you love animals and that's why you don't want to kill one, but the fact is, you are responsible for the deaths of a hundred or so animals a year, and that's just from eating, that's not counting shoes and gloves. You're just squeamish because you're not used to taking responsibility for what you eat."

It wasn't a subject Nikki had given a lot of thought to. All she knew was, it didn't feel right to be waiting for a rabbit in order to kill it. Anxiety stirred in her belly. She needed to pee, and she didn't fancy doing it in the snow, but she didn't want to irritate Papa by mentioning it.

Papa shushed her, although she hadn't said anything. He nodded slightly, the smallest incline of his chin toward the trail. A grey rabbit rose on his back legs, sniffing the air, pink nose twitching with the thoroughness of a connoisseur's. He was maybe twenty yards away, slightly below them.

"We're downwind," Papa said, barely audible. "He won't smell us. You have him in your sights?"

"Uh-huh." He was cute, this bunny, but Nikki felt that consideration leaving her as tangibly as someone slipping out of a room. The mechanics of getting his torso between the V of her sights, setting the bead on him, pressed other thoughts from her mind.

"You're too loose," Papa said. "Pull the stock into your shoulder. Hard. You want the recoil to pass through you, not kick you."

She did as he said. The rabbit made three hops and stopped once more to sniff the air. Nikki was on him. Her heart was beating hard, insistent.

"Any time," Papa whispered. "No point waiting."

"I can't."

"If you can eat chicken, you can kill a rabbit."

"I can't."

"Can't doesn't cut it. Can't doesn't contribute to the common good. Can't doesn't feed your brother. Can't is for weaklings and hypocrites. Take responsibility for your life. You're flesh and blood, and you live on flesh and blood."

"I'm gonna feel like shit if I shoot him."

"Do it."

"I can't."

"Do it."

She squeezed the trigger, and then everything happened at once: the recoil shoving her shoulder back, the slam of sound in her eardrums, and the rabbit, lifted off his feet and flung sideways, red spray hitting snow.

"And that's dinner," Papa said.

He turned and looked at her, but Nikki stayed motionless, still sighting down the barrel as feeling returned to her shoulder.

"He's still moving." She could hear the panic in her voice, the higher pitch and the approach of tears.

"Go and finish him off."

Nikki was on her feet, kicking at snow, looking for a rock, a large stick, anything. Everything was hidden under snow. The rabbit was struggling to get up, but he was hit in the shoulder and his forepaws wouldn't work.

"Oh, Jesus," Nikki said. "I can't find anything. There's nothing here."

"Shoot him again. Get close and give him one in the head. And don't shoot your foot."

Nikki climbed over the log. It was difficult in snowshoes, and she nearly twisted her ankle. She went down the slope and the rabbit struggled harder. His whole left forepaw was slick with blood and there was a red bloom on the snow around him.

Nikki sighted down the barrel. The rabbit's black, glistening eye looked at her wildly, and even though she was only thirteen, Nikki recognized the universal cry of nature for more life. She took aim, but before she could pull the trigger, the rabbit laid his head back down on the snow and whatever it was that had made him a living creature and not a rock or a stick or a stone left the small body. The black, glistening eye went dull, and ceased halfway in its final effort to close.

33

ON THURSDAY, CARDINAL AND Delorme flew to Toronto and drove a rental car to the morgue. The pathologist had no surprises for them. Irv Mendelsohn died as a result of the bullet wound to the head. The chest wound would have killed him by itself had the cranial devastation not done the job first.

In Firearms, it was Cornelius Venn's conviction, expressed with his patented mixture of paranoia and hostility, that the recovered slugs had been fired from a Browning Hi-Power nine-millimetre—the same make and model as the gun that killed the Bastovs, but not the same individual firearm. It was, however, the same weapon that was used to kill the boy at the ATM.

Half an hour later, they were driving up the 427 toward the airport.

"We know the kid was with whoever killed the Bastovs. And whoever killed him also killed Mendelsohn, making it likely it was either the guy who helped him steal the car from the airport or someone else who joined them later. But why would he or they kill him while he was robbing a cash machine?"

"Thieves fall out," Cardinal said. "It happens all the time." He changed lanes and made the turnoff to the airport.

Delorme continued thinking aloud. "How did this person or these persons even *know* about Mendelsohn?"

"Well, they're not dumb," Cardinal said. "Obviously, they know how to find people. I didn't tell you, but the other night that American reporter was followed—or at least thought she was—by a guy in his mid-fifties."

"She was? When did she tell you this? And why wouldn't you mention it at the morning meeting?"

"Because she admitted she was probably just being paranoid. She's been writing about the Russian mob, and maybe the horror stories got to her."

"How would they even know about her? It's not like she's Diane Sawyer."

"She's been following the Bastovs. Following the fur business. She's tenacious, same as Mendelsohn. Maybe these characters knew the two of them were closing in. Maybe they were even interviewed by them at some point—who knows? The Bastovs were at least partly connected to Russian organized crime, and those people kill cops and journalists whenever they feel like it."

Delorme pointed to the sign for rental returns, and Cardinal drove into the underground lot. He parked under the Avis sign and an attendant trotted over to take their mileage. While they were waiting for him to print out a receipt, Delorme said, "I still don't see why you didn't tell me about Donna Vaughan being followed."

"I have no explanation, Lise. Maybe I was just overwhelmed with Scriver."

"You haven't spent five minutes on Scriver since this case hit the fan."

"Lise, I was *kidding*."

"*Ouais, ouais — t'es bizarre, tu sais?*"

"I do know what that means."

"Good."

—

The Peel Regional Police, Airport Division. Cardinal had arranged to meet Rob Fazulli in Terminal One. He took them into his office, which managed to be glass-walled and claustrophobic at the same time. Flight announcements echoed beyond the walls.

"Funny thing," Fazulli said. "I was convinced I would hate working at an airport. But you know what? Airports are great places when you don't have a flight to catch. You truly get to watch the world go by."

He put a disc into a player and turned on the monitor. The image was surprisingly sharp: a line of travellers with shoulder bags and carry-ons in postures of weary resignation.

"Passport control," Fazulli said. "Terminal Two. Twenty-seven minutes before your suspect vehicle was stolen. Note the guy with the hoodie and the backpack. Parking lot image was too low-grade for facial recognition, but he could be one of your perps, right? Guy who jimmied the car?"

"Could be," Delorme said. "But lots of people dress like that. Practically everyone under twenty dresses like that. Certainly can't tell from this distance."

Fazulli looked at Cardinal. "She always this impatient?"

"Always."

Fazulli hit fast-forward. Now the kid was before the immigration officer, maybe four feet from the camera.

"It's him," Delorme said.

"Such certainty all of a sudden," Fazulli said.

"We've seen him up close," Delorme said. "He got himself killed robbing an ATM. That's definitely him."

"I don't suppose you have the flight number," Cardinal said.

"You seem to have forgotten what an ace crime fighter I am," Fazulli said. He picked up a folder, opened it and read aloud, "Liam Rourke. Age sixteen. American Airlines flight 592, La Guardia to Toronto."

"Fantastic," Delorme said. "You guys're better than TV cops."

"Better-looking, too," Fazulli said.

"This is great, Rob," Cardinal said. "Now all we need to do is look for two single male passengers on that flight who purchased their tickets probably at the same time."

"We already did that. And it's a good thing we did, because we could never have matched up the images from that parking lot video. I've been pushing for new equipment over there, but car theft is not exactly a priority with the TSB. Here's what we got." He switched the video to another image. A man in his fifties, salt and pepper hair, close-cropped. Handsome and fit.

"Facial recognition any good on this one?" Cardinal said.

"Totally useless. So much for TV cops. Those guys can extract DNA from a postal code. But almost as good—same flight, same ticket purchase. This is Curtis Carl Winston, fifty-eight."

"Winston?" Cardinal said. "Winston sounds kind of familiar."

"I believe there was a British prime minister by that name. Fat guy with a cigar?" Fazulli handed over the folder with a flourish. "Sir? Madam? Thank you for using Peel Regional Police, Airport Division. We accept MasterCard, American Express and most forms of alcohol."

Cardinal thanked him. "And listen, Rob. Next opening comes up in our department, I'm starting a Draft Fazulli campaign."

"Appreciate it, but I could never live up north. Too much crime."

—

"Is there something going on with you, John?"

They were sitting at the Air Canada gate, waiting for their flight to board. Cardinal watched a little boy stumble toward the window, gripping a teddy bear. He told her he was fine.

"You seem distant."

"This case is taking up a lot of mental space."

"But suddenly you're not talking to me, you don't want to watch videos together, you're not calling. And when I call, you're either too busy or you don't answer. Have I done something to upset you?"

"I'm just preoccupied with the case, that's all."

Delorme pulled out her BlackBerry and scrolled through her messages. After a while she said, "I know we're just friends, but we see each other a lot—twice a week usually, outside of work. We've been doing that for, what, nearly a year now? But suddenly you change the rules, and you won't even talk about it. Just because you're seeing Donna Vaughan doesn't mean you have to stop talking to me."

"I haven't stopped talking to you."

"Is she the jealous type? Wants you all to herself?"

"There's nothing for her to be jealous of. I haven't even mentioned you." Cardinal felt bad before he had even finished saying it.

Delorme looked at him, scanned his face once and looked back down at her BlackBerry. She pressed the dial button and put the phone to her ear, got up and walked over to the window.

34

Lloyd Kreeger was talking to him, but Papa was not paying a huge amount of attention. He was writing a murder story in his head. Setting pen to paper had never interested him, but he took an authorial pleasure in the orchestration of violence. His victims and perpetrators may have been real people, but they had no more knowledge of his intentions than characters in a book.

"Here's my proposal," Lloyd said. "Why don't you do this?" The old man was in the rocking chair, rocking in a manner that Papa would have described as overwrought. Obsessive, even.

Papa was lying on the couch, flat on his back with his feet raised at one end. It was his belief that this posture offered certain cardiac benefits. "I had a proposal for you once, Lloyd."

"It's not the same. That was just a business proposition. This is—"

"What's your idea, Lloyd?"

"You could secure me somehow in the bathroom. Leave me enough food so I wouldn't starve. A mattress. And you could arrange it so someone was alerted two days later. Doesn't have to be the law. Just someone who will let me out."

Papa was outlining in his head a very different scenario. The old man lying in bed asleep. Nikki sneaks in, dead quiet, and shoots him under the jaw. Does it in such a way that it could be suicide. Of course, that would require that the weapon be left behind.

"Are you listening?" Lloyd stopped rocking. "It would give you time to get away. Lots of time. Two days, you could be in Paris, Rome, Mumbai—how's anyone going to catch you?"

An amateur—your average spouse-killer, say—would put the gun in the deceased's hand. No, thanks. Papa had a rule never to leave a gun behind. He was not a superstitious man, but he had an almost mystical relationship with the Browning HP nine-millimetre, and he was not about to hand one over to the enemy.

A typed suicide note? That would raise immediate suspicion. On the other hand, that could be exactly the point: make it *look* like some amateur was trying to make it *look* like suicide. Layers within layers.

"What I'm saying is, it's not essential to kill me."

Papa turned his gaze from the ceiling to Lloyd. "Nobody said anything about killing you."

"You killed Henry. Why would you kill him and not me?"

"Henry made threatening remarks."

"That's highly unlikely. Henry was the most gentle man I ever met."

"Maybe that's what got him killed."

"Well, now you're contradicting yourself."

"Life contradicts itself all the time. Rosy sky at dawn, lightning at noon. Snow in the middle of May. A quiet postal employee suddenly slaughters his colleagues. A mother kills her daughter. Any man who speaks the truth is going to contradict himself."

"One minute Henry's making threatening gestures, the next minute he's too gentle to live. Why can't you just admit you killed him? Clearly you're not ashamed of it."

"I never killed anyone."

Papa liked the idea of the inept amateur up to a point. But what if they bought it? It was boring; there was no wit to it. Suppose Nikki were to put a *different* gun in his hand, some run-of-the-mill street weapon. The cops would know pretty fast that it wasn't the murder weapon. Then it would look *really* amateurish.

". . . could alert my lawyer two days later. You're safely out of the country."

"We're not worried about getting out of the country."

"Maybe you should be."

"We're not."

What would make it really clever, what would make people sit up and take notice, would be if Nikki didn't leave *any* gun. She could make it look like a suicide in every way but not leave the gun. Then—assuming the cops wouldn't theorize that some thief came in later and stole it— they would have to know the whole scene was constructed. Designed. You go to all that trouble and then you undercut it. They couldn't ignore that. They would know this was a crime with an author—a controlling but invisible hand—and intelligence outside it, beyond it, directing the whole thing. And yet above it.

Lloyd was still talking, trying to force alternate endings.

"Lloyd," Papa said, "I'm not going to kill you."

—

When Papa asked Nikki to meet with him alone, in the basement, she knew what was coming.

"You've been with us a while now, Nikki."

"It doesn't seem that long."

"That's good. The time's going fast?"

Nikki shrugged.

They were each sitting in an armchair angled toward the basement fireplace. Like an old married couple, Nikki thought.

"Do you see yourself ever going back to your former life?" Papa didn't look at her. He kept his eyes on the flames.

"Never. Hustling again? No way."

"You want to stay with the family?"

"Well, yeah. I've never been this happy in my entire life."

"To stay with the family, you have to be loyal to the family. Loyal to the family above all else."

"I know that. I'm loyal."

"Nothing comes before the family. Not love, not hate, not the law. The family always comes first."

"Cool. That's exactly how I feel."

"Are you ready for an assignment?"

"I'm ready."

"Mr. Kreeger is not part of the family. He is an enemy of the family. A danger to the family. As soon as we leave this place, he'll go straight to the police and give them everything they need to put all three of us away for a very long time—possibly for life. The time will come—and it's going to come soon—when he will have to be killed. Are you prepared to do that?"

"Oh, man, I don't know. I don't think so."

"You don't think so?"

"Well, not a hundred percent. I don't want to get in over my head. I don't want to make a mistake, mess everything up."

"It'll be for the safety of the family. Lemur was going to do it. He volunteered, in fact. But Lemur's not with us anymore. Jack could do it, obviously. Or I could. But I'd like you to do it. That way your loyalty is proven, and you have a home for life."

35

AT HOME—IF YOU COULD CALL this overheated, jungle-humid apartment any kind of home—Cardinal was finding it difficult to focus. For one thing, there were three women in his head. Delorme, with that impassive look in her brown eyes, the look she had given him in the airport. A look that said he was not the man she had thought he was. And Donna Vaughan. The remembered heat, her intensity, kept reaching into his mind in a way that stirred him physically.

And Catherine. Would there ever come a time when he would close his eyes and not see Catherine's face? Their life together flashed before him every night. And every night, as if he were an obsessive accountant gnawing at a statement that refused to balance, he found his own contribution to that life wanting. "I did my best," he said aloud, and his words echoed off the window, the fridge, the kitchen table cluttered with the creased and dog-eared Scriver file.

He had dug Scriver out again for one reason: the name Winston. He was sure—well, almost sure—that he had come across the name in the stack of folders with their faded type, their broken rubber bands. Winston. Not exactly a rare name, but not common either. There were no Winstons listed in the Algonquin Bay telephone directory; he had checked.

Walt Scriver, his wife Jenny, their son Martin. No Winston there, and none among the many neighbours who had been interviewed, people who lived in the same block as the Scrivers in town. Out on Trout Lake they had had no neighbours. Their cottage had been located on the island at the end of Island Road. It might well have been visible from the Schumacher place, had the Schumacher place existed back then. Cardinal looked again at the black-and-white photos of the exterior. A small, unassuming cottage, in need of paint and a new porch. Large woodpile neatly stacked under the overhang, a canoe hull-side-up on a couple of sawhorses, bathing suits strung on a line. A rickety dock hanging in the water off the rocky beach. Duly noted, indeed emphasized, in the file, the Scrivers' aluminum outboard—not there.

Cardinal's cellphone started to vibrate and turn on the kitchen table.

"I knew you'd still be up." Donna Vaughan.

"You want to come round a little later? Say in an hour?"

"Can't. I have to rewrite a piece for *New York* magazine. I get it in tonight or it doesn't run and I don't get paid."

"Russian mob?"

"Just the fur business. I filed it months ago and they're just getting around to running it. I'm adding a sidebar about the Bastovs—and don't worry, it won't mention anything off the record."

A sudden longing for her took Cardinal by surprise, but he said nothing. Uncertainty over a woman was unfamiliar terrain, untrodden since before he met Catherine. He wasn't sure if it was longing for Donna Vaughan or just a longing to not be alone in his humid apartment with his ancient file and his dead-end ideas. Or just longing, another word for being alive.

"I have to get off the phone," she told him, "or I'm going to get too distracted by you."

"Good," Cardinal said.

"I hate self-discipline. What little I have."

"Maybe we can make up for it soon," Cardinal said.

Interior photos showed a scene of abandoned tranquility. Dishes in the sink, three coffee mugs still on the dining room table, *The Algonquin Lode* open on the table. Fishing and hunting trophies on one wall, a locked gun rack, rods and tackle. A tiny rabbit-ears television in one corner, lumpy-looking furniture arranged around it. Large wood stove.

The hunting gear interested Cardinal. There was a note in the file that Mr. Scriver had been an occasional trapper, nothing too serious. Lots of guys go trapping just as a way to spend time outdoors.

The newspaper on the table was open to the movie listings. Algonquin Bay's theatres had long ago been relegated to the shopping malls, but back then the city had had four, three on Main Street and a drive-in on Trout Lake Road. Someone had circled the ten p.m. showing of *Butch Cassidy and the Sundance Kid* at the drive-in. To make the show, the Scrivers would have had to take the boat out around 9:45, head over to the marina where they kept a parking spot, and drive to the theatre. They never got to the car.

There was no guarantee that they had in fact set out for the movies. No one in the few cottages on Island Road recalled hearing or seeing them on the water. The property was thoroughly searched. A stack of file photos showed layers of excavation. There were close-ups of bones that proved to be those of a moose long buried—something that happens to moose remains when hunters lug home more than they can chew. These dated from long before the Scrivers bought the cottage.

Their house in town had shown no signs of recent occupancy. It was the Scrivers' summer routine to move to the cottage at the end of June and stay there until the school year started in September. And so, lacking any signs to the contrary, the Scriver case became Algonquin Bay's most famous presumed drowning.

The lake had been searched by divers, and dragged, but no trace of the Scrivers or even their boat turned up. Mr. Scriver was a long-time employee of Lands and Forests, and the department had pulled out all the stops in the search, but even their sonar remained stubbornly silent.

Cardinal flipped through report after report. Interviews with relatives: yes, the Scrivers all got along well. Friends, neighbours, employers—all the interviews pointed to the Scrivers as a happy family. Martin, the son, fishing and hunting with his dad all the time, mother a good teacher, father a reliable employee devoted to the outdoors. Martin had caused some anxiety— thrown off the school hockey team for putting a referee in hospital, a juvenile charge of break and enter. And then there it was: supplementary report filed by one Detective René Proulx, interview with the son's girl-friend, Cecilia Winston.

Martin Scriver had found summer employment in a deer census project north of Temiskaming. Cecilia Winston lived in the area. She was interviewed at a memorial service for the Scrivers that had taken place nearly a year after their disappearance. Inexcusable that she hadn't been interviewed earlier. No, she had never seen any violence or anger in Martin. If anything, he was extremely protective of her in a mostly male environment. No, of course she hadn't heard from him after the disappearance. *Subject agitated and tearful. Related devastated by Martin S's presumed demise. How it came just a week after the death of her brother (Kurt, 18. Leukemia).*

Cardinal pulled the folder from his briefcase and opened it to the airport image of Curtis Carl Winston, age fifty-eight. That made him eighteen at the time of the Scrivers' disappearance.

—

Cardinal spent the entire following morning on the Internet and the telephone. The Registrar General's office confirmed that one Curtis Carl Winston of Temiskaming, Ontario, had indeed died on July 5, 1970, at the age of eighteen. The facsimile showed cause of death as leukemia. The certificate had been issued three months after the boy had died.

Cardinal called Jerry Commanda at OPP. "Jerry, there's a private contractor called DeepTec in Toronto that does a lot of salvage in the Great Lakes. They have a new gizmo called a side-scanning sonar we're going to need, and it'll be way out of our budget. Can you guys swing it?"

"Why? Did Chouinard put you on the Scriver case or something?"

"As a matter of fact, he did."

"Wow. I was actually joking."

"There's a connection to the Bastov murders. And if the Scrivers' boat is on the bottom of Trout Lake, this sonar might be able to find it."

"John, the lake is frozen."

"Scriver was a long-time Lands and Forests guy. I'm thinking they'd be willing to help out."

"Well, you don't need a private contractor," Jerry said. "Orillia HQ bought one of those units in the summer. If it's not in use, I should be able to get it up here today."

Things didn't go as smoothly with the Armed Forces. Cardinal had to call many different numbers before he finally got through to an actual human being in the archives who could answer his questions, which were very few. Did they have any record of a soldier by the name of Curtis Carl Winston? *Yes, they did.* When had he enlisted? *September 15, 1970. Mobile Command, Petawawa, until 1972, by which time he had attained the rank of corporal. He trained briefly with the U.S. Army Rangers as part of a JTF known as the Northern Rangers — specialists in survival, sabotage and CHC — combat in harsh conditions — since disbanded. Discharged in 1974.*

"Thank you," Cardinal said to the female civilian who had dug all this up for him. She sounded young, and Cardinal had an image of a girl with a laptop, an iPod and a Starbucks mug on her desk. She also sounded smart. He told her he had another question.

"I'm listening, sir."

"I need to know what was the sidearm they carried at that time."

"In Mobile Command?"

"And in the JTF."

There was silence at the other end.

"I've stumped you," Cardinal said.

"No, sir. Just contemplating the best way to run down this information. You know what? It's not my department, but it may be under Logistics and Weaponry, or whatever it was called way back then. Let me see if I can go through them to pull up some stuff—or actually, the Web may be faster. Can you hang on?"

—

"This is what I don't understand," Delorme said. She had to speak loudly over the noise of the icebreaker's engine. "I don't understand what made you go to the Armed Forces in the first place. Why did you even think of checking the military?"

They were ploughing slowly through the ice surrounding the island where the Scrivers had spent their last summer. An OPP diver sat silently beside them like a lonely astronaut in a penumbra of tubes, his helmet on his lap. Sunlight flashed off the snowy surface of the lake, making their eyes water.

"It was a lucky guess," Delorme said. "Admit it. It was an incredibly lucky guess."

"It was Mendelsohn's idea," Cardinal said. "I read an entry in his notebook that said Check Canadian military weapons, and it took me a while to realize what he meant. He had two cases of beheadings where there was also a firearm involved. And in both of them, that firearm was a Browning HP. Not the same gun, but the same model. Same as with the Bastovs. Same as at the ATM. And you have to wonder how and where someone becomes so devoted to a particular weapon. It's not like it's the most common firearm in the world, but in the early seventies it was standard issue for the Northern Rangers."

Two dark figures stood on the rocky beach of the island, Jerry Commanda and Ian McLeod. Behind them, a beautiful summer house of red cedar had replaced the homely Scriver cottage. The Schumacher property was visible across the short stretch of ice that was now churned and broken as if it had been jackhammered. Jerry Commanda was a persuasive guy, but it must have taken a star performance even by his standards to persuade Natural Resources to produce their breaker. It was nothing like a Coast Guard boat, amounting to little more than a modified outboard with a reinforced, sharpened prow, and another two weeks of winter would have rendered it useless. Progress was noisy but slow.

At Cardinal's request, their pilot steered the boat around the elongated tip of the island, opposite to the direction the Scrivers would have taken had they been crossing the bay to get to a movie. Cardinal tapped on the door of a squat, telephone booth–like structure in the middle of the boat and spoke to the OPP technician inside.

"Anything yet?"

The tech shook his head. "Just a lot of logs. Amazingly well preserved, considering there hasn't been any logging here for at least sixty years." Cardinal could see over his shoulder that the images were crisp and clear.

"How deep?"

"Ninety, ninety-five feet. It'll get deeper real soon."

"Scriver senior helped map the underwater geography," Cardinal told Delorme, "and his son worked with him a couple of summers on fish surveys and so on. They both would have known the lake very well."

They came around the tip of the island and the wind picked up. A slice of black water eased the way for fifty yards or so.

The diver spoke up for the first time. "Deepest part of the lake coming up. Hundred, hundred and twenty metres. Current moves in the opposite direction, so they likely wouldn't have searched this area back when."

"And they assumed the Scrivers were headed toward town," Cardinal said.

On the island, Jerry Commanda and Ian McLeod emerged from the trees and stood on the beach. Both folded their arms at the same moment against the wind, as if they had rehearsed.

The booth door opened and the tech called out, "Got something."

Cardinal leaned in. Again he marvelled at the clarity of the image. "Delorme, you gotta see this."

Delorme stuck her head in. "Can we get closer?"

"Hell, yes," the tech said. "Closing in as we speak. It's snagged under an outcropping. No way the old sonars would have detected it."

The image took on greater contrast and definition. An oar hanging over a gunwale. An outboard off the stern.

"Two hundred and thirty feet," the tech said. "You see what's *in* that thing?"

"Yes," Cardinal said. "I do."

They helped the diver screw on his helmet. He switched on his lights, and the red LED began to flash on his tiny videocam. He climbed over the side and lowered himself into the water, and they watched him sink into darkness. He had to pause several times on the way down to adjust to the pressure.

Cardinal's phone rang and he took it from his inside pocket and opened it. It was Ian McLeod, wanting to know how long he was expected to hang out on a beach in the middle of goddam winter. He could see McLeod giving him the finger across the water. "Hang in there," Cardinal said.

"By the way—checked out Divyris's so-called business contacts. He's dreaming. Yes, he has been meeting with people, talking with people, hounding people, and they're totally sick of him. Apparently he won't take no for an answer. One guy's threatening to sue the bastard for harassment. Are you having fun out there?"

"Hell, yes. This'll be in the papers tomorrow."

"Yeah, but in a good way?"

Cardinal clicked off and watched the video monitor, the sunken boat coming into view.

"Are we sure it's the Scrivers?" Delorme said.

"Fourteen-foot aluminum. Evinrude thirty-five on the back," Cardinal said. He asked the tech to get the diver to scan the motor. A couple of seconds later the image changed and the motor filled the screen. Cold and depth combined make an excellent preservative, and the lettering was still visible after forty years. Evinrude thirty-five.

When the diver turned back to the boat, Cardinal heard Delorme's sudden intake of breath and felt his own pulse jump.

"There are only two bodies," Cardinal said. "Ask him to get close on the faces."

It took the pilot a moment to respond. "He says they don't have any faces." The image drifting lazily across the monitor screen confirmed this. "They don't even have any heads."

"I have a feeling," Cardinal said, "that this is not the usual disarticulation you get with drowning victims."

The tech shook his head. "Too deep. Too cold. Anyway, the feet would have detached first, then the hands, and as you can see, the extremities are still intact. Minus a finger or two."

"Forty years," Delorme said. "Incredible."

No sound but the scrape of ice against their hull. Hundreds of feet below, the water was perfectly clear. The zoom lens lurched into extreme close-up, swerving from one detail to another: a jagged hole in the hull, then another, both made from the inside. The diver's light flared off sharp edges of aluminum. Then a third gash.

"Look at that," Cardinal said. "The axe is still wedged in it."

The view swung back to the bodies, extreme close-up, the white gleam of neck bone.

—

Aromas of fresh coffee and pastries filled the meeting room. All the CID personnel were there, and Chouinard was so excited he had even called Police Chief R. J. Kendall to sit in on the debriefing. The mood was festive, even triumphant.

"You're losing me," Chouinard said, in urgency, not anger. "Who was it dies of leukemia?"

"Curtis Carl Winston. Eighteen-year-old brother of Martin Scriver's girlfriend. Never did anything suspicious in his life until he joined the army—which wouldn't be suspicious either, except for the fact he did it two months *after* he died."

"So we think Martin Scriver killed his parents and took off? He joins the army using someone else's identity?"

"Back then, all you needed was the name of a dead person close to your own age. He gets a few years in the military, Northern Rangers— where, incidentally, he becomes intimately familiar with the Browning HP nine-mil, their official sidearm at the time."

"And he keeps the name ever since?"

"There'd be no need to change it. No one was looking for Curt Winston, and it's not like it's such a peculiar name there couldn't be more than one person with it. Also, he moved to the States soon after discharge. FBI New York is pulling out all the stops for us on this. They've already traced Winston back to several different businesses going back to the seventies— tanneries, fur farms, always stuff connected to the fur trade. He was located for a long time near Seattle, and also just north of New York—both fur auction centres. We're making a list of our locals who've been in the business for decades and we're going to start talking to them tomorrow."

"Back up a minute." Chief Kendall raised his hand as if to halt oncoming traffic. "Just because the boy's body is not found with his parents doesn't make him a murderer. His body could have drifted away. He could have been kidnapped. He could have been killed somewhere else."

Cardinal pulled a photo from the folder in front of him. "Got this from Armed Forces archives. Curtis Winston's enlistment photo." He handed it to the chief and reached into his briefcase and pulled out a book. "Chippewa High School yearbook, 1969. Take a look at Martin Scriver's picture. It would have been taken about a year earlier."

"Fantastic," Kendall said. "This is very good work."

"Martin Scriver had some problems with violence—put a hockey referee in hospital, for example. I'm thinking he lost it with his parents, possibly over something trivial, and he went crazy with the axe. We've got two cases in the States where a couple and their child are murdered. And Bastov would have been a third, except the son had to miss his flight. In some screwed-up way, he could be re-enacting the crime over and over again."

"Why would he do that?"

"I'm not saying it's sane. Maybe to suggest there are other killers out there—killers who attack couples and their kids and chop them up. A twisted way to imply he never killed his parents, that it was the work of itinerant strangers."

"He's murdering people to prove his innocence? Until today, nobody even knew for sure the Scrivers had been murdered."

"He did. It's himself he'd be trying to convince."

Chouinard nodded at Jerry Commanda. "The lake is OPP territory. Are you guys going to boot us off?"

"Oh no, sir. Scriver's been a joint operation since the beginning of time. We're happy to keep it that way. Besides, it's totally bound up with Bastov."

"I take it that's from your evidence warehouse?" Chouinard pointed at the banker's box on the table in front of Jerry.

Jerry tapped the top with a long index finger. "Martin Scriver's stuff from the cottage. He left everything behind, even his wallet—probably to make it look like he was a victim. We got a toothbrush, and a hairbrush with some hairs in it could be useful for DNA. It's at the Orillia lab. We have prints that were lifted from the cottage and from his wallet."

"I love this," Chouinard said, and turned to Chief Kendall. "Don't you love this?"

"I'll love it more when we have someone behind bars."

36

CARDINAL WAS NOT MUCH GIVEN to parties or celebrations. But police work rarely went better than it had gone this day, so when Donna came round that night with a bottle of champagne in one hand and her notebook in the other, he was uncharacteristically effusive.

They clinked glasses and he sat in the recliner and she sat on the end of the couch, pen poised above her notebook. She wanted to use a recording device but didn't protest when he said no. "Learning shorthand," she said, "is my one undeniable achievement in life."

Cardinal related the day's events, beginning with his search through the ancient Scriver file. "It's amazing," he said. "When you get right down to it, a good file is a cop's best friend. Routine interview, forty years ago, but the guy who did that interview made a careful note of a name. Completely peripheral—the son's girlfriend's *brother*, for God's sake, you can't get much more peripheral than that—and there it is, waiting for me forty years later."

"But it was you who thought there might be a connection," Donna said. "Let's not be too modest here."

Cardinal shrugged. "The name Winston rang a bell, that's all." He sat up and pulled the champagne from the ice bucket and filled her glass. "Champagne in the middle of the week. I can't believe I'm this decadent."

It was making him light-headed, not his usual response to alcohol. Or perhaps it had more to do with this extremely attractive woman and her serious grey eyes. He told her about the new sonar, about the diver sinking into the black water, and about everything else, right up to the matching photographs. Then he sat back and said, "I never talk about my cases. I feel like a blabbermouth."

"But you're hardly saying anything at all." She tipped her head back in a silent laugh, exposing that pale throat, the perfect sculpture of neck and collarbone.

The phone rang and Cardinal talked to Jerry Commanda for a few minutes, about their plan for the next day. "I got your list of the fur business lifers," Jerry said. "You want some help interviewing them? Could generate a lead on where the guy's holed up. Of course, if he has any sense, he'll be long gone by now."

"I don't think so," Cardinal said. "I think he has unfinished business here. He killed Mendelsohn, and he may have come after an American reporter who's been covering the fur business and the Bastovs for a couple of years."

He was looking at Donna as he spoke. She came over and knelt beside his chair and started undoing the buttons of his shirt.

Jerry asked if the reporter was getting extra protection.

"I'm working on that." The heat of her fingers on his skin, undoing his belt. He grabbed her hand and held it while he finished with Jerry. "Listen, tomorrow I'm going to have the FBI's complete file. It should arrive before ten. I'll be taking a quick look at that and then I'm heading out to Lloyd Kreeger's place. He's the oldest guy on our list."

Jerry agreed to assign some of the others to OPP detectives and they would confer again in the afternoon.

"What list?" Donna said when he hung up. She was still kneeling in front of him, hands on his thighs. "Who's Lloyd Kreeger?"

"Lloyd Kreeger is the oldest living man in the fur industry, at least around here. Also the richest. We've got a list of old-timers in the business who might recognize the airport security photo of our suspect. Until we get a direct lead on this guy's whereabouts, it's back to plod, plod, plod."

"You have a photo of your suspect and you weren't going to show me?"

"Didn't even think of it, I got so excited about Scriver. We even have a name now. I can show you, but you can't have a copy and you can't tell anybody."

"No, that's all right. Show me when you feel comfortable with it. Right now I'd rather just undo this belt."

Later, when she was putting on her clothes, Cardinal asked her to stay. "Look, the guy may have come after you before. He could try again."

"He chopped up a couple of people, he killed a cop and that ATM kid—do you honestly believe he's still in the area?"

"The OPP doesn't. But I think he might be."

"I don't."

"Yeah, but you also thought he was Russian *mafiya*."

"Touché." She zipped up her jeans and pulled on her sweater.

"Really, Donna—you might not be safe out there."

"All right, all right. Enough already." A glint of anger in those grey eyes. "Sorry," she said, and her face softened. "I've had bad experiences with people looking after me. I guess I overreact. Don't get up. What are you doing?"

"I'm walking you to your car." Cardinal pulled on his pants and a sweater. "And don't overreact."

⁓

In the morning, Cardinal had Mendelsohn's copy of the FBI file spread out on the meeting room table next to the new copy that had just arrived. Using both hands, he was turning over pages one by one, old file to the left, new file to the right.

Also open on the desk, Mendelsohn's tiny notebook. He had flipped through it again and found a note that he let linger in the back of his mind as he scanned the FBI files. *Simultaneous crimes,* the note said, *from major to petty. Check. THINK!* Mendelsohn's notes were in the same emphatic voice as his speech, and Cardinal had a vivid image of the man in Morgan's Chop House, explaining, italicizing, gesturing with his fork.

Mendelsohn was right about the simultaneous crimes, of course. They knew the ATM robberies were committed by Winston's young associate. But other crimes? Maybe in New York, but right now in Algonquin Bay there was nothing. As far as they knew.

Cardinal paused, a hand on either file. Under both hands a handwritten note scrawled across an otherwise blank page: *Begelman — photos to ViCap*.

Under his left hand, a file of some fifteen hundred pages. Under his right hand, the same thing—plus a manila envelope. He lifted it out from under the stack and opened it and pulled out scans of original photos. The scans were excellent, the U.S. federal government being significantly better funded than a small Ontario police department. Even the captions at the bottom of each one were sharp.

Some were crime scene photos, courtesy of the NYPD. Nine-mil casings, headless torso, shattered computer screen. Cardinal flipped through these quickly. Then he came to a picture of a ramshackle old house partly hidden by trees, the caption *Zabriskie Farm. Search following phone tip.*

Cardinal read the note on the search. They were looking for a young man named Jack, who according to the anonymous caller lived at the Zabriskie farm and seemed to know a lot about the Elmira murders. The place was occupied by a bunch of young people, most of them students at the state university located a few miles up the Hudson. Jack had come to the farm after meeting one of the students in a local bar. He'd only stayed two days, and they were glad to see him go. Photos of his room showed a bare mattress, a bare floor, a dog-eared copy of *The Art of War*.

There were pictures of the residents, three on the porch steps, another couple in the kitchen. Cardinal could picture the police technique. They had no reason to arrest these people, but they wanted a record—faces to go with names—so they had taken the pictures in a casual way. It was something cops did for the sake of a complete file. There were two young women and two boys, early to mid-twenties all of them, and none looked like the vague description from the anonymous call: eighteen-year-old white male, five-ten, short hair. But Cardinal returned to the photo of the group on the porch and looked closer. He went very still and held on to it for a long time.

—

As far as Lise Delorme was concerned, Cardinal was behaving oddly. They had been scheduled to drive out to the Kreeger place, but instead of leaving together, he had told her to pick him up at the Highlands Lodge; he had to go out there and interview the manager again for some reason. It would have made more sense for them to just stop on the way, but he didn't want to hear about it.

So here she was parked in the Highlands parking lot, watching the skiers riding the hoist to the top of the escarpment. They were dressed in all manner of the latest gear, some even wearing balaclavas. The temperature was dropping and showed no sign of doing anything else for the rest of the day. Storm clouds were cascading over the hills, heading for Parry Sound, according to the radio.

When Cardinal finally emerged, he pointed to his red Camry. Delorme got out and locked the unmarked. She went over to the Camry and opened the door. "Shouldn't we use the company car?"

"Mine's got better snow tires."

She got in and he had the car moving before she had the belt done up. He took a right on Sutton, merged onto the highway and headed north. She was curious about his stop at the Highlands, and normally she wouldn't have thought twice about asking him. But Cardinal didn't speak or even look at her, and his mouth was set in a hard line. She was fed up lately with trying to pry answers out of him, so she made an inner vow to say exactly nothing unless spoken to.

They passed the first subdivisions, and then Trout Lake on the right.

"It's getting so dark," Delorme said, and then remembered she had meant to stay silent.

Cardinal didn't respond. She couldn't tell if he was angry or worried. He was utterly transparent about small things; whenever he was irritated or impatient, she knew instantly. But it was precisely when he was feeling the most that he became most unreadable. All those times his wife had been admitted to hospital, you never would have known from his day-to-day behaviour. A little quieter maybe, nothing more than that.

The only exception was when his wife had died. Even a stoic like Cardinal couldn't keep that to himself, and it had been heartbreaking to watch. He continued working right through his grief, of course, which was his way of dealing with it. Delorme thought she would have done the same thing. No, she corrected herself, I would have *tried* to do the same thing.

They drove out past Island Road, out past Clayton Crossroads, until they were well beyond the built-up areas. The forest closed in around the highway, the rock cuts glistened, ridged with snow. A uniform greyness descended, grew darker and seemed to grip the road. Storm.

"This is looking serious," Delorme said. "I thought it was supposed to hit Parry Sound, not us." Weather didn't usually make her nervous, but the onset was sudden, the change in light dramatic.

Cardinal's expression, or his lack of one, did not change and he did not speak. He kept right at the speed limit, slowing slightly and without comment when it began to snow. The first flakes were large, swaying leaflike as they fell. But as the colder temperature took hold, the flakes got smaller, the wind blowing them into fine slanting lines.

Delorme had never been to Black Lake, had never even heard of it before that morning. She had googled it and found it to be little more than a black dot surrounded by white, a full stop on an empty page. Except the page was actually forest.

She didn't know how Cardinal even saw the sign, which was small and obscured by clinging snow, but he turned off the highway onto a road that was deeply rutted under the snow.

"Four-by-four territory," she said, and put a hand on the dash.

"Lots of people come out here," Cardinal said. "Popular area with hunters."

"Not in this weather."

The car dipped and jounced and Cardinal had to slow to a crawl. The snow was falling so thick and fine, it was almost like looking into fog.

Cardinal's phone rang and he unzipped his coat to reach inside. He checked the readout, but they hit a bump and he had to grab the wheel. "It's Chouinard. You take it."

"Where are you?" Chouinard said. "Where's Cardinal? Why aren't you on radio?"

"We're in John's car, heading out to Black Lake."

"That's unfortunate—you're going to miss the big show. Suspect's been sighted on 124, big fur farm down there. OPP SWAT team should be hitting it in about fifteen minutes."

"Damn," Delorme said. "We'd never make it. Hold on a sec." She told Cardinal what was going on, asked him what he wanted to do.

"We're out here now, we may as well interview Kreeger. If he knows Winston from way back, it could be useful in court."

Delorme related this to Chouinard.

"Stick with it," the D.S. told her. "Oh, and keep an eye out—we got a report on a couple of lost hunters. Tony and Gary Burwell. Last the family heard, they thought they were near Black Lake, but they're not sure. I thought everybody had GPS these days, but apparently not. No way we can mount a search party in this weather. How's the driving?"

"It's shit."

"I figured."

Delorme closed the phone and dropped it into Cardinal's outside pocket. "D.S. says to keep an eye out for a couple of lost hunters."

"Actually, I'm thinking we should head back. Clearly the weatherman was stoned when he called this one."

"If you can find somewhere to turn around."

He steered them slightly toward the right then hard left and came to a stop.

"Did you hear that?" Delorme said.

He paused with his hand on the shift. Delorme rolled down her window a couple of inches. Snow swirled in. The cry came again, a man's voice. Distant enough to be faint, close enough for them to hear the distortion of panic.

"That way," Cardinal said, indicating west, the forest.

"I hope you have snowshoes in the trunk."

"I don't."

37

OPP Sergeant Tyler Adams used his right-hand tactical glove to pull back his sleeve and check his field watch. He was on the ground in a specialized assault vehicle along with five members of a Tactics and Rescue Unit, three guys and two females. They were as fit as a SWAT team could be, as highly trained. All of them were expert in special weaponry, explosives and marksmanship.

They were crammed into the Forced Entry and Rescue truck, parked in a field behind a barn off Highway 124, waiting for the chopper that would carry the other half of the team. The FEAR truck is a highly modified Hummer that can drive through pretty much anything. It features a hydraulic lift system that is useful for surprising an enemy by ignoring the ground floor and inserting personnel directly into an upstairs bedroom.

The team were double-checking their weapons and supplies, the flash-bang and Stinger grenades, the nine- and ten-millimetre Heckler & Koch submachine guns along with the sniper rifles, and a bulky infrared motion sensor that filled up most of the interior. Adams checked his watch again. The chopper was due in three minutes.

Information was thin. A man in his fifties, armed to the teeth, had taken over the Magnet-One Ranch three miles up the road, one of the bigger mink-farming outfits in the province. Husband away at the auction in Algonquin Bay, wife and kids possible hostages. According to the 911 call from a terrified ranch hand, the guy was claiming credit for chopping heads in Algonquin Bay.

Adams was new to the position as commander of the TRU team. The last commander, Glenn Freitag, had successfully taken down many highly defended grow ops and defused his share of nasty hostage situations, but his last deployment was to take back a park that had been commandeered by militant Mohawks, and it had gone terribly wrong. A couple of Indians were shot dead and Freitag was reassigned and off the force long before the SIU and all the public inquiries had finished digesting it.

A SWAT team is not for show, Adams thought. It's a loaded weapon and you don't draw it out of the holster unless you're serious.

He heard the *whup-whup-whup* of rotors and stepped out of the truck. He had to squint, his eyes dazzled by sunlight on snow. The Eurocopter TwinStar came over the trees, scarlet against an indigo sky, low enough for its twin engines to kick ground snow into Adams's face. His number two's voice came over the radio, crystal clear on the new FleetNet frequency. "So what happened to the blizzard?"

"We shipped it to Algonquin Bay. They responded by sending us a total wacko."

"Nice. We're ready to rock 'n' roll in here, just tell us where you want us."

—

Cardinal and Delorme were only a couple of hundred yards into the bush, but already you would never have known there was a highway nearby. The snow was mid-shin level, just high enough to get into their boots. Cardinal pointed to the west where a line of hydro poles stretched over a slight rise in the terrain. "Keep those as a landmark. Even if we get totally disoriented, we can follow them home."

"I plan to stay oriented, thanks."

They walked on, enveloped in the deep hush of snowfall, the only sounds the nylon of their parkas rubbing against itself, the occasional muffled snap of a twig, and the huff of their breathing.

They passed a dilapidated shack on their left, all but hidden among the trees. In summer it would have been invisible.

"Trapper's cabin," Cardinal said. "Totally illegal, no doubt."

For a while the wind was somewhat baffled by the woods, the odd breeze causing a sudden vortex of snow. But soon it came in earnest and drove the snow into their faces. Cardinal could no longer hear their steps, or Delorme's breathing, only his own.

They stopped and listened. Cardinal called out—once, twice—and they waited for an answering cry, but none came.

"This is *so* not good," Delorme said.

Cardinal pointed to the hydro wires, still faintly visible. A single heavy wire branched off. "That'll be for Lloyd Kreeger's place. Black Lake's the only thing on the map around here."

"Well, if those hunters are here, presumably they'll figure that out too." The fur trim of Delorme's hood was entirely white, as were her eyebrows and eyelashes.

"I'm still not seeing any tracks. Not that they'll last long in this. Let's follow the wire. They could be further up ahead. If they're not, we'll stop at Kreeger's and get warm and alert search and rescue. They'll come out the minute this is over."

Cardinal angled off to follow the direction of the new hydro line. The snow flew thick and wild. The hydro line was getting harder to make out.

Cardinal stopped and called out again. Even though the temperature was now well into the sub-zero zone, he was sweating. "Voice isn't going to carry far in this. Are you up to keep moving? We could go back to the trapper's shack, wait till visibility improves."

"We must be pretty close to Kreeger's, no?" Delorme's white eyebrows looked like stage makeup. "I say keep going."

She pressed on ahead of him.

Every few yards they had to pause and wait until the wind dropped or changed direction enough to allow a glimpse of the hydro wire. It too was covered with clinging snow. There was a broken birch up ahead, one large branch angling down to the ground. Cardinal made note of it, happy for anything that might be a landmark. He called out again. They waited. Heard nothing. Moved on.

The shriek when it came was so loud, so inhuman, that Cardinal did not immediately associate it with Delorme. She staggered and fell in front of him, but he thought that was in response to the scream. He scanned the forest, but the world around them was a grey-white nothing.

Delorme was writhing on the ground. She was screaming again, but suppressing it so that it came out as a desperate growling.

Cardinal went to her. The iron clamps of a bear trap were closed on her shin.

"Try to hold still," he said.

Cardinal was no hunter. He had never even seen a bear trap up close. He brushed snow away. The thing looked ancient, a malevolent jaw of black iron.

Delorme was hyperventilating, growling through her teeth.

Cardinal searched for a release mechanism amid the springs and levers. He found a loop of metal and pulled on it. It was rusty, but finally the long pin came free. He pulled the clamps apart and Delorme fainted, her head lolling to one side. Cardinal gently felt her shin. The break was palpable through her jeans.

Her face had gone white. That would be shock, the blood retreating from the extremities. The unconsciousness was merciful, but she was more vulnerable in this condition to hypothermia and frostbite.

Cardinal sat on his heels and pulled Delorme into a seated position so that her head hung down over her outstretched legs. He rubbed at her wrists and slapped her face lightly to bring the blood back.

She came to and vomited, choking. Cardinal turned her on her side and she cried out and vomited again, coughing into the snow. "Sorry," she said. "Sorry. Oh, fuck, it's bad, John."

"We're going to have to get you back to the trapper's shack. I could try to carry you."

"No. That would hurt worse."

"Can you get up on one leg?"

Delorme grabbed a handful of snow, reaching past the steaming vomit, and washed it over her face. She took another small handful into her mouth.

"Pull me up."

Cardinal got to his feet. He took off his glove and reached down. Delorme took off her mitten and put it in her mouth and bit down on it. Their hands locked together.

"On three," Cardinal said. "One. Two . . ." On three he pulled hard and Delorme raised herself on her good leg, growling through the leather mitten.

She swayed against him and Cardinal thought she was going to faint again, but she didn't. They arranged themselves so that Delorme had one hand on Cardinal's shoulder and he had an arm around her waist. Every time she had to take a step, he held her tight, taking her weight.

Their tracks were already nearly obliterated. It took them more than half an hour to cover ground that had taken ten minutes. Delorme had to pause after each step and take deep breaths. Blasts of wind hurled the snow into their eyes, obscuring all but the few feet in front of them. Panic began to crash through Cardinal's bloodstream. Finally the cabin came into view, pillowed in snow. It was boarded up, padlocked.

"Do you want to lie down while I try and open this place?"

"If I lie down, I'll just have to get up again." She leaned against a tree. Cardinal pulled her hood forward and fastened the snaps.

He examined the padlock. It was not the biggest lock he had ever seen, but he had nothing to bash it with. There was nothing under the overhang except firewood. He unzipped his parka and took out his Beretta. The first shot dented the lock. The second broke it open.

The shack wasn't much, two tiny rooms with two bunks in each, a wood stove in the middle. Cardinal left the door open so he could see, and helped Delorme inside and onto the closest bunk. He wanted to ease her broken leg onto the bed, but she wouldn't let him. She lay there, barely conscious, wrapped in her parka.

Cardinal went back out and pulled some firewood from the middle of the pile. He found a small hatchet and used it to split one of the logs into kindling. He primed it with some charcoal starter, lit it and closed the stove door.

Blankets were piled up on one of the bunks. Cardinal spread one over Delorme. He found a Coleman lantern that still had fuel in it and got it going. The cabin was lighter, but with the door closed and the windows boarded up, it still looked like midnight.

"You want me to try and take your boots off?"

Delorme didn't open her eyes. Her cheeks were wet with melting snow. Cardinal got a towel, almost clean, and wiped off her face. Shadows pulsed around him.

There was nothing to do now but wait out the storm. He lay down on the other bunk and, without intending to, fell asleep.

"John. John, wake up."

It was warmer now. He didn't know how long he'd been asleep.

"John, wake up."

He sat up and rubbed his face.

"I heard something." Delorme spoke in an urgent whisper, as if someone might be listening. "Someone in trouble."

Cardinal pulled on his boots.

The cry came again, muffled, all but lost in the wind.

"Must be close," Cardinal said, "or we wouldn't even hear it."

Cardinal stepped out into the storm. Snow blew hard across the opening in his hood. He had no peripheral vision at all. He made his way back the way they had come as far as the broken birch. The cry came again. Cardinal strained to see through the snow. A dim flash of orange.

"Hold on there," Cardinal called out. "Police."

The figure came lurching toward him, yelling incoherently, a man in a hunter's vest.

"It's okay," Cardinal said. "You're okay. Police."

"There's a man. You have to help me. A man. He killed my brother. He killed him. He's insane. He's going to kill me too." The man ran toward Cardinal, tripped and sprawled into the snow.

"Are you one of the Burwells?" Cardinal said.

"What?" The man was on his knees now, swaying, stunned. "Yes. Tony Burwell. Please, you have to help me. There's a fucking lunatic out there. A bunch of them. They shot my brother. They tried to shoot me."

"All right, you're okay now." Cardinal had drawn his Beretta, safety on. "Where's this man?"

Burwell didn't appear to hear him. He scrambled to his feet. "They took our wallets, they took our guns, they took everything. They killed my brother! Get me the fuck out of here!" The man broke into sobs. "Oh, Jesus . . ."

"It's okay. You're all right. There's a cabin nearby."

"Jesus, my brother. Fucking insane people out here."

Cardinal led him to the cabin. The moment he opened the door, the man sank down in a corner and hugged his knees to his chest. "Shut the door, man. Shut the door. They're gonna find us."

"What happened?" Delorme said.

"Mr. Burwell was attacked, along with his brother. His brother's dead."

"You got to get me out of here," Burwell said. He seemed unaware he was shouting. "I do not want to be here. Can't you radio for a helicopter or something? I need to not be here."

"There's nothing flying in this weather. We're just going to have to wait it out. Tell us how it happened."

"Oh, God. We got lost. My brother and me. It was my fault. I was supposed to bring my GPS and I forgot—I just fucking forgot. We didn't have a compass or nothing. Storm's about to hit and we see a hydro wire. Follow it a ways until we come to this tiny lake. House on the far side. Like a real house, not a cabin. So we head for it and—Jesus, I still can't fucking believe it—my brother ends up with his leg in a trap. Can you believe that? A fucking trap."

"I can believe it," Delorme said faintly.

"Go on," Cardinal said.

"Oh, God." The man squeezed his eyes shut. "Oh, God. I panicked. I just totally panicked." He turned pleading eyes to Cardinal. "He was screaming. My brother was screaming and I was trying to figure out the trap and I couldn't. I mean, I've never even *seen* a trap like that.

"So I run to this house, screaming and yelling for help, and bang on their door. Guy answers. Big guy, maybe fifty, fifty-five, and he's got a gun in his hand. That should have clued me in right there."

"Did you see anyone else?"

"A girl. Girl maybe thirteen."

"Was she with him? Was she a hostage? What was the situation?"

"Fuck, I don't know, man. My brother was in a fucking trap, I was in total panic mode. I just wanted someone to come and help." Burwell squeezed his eyes shut and pressed his forehead into his knees. When he looked up again, there were tears in his eyes. "She called him Papa."

"Papa."

"Papa. 'You want me to go, Papa?' But he said no. He throws on a coat and comes with me." He collapsed once more into sobs.

Cardinal found a bottle of whisky and poured some into a glass. He handed it to the man and he drank it down in one shot. He poured him another and offered some to Delorme, but she shook her head.

The man started to calm down. "Sorry," he said. "Didn't mean to get hysterical."

Cardinal went to the door and opened it a crack. "The storm's easing off a little. I'm going over there."

"Don't do that. I can't go back there! You can't make me go back there!"

"You don't have to." Cardinal pointed to the other tiny room. "There's another bunk in there. You'd better lie down. You've had a terrible shock."

"Oh, man. Shock is not the word. I think I'm gonna go out of my mind."

"So go lie down."

The man went in to the other bunks and threw himself down on the bottom one.

"John," Delorme said in a low voice, "you can't go alone."

"They won't know I'm alone—and they won't be expecting police anyway. They won't be expecting anyone. Not in this weather. You'll be all right with him."

"I'm not worried about him. I'm worried about you."

"They have an old man hostage. I have to at least take a look."

"John, we have to call for backup."

"They won't come. Look, it's one man and a girl. And they don't know we're out here."

—

Once Cardinal had closed the door, the only sounds Delorme could hear were the hiss of the lamp, the wind outside and the occasional crackle from the stove.

From where she was lying, she couldn't see into the darkened other room. She called out, "Are you okay?"

No answer. She lay listening, the pain in her leg a deep throb. The sounds of the wind and the stove reminded her of camping trips she had taken with her parents as a little girl. The guy in the other room began to snore.

After a time she realized she was hungry and very thirsty. There would be nothing to eat in this bare-bones shack, but there were a couple of large bottles of water on a shelf near the stove. Beside them, a box of Lipton tea.

She pushed herself into a sitting position and nearly passed out from the pain. She gripped the iron frame of the bunk and waited for it to settle back into its former throb. She pushed herself to a standing position, putting all her weight on her good leg and leaning against the wall. It wasn't much worse than sitting down.

The stove and the water were a couple of hops away. The first hop got her as far as the door frame between the two tiny rooms. She gripped the frame, sucking air through her teeth.

The man was flat on his back, his mouth open slightly. He was not that old, maybe thirty, but his features bore the bruised look of the utterly exhausted. He still had his coat on, the orange hunting vest closed over it.

Delorme took three deep breaths and made the next hop. She nearly fell, and had to grab onto a wall stud. A sliver bit into her hand.

She reached for a water bottle and got it and twisted the cap off. She poured water into a saucepan and put it on the stove. There was a tremendous crack of thunder and there must have been lightning, but through the boarded-up windows nothing of the outside world could be seen.

—

Cardinal stopped to wipe snow from his eyes. There were ice pellets mixed with it now that stung as they hit his face, but visibility had improved. He could see the hydro wire again, much farther away than he had thought. His feet were wet and cold, and he wondered how long he would have before frostbite set in.

An odd shape materialized amid the diagonals of snow, about twenty yards off. Dark grey on light grey, hanging like an ink blot among the trees.

As Cardinal approached, he saw that it was human, a man dangling upside down, his hands hanging as if in surrender toward the forest floor. One of his legs was folded down, the other was held fast by a rope that stretched upward into the higher limbs. The body swayed and turned.

Cardinal gripped his Beretta. The man's face, inverted, was at the same height as his own. Cardinal took hold of one of the arms to stop the swaying. The eyes were open, a black, gleaming hole in the forehead.

Off to Cardinal's right, faint depressions in the snow led in the direction of the trapper's shack. Impossible to tell if there had been one set of tracks or two. He turned back to his original direction. There was something

orange on the ground—possibly the hanging man's safety vest. Cardinal
went to it and started brushing snow away.

It wasn't just a vest. Cardinal reached under the shoulder and turned
it over. The hat fell off, and snow slid from the features. Again a bullet
wound between the eyes. Cardinal found a wallet buttoned in the man's
cargo pants. Tony Burwell. The similarities to the hanging man beside him
were those of a sibling: same widow's peak, same dirty blond hair, same
slightly protuberant eyes, long upturned nose, small ears. Brothers.

Cardinal reached into his parka for his cellphone. Not there. He found
it in his outside pocket—not good in this weather. He hit the speed-dial
for Delorme's number. He listened to it ring five, six, eight times. The tiny
screen showed strong signal, weak battery. That would be the cold; he had
charged it the previous night.

"Delorme." Her voice was all but lost in static.

"What's your guest doing? Can you talk?"

He didn't get much of her reply. He thought he heard the word "sleep."

Cardinal spoke as quietly as possible. "Can you get outside? Signal's
breaking."

The phone crackled. Delorme's fractured voice: "hear you."

He repeated his message. "The hunters—the Burwells—are both dead.
They're both dead. Murdered. Can you hear me? Get cuffs on him if you
can. I'm heading right back."

No response except the hiss of dead air.

He put the phone in his inside pocket. Maybe his body heat would
revive the battery.

Snow was jammed in the tops of his boots. He knelt to tie a lace, and
as he did so, a sudden burn on his ear. He heard the *crack* a second later.
A powerful weapon, fired from some distance. The snow had dropped for
the moment, improving visibility. Cardinal ducked behind a tree that was
not big enough to cover his entire body.

The shot had come from somewhere between him and the trapper's
cabin. Gusts of wind kept changing the visibility. He thought he saw a
hooded figure bent low and moving. He took aim and fired. Cardinal was
a good shot in a controlled environment, but he had no confidence in his
talents under these conditions. What are you going to do now? he asked
himself. What's your next brilliant plan?

He scanned the trees. Nothing moving but snow and sleet. A stump and a fallen tree about ten yards up the trail. If he could get past that, he might have enough cover to get back to Delorme. Keeping low, he moved back slowly, keeping the tree between him and where he thought the shooter was positioned. When he was close enough, he jumped across an open space and landed hard behind the stump.

Another round whizzed by. The crack of the shot. Closer. Making a run for the cabin—left or right made no difference—would put him in plain view.

38

NIKKI BRUSHED AT HER HAIR, patted it down with her left hand, and brushed at it again. She attacked first one side, then the other, then the back. Brush, brush, brush, it made no difference. No matter what she did, it stuck out from her head in wiry tufts. The only time it looked good was when it was soaking wet, and even then it was only a matter of minutes before it started to frizz out.

"Bozo," she said to the mirror. The last time she had been called Bozo, she had nearly throttled the girl, a total skank named Charlene two cells down from her in juvie. But she said it to herself all the time. She'd had a laptop for a while—stolen, of course, but it still hurt when it got stolen in turn from her—on which there was a program where you could change your hair, your makeup, your clothes. She wished she could really do that—replace her nose, her cheekbones, her piggy eyes, and most of all this hideous hair.

Nikki curled up on the bed and held Lemur's iPod. Turned out he had liked a lot of the same songs as her. She wasn't listening to it right now because she'd forgotten to charge it, but she held it anyway.

The family was coming apart. Lemur dead, and now Papa and Jack had had another fight. Even worse, this time. Jack must have thought Papa was out hunting, because he came on to her at exactly the wrong moment. She had stepped out of the shower, dried off and—wearing her bathrobe—gone straight to her room. Jack was in there with the door shut behind them in a split second. Pulled the bathrobe off, big hands squeezing her tits then shoving her onto the bed.

The funny thing was, she'd been fucked so many times that if Jack had only *asked* her, she'd probably have fucked him too, just to keep the peace. Or at least she would have before Papa began to get to her about self-respect. But Jack wasn't asking and she fought and it was noisy and Papa burst in.

Usually when people fight, it lasts about thirty seconds. A couple of wild punches, a kick in the balls, and it's over. But this went on and on. She thought Jack would win, since he was younger than Papa, and crazier. He picked up the entire coffee table and swung it at him, Papa stepping back cool as you please—then stepping forward and shoving Jack headfirst into the wall. Jack came back at him with a knife that caught Papa in the fore-arm a good one. Blood everywhere. Papa took it away from him, but when Jack snatched up the poker, she thought Papa was as good as dead.

Papa took the poker from him too. He could have killed Jack then; he had the opportunity. All it would have taken was a crack on the head with that length of iron, but he didn't seem to want to—it was like he was being held back. He grabbed Jack from behind—by the nuts must have been, judg-ing by the way the fight went out of him—and threw him to the side door. Opened it, shoved him out with his boot and tossed his coat out after him.

There was a knock at the bedroom door, and Nikki said to come in. Papa never came in without knocking. He entered and sat beside her on the bed and put a hand on her shoulder, as if she was the one needed com-forting. He was wearing a clean shirt, well ironed—he was fanatical about ironing his shirts—and you'd never have known he'd been in a brawl and got his arm slashed.

Nikki asked how the arm was doing.

"It's fine. It's nothing. How are *you* doing?"

Nikki shrugged.

"Thank you for standing by me," Papa said. "For helping me."

Nikki didn't know what he was talking about. Sometimes Papa saw things totally backwards. "I didn't do anything," she said.

"Nikki, Nikki, what am I going to do with you?" He squeezed her shoulder. "Always putting yourself down. Minute Jack was out the door, you were right there for me. Whisky in one hand, clean towel in the other. You were my battlefield medic. I could not be more grateful."

"If I'd been thinking, I'd have got the hunting rifle and put one in his head."

"Jack's your brother. No one wants that."

"*Was* my brother."

"Oh, don't be surprised if Jack comes slinking back. I've seen it happen before, and he's not going far in this storm. When he does come back, he'll need forgiveness, and you know what? He'll get it."

He handed her the box of Kleenex and she blew her nose and tried to get hold of her feelings.

"Sit up, now. There's no call for a posture of defeat." He gripped her biceps and hauled her into a seated position beside him. He draped a comradely arm over her shoulders. They were facing the dresser mirror. "You're looking so pretty today. Did you do something to your hair?"

She pressed at the frizz. "My crazy hair."

"Crazy beautiful. That hair's got spirit, kid, same as you."

She met his gaze in the mirror and smiled.

"You don't know how proud I am," he said, "how grateful I am, that you've shared your beauty and your spirit with me. I know I don't deserve it."

"But you do everything. You look after everyone."

"Not so well sometimes, the way it seems lately."

"Jack's just psycho. He's not your fault."

"I was hoping to be a better influence."

"You are, Papa. You *are*. Like you say, he'll probably come back."

"You think so?"

She nodded.

"You're a fine individual, Nikki the Kid. You truly are, and you make me one proud Papa."

Nikki's heart was full and she wanted to give him something. Sex was the only thing she had of any value, and she would have really liked to show him what she could do in that regard. But Papa didn't want sex from her.

"I need you to do something, Nikki."

"Sure. Anything."

"We talked about it before. It's something for the family. It was going to be Lemur's job, but Lemur's no longer with us."

"What is it?"

"Well, it's a hard thing and it's crucial and it just absolutely has to be done. And to be honest, Nikki . . ." He looked at her, those honest blue eyes creased with worry. "To be honest, I'm not a hundred percent sure you're ready."

—

Delorme tried her phone again. She got crackle and fizz and nothing else. Cardinal had been trying to tell her something. Something he didn't want the man sleeping in the other room to hear. *Go outside,* he had said.

She got up on her good foot again and steadied herself against the wall, waiting for the pain to subside. It didn't, but she moved anyway, taking a quiet hop into the other room.

The man had turned on his right side. His mouth was open, but he had stopped snoring. In his left hand, an automatic. Well, you could have an automatic with you in case you wounded an animal and had to finish it off, Delorme told herself. Not exactly a sporting weapon, but possible. Balancing herself against the door frame, she took a short hop forward, noisier than she wanted.

The man stirred but did not wake.

Another hop. Delorme nearly fell, and touched the end of the bunk with her fingertips to keep her balance. She held her breath. The man didn't stir. She bent forward, fingers still on the end of the bunk, to try to see the make of the gun. It looked almost identical to the one at the ATM scene, but she had to squint to be sure of the manufacturer's imprint: Browning Hi-Power.

The man's eyes opened. "You got a problem?"

"I was just trying to see if you were awake. You want some tea?"

"Thought you had a broken leg."

"I'm thirsty. I'm going to make some tea."

"You look like you're in pain. Maybe you should lie down."

"I'm all right."

"Plenty of room right here." He tapped the bunk with the gun.

"I don't think so."

"Come on. See if we can make that leg feel better."

"You want some tea or not?"

"Tea. Sure. Why the fuck not? Where'd your partner go?"

"He went looking for the house," Delorme said, and regretted it right away. Wished she'd said something that meant he'd be back in one minute.

"If he finds it, he's gonna wish he had an army with him."

Delorme turned and took a hop toward the door.

Behind her, a creak, and the sound of the man's feet hitting the floor.

She hopped as hard as she could and that got her into the other room, but the man's full weight hit her and slammed her to the floor, the pain forcing a scream out of her.

He pulled back hard on her hair. "Hold still."

Delorme twisted onto her back and brought her good leg up and around his face. She forced him back and he let go of her hair, but as he fell he yanked at her broken leg and she shrieked in agony.

When Delorme regained consciousness, he had her belt buckle undone and was trying to slide her pants down. He had put the gun aside on the floor. Delorme reached for it, but he got to it first and clouted her in the temple.

She hit him a hard backhand, her knuckles catching him in the eye.

He swung again with the pistol, but the floor took most of it. Delorme got hold of the barrel and twisted and the man let go. The gun flew out of her grasp and hit the floor somewhere behind her head. The man lunged for it, his face so close she could smell his breath. She pulled him closer and bit his cheek. The sudden heat of his blood on her face.

The man roared and clutched his cheek, blood spilling through his fingers. Delorme reached back for the gun and the man grabbed her throat and punched her face. His knuckles slid on blood.

Delorme grabbed his waist and felt the knife handle. The man lunged for the gun and she undid the snap and got the knife out. He reared back with the gun in her face and she brought the knife up and jammed the blade just under his arm.

He screamed and dropped the gun and fell sideways to the floor. When he reached for the gun again, Delorme twisted and brought the knife down hard on the side of his head. The bone gave way and she could feel the blade lodge in his temple.

She held on to it and felt the force drain out of him. It was as if he were becoming smaller under her hand. He lay there, half curled, still breathing, staring at some fixed point through and beyond Delorme. Blood flowed from his face wound into his eye, but the eye didn't blink. Delorme kept her grip on the knife until he stopped breathing, and for a while after.

She rolled back and dragged herself toward the bunk. She took up the gun and, when she had twisted herself into a seated posture with her legs out in front, held it in her lap.

"Fucker," she said. Her breath came in ragged gasps. "Teach you. Fucker."

39

"We're never going to get to the highway if you keep falling on your face," Nikki said. The old man was floundering just ahead of her. The storm had abated somewhat, but the snow was still flying and sticking to Nikki's eyelashes so that it was hard to see. And it was deep. Their snowshoes sank six inches and more into the top snow, making progress difficult for Nikki, let alone for an ancient geezer like Mr. Kreeger.

He staggered to one side, nearly toppled, but finally managed to right himself.

"The sooner I get you to that highway," Nikki said, "the sooner I can get back and curl up in front of that fireplace."

The old man turned to face her. "If we were really going to the highway, the obvious way to go would be the road. There's a plough blade on the front of the Range Rover, you know."

"I'm not old enough to drive."

"I am."

"We're going this way."

"Even on foot, the road would be faster."

"For the last time, we can't take the road. Papa will be coming back that way, and if he sees me helping you escape, it'll be game over for both of us. Jack could come back that way too, and I don't want to die, Mr. Kreeger, do you?"

Papa said the old man had to die but how she did it was up to her. So she had come up with this phony escape plan. There was no reason why the guy should die miserable. This way he would go out happy at least. He thinks he's finally free and *boom*, she shoots him in the back of his head and puts him to sleep.

"When did your so-called Papa go out? I didn't hear him leave."

"You didn't hear the fight? He booted Jack out and then he took off himself."

"Uh-huh. Drove out into the blizzard, did he?"

"As a matter of fact, someone came to pick him up. Guy in a Jeep."

The old man looked at her and shook his head in disgust.

"Yes, sir. They took off right after Jack did. Guess those Jeep tracks got covered pretty fast. I have no idea where they were going or when they might be coming back, but this is the first and likely only time I'm gonna be on my own with you, so would you please for Christ sake take advantage of it and keep your skinny butt moving? I thought old people were supposed to be wise."

"That's right. And young people are supposed to be innocent."

"Okay, so we're even."

The old man kept looking at her. His face was thin, elongated, and his papery cheeks were blotchy from the cold. He put Nikki in mind of a rabbit, and she was about to yell at him to turn around when he finally did so. Turned and took a step through the snow, then another, wide-legged, duck-like.

"See, it's not so bad," Nikki said. "We'll have you on that highway in no time. Someone'll come by and pick you up." She knew it didn't really make sense. What possible reason could she have to send him safely into town? She'd made him solemnly promise that he'd wait a day before he called the police, but obviously he'd call them first thing. He must know Papa was at the house waiting for her to come back and announce she'd done it. Meanwhile she was terrified of bumping into Jack. Jack clearly inhabited the boundary line between the kind of craziness you can live with, and the kind you can't.

The old man stopped. Even through his heavy parka she could see his shoulders heaving. He turned to her again.

"Dude, are you on crack? We have to keep moving. Or have you just not noticed we're in the tail end of a blizzard?"

"How old are you, young lady?"

"I'll be fourteen in February."

"Fourteen in February." He smiled, long rabbity teeth amid cheeks of high pink. "In February I'll be seventy-six years old."

"OMG, we have such a lot in common! Would you keep it moving, please."

The old guy didn't move, intent only upon her, the hunting rifle in her hands—in case she saw a pheasant for dinner, she'd told him. "That man isn't your father."

"Yes he is. In every way that counts, he is."

"Raised you, did he? From the time you were a baby? Changed your diaper? Got you into school? Made you do your homework? Read to you at night? Taught you to read and write, and how to get along with people? Raised you like a dad?"

"Raised me, no. Rescued me, yes. I was one death-bound fuck-up, Mr. Kreeger, and Papa saved me from the solid brick wall I was smashing my head into."

"You were living on the streets?"

"Anything bad you can imagine, I was doing it. Now get moving before I become hostile."

"I wouldn't call where you are right now rescued."

"What?"

"I wouldn't call the place where you find yourself right now being rescued."

"You don't know the place I was previously."

"And I wouldn't call Papa anything resembling a father."

"You don't know the man."

"Have you looked in the bunkhouse, Nikki?"

"I had no reason to."

"You mean you were told not to."

"I don't care what's in the bunkhouse."

"Not what—who. His name was Henry. He was an Indian—a First Nations person, though he always referred to himself as Indian. He'd be about forty-four, forty-five. Younger than your self-styled Papa by quite a bit. He was probably about your age when he discovered he was alcoholic. Just couldn't let it go. He had some pain raging inside of him that only alcohol would stop. Imagine that. Only alcohol could stop it. But it also made it worse."

"Uh-huh. And I'm supposed to care about this drunkard why?"

"Imagine having a constant pain. A burn, say—your skin feels like it's on fire. Or maybe not so dramatic. You just feel that your heart is breaking. All the time, every day, for no reason—and the only time this pain stopped was when you were drunk. That was Henry's life. It rendered him uncongenial and unemployable. It got him thrown off the reserve. It got him thrown in jail countless times. And all the time, that burn, that heartache. He got himself sober for a time. By some Herculean effort of will, he managed to do that. He even got himself married and got a job. The job didn't last. The kind of work he could get never does. So he started drinking again. His wife left him."

"A loser. What you're describing's a loser."

"What I'm describing is a human being. Henry quit drinking. And no, it didn't happen overnight. It took him many tries and many setbacks, many failures, but the man stopped drinking. Sober, Henry was good with his hands, a skilled carpenter. He did some work on the house. How I met him. He knew lots of things: electricity, plumbing, hunting, fishing. And he was a big reader. Liked books. Liked a good story. Liked a good joke. Nice sense of humour. Kinda dry.

"He came to work for me. Just doing whatever needed doing. I don't pay him much—didn't pay him much—but his rent was free and he liked the quiet. Liked the woods. I think maybe he even liked me. Seemed to, anyway. I asked him once what he did about all that pain, where it went, and he told me it never went anywhere. It was still there. Every day. He just didn't do anything about it anymore. He just let it be, and sometimes he forgot about it. He had a hard life. Incomprehensibly hard to someone like me, a lucky person. But he found a way to smile now and again. A way to laugh. And he took pleasure in small things—making breakfast, hanging a door. In keeping an old man company. I can't say he was a happy man, Henry, but he was a good man, and he thought that little bunkhouse was the finest place he'd ever lived. And now he's lying dead in it with a bullet hole in his forehead because your so-called Papa preferred him that way. There was no reason for it, and that was the end of Henry's life."

"You don't know that."

"I do. So do you."

"The highway's that way, Mr. Kreeger. Would you turn around, please?"

He turned and took exactly one step and stopped again and looked at her. "Is this really who you want to be?"

"What I am is not something I have any say over."

"But what you do—what you do is under your control."

"If you've got such a rosy view of life, why are you having such trouble believing anything I tell you? Just keep your head down and keep those snowshoes moving one step ahead of the other and we'll get you to the highway safe and sound. I know, how about maybe we sing a little bit? You wouldn't happen to know any snowshoeing-through-the-woods-type songs, would you? We sing those the rest of the way, we'll keep warm and cheerful, and I can't think of a better way to get us through, you know . . . whatever."

40

KEEPING LOW, CARDINAL MADE IT to the edge of the ravine and jumped. He slid down, hidden rocks chomping at femur and tibia. The line of trees above would give him some cover, unless whoever was shooting at him slid down into the ravine too. You got yourself into it this time, he told himself. You got Delorme into it too.

The ravine bottomed out at a small creek that was only half frozen. Swift black water, silver where it splashed over the rocks. Cardinal hunkered behind some thick brush and tried his phone again. Stone dead. Practically crawling, he made his way back toward the cabin, praying that Delorme was still alive.

This time the shot actually creased his arm, tore through his parka sleeve. It didn't hit bone or even muscle, but ripped a hot line in the skin just above his elbow. He lay flat and peered through the bush toward the top of the ravine. The sniper was a ghost, a wraith out of Native folklore wafting soundlessly through the forest.

If it was the man who had bluffed his way into the cabin, either Delorme was already dead or she had forced him out into the woods. Another shot tore through the branches just above his head. Cardinal plunged back the way he had come, away from the cabin. If he could get to the Kreeger house, he might be in a stronger position to deal with this maniac, then come back for Delorme. It was not an idea that would withstand analysis, and he didn't submit it to any. He just kept moving through brush and rocks and water.

A little farther on, the wide white platter of a lake opened up and across it Cardinal could see the house, a dim outline behind diagonals of falling snow. A crack of thunder split the air and lightning sparked wide over the trees. If whoever's behind that rifle comes down this way, I don't want to be out in the open, Cardinal thought. I really don't.

Keeping well inside the tree line, he moved clockwise around the lake. That would take him behind the house and provide some cover. By the time he made it to the trees behind the house, the lightning had come west too, as if it had personal business with him. Several bolts lashed at the trees and the thunder sent shock waves through his diaphragm. It set off a car alarm in one of the snow-covered vehicles out front.

The snow had now changed almost completely to rain. Cardinal's parka was not waterproof. Within minutes, icy water glazed his shoulders.

He moved farther around until he could see the side door of the house. To his left, a bunkhouse. If you were holding a hostage, he asked himself, where would you be most likely to keep him?

He got to the bunkhouse and scanned the trees in either direction. No sign of the rifleman. The car alarm still throbbing. He stepped up to the back window and peered inside. He was looking into a bunk room. Unoccupied and not much of anything in it. Beyond this, a table. It was dark, but not so dark he couldn't make out a body lying on the floor. He could see enough to know that it wasn't Lloyd Kreeger and that whoever it once was had been dead some time. There wouldn't be anybody else in the bunkhouse, not with that.

He stepped back into the trees. Rolls of thunder, moving off now, rain soaking through to his back, his chest. His arm stinging. The car alarm shut off and the rain was louder hitting the bunkhouse, the trees. He scanned the woods once more and ran to the side door of the house.

He tried the handle. Unlocked. He pushed the door open.

Dim interior. Table right in front, living room beyond, a bedroom or two off a mezzanine to the right. It was the kind of test scenario they might set up for you at the academy in Aylmer. Be ready to shoot, and if you do, shoot to kill—but know that it could be a victim or a bystander coming through any one of those doors.

Cardinal moved into the kitchen area, acutely aware of the stairs in the corner behind him, the basement they would lead to. The bathroom was empty. He got to the first bedroom door and opened it and checked inside. No one. He stood listening, the shiver in his knees only partly from cold.

He moved on toward the last door at the end of a short hall.

A voice behind him said, "Put the gun down."

Cardinal whirled and dropped to his knee in one motion, Beretta at the ready.

"Very impressive," the man said. He was in his late fifties. Bigger than Cardinal by a lot. Short hair and a military look to him, a shotgun at his shoulder—a shotgun being the exact tool for the situation. Fill a room with buckshot and no one gets away.

"Curtis Winston," Cardinal said.

"It doesn't matter who we are. It only matters what we are."

"I know what you are, and you're under arrest."

The man came closer. "Cop," he said. "Society's lackey. Lickspittle. A no-account backer of the status quo."

"Somebody has to take out the garbage."

"Garbage is just material you don't personally value. Others might take a different view."

"Put down the weapon."

"No."

"You're not getting out of here."

"You might want to recalculate those odds. Shotgun versus pistol. Pathetic little cop versus . . . what? A force of nature. A united family."

"A family is not what I'd call you."

"What would you call us?"

"Just put down the weapon."

"Negative. What would you call us?"

"I don't see any us. I just see a gangster minus a gang."

"Family, not gang. Our loyalties run deep. Now drop the Beretta."

A hooded figure came in from the side door. "It's the girl you have to worry about," she said to Cardinal. "Not Papa."

"Hello, Donna," Cardinal said.

"You don't seem surprised to see me."

The man called Papa did. "Christine," he said, keeping the shotgun trained on Cardinal. "Christine, what are you doing here? Have you forgotten the rules?"

"I know the rules," she said. "'You leave the family, you leave for good.'" She turned to Cardinal. "How'd you figure it out?"

"Mendelsohn. You killed him because you knew he was going to recognize you. You took the photos from his file. What I don't understand is why you killed the kid at the ATM."

"He wouldn't tell me where Papa was."

"You kill a kid? To have Papa bear all to yourself? You're that desperate to run with this guy again?"

"Not run with him. Kill him." She pressed her gun to Papa's head. "He won't shoot. Papa never shoots anyone." She lifted the shotgun out of Papa's grasp and stepped around him. He stared at her with hatred. "You're not the easiest man to find," she said.

"You led a cop here? Are you that much of a traitor, Christine?"

"It was the other way around," Cardinal said. "She followed me. Tried to shoot me, too, if that's any consolation."

"To warn you away," Donna said. "If I'd wanted to kill you, you'd be dead."

"That is true," Papa said. "Meet Christine Rickert—best shot I ever saw. Best tracker, best fighter, best I ever trained. It broke my heart when you quit the family."

"*Family*," Donna said. "Always *family*. What a joke."

"What do you want, Christine?"

"I want my life back, *Papa*."

Papa laughed. "I gave you your life back. Years ago. What were you? A juvenile delinquent. A petty thief. Drug dealer, street slut, a human spittoon. We took you in, gave you a home, something to belong to. Something to believe in. You could have become anything—special forces, undercover cop, the failsafe assassin. We trained you until you were the absolute best you could be."

"Trained me to kill without mercy."

"You were good at it. You were the best."

"Trained me to believe that the slightest discomfort could be solved with a bullet."

Winston shrugged. "So you threw it away. Now what are you?"

"Daddy's girl."

"You're nothing. You're a zero."

"You made me in your image. Trained me for slaughter. I never learned any other way to meet the world. What are you supposed to do when your lover upsets you? You kill him. What do you do when you don't get the job you want? You kill. What do you do when your husband isn't a saint? You kill him. I just spent eight years in fucking prison, *Papa*."

"Not for anything you did with me."

"It was the culmination of everything you taught me." She looked at Cardinal. "That's right, John. My husband didn't leave me. I sent him on his way." She gestured with the gun. "With this. It's one thing when you kill a stranger. That's relatively simple to get away with. Unfortunately, when you shoot your husband in a fit of rage, you tend to get caught."

Cardinal spoke quietly. "How did you know where to find the ATM kid?"

"Papa here's a creature of habit. Always tells them to hit the first ATM again. After the second one. Every time. Kid wouldn't tell me anything. But like I say, Papa's a creature of habit. I don't know how far Mendelsohn got with this, but you check back, you'll find that aside from his habit of beheading people who annoy him, Papa likes to storm someone's house and drain every dime out of every account they ever opened. As soon as you said Kreeger was wealthy, in the fur business, I knew he'd be here. The kid didn't tell me a thing. Just stood there waiting for it. He knew if he got into his car I'd follow him."

"Lemur was loyal," Papa said. "Unlike you."

"And look where it got him," Donna said. "Are you proud of your children, Papa?"

"Donna—Christine," Cardinal said. "Whatever you have in mind now, don't do it."

Donna laughed. "He took my life. Why shouldn't I take his?"

"If not for me," Papa said, "and the family I gave you, you'd have been dead at fifteen."

"You're an assembly line for murderers. You'll just keep turning out more like me. Taking you down will be the one good thing I've ever done."

"Don't do it," Cardinal said.

"Why, John? You have a happy ending for me? You marry me and take me away from all this? I don't think so. In a way, you're partly responsible. You gave me a glimpse of real love, real loyalty. You would have figured me out quick enough—but it was just so obvious you loved your wife. Real love. Not the fake stuff Papa deals in, the real thing. That's something I've never had, never will. You can't imagine how that feels."

"You kill a boy and a law officer and God knows who else," Cardinal said, "and you blame it on your childhood?"

"You can't imagine the things I've seen. Either of you. You can't begin to guess the places you travel when you've had the benefit of Papa's training. I've seen fathers clasp their hands in prayer and beg, beg not to be killed—not for their own sakes, for the sakes of their children. I've seen young mothers sprawled on the ground, blood spilling from their heads, their babies wailing in the next room. I've seen teenagers, a teacher, an architect, at least one doctor—all dead for the same reason. The same simple reason. Because Papa wanted it that way. It was never for anything that mattered, anything that might make sense as a motive. They looked at him wrong, they didn't bow down to him, they didn't recognize that he was God, obviously they were not fit to live. I lost interest when he started cutting people's heads off. Not personally, of course. Why kill anyone yourself when you can have a so-called son or daughter do it for you?"

"Look at you," Papa said. "You're magnificent. An implacable force. Come with me up north. We'll work together. We'll raise a family the like of which has never been seen, and we'll take over whatever's left of the world."

"Big talk from a guy who's never killed anyone."

"He did," Cardinal said. "Martin Scriver—later known as Curtis Carl Winston—murdered his parents forty years ago. Took them for a ride on the lake and chopped their heads off and sank the boat. Why'd you do it, Martin?"

"I didn't. I didn't kill my parents," Papa said. "I never killed anyone."

"Nobody did it for you," Cardinal said. "Not that first time. You did it all by yourself."

"My parents died. I didn't kill them."

"What did you do with the heads, Martin? Not that I suppose we'll find them at this point."

"I didn't do that. I didn't do anything." For a moment at least, all arrogance and authority seemed to drain from the man, leaving nothing but faint denial.

"Then how come you changed your name to Curtis Winston? We have the DNA, by the way."

Papa shook his head.

"In some weird psychotic way, you've been trying to prove that ever since. It's always somebody else doing the killing, right? You have them kill the couple. You have them kill the kid. You would have had Bastov's son killed too, if he hadn't got sick and missed his flight. But that first time, nobody did the killing for you. That was all you."

"No," Papa said, still shaking his head. "No."

"That's how you knew the house was for sale, right? Took a drive out Island Road to get a look at the old cottage? Last place you saw your parents alive? The Schumacher property was the best place to get a look at it."

A girl of about thirteen stepped into the kitchen from the basement stairwell. She had a gun gripped in her two hands and aimed at Donna. Even from where he stood, Cardinal could see it shaking, but her arrival seemed to breathe life back into Papa. "Nikki," he said. "Kill this woman."

Donna kept her gun pressed to the side of his head. She looked the trembling girl up and down. "You're losing your touch, Papa. This one's not ready to kill anybody."

"You're wrong," Papa said. "She already has."

"I don't think so."

"Do it, Nikki."

Nikki swallowed. She kept the gun trained on Donna.

"Do it," Papa said again.

Nikki adjusted her stance.

"Dear me," Donna said. "At her age I'd already killed at least two people for you."

"Christine, this family is on the cusp of greatness. A pure existence in the clarity of the north. We can sit there in comfort and watch the entire planet go to hell."

Donna laughed. She looked at the girl. "He's been going on about the Pure White North for decades. Did he give you the story about so-called guided chaos too? Stir things up, then retreat to the north to wait out world war?"

"It's such a shame," Papa said. "We made you into something real, Christine. Lethal, yes, but real. We made you into travelling darkness, the agent of destiny, death incarnate. You had the power, not me, and that's as close to God as it gets."

"Not human, in other words."

"A force to be reckoned with."

"And now I'm reckoning with you."

Donna shot him through the temple and he crumpled to the floor. Random nerve and muscle spasms jerked the arms and legs. Before Cardinal could move, she had the gun, still smoking, trained on a spot between his eyes.

The girl was trying to keep Donna in her sights, but her arms shook and wavered with her sobs.

Donna ignored her. "You've investigated a lot of murders, John. Now you've actually witnessed one up close. How do you like it? Would you like to make a career out of it?" When he didn't respond, she said, "Didn't think so. It's an acquired taste. That bastard made sure anyone near him acquired it pretty fast."

"You think I'm going to let you go because we slept together?"

She shook her head. "Never. Sorry, John."

"Kill me and you won't get away with it."

"Who's going to know? I'm willing to bet you haven't told anyone else what you figured out. It makes you look too dumb. What was the clincher for you?"

"Zabriskie Farm. The pictures you stole from Mendelsohn's room."

"How long have you known?"

"A couple of hours. Other people will know soon enough."

"It's too bad," Donna said. "I liked you. Admired you. I still admire you."

The girl made a move—it was only a sob, but it made her gun hand jerk—and Donna whipped around. In that splinter of time Cardinal had no opportunity to judge whether she would actually shoot the girl. Instinct took over. His gun hand came up and his finger squeezed the trigger.

Donna stumbled and fell back against a table. She started to raise the Browning toward Cardinal and he shot her again, catching her in the arm. She lifted the gun again. Her knees gave out and Cardinal's final bullet went into her skull just above the left eyebrow.

41

"Look at this condensation." Cardinal drew his forefinger down the foggy surface of his picture window and added a dot underneath. He added a question mark next to it. "You think I should move again?"

"Back out to the lake? You'd lose a ton of money, wouldn't you?" Delorme was lying on his couch in blue jeans and a red Christmas sweater. She had her left leg, in its plastic and foam cast, propped up on the back of the couch. Her honey-coloured hair flowed over the cushions beneath her head. "Don't move again. I'd miss having you just down the street."

I would too, Cardinal nearly said, but didn't. Then he wished he had. And then it was too late. Instead, he told her about Sam Doucette. She and her mother were back in town. He had stopped by to tell them about developments. "I met her father too."

"He finally came back from the Yukon or wherever he was?"

"Said he's trying to get Sam a sponsorship deal with a crossbow manufacturer. I'm not sure, but I think he was joking. You ready for more coffee?"

Delorme picked her mug up from the floor and held it out in a languid hand. "I could get used to this, having a man wait on me hand and foot."

"Shane doesn't do that?" Cardinal took the mugs into the kitchen and picked up the coffee pot and started to pour.

"Shane and I broke up."

Cardinal put down the pot and went back to the doorway. Delorme was twisting a lock of her hair, examining it in the light as if it were far more interesting than her romantic fortunes.

"He dumped me."

"Then he's an idiot."

"Yes," Delorme said, still contemplating the lock of hair. "I think so too."

"Are you upset about it?"

She held the hair still, then let it fall back to the cushions. "Yes."

"But you weren't too excited about him, you said."

"It always hurts to be dumped—even though I have a lot of experience at it. I don't like being on the other end of it either, but it beats being the dumpee."

Cardinal went back to the kitchen and finished pouring the coffee and handed her her mug. Delorme sat up awkwardly, bad leg out to one side.

"You want to sit in the recliner?" Cardinal said. "You'd be more comfortable."

She sipped her coffee and shook her head. "That's your spot."

Cardinal was about to sit down when the phone rang. He talked to McLeod for the next few minutes, aware that Delorme was watching his face, reading his reactions.

"So?" she said when he hung up.

"You remember our fur protester—Chad Pocklington? OPP just figured out that's who they swooped down on with their SWAT team."

"Wow. I bet they're pissed. Any news about the girl—Nikki?"

"They still haven't tracked down her parents. They may not want to be found. She'll be stuck in detention for now. Kreeger apparently doesn't want to press charges, but the Crown is not going to ignore kidnapping and false imprisonment even if she did let the old guy go."

"What do we hear from Forensic?"

"DNA from the Scriver cottage matches Curtis Winston. There's no criminal record under either name, but he's now the chief suspect in several gruesome murders in the States—all of them where he has a slight connection but no obvious motive."

"People annoy him, so he cuts their heads off."

"He has his so-called children do it. The guy who attacked you was one

Jackson Till. He's done time in the Texas state pen for rape, manslaughter and aggravated assault. Are you okay? How are you holding up?"

Delorme had gone pale. She closed her eyes and shook her head. "I can't stop thinking about it. Seeing it. Over and over again."

"You didn't have a choice. You know that."

"I do know that. It doesn't seem to make any difference."

"If it's any comfort, SIU's initial take is they believe you killed him in self-defence. The final report'll take weeks. Same for me and Donna Vaughan."

A wave of nausea or something like it passed through Cardinal and he sat down on the couch beside her. Neither of them spoke for a long time. Finally Cardinal said, "I never thought I'd see the day I'd shoot a woman."

"Like you say," Delorme said, "it's not as if you had a choice."

Another silence.

Eventually Cardinal said, "You know, I spoke to the real Donna Vaughan. She's a freelance journalist in New York who covers fashion and has no interest whatsoever in the Russian mob. She also had no idea that Christine Rickert borrowed her identity about two weeks after she got out on parole. I'm telling you, Lise, sometimes my own idiocy takes my breath away. I can't believe I didn't see through her."

"Why, John? You had no reason to suspect her of being anything other than an aggressive journalist." Delorme placed a warm hand on Cardinal's shoulder. "And it's not so long ago your wife died. You were vulnerable."

"Stupid, you mean."

"You broke a major case. Two major cases. I don't think that qualifies as stupid." She gave his arm a squeeze. "You want to watch a video tonight? Do the popcorn thing?"

Cardinal shrugged. "I don't know . . ."

"Come on. What do you feel like? An old classic? A comedy?"

"I really don't mind," Cardinal said. "Something without monsters."

GILES BLUNT grew up in North Bay, Ontario. After spending over twenty years in New York City, he now lives in Toronto. He is the author of *Forty Words for Sorrow*, for which he won the CWA's Macallan Silver Dagger; *The Delicate Storm*, winner of the Arthur Ellis Award for Best Novel; *Blackfly Season*, one of Margaret Cannon's Best Mysteries of the Year; *By the Time You Read This*, a national bestseller; *No Such Creature*, one of the *Globe and Mail*'s Top Ten Crime Books; and *Breaking Lorca*, which the *Globe* called a "tour de force."